WHITEOAK HERITAGE

WHITEOAK HERITAGE

MAZO DE LA ROCHE

DUNDURN PRESS
TORONTO

Project Editor: Michael Carroll
Copy Editors: Kelvin Kong and Jennifer McKnight
Design: Erin Mallory
Printer: Webcom

Library and Archives Canada Cataloguing in Publication

De la Roche, Mazo, 1879-1961.
   Whiteoak heritage / by Mazo de la Roche.

ISBN 978-1-55488-411-7

   I. Title.

PS8507.E43W46 2009   C813'.52   C2009-901988-4

I   2   3   4   5   13   12   11   10   09

Conseil des Arts
du Canada

Canada Council
for the Arts

ONTARIO ARTS COUNCIL
CONSEIL DES ARTS DE L'ONTARIO

Canadä

We acknowledge the support of **The Canada Council for the Arts** and the **Ontario Arts Council** for our publishing program. We also acknowledge the financial support of the **Government of Canada** through the **Book Publishing Industry Development Program** and **The Association for the Export of Canadian Books**, and the **Government of Ontario** through the **Ontario Book Publishers Tax Credit** program, and the **Ontario Media Development Corporation**.

Care has been taken to trace the ownership of copyright material used in this book. The author and the publisher welcome any information enabling them to rectify any references or credits in subsequent editions.

J. Kirk Howard, President

Printed and bound in Canada.
Printed on recycled paper.
www.dundurn.com

Dundurn Press
3 Church Street, Suite 500
Toronto, Ontario, Canada
M5E 1M2

Gazelle Book Services Limited
White Cross Mills
High Town, Lancaster, England
LA1 4XS

Dundurn Press
2250 Military Road
Tonawanda, NY
U.S.A. 14150

Mixed Sources
Product group from well-managed forests, controlled sources and recycled wood or fiber
www.fsc.org Cert no. SW-COC-002358
© 1996 Forest Stewardship Council

FSC

99%

ANCIENT FOREST ™
FRIENDLY

To the memory of H.E. in abiding friendship
Windrush Hill
June 1940

Contents

I

REUNION

THE TRAIN WAS nearing its destination and the three men lighted cigarettes and fixed their eyes on the swiftly passing fields, expectant of the first glimpse of the town. The expressions on their faces were remarkably different. Their very attitudes showed something of the contrast of their feelings. For two, it was a return; for one, the introduction to a new country. All three were in khaki. One wore the uniform of a captain, one of a sergeant, one of a private. The last sat by himself and, even though he stared through the window, his ears were alert for anything the others might say. He sat, tense and neat-looking, in spite of the clumsy cut of his uniform. He had mouse-coloured hair, pale eyes with fine lines about them, an inquisitive nose, an impudent mouth, and a jutting, obstinate chin. His name was John Wragge.

The sergeant, Maurice Vaughan, was thirty-four and heavy for his age. His brows were dawn together by a deep line above his fine grey eyes. His mouth wore a look of somewhat sullen endurance but had lighted boyishly when he smiled as he was now doing. He had had an officers' training course before leaving Canada but, in England, had reverted in order to get to the front. He had risen to the rank of sergeant, been twice wounded and brought back with him, as souvenir of the War, a crippled hand which wore a leather bandage, and which he was just beginning to use again, clumsily and not without pain.

The third member of the party was Renny Whiteoak, lifelong friend of Vaughan and two years his junior, being just past thirty. He had been educated in a military college and, at the outbreak of the war, joined the Buffs, a regiment with which his family had long been associated. He had been awarded the DSO for an act of distinguished bravery. The officer's uniform well suited his lean body of which the flesh seemed rather a weathered and durable sheath for the active muscles beneath, than the evidence of good nourishment. His strong, aquiline profile, his close-cut dark-red hair, his vivid brown eyes added to the impression of nervous vitality. He was saying:

"I'll bet that the first person to meet me, inside the house, will be the old lady. When the door opens there she'll be, with both arms stretched out to hug me."

Maurice Vaughan smiled. "I can just see her. What a fine woman she is for her age! As a matter of fact, for any age. I wonder if she's failed much while you've been away. Four years is a long time for a person of ninety. She is that, isn't she?"

"She'll be ninety-four next September. But I don't think she's failed. The last letter I had from her was full of news about the family. And it was perfectly legible, except toward the end. She said how glad she was spring had come. She never sets foot outdoors till the snow has gone."

"It must be nice," said Maurice, "to know that such a welcome is waiting for you. Relations of all ages — right down to the kid you've never seen."

He instantly wished he had not said that. It would bring to Renny's mind the loss of his father and his stepmother while he was away. His father had died before he had been absent a year. His stepmother had survived the birth of her last child for only a few weeks. Renny Whiteoak, however, answered composedly:

"Yes, it is nice." His face softened and he added — "I'm keen to see the youngster. Wakefield they named him. His mother's maiden name."

"I might as well," said Maurice, "have been killed for all the rejoicing there will be over my homecoming."

His friend drew down his mobile brows and bit his lip in embarrassment. He could think of nothing to say for a moment, then he got out:

"I'm mighty glad you're here."

Still embarrassed he turned to Wragge. "What do you think of this country?"

Wragge had, before the War, been a cellarman in a London wholesale wine merchant's establishment. He answered with a grin:

"Well, sir, I used to spend my days underground before I went to France. After that I lived in the trenches. I'm not much of a judge of landscapes but those rail fences do look funny after 'edges and walls."

"They look good to me."

"I expect they do, sir. It's all wot you're used to. That's a pretty bit of woodland there. It's a nice colour."

"Those are young maples, just coming into leaf. The tips are red. Look, Maurice."

"Yes, I was just admiring them. And the blue of the sky."

After a pause Renny said — "There's young Pheasant. She'll be glad to see you."

"I don't think so. Why should she? We have been separated for four years, and she's only twelve now."

"But you've written, haven't you?"

"I've sent her a few picture postcards."

"Christmas presents?"

"I wasn't where I could buy anything suitable. I didn't think of it and that's the truth."

"Well — I'll say you're the world's worst father! If I had a kid — " He saw that Wragge was straining to hear what was said and broke off with a frown.

"I know — I know," said Maurice. He nervously fingered the leather bandage on his maimed hand and his mind turned back, in self-condemnation not untouched by self-pity, to the time of his early manhood when he had been engaged to Renny's sister, Meg. Meg and he had been perfectly suited to each other, he was sure of that. Both families had been delighted by the prospective union. He had wrecked it, made a fool of himself, by getting entangled in a momentary passion for the niece of the village dressmaker.

It was an experience he had thought to leave behind undiscovered, except as it had affected his own maturity. But a child had been born of those few meetings in a summer wood. The girl had taken the child to his parents' house. Maurice had confessed his fatherhood. The engagement had been broken of by Meg who ever since had been inaccessible to him as if she lived in a foreign country and knew no word nor wanted to know a word of the language he spoke.

That Maurice could continue to love Meg after twelve years in such a situation was a miracle to Renny, and not an edifying one. Maurice should have broken down her resentment by a more flamboyant constancy or simply found someone else to love, someone who would be a mother to his child. Still, Renny cherished Maurice's fidelity as something unique, the proof of Meg's desirability, even a tribute to the Whiteoak family.

He leaned toward his friend and said in an undertone — "Perhaps it will be different with you and Meg now — the War and all that ... your being wounded ... Well, I think you ought to fix it up somehow."

"God, I should like to!" said Maurice, "but I have no hope at all."

A movement was going through the passengers, a tentative reaching out toward their belongings, a searching of the narrowing fields for the first ugly intrusion of suburbs.

A few minutes more and they were indeed arriving. The three men in uniform stood up, put on their caps with characteristic gestures; Wragge, the Cockney, slapping on his jauntily, as though with it on one side of his head he was prepared for anything; Maurice Vaughan, deliberately, as if he assumed with it the burden of what lay ahead; Renny Whiteoak, with a decisive movement in which his hair seemed to join, clinging against the rim of the cap as though to clamp it the more closely to the sharply sculptured outline of his head.

He was the first of the three to stride through the railway station, eager to see who was there to meet him. As he reached the barrier his progress was hindered by a straggling group composed of a man in private's uniform, a woman and five children, ranging in age from three to ten years. The man was plainly embarrassed by the six pairs of eyes turned up to him as his family crowded about him like sheep. They were strangers to him and he did not know now to reunite himself with them. His face was a blank. His wife wore an apologetic smile as though it were her fault that the children had grown beyond his recognition.

But now Renny discovered those who were waiting for him. He pressed his way through the straggling family and went eagerly to meet his sister and his three brothers. He had expected that Eden and Piers would be there, possibly one of his uncles, but he had not expected young Finch. The sight of Meg was a happy surprise. And looking just the same — after all she had been through! Her complexion as fresh, her hair the same soft light brown, the curve of her lips as full and affectionate. Her lips parted in a tremulous smile when she saw him and she raised her two arms ready for the embrace. Now he had her in his, pressing her close. He felt that there was perhaps a little more body to her. She had, he guessed, put on six or eight pounds in his absence.

"Oh, Renny, my dear, how thankful I am!" She clung to him, unwilling to surrender him to the others. He was her own, her very own brother. They had had the same mother. As she pressed him to her the painful imaginings of what might happen to him in the War melted away and her one thought was — "I have him safe, and quite unchanged."

But while she savoured the first joy of this reunion she saw, over Renny's shoulder, the figure of Maurice — looked straight into his eyes. She had not known he was returning with her brother. She had not given him a thought.

Renny felt her go rigid in his arms. Then she burst into tears.

"It's all right, old girl," he said, his voice husky "I've come home and you'll never get rid of me again."

"It's not that," she sobbed. "It's Maurice. I can't meet him! Please don't ask me to."

Renny screwed round his head and gave his friend a distracted look. Then he loosed himself from Meg's arms and returned swiftly to Maurice. He said:

"Look here, I can't ask you to come with me. Meggie's too upset, seeing me again and all that."

Maurice, very white, returned — "Seeing me again and all that, you mean! Never mind, I'll go on a local train. It's all right. Tell Meg I'm sorry to have appeared at such an inopportune time."

His sympathy torn between the two, Renny exclaimed, almost in exasperation:

"Do what you think best and don't talk like a fool!"

"It's true and you know it. Well, I'll see you later. Lord, how those boys have grown."

"Haven't they! The car will be packed. Will you take Wragge with you? I'll send for him when we get home."

"Righto." Maurice turned away, the lightness of his tone contrasting with his look of hurt. The Cockney, Wragge, followed him, his shrewd eyes having absorbed the strangeness of the meeting. He threw all he could of devotion into the parting glance he gave Renny Whiteoak. He had been his batman in the War and now his look said — "Whatever 'appens you can count on me, sir."

Renny rejoined his family. Meg had conquered her agitation and taking his arm drew him toward the three young brothers eagerly waiting to greet him. He kissed each in turn.

They had so developed since he had last seen them that it required an effort of will to place each in the cherished niche where he belonged. It was hard to tell which had changed most. He grinned, almost in embarrassment, as he looked into their three faces.

If it was a matter of mere growth Piers had it, he decided. From a sturdy little boy of less than eleven he had grown to a strapping youth of almost fifteen, with broad shoulders and head well set on a strong neck. His full blue eyes were bold and there was a look about his mouth that hinted that he would not be too eager to do what he was bid. And his hands — well, they looked ready for anything — muscular, brown, vigorous.

But could he give the palm to Piers with Eden standing there, almost as tall as himself? He had last seen Eden as a slender, fair boy of fourteen and here he was a man and almost too good-looking for he was like his poor mother who, if she had not been so delicate, would have been beautiful. Of the three young brothers Eden gave Renny the most eager, the warmest welcome, gripping his hand, looking into his eyes with a swift, penetrating glance.

Finch had changed the least; but even he was grown almost out of recognition. His hand lay small and thin in Renny's. His teeth looked big and new between his parted lips.

"Hello!" he breathed. "Hello! I thought I'd come to meet you."

"Good fellow." Renny still held his hand as they all moved through the station.

Again the family which had impeded his entrance appeared on the scene. The man had placed a heavily shod foot on a bench and, elbow on knee, was staring over the heads of his family, whistling through his teeth, while children and wife in dumb resignation waited to see what he would do next. Renny nudged Meg, with a nod in their direction.

"Poor things," she exclaimed. "How happy they are." She smiled at the children, then glanced apprehensively over her shoulder. Her brow cleared as she saw that the crowd had closed between her and the figure of Maurice Vaughan.

Porters had arrived with Renny's luggage. Eden and Piers were fastening the trunk to the back of the car. It had been washed for the occasion and though Renny disliked it he gave a glance of approval at it. He, Meg, and the small boy got into the back seat. Eden was a good driver. They sped smoothly along the road that lay beside the lake. It was noonday and there was little traffic once they reached the suburbs. Then there were trees in their budding leaves in front of the houses and, glimpsed between them, the lake, fluttering little bright waves.

This moment which Renny had so often pictured, strained toward in homesickness, now seemed unreal. The scene, the backs of the two youths in the front seat, the thin body of the child beside him, the clasp of Meg's hand across the child's knees, might, he thought, dissolve into the vapour of a dream and he find himself once more in France, with war the only reality. His weather-seasoned profile looked so aloof to Meg that she leant toward him and asked:

"Aren't you happy to be home?"

He pressed her fingers and nodded. She felt that he was thinking that their father would not be waiting to welcome him. She herself had got used to the loss but of course it was fresh to Renny. She said in her peculiarly comforting intonation:

"We've made *such* preparations for you! Gran and the uncles and Aunt Augusta have been counting the hours till you come. Everything has been done — even to washing the dogs."

"It's grand to be home!" Again his hand pressed hers. He grinned down into Finch's face. "Eh, Finch? What do you think of me?"

The colour rose to Finch's forehead. He could not speak. Meg spoke for him.

"You're a hero to Finch. Of course, you're a hero to all of us but you know what small boys are. Who do you think he is like, Renny?"

Renny's vivid brown eyes scrutinized the child's long, sensitive face. "I'm damned if I know. Well, he's got the Court nose. He's got grey-blue eyes. Who has grey-blue eyes in our family?"

"No one. Both his parents' eyes were blue. Isn't Eden like his mother? But so different in disposition. He's full of character. I can tell you, Renny, those two in the front seat are a handful. I shall be glad to have your help with them. They've wills of iron."

The elder brother's eyes turned to the two pairs of well-shaped shoulders, the bright hair and strong necks of the two. "They had better not try any of the iron-will stuff on me," he said.

As though conscious that they were being talked about, Eden and Piers glanced toward each other, the first with a mocking smile, the second with a look half mischievous, half daring. Eden increased the speed of the car, for they were now driving between the lake and the fields that lay dark and receptive after the plough. The air was fresh, sweet with the scents of May, and the sun gave promise of summer heat. An approaching team of farm horses stirred the dust to a low cloud about their shaggy feet. Finch found his voice and shouted:

"There's one of our wagons, Renny!"

Again Eden increased the speed.

Giving him a poke between the shoulder blades Renny exclaimed — "Stop the car!"

They were now beside the horses. He gave an admiring look at their sleek sides then noticed that the load they drew was a dozen fat pigs, shouldering each other in the straw, peering at him in a mixture of impudence and foreboding. The driver was new to him. He did not like his looks.

"By George, those are fine pigs!" he said.

"I helped to feed them," put in Finch. "I often gave them extra feed."

"Shall we go on?" asked Eden.

Renny enquired of the driver — "Where are you taking the pigs?"

Eden answered for him — "To market. He'll not get much for them. We'd better be getting along. They'll have lunch waiting at home."

"Yes, go on."

A sudden sense of reality swept over Renny. The sight of the farm horses, their honest eyes beneath their blond forelocks, the smell of their harness, their most hides, the jostling pigs, swept his future toward him in a living tide. There was an end to war. Life on his own land, his sister and young brothers about him. He realized for the first time that he must be a father to these boys, take their dead father's place. He must find out what each was and do the best he could for him. The bond already existing between him and them tautened and sought strength in his heart. He drew a deep breath and took Finch's thin hand in his. He felt its pliable bones quiescent in that clasp. He saw the childish bare knees, close together like twin chestnuts smooth and brown.

Piers hooked his arm over the back of the seat and turned to point out the changes that had taken place since Renny's leaving. At each Renny gave a grim nod, thinking none of them for the better. He was glad when the car turned into the quiet country road where the great trees still spread their branches and caused a moment's slackening of motorists' speed. "I'll protect them always," he thought. "There'll be one road that isn't mutilated."

As the car turned in at the gates the sense of naturalness that had come to him with the sight of the farm wagon increased. He felt as though he had never been away from Jalna. Why, there was the old silver birch tree with the circular white seat beneath it, the lacy new foliage moving delicately in the breeze! There was the house itself, the rosy brick a rich background for the spreading Virginia creeper that massed itself about the windows but saved its most delicate tendrils to drape above the porch. There were the dogs stretched in the warm sunshine on the steps, rousing themselves to join in a concert of barking about the car. There were two newcomers that raged about his heels till he put his hand down to them palm upward and they touched it with their nostrils and were satisfied to welcome him as having the true scent of the family.

Then he saw his father's Clumber spaniel, Fanny, standing quietly by herself in the shadow of the porch, her fringed tail drooping, her eyes questioningly raised to his face.

"There's old Fan," said Piers. "She's forgotten you."

"Forgotten me! No — she couldn't! Hello, Fan, old girl! Hello, old pet! It's me — Renny!" He bent over her, his lean hand running the length of her silky coat.

She reared herself against his legs, her pensive spaniel's face regarding him from the frame of her long ears. Her eyes were full of a mournful recognition. It was not enough to stroke her. He took her up into his arms and held her close to his breast. And his father was dead! He felt the tears rising in his throat as he hugged the spaniel close. He hid his face against one of the long ears. He heard Meg's voice.

"Isn't she an old dear? Oh, how she missed Papa! No one can take his place with her. I think we ought to ring the bell and give them warning inside that we're here."

"They've had warning from the dogs," said Eden. "I hear Gran's voice."

Meg, however, rang the bell and an instant later the door opened and an elderly maid who had been with the family for nearly thirty years stood smiling a tearful greeting to Renny.

"Eliza!" he exclaimed. He still held the spaniel in his arms, and holding it strode toward the woman, his face alight.

"Keep that grin for me," said a harsh voice. His grandmother pushed the maid aside with her ebony stick and herself advanced with a vigour that defied her ninety-three years. Her face, invincibly handsome because of its superb bony structure, was creased into a network of lines by her wide smile which displayed her double row of strong artificial teeth. Her brows, though shaggy, still showed their fine original arch above her dark eyes, as might the Gothic arches of a ruined cathedral through their growth of ivy. She wore a much-trimmed cap, a cashmere shawl and large woollen bedroom slippers.

Before her stick had tapped thrice on the floor of the porch she discarded it and it fell with a clatter. She opened wide her arms and Renny, setting down the spaniel, buried himself in her embrace. It was as though the gates of his past had opened, the past of his father and his grandfather who had lived and loved and begot children under this roof, to claim him to carry on their tradition. The memory of what he had witnessed in Europe, of despair and disintegration, he would throw off with his uniform and turn wholeheartedly to the stability of this dear place.

He forgot in his ardour the weakness of the symbol of this life which he embraced in the person of his grandmother. Her shawl fell off, her cap was askew, she was gasping for breath.

"Lord, what a hugger you are," she got out. Then hastened to add — "But I like it. Don't you ever be afraid to squeeze my ribs. I'm not made of such delicate stuff as my daughter and granddaughter. If I was I'd not have had three such big sons."

She kept on talking, as though she would by the flow of her words exclude the rest of the family from their reunion. But her daughter, Lady Buckley, and her sons, Nicholas and Ernest, were close behind her and now claimed their share of Renny's attention. They were tall handsome men in their middle sixties, Nicholas with a mass of iron-grey hair, a strong aquiline profile and deep-set brown eyes; Ernest blue-eyed, fair-skinned, his fine grey hair brushed smoothly over his narrow head, his sensitive lips trembling a little as he put his arm about his nephew's shoulders.

"Welcome home, my dear fellow," he said — "Welcome — welcome. To think we have you back at last!"

Nicholas added, in his deep voice — "By gad, Renny, it's good to see you! And just the same!"

Renny gripped his uncles' hands and then embraced his aunt, pressing fervent kisses on her sallow cheek. She was in mourning, her husband having died less than two years before. She held Renny close while her breast, above her high-corseted body, rose and fell in her emotion.

"My dear boy," she said, in her contralto tones. It was all she could say and she repeated the words several times. "My dear, dear boy!"

It irritated her mother, who exclaimed brusquely — "One would think you'd given birth to him, Augusta! The way you go on! Let the lad loose. You're smothering him. Haven't you a word for poor Eliza, Renny?"

He detached himself from his aunt, who drew herself up, with an offended look at her mother. He turned to the maid.

"Just the same old Eliza!" he exclaimed, patting her shoulder.

"That's right," said his grandmother. "Tell her she is just the same. She's got the notion that she's worn out with working for us and needs to retire. It's nonsense."

Eliza smiled palely and handed the old lady's stick to her. The entire group moved toward the dining room where the one o'clock dinner was laid, the dogs jostling each other alongside. A tawny cat belonging to Ernest glided down the stairs to a convenient height and from there jumped to his shoulder, arching herself and beginning to purr in anticipation of the meal.

Old Adeline, in the heart of the group, declared:

"I'm starving. It's not right for a woman of my age to wait so long for her food."

"It is very bad for you, Mamma," said Ernest. "It simply means that, when you do get food, you will eat too much and eating too much produces flatulence which is dangerous."

She stared impatiently into his face as he made his pronouncement, then exclaimed:

"I've had wind on the stomach for twenty years. It doesn't harm me. I'm like an old sailing ship. Wind *moves* me!" Chuckling, she shuffled in her woollen slippers toward the agreeable odour of roast chicken that came from the dining room.

"Look here," said Renny, "give me time to wash my hands. I'll just be a moment!"

He sprang up the stairs and went to his old room.

"You'll find hot water waiting there," called Meg after him.

"And do make haste," added his Uncle Ernest. "My mother is faint for food."

"I'll be down in a jiffy," returned Renny.

"How wonderful it is to see him running up the stairs again," said Meg. "Oh, I shall be so glad to have him home; there'll be someone to lean on."

"More likely someone to order you about," said Eden.

"I heard him say," put in Piers, "that he had only a roll and coffee on the train. He'll be hungry."

"Rolls and coffee," exclaimed the old lady. "What a Frenchified breakfast! But it's well if he is hungry. We have plenty for him to eat."

"I think we had better seat ourselves," observed Lady Buckley. "It will save time when he comes down."

But when they reached the dining room where the spring sunlight poured between the yellow velour curtains on to the table, shining on silver and smooth damask, a surprise made them halt, almost in consternation. Eliza, when laying the table, had placed Renny at its head.

On the death of Philip Whiteoak, early during the War, Nicholas and Ernest had returned to Jalna from England. To the household of women and young boys left behind, their coming had been a bulwark against the world and a restrengthening of family solidarity. There was their old mother bereft of her youngest son, eager to have one of his older brothers on either side of her. There was Meg who had lost a tender and indulgent father, whose favourite brother was in constant danger of his life in France, ready to throw both arms about her uncles' necks and absorb the comfort of their nearness. There was Mary, Philip's widow, soon to give her life for her child, tremulously welcoming their strong masculine presence. Their return had been a success both from the point of view of the family and their own finances. In these last years the income of each had been sorely depleted from earlier extravagance and bad investments. Life at Jalna cost them next to nothing.

Nicolas had become so used to sitting at the head of the table, facing Meg at the other end, his mother on his right hand, that the thought of relinquishing this place to Renny, who, by his father's death, had become owner of the house, never entered his head. Neither did it enter the head of his ancient mother, peering at the joint or roasted fowls he carved so skilfully. The tender slices went to her and to Ernest and Meg, while the tough, smothered in gravy, were given to the three strong-toothed boys. Ernest, on old Adeline's other side, thought the arrangement admirable, he taking the place of Nicholas when an attack of gout kept him in his room.

"Boys, put out the dogs," ordered Nicholas.

There was a skirmish while Piers and Finch tugged several terriers and the spaniel by their collars from the room.

"Don't shut the door," said Lady Buckley. "Stand on guard so that the animals shall not re-enter. It will be more polite to Renny."

It was in this moment of confusion that the elders discovered the new order in which they were placed at the table. Nicholas was the first to notice it. He saw that his massive silver table napkin ring which represented a classically draped female figure reclining against a heavily chased cylinder, had been removed to the first place on the right of the carver.

His hand went up to his grey moustache and he gave it a tug of chagrin. His voice, a deep one, expressed his feelings in a sonorous "Ha!" His brother's expression was a mingling of annoyance that Nicholas was displaced and a Puckish pleasure in his discomfiture. Meg stood imperturbably by her chair.

Lady Buckley, looking her straight in the eyes, asked —

"Was it you, Margaret, who ordered my brother's napkin ring to be displaced?"

The stilted expression brought a chuckle from Eden. Lady Buckley turned to him with some severity.

"There is nothing to laugh at," she said. "Your uncle has filled your father's place with dignity for almost four years. I see no reason why he should be put out of it the moment Renny returns."

Old Adeline now became conscious that something was wrong. She peered excitedly from one face to another.

"Who's put you out of where?" she demanded, supporting herself by the table when halfway into the chair.

"It doesn't matter in the least," said Nicholas. "Now then, old lady," — he took his mother by the arm — "you must move along one place. You're to sit between Ernest and me now."

But she would not budge. "Who's being put out of where?" she reiterated. "Not me, I hope. I won't have it."

"It is evidently considered," said Ernest, "that Renny is the master of the house."

The old lady was making a gallant effort to retain her former place at the table but Nicholas urged her toward the next chair. Eliza moved forward from the serving table. She said, addressing Adeline:

"I placed Mr. Renny at the head of the table of my own accord, ma'am. I thought that as it is him that owns the house it was natural he would like to carve."

"Well! Well!" said Ernest. He eyed the pair of juicy roast chickens almost accusingly, as though they had in some way been disloyal to the established order of things. Although he and Nicholas had had their fair share of their father's money, they could not help the inward twinge of mortification at their younger brother's inheriting of Jalna. But he had been dead for four years and the sting of it had subsided. Renny's return, his inheritance through his father and this pointed reminder of it, made them uncomfortably aware of the change in family relations.

"You should not have done such a thing without an express order," said Lady Buckley.

"Certainly not, certainly not," agreed Ernest.

"It doesn't matter," growled Nicholas.

"An order from me!" exclaimed old Adeline. "Nothing's to be changed without an order from me. But it's right for Renny to be at the head of the table. He's his father's eldest son. Jalna is his … Well, now, where do you want me to sit? I begin to feel very weak. I need food." She peered eagerly at the full-breasted birds on the platter.

Nicholas got her into her chair. She unfolded her napkin and tucked it deftly beneath her chin.

"Don't let those dogs in, boys," she commanded.

Eliza stood rigid, her lips puckered, on the defensive against criticism of her act. All eyes were fixed expectantly on the stairway which could be glimpsed through the open door. Ernest kept repeating under his breath — "Well, well!" Nicholas drummed on the table with his fingers. Eden looked slyly at Meg, urging her to laughter, but she kept her countenance. The dogs made a concerted effort at return but was repulsed by the boys. The shadows of their waving tails were thrown against the pale woodwork of the staircase.

Renny's feelings as he went up to his old room were a strange mixture of the familiar and the dreamlike. He had so often imagined it in his years of absence that now in its reality it was dwarfed and pressed in on itself. His own reflection in the mirror stared out at him like a stranger.

The shiny lithographs of famous horses that adorned the wall seemed ready to rear in astonishment at his claim to be flesh and blood.

But he must not keep the family waiting. He went to the washstand and poured warm water from the can into the basin. He had a sudden feeling of childhood, of being sent from the table to wash his hands. But these hands that he now lathered were the weather-hardened hands of a soldier. They had to take into their grasp the reins of a new life.

As he inadequately rubbed a towel between his palms, his eyes fixed on the fields that spread beyond his windows, he suddenly felt that he was being watched. He wheeled and discovered a tiny figure standing in the doorway. It was a little boy of less than four years, dressed in a white knitted suit, his mass of brown curls and his bright dark eyes contrasting in their vitality to the fragility of his body, his small pale face and his thin little legs. For an instant he could not think who the child was, then it rushed upon him that it was the brother he had never seen, his father's posthumous child.

"Hello!" he got out. "And what's your name?"

The mite stared at him, his eyes becoming larger, his mouth smaller and rounder in his astonishment.

"Hello!" repeated Renny, with what he imagined was a friendly grin. "I'll get you!"

He dived at him and tossed him up. Well, that was what he did to little boys. But this little boy was evidently different. Instead of squealing in delight and crying "Do it again! Do it again!" he gave a scream of fright and then burst into tears. Renny did not know whether to set him down and leave him or carry him downstairs. He decided to do that last. Tucking him under his arm he ran quickly down the stairs. Wakefield had apparently stopped crying but he was only holding his breath. They reached the dining room.

"Sorry to keep you waiting," Renny began, then the screams broke out afresh. The little boy kicked and struggled. The dogs followed them into the room. The spaniel, fearful that Wakefield was being hurt, stood on her hind legs and pawed at the intruder. Her nails scratched Wakefield's bare leg. He kicked and screamed more loudly than ever. The dogs barked.

Meg rose from her chair and flew to her darling's rescue.

"Come to Meggie then! Meggie's pet!" She took him to her breast.

"Why, his leg is bleeding!" exclaimed Ernest. "Whatever have you done to him?"

"Good God!" said Nicholas. "It's enough to give him a fit."

Eliza was examining the scratch.

"I'll get Vaseline and a bandage," she said. "Come with Eliza, my pet."

"No, no!" he shrieked. "Won't go! Send the bad man away!"

"Give him to me," commanded Lady Buckley. "I can quiet him when no one else can."

It was true. On her ample lap, her clean handkerchief bound about his leg, he became tranquil and beamed at the faces about him. His grandmother was only half sympathetic. She did not like the delay. She wanted her dinner. She looked critically at Renny as he prepared to take his place. He himself was concerned at the unfortunate introduction to the last-born of the family. He dropped into his chair with an apologetic air.

"Put the dogs out," said Ernest. "They are irritating Sasha." The cat was indeed arching her back and swinging her tail on his shoulder.

"Must they go out?" asked Renny. "They used to stop in. Do you remember how Dad used to pull burrs out of them and hide the burrs under his chair?"

This sudden unexpected reference to the dead Philip fell almost brutally on the ears of those about him. The tremor of laughter in his voice shocked the elders and made the three boys grin in response. In truth Renny had not yet come to believe in his father's death. Jalna was so bound up in his thoughts of Philip that to return to the one was to bring the living presence of the other to his mind.

But how he felt that he had said something unseemly. His already high-coloured face took on a deeper tinge. He picked up the carving knife and said nervously — "So I am to do this job! Well, I'm afraid I shall make a hash of it." He talked excitedly of his journey while he carved.

His uncles, his aunt, and Eliza standing by, thought he showed no proper appreciation of the honour done him. They were not consoled by the fact that he showed little discrimination in his apportioning of the birds. It was disconcerting to see eleven-year-old Finch stuffing his greedy young mouth with the tenderest breast. It was annoying to see heedless Piers devouring those juicy ovals of flesh dug out of the back which the knife's tip, just north of the Pope's nose.

But his sister and his grandmother were satisfied. To Meg the sight of him opposite her, his red head bent above his task, his eyes, under their dark lashes, giving her quick glances of affection, filled her with bliss. She could not eat.

"You're eating nothing, Meggie!" he exclaimed.

"I'm too happy," she answered. "Besides I never eat much. And I've Baby to feed." She was offering morsels to the little boy, who refused them, turning his face against his great-aunt's breast with petulance.

"I hope you are not spoiling him," said Renny.

A derisive laugh came from Piers. "Spoiling him!" he exclaimed. "He's the most spoilt kid in the world."

"No, no," said Lady Buckley. "His delicacy makes a certain amount of humouring necessary."

"It is not well to cross him," agreed Ernest. "He needs encouragement. I was a delicate child and I know how such a one can suffer at the hands of people of coarser grain."

"I should like to know who caused you suffering," rumbled Nicholas. "I seem to remember how you always had the best of everything because you were ailing."

Their mother spoke in a tone of surprising energy. "I took great care of my children. I wrapped 'em up against the cold. I kept 'em out of the heat of the sun. I dosed 'em with sulphur in the spring and senna in the fall. I never lost a child. My mother lost five out of sixteen.... Hm, well, I don't know what this is you've given me but I can't eat it at all. You don't carve the way your uncle did."

"Sorry," said Renny. "I know I'm damned awkward but I shall get used to it."

"There's a nice bit of breast," said Nicholas, pointing with his fork. "Cut that off for her."

Renny complied.

"Renny," said Finch, "when can I see your wounds?"

Meg turned horrified eyes on Finch.

"How *can* you say such things? It was bad enough to know that Renny was wounded without speaking of it the moment he arrived."

"I always say," declared Lady Buckley, "that delicacy of mind cannot be instilled too early. I don't see much of it in these boys."

"What we want," said Piers, "is to hear Renny talk about the War. We want to hear how he carved up the Germans. Tell us about when you won the DSO, Renny."

"Time enough for that later," answered Renny gruffly.

"You must come to my room," said Eden, "and tell everything."

Meg interrupted — "Isn't Wakefield pretty, Renny?"

"Pretty as a picture. Are you going to make friends with me, you young scamp?"

"Whom do you think he is like?"

"Renny considered the little face. "I don't know. Me?"

"A little. He's got the Court nose."

"Rot," said Eden. "His nose is like mine."

"He has glorious eyes."

"He looks like my brother Thaddeus," said their grandmother, peering round her hawk's nose to stare at him.

"Who are you like, you rogue?" cooed Meg.

Finch stared pessimistically at his little brother. Why all this fuss? Why should he have been so important from the day of his birth while himself had such casual treatment? He gave Wakefield's empty high chair that crowded his elbow a push, then helped himself liberally to chow-chow.

"Renny," he said, with his mouth full, "I do want to see your wounds!"

"Now," said Meg, "you may leave the table. You're a naughty boy."

He flushed and began reluctantly to drag himself out of his chair.

"Please don't send him away," exclaimed Renny; "not at my first meal at home."

"But he's making me feel faint."

"Nonsense, Meggie, — you're made of better stuff than that."

"Very well. If Renny wants you to stay. But see that you behave."

Wakefield's little voice penetrated. "Baby wants to go to Uncle Ernest." He struggled from Lady Buckley's lap.

Ernest was flattered. He took the child on his knee and mounded his own fork with mashed potato for him.

"More g'avy," demanded Baby.

Ernest plastered gravy on the potato. The little mouth opened wide. The fork was inserted. Baby beamed at everyone.

"Gad!" ejaculated Nicholas. "I'd almost forgotten the champagne!"

He rose and limped to a side table where the bottles were cooling on ice. "This is my contribution to the feast. Renny, we're going to drink to your health, my boy."

They did. All the family stood about him, wishing him prosperity and a long and happy life. He was moved. His eyes glistened and his mouth softened to an expression of protective tenderness. There they were — his own flesh and blood — clustered about him, wishing him well, drawn close to him in the bond of kinship, from the old, old grandmother down to the baby, Wakefield. The years of separation, of confusion, were over. Now there would be peace for the rest of their days. The roof bent over them. The walls closed about. He had taken his place as the head of the family. He would be a father to these boys. As he raised his own glass to his lips he had a physical sensation of the tightening bonds between himself and each of the others about the table, as though his very sinews were taut in the dark close bonds.

Old Adeline left her place and came in the voluminous folds of her dress to his side. She took him in her arms.

"Ha!" she exclaimed, kissing him almost vehemently on the mouth. "I've lost my son … Philip is gone … but I've got you!" She hugged him close. "Lord, how hard you are! You give me strength…. This old body of mine hasn't lived in vain! The lot of you … you'd never have been … if it wasn't for me!"

Still clinging to Renny she looked triumphantly about. "Augusta, Nicholas, and Ernest…. Not a child among 'em! Well — I'm rotting old timber but you're young and tough, Renny. Bless you!"

"Champagne," whispered Ernest to Meg, "always goes straight to Mamma's head."

II

Father and Daughter

PHEASANT WAS THINKING, to the rhythm of swinging legs that dangled from the broad damp bough of an old apple tree: "This is a wonderful year for me. In a month I shall be thirteen — in my teens — and in an hour I shall see Maurice. I don't know which amazes me most."

Her expression, always rather startled, became amazed, by her own will. She sent up her eyebrows, parted her lips and breathed pantingly. As though amazement was transmitted through her into the old tree, a tremor ran through it and it scant pinkish-white blossoms filled he air with a startled scent. Her thin legs, in the brown lisle thread stockings, swung in a kind of syncopated rhythm, as though beyond her control. She thought: "In a few minutes I shall go in and brush my hair and clean my nails and put lots of scent on my handkerchief."

The apple tree stood by itself in a small irregular field by the side of the creek. She always thought of it as her own tree, for none but she paid any attention to it. The apples it produced were small and warped and rough-skinned but to her taste had the sweetest flavour of all. If she shut her eyes and tasted carefully it was almost like a pear but far better. The trouble was that the old pony, which pastured in this field, was just as fond of the apples as she was. He would stand beneath it, waiting for them to fall, or stretch his rough-maned neck to tear them from the bough.

He ambled toward the tree now and rolled his full, blue-black eyes at Pheasant with the look of a conspirator, as though they were both thieves. Yet the apples were still no more than ideas in the heads of the buds.

"Hello, you old rogue," said Pheasant. "You don't know who's coming home today!"

The pony blew out his lips and the faintest whicker stirred his insides. Little drops of moisture hung on the hairs about his mouth. She put down a foot and scratched his back with it.

"It's Maurice who's coming," she said. "I suppose you know more about him than I do. I wish you could speak, Sandy. You could tell me a lot."

The pony was twenty-eight years old and had belonged to Maurice when he was a small boy. Pheasant in her turn had ridden him about the fields but he was fat and lazy and would not move out of a protesting jog-trot. Now Pheasant pictured him young and feeling his oats, with little Maurice on his back, galloping along the country road where there were no motor cars, Maurice laughing and happy.

Sandy moved from under her foot and began to crop the scant young grass. He gave a look askance at her when she caught him by the forelock and told him: "Your master's coming home! Do you hear! Your master and my father."

There was a strange lightness inside her, half fear and half joy. She had lived so solitary that the thought of sharing the house with a large, almost strange man, changed the very aspect of the spring day for her. Colours were deeper, more intense, there was mystery in the murmuring of the creek. Father — father — father — it kept saying. Yet she had never called him anything but Maurice. Mrs. Clinch, the housekeeper, was getting old. She was hard of hearing and suffered from lumbago. She had lived in the Vaughans' house for forty years and seemed as permanent as the very walls to the little girl. Mrs. Clinch looked on Pheasant as a disgrace to the name of Vaughan and, while to the outer world she carried herself proudly, she never came suddenly on the child without a shock to her innermost self, and the thought: "This is the skeleton in our cupboard and it's my duty to care for it...." If only she might have had a properly born, greatly welcomed child to look after!

She was kind to Pheasant, without tenderness. Her idea of a child's goodness was that it should be keeping still. Pheasant's idea of getting on with Mrs. Clinch was to stop doing whatever she happened to be doing, when Mrs. Clinch appeared, and stand quite still. The housekeeper would scrutinize her, appear satisfied and return to her little sitting room off the kitchen. She had a rocking chair there that gave a sharp crack each time it swung backward. When Pheasant heard this noise she knew she would be unobserved for the next hour.

Till she was eight Pheasant had spent much of her time in keeping away from Mrs. Clinch and in watching Maurice, unseen. She would follow him through the fields, hiding behind blackberry bushes or among the tall corn, sometimes in the house, always in the room he had just left. Everything he did fascinated her. She would stand with her eye to the crack of the bathroom door watching him shave, watching the deft lathering of his face, the controlled sweep of the razor, the smooth-skinned face that emerged. She would spy on him as he cleaned his gun, read his paper, or mixed himself a drink, always trying to imagine what it would be like if he was fond of her and wanted her near him. Pheasant knew that in some mysterious way she had spoiled Maurice's life. She was sorry for him and wished she could think of something to do to make up for this.

Now this morning she stood in the dining room taking in the unaccustomed brightness of the room. During Maurice's absence the blinds had always been drawn except when Mrs. Clinch had opened up the room for airing and cleaning. The sideboard had been bare, the table covered by a sheet. It had been a game of Pheasant's to dare herself to lift the corner of the sheet and look beneath it. Once, rigid with fear, she did. There were some cushions beneath. That was what had made it look as though a body lay there. But she had run from the room terrified. What might not lie beneath the cushions. This morning bright sunlight flowed into the room, caught and held by the polished silver on the sideboard, making a shining shield of the walnut top of the table. Silver and wood were evidence of the state of Mrs. Clinch's hands. She now came into the room just in time to see Pheasant run her palm over the table top.

"Don't touch!" exclaimed Mrs. Clinch, as though speaking to a child of three.

Pheasant drew back and stood still, her arms at her sides. She saw that the housekeeper was shiny and neat as the room, her grey hair flattened, a stiff white apron over her grey dress. Her hands, clasped in front of her, were her only spot of colour. They were a greyish pink from the silver cleaning powder.

"It all looks lovely," said Pheasant, speaking loudly because Mrs. Clinch was deaf.

"It ought to," returned Mrs. Clinch. "I've been rubbing and polishing for three days. You'll have your lunch in here with him."

"Me?" Pheasant turned pale with excitement. "I couldn't eat. I'd be too frightened."

"Nonsense. There'll be no more meals with me. Your place is here from now on. You had better dress yourself now. There's no time to spare."

"Shall I put on my white dress?"

"Goodness, no. The plaid one. Then come to me and I'll give your hair a good brushing."

Pheasant flew upstairs. There was a fluttering in all her pulses. She felt that she surely must weigh less than usual. She felt as though she were blown up the stairs and into her room.

She put on the plaid dress and tried to find a pair of stockings without a hole in them, but could not. She ended by putting on one each of two different pairs. The shades were not an exact match but she thought the difference would not be noticed. She looked at herself in the glass and saw a face, two eyes that sparkled back at her and a mass of brown hair. There seemed to be more plaid stuff than features to her. But she was not dissatisfied with her appearance. She snatched up her hair brush and ran down to the kitchen.

There were agreeable smells about. Coffee was bubbling in the pot. Mrs. Clinch ignored Pheasant and the hair brush. She seemed to take a pleasure in walking about, doing things, with the child dumbly following her. Then suddenly she turned abruptly and said:

"Well, then, let's have it."

She swept the brush ruthlessly over smooth locks and tangled locks alike. Pheasant set her teeth and her eyes watered as a twig from the apple tree was detached from a tangle.

"No wonder the birds are building nests in your hair," Mrs. Clinch said.

She had barely given a dozen strokes when the sound of a motor was heard and voices at the front of the house. Mrs. Clinch exclaimed:

"There he is now! Poor young gentleman!" Mrs. Clinch usually ended any remark she made about Maurice with the words "poor young gentleman," and for some reason they always made Pheasant ashamed. Now she stood hesitating, not quite knowing what to do. The housekeeper hurried to the door.

Pheasant went slowly into the hall.

The front door had been opened wide. The fresh spring air, as though it had been shut out to long from that gloomy house, rushed in, freighted with the scents of warm earth, opening buds, and damp leaf mould. It was as though the side of the house had been taken out and all secrets, all unhappiness blown away.

Maurice, stalwart in his uniform, came in. He was followed by a small wiry man laden with luggage. Maurice shook hands with the housekeeper. He paid the taxi driver. The door closed and Pheasant felt suddenly too shy to face Maurice. But he saw her and came down the hall.

"Hello," he said. "How you've grown!" He took her hand in his left hand. She saw that he wore a leather bandage about his right wrist and that the hand looked helpless.

"A piece of shell crippled my hand," he said.

Pheasant felt weak with the love that surged over her. She longed to kiss the poor hand. She longed to draw his head down to hers and hold it close. But he moved away and began to explain to the housekeeper about John Wragge. These two went to the kitchen and Maurice up the stairs. The meeting had taken no more than a few moments and was over. Pheasant stood irresolute.

She longed to follow Maurice to his room but she dared not. She clasped her hands about the newel post and swung her body from side to side. Swinging so, she sometimes saw up the stairs and sometimes into the dining room. A strange new life had come into the house. She sniffed. It even smelt different. Then she saw the luggage mounded in the hall. It smelt of leather and strange adventure. In the dining room Mrs.

Clinch was placing a platter of cold meat on the table and a glass jar of red pickled cabbage. A good smell came from some hot escalloped dish. Everything was so clean, shining, and attentive for the new life to begin. What would it be like to have a man in the house?

She heard his step above, then he came slowly toward the stairs. She loosed herself from the newel post and fled to the passage that opened into the kitchen. At that moment the kitchen door opened and Mrs. Clinch stared at her as though surprised.

"What are you doing here?" she demanded.

"Nothing. Why?"

"Your place is in the dining room now."

The housekeeper's tone was so final that Pheasant seemed to hear the slamming of a door. But she did not know what her place in the new life was to be.

"Lunch is ready." Mrs. Clinch said this to Maurice who was now at the bottom of the stairs.

He glanced uncertainly at Pheasant.

"I've set a place for her," said the housekeeper. "Was that right?"

"Of course."

"I'm feeding the man you brought, in the kitchen."

"Good."

Mrs. Clinch gave Pheasant a slight push in the direction of the dining room. Maurice drew out a chair for her. He was embarrassed. He did not know how to talk to children.

"What will you have?" he asked, when they were at table. "Ham? Tongue? I don't know what the other stuff is. Should you like a mixture?"

"The other meat is brawn," answered Pheasant faintly. "I'll just have ham, please."

They ate in silence.

Pheasant was fascinated by Maurice's crippled hand. She saw that he had difficulty in using his knife and fork. Her own hand felt weak, in sympathy. She longed to cut his food for him.

Her fork fell from her hand and clattered to the floor. A hot tide rose to her cheeks and she bent double, trying to retrieve it. Maurice remarked curtly:

"Well — I can do better than that."

She felt disgraced.

Maurice was oppressed by recollections of his parents who had lived in this house. They had died years before the War but his absence from home had brought them near, on his return. They were much nearer to him than Pheasant was. He wondered what Renny Whiteoak was feeling, whose father and stepmother both had died while he was in France. Then the remembrance of Meg's shocked look when she saw him at the station stabbed him with a chagrin so keen that he uttered an incoherent exclamation and pushed his chair back from the table. This homecoming was horrible. This house was deadly.

He rose and went to the sideboard. He was relieved to find that the whiskey decanter had been filled. He found a glass and half filled it. Pheasant watched his every movement. He went to the door of the pantry, opened it a few inches, and called loudly:

"Mrs. Clinch!"

She came running, as though he had shouted "Fire!"

"Is there any soda water?" he asked.

She looked blank. "I never thought of soda water," she answered. "I'm terrible sorry."

"It doesn't matter." He returned to the table and filled his glass with water.

The spirits cheered him and he tried to think of something to say to his child…. Lord, he should have brought her a present. Children expected presents. "You've grown like anything," he offered.

She sat straighter. "Yes. I'm tall for my age."

He looked her over critically. "But you'll not be a tall woman."

He realized by her expression that he had said the wrong thing and he added:

"I don't like tall women."

Mrs. Clinch brought the pudding.

When they were alone again Pheasant asked, in the voice that still did not sound like her own — "Are you glad the War is over?" She was pleased with this question which sounded really grown-up.

He considered it with his brows knit.

"No," he answered at last. "I don't think I am."

Pheasant kept her eyes on her plate. Then he was not glad to see her! He would rather be thousands of miles from home, fighting in a war, than be with her. Tears crept slowly, painfully into her eyes. A deep flush covered her small pointed face.

"The war wasn't so bad," he said. "But when I've settled down I daresay I shall be glad. How are you getting on with your lessons?"

Pheasant had lessons from Miss Pink who was the organist of the Church.

"Do you mean the school lessons or the music lessons?" she asked, after a silence in which Maurice almost forgot he had asked the question.

"Both."

"I'm pretty good at literature and history. I'm not much good at music." She could control her tears no longer. They ran swiftly down her cheeks and dropped on to the rather soggy spice pudding.

Maurice stared at her embarrassed and annoyed. Did the child think he was a brute?

"It doesn't matter," he said. "You may stop the music lessons if you wish."

She took a large spoonful of the pudding and, in the effort of swallowing it, found self-control. Maurice left his unfinished and lighted a cigarette. He wondered if there were any way out of having the child with him at meals. Pheasant made a resolute effort to carry on the conversation.

"Finch Whiteoak likes music," she said. "He sits by the organ in the church while Miss Pink plays. She says she can hardly play for looking at him. He throws his whole soul into his eyes, she says."

"Hmph…. He was at the station to meet Renny…. Do you see much of the Whiteoaks?"

"Not very much. Wakefield is the sweetest little fellow. Once he ran away and came here, all by himself. When he can't have what he wants he just lies down on the floor and rolls over and over till he gets it."

"Do you ever see Miss Whiteoak — Meg?"

"No. I never see her. But once I met one of the uncles — the one called Nicholas — and he was very nice. Two days afterward a parcel came addressed to me and, when I opened it, there was a beautiful doll!"

"That was kind."

"Shall I fetch it and show you?"

"If you like."

She pushed back her chair and left the room. Upstairs she stood breathing quickly, trying to keep back the tears. She was not sure why she wanted to cry. She drew out the bottom drawer where she kept the doll, for she no longer played with it. It lay with closed eyes like someone dead, she thought. She felt suddenly very sorry for it. She took it up and buried her face against it. She no longer tried to control herself.

She did not go back to the dining room and after a little she saw Maurice walking slowly along the path that led to the wood.

A dimness came over the sun and a few drops of rain fell. There was a deep silence except for the chirping of a small bird. Then the rain came swiftly, lightly, as though not to injure the delicate blossoms of May. Pheasant wondered if Maurice would get wet. But he seemed unreal suddenly. Had he really come home? Was the meeting with him, which she had strained toward so long, already over? A cackling laugh came from the kitchen. Wragge had found his way into Mrs. Clinch's good graces!

III

NEWCOMERS

As PHEASANT HAD in earlier days followed Maurice about, she now shunned him. The sound of his step sent her flying, with beating heart. She ate her tea alone and was in bed when he had his dinner. She had left for Miss Pink's when he appeared the next morning. Eating his bacon and eggs he thought that after all the kid was not going to be greatly in evidence. If she had had any look of his family he should not so much have minded her presence, but she bore no resemblance to anyone except the girl who had, for a brief season, made him forget his loyalty to Meg. Yet there was something in the child that was like no one. That look of a young wild creature that watches you with no understanding, yet seems to see right through you. She made him uncomfortable, and that was the truth.

It was late in the afternoon of the next day before they met again.

She had had her tea and was writing in an exercise book on the dining room table when he came into the room. The light was fading and she was bent over the book, her thick, brown hair falling over each cheek, so that her face appeared very pale and narrow, as though between bars. On the wall opposite her was a patch of dusky-red sunshine. A plate of bread and butter, a pot of strawberry jam and a jug of milk stood on the table. A half-eaten cookie lay beside her and just as he came in she reached for it, her eyes still on her book, and took a bite.

His step startled her and she stared at him, the bit of cookie distending her cheek. She was so unused to sudden sounds in that quiet house that it took little to startle her.

"What are you jumping for?" asked Maurice irritably. "I'm not a burglar."

"No, I know you're not," she stammered. "I just … I wasn't expecting you."

"I can't send word that I'm coming very time I enter a room, you know."

"Yes — no — of course you can't."

She had spoken indistinctly through the bite of cookie. Now she swallowed it and looked at him as though asking whether she should stay or go. He dropped into an armchair and took a note book out of his pocket. He fluttered the leaves, in search of some entry. Neither heard the new step in the hall. A moment later the door opened and Renny Whiteoak stood before them.

"Hello," he said. "I didn't ring because I saw you through the window. All settled down, eh? Hello, Pheasant!"

She rose and went to him, shyly holding out her hand. Maurice's face lightened at the sight of his friend. "It's about time you showed up," he said.

Renny shook hands with the little girl. "If you had been through what I have —" he said.

"I suppose they've fairly eaten you up."

"I've been like a scrap of bread on the duck pond. Among them — from Gran down to the baby — I haven't had a moment to myself. I've talked myself hoarse. I've stripped to display the marks of battle. That was for the old lady. She wasn't a bit shocked. She just ran her fingers along the scars and said — 'Ha! We were always good fighters!' I was out in the stables by seven this morning. I've been all over the farm."

"It sounds just like my homecoming…. Sit down and have a drink."

Maurice went to the sideboard and filled two glasses. "Happy days!" he said.

"Happy days!"

They sat down.

"Pheasant," said Renny, "come and sit on my knee, if you're not too grown-up."

"I shall never feel too grown-up for that," she answered seriously.

"That's the right spirit."

She came to him and seated herself sedately on his knee. They looked into each other's eyes. He had taken a chair by the patch of sunlight on the wall. His head and shoulders were illuminated as though by a spotlight. Pheasant thought: He looks like a *really red* Red Indian, in this light.

"I wish I had a little girl," said Renny. "All those boys of mine ..."

Maurice thought: If that isn't like old Renny — calling them *his* boys, already! He'd be paternal toward his grandmother if she'd let him.

"You're too young to be my father," said Pheasant.

"I'm just two years younger than Maurice."

"You seem a lot younger."

"Do I?"

"Yes. I think it's because ... I don't know —"

"Tell me."

"I can't."

"Yes, you can.... Whisper it."

She bent her face to his ear, smiling.

"Don't mind me," said Maurice. But he felt a moment's perverse jealousy. How easily Renny had got round the kid!

Pheasant whispered — "Because I think you feel about things more like I do."

Renny threw an arm about her and pressed her against his shoulder. He whispered in return: "I'll bet I do. I think Mrs. Clinch is a killjoy. I think Maurice is a duffer, I think I'm a fine fellow and you're the most clever and interesting child I know."

Pheasant gave a gay little laugh. They laughed into each other's eyes. It was funny, she thought, that Maurice gave her the feeling of being almost grown-up, while Renny made her feel very young and rather reckless.

Maurice puffed at his pipe and regarded the two somewhat sombrely. He wanted his friend to himself, yet did not quite know how to get rid of the child.

"Have you finished your tea?" he asked.

"Oh yes."

"What about those lessons?"

"They are done."

She felt the wish in his tone and slid from Renny's knee.

Renny asked — "Did that father of yours bring you a present?"

She shook her head.

"Not even a German helmet or something made out of an empty shell?"

"No — I don't think so."

"Do you know, I should never have dared show my face at Jalna without a present for every single one of them, from my grandmother down to the baby!"

"Did they like their presents?"

"Yes. And I've brought a present for you."

"Don't tease her," said Maurice.

"I'm not. Look here!" He put his hand in his pocket and brought out a small silver fruit knife in a chamois case and gave it to her.

"Open it."

"Oh, how pretty! Did you bring it all the way from France for me?"

"Yes."

"I've never seen anything so lovely." She put both arms about him and kissed him on the cheek. "Thank you — thank you…. Look, Maurice!"

When she had gone with her books, Maurice said:

"You are a good fellow!"

"Well," said Renny, "the knife was a little extra present for Meg but I thought she could do very well without it."

"It's a good thing she doesn't know…. I saw her face when I suddenly appeared at the station."

"Well, it was a bit of a shock to her. But she was strung up at the time. I shan't be surprised if she forgives and forgets — after the years you've been away."

"I shall."

Renny gave his friend a look of intense irritation. "Then for God's sake," he ejaculated, "forget her! There are other women in the world."

"Not for me. Other women simply don't count…. She might be reconciled to me if it weren't for Pheasant."

"Send her away to school."

"I can't afford it. Besides there are the holidays. No — there's nothing to be done about it. I must just settle down and make the best of things." He rose heavily and poured out a fresh drink for each of them. After a pause he asked:

"How have they been managing things at Jalna?"

"Pretty badly from what I can make out. My uncles have always been extravagant. My grandmother has her nose into everything and she has the ideas of fifty years ago. Meg and Eden have been looking after the farmlands. Good Lord, they have the apple house stored with hundreds of bushels of rotting apples — holding them back for high prices! They have sold good horses for too little money. They sold my father's grand old stallion last winter. Each one has a different tale to tell about that…. Well, you can't be aggressive the moment things come into your own control but there must be a change. I shall buy a new stallion and one or two promising colts and see what I can make from show horses and hunters. Piers is going to be a help to me. I can see that."

"There was a fellow," said Maurice, "who came to see me this morning. He might be of some use to you. He wants work and he seems to know a lot about horses and farming. He says that his sister is just as capable as he is."

"Where do they live?"

"In that white house behind the church. It stood vacant for years, you remember. Then a Mrs. Stroud bought it. She divided it, so she could let half of it."

"Oh yes, Meg told me that in a letter."

"Well, this fellow — Dayborn his name is — lives in the other half. He has a widowed sister and her child with him. They're English. They're quite young. He looks about twenty-six. I gather they're hard-up and Mrs. Stroud is very good to them."

"Is she another widow?"

"Yes."

"I'd like to see them. Could we go there now?"

"All right."

"If you think it's safe for us. Two widows! God knows what may happen to us."

"I'll look after you," said Maurice.

He would have preferred to stay where they were and talk over their whiskey and soda but he knew what Renny was. If he got an idea in his head ... They emptied their glasses and set out across the fields, Maurice accommodating his slower step to Renny's urgent stride.

Renny had many qualities in common with his Irish grandmother and one of them was to let no scheme of his languish for lack of swift attention. Now, in his mind, he saw this young Dayborn as the very man he needed to help him in the work of putting his estate in order. And there was the sister! A girl like that might be a lot of help in schooling ladies' mounts. He felt full of goodwill toward them. This meeting was to be propitious.

They walked along a path that ran by the side of a field where the delicate spears of fall wheat were an emerald green and the earth took on a warm mulberry tint from the glow in the west. The path mounted gradually to a distant rise of ground, and reaching this they looked back on the house which stood half-hidden. Maurice's grandfather had built it ninety years before. He had planted sturdy young conifers about it, as though it were not snug enough in its hollow. They, in the long decades, had grown towering peaks, had clasped bough to bough, twined root about root, till there was a prickly wall that not only kept out the cold winter winds but arbitrarily advanced the evening, long before the sun had set.

"You should get some good exercise," said Renny, "thinning out those evergreens."

"Yes," agreed Maurice but without enthusiasm, "they're far too dense."

"Now look at Jalna," wheeling to face his own domain. "There's light there. We get all the sun, while we've lots of trees."

The house was indeed at this moment almost flamboyantly gay in its setting. The double row of tall balsams and hemlocks that bordered the drive stopped short at the gravel sweep. The lawn was open to sun and a group of silver birches showed trunks as white as the petals of narcissus, while their pointed leaves fluttered in palest green. The vast Virginia creeper that enriched the walls had placed its glittering young leaves with such precision against the old bricks that it seemed a calculated adornment. Certainly the fresh paint of the shutters and porch was in honour of Renny's return, and the shine of every windowpane from polishing. Behind the house the cherry orchard spread the white veil of its blossoms and, in the ravine that divided the two estates, there were the red stems of willows, the purple and gold of flags that bloomed by the stream, and the stream's own May-time blossom of foam. The energetic tapping of a woodpecker was the only sound.

"It seems strange," said Renny, "to own the place. When I left home my father was as sound as a nut. I thought he would live to be as old as my grandmother. I was satisfied to be his eldest son and to be a part of the place."

"I always admired your father," said Maurice. "He had a fine physique and that beaming look you seldom see in faces nowadays."

"Well," Renny spoke almost brusquely, "he's gone and I've got to get used to it.... Come along, Maurice. Let's see this fellow. What's his name?"

"Jim Dayborn. I forget his sister's name. It was a little short name. Oh yes — Chris, he called her."

"I'm glad that house is occupied. I remember how desolate it looked standing there."

"Mrs. Stroud has made the place look very nice, my housekeeper tells me. She had a sort of party there for the Women's Institute."

They walked on in silence.

Coming out on the quiet country road they crossed it, and Maurice was about to suggest that they should take a short cut through the churchyard when he remembered the new graves there and turned abruptly toward a narrow path that crossed a field. Renny hesitated a moment, his eyes fixed on the church surrounded by white gravestones, now flushed pink in the sunset. Then he followed Maurice. In a short while they stood in front of the now inhabited white house. It had once been the home of Miss Pink, the organist, but when her parents died she could no longer afford to live there and its rental had been her chief income. She had suffered privations during its vacancy and the fact that it was now sold was as a new lease of life to her.

The two men stood looking at it, remarking, with the interest of those whose roots have long been in the one spot, the alterations that had turned it into a two-family house. Also it had a fresh coat of paint, two green front doors against the fresh whiteness of the walls.

"I'll make a guess," said Renny, "that Mrs. Stroud lives in the right-hand side."

"That's easy. You can see the man moving about the room in the other half."

"No. I guessed from the curtains. A woman with a baby wouldn't have had time for all those frills."

They strode through the gate and rang the bell. The door was opened almost at once by a very thin young man wearing loose grey flannel trousers and a rough grey pullover. His colouring was nondescript but his movements were so graceful and the bones of his face so fine that he gave an impression of elegance. His expression was gloomy. This changed to a look of expectancy when he saw Maurice Vaughan.

Maurice introduced him to Renny.

Jim Dayborn invited them indoors with no apparent embarrassment for the sparsely furnished, untidy room, the scant meal which looked as though it might have been thrown on to the bare table, and the baby's diapers drying before the stove. Renny's first thought on seeing these was — "Why the devil didn't she dry them out in the sunshine?" He said, when they were seated:

"I hear you understand horses and that you're looking for a job."

"Yes," said Dayborn, "I'm terribly anxious for work. You see, I have my sister and her baby to support. Not that she wants to be dependent. She's ready to do anything. She's absolutely at home with horses."

"Who could look after her baby?"

"Oh, he's no trouble. Put him down anywhere and he'll amuse himself."

"In a stable?"

"If necessary," answered Dayborn laconically.

"Where did you get your experience?" asked Renny.

"We were brought up in a rectory in Suffolk. Our neighbours kept large stables and we spent half our time in them. We met an American who raised show horses and we came out to work with him. Well, that didn't last and —"

"Why didn't it last?"

"The owner was paying attention to my sister. But she didn't like him. She liked a chap named Cummings. She married him and then Cummings died and my sister could not stick the place without him. The baby was just a few months old. We knew a horse breeder in Montreal and got a job with him. My sister can break in any sort of colt. She's wonderful. But the man lost a lot of money and sold his horses. We've had bad luck since then. If you are wanting two people who aren't afraid of work, and who understand horses, I hope you'll give us a chance."

"I'd like to meet your sister," said Renny.

"Good." Dayborn left the room with a hangdog grace that repelled Renny, even while he was attracted by his candour. There's something queer about him, he thought.

Maurice's eyes swept the disorderly room. He gave Renny a significant look. "If this is an example of her work ..." he said under his breath.

"Sh ... they're coming."

But the young woman who returned with Dayborn was the opposite of slovenly. Her khaki breeches and shirt, open at the neck, were well-cut and clean. Her pale fair hair hung straight and sleek about her small head. She was tall, like her brother, but their only resemblance was their extreme thinness. Compared to them, the baby of fifteen months she carried in her arms, was almost aggressively plump and rosy. He wore white flannel pyjamas, and his golden hair stood moist and curly from his bath.

Dayborn introduced the two men to his sister. As Renny looked into her long amber-coloured eyes, he noticed also the fine line of her nostrils and the firm clasp of her thin calloused hand. When she smiled she showed good teeth with a small corner broken off one of the front ones.

"What a fine child!" exclaimed Renny. "What is his name?"

"Tod."

"Hello, Tod!"

The baby leant forward and grasped Renny's nose. He pressed his tiny nails into the flesh and crowed in pleasure.

"No, no, Tod!" said his mother, unclasping the little fingers.

"Come along, then," said Renny. He took the baby into his arms, where he jumped and chuckled as though that, of all places, was where he most wanted to be.

Renny gave a pleased grin. "He's taken to me at once," he said. "I wish my baby brother were half so friendly."

"Tod is like that with everyone. He has knocked about so much."

Renny gave her a swift but penetrating glance. "I'm afraid you've had rather a rough time."

She laughed shortly and a faint colour came into her thin cheeks. "It has been pretty bad — but I shouldn't complain to one who has just come back form the War."

"But that's different. You're a woman and a very feminine one, in spite of your clothes. I'm wondering if the people about here approve of you. They're very old-fashioned."

"Mrs. Stroud, our neighbour, seems not to mind. And of course she's the most important to us — owning the house."

"I'd like to meet her."

Dayborn who with Maurice had been standing by the window, exclaimed — "There she is! I believe she's coming in."

"She has seen the visitors," said Chris Cummings. "She's eaten up by curiosity. No one enters this door but she knows it."

"I'll not hear a word against her," declared Dayborn. "Think of the eggs and fruit she's given us!"

"Yes. She is kind. But behind her good nature I'll bet there's a hell of a temper."

The girl was unconventional — swearing like that! Renny wondered how she would get on in this Victorian backwater. It was all very well for his grandmother to rip out an oath on occasion but she held a position unique in the community.

She continued — "I'm afraid of people with tempers, aren't you?"

He said — "If I were my life wouldn't be worth living."

"Do you mean that your family have tempers?"

"Yes."

She eyed him critically. "I'll bet you have one too."

He laughed. "Oh, I'm a terror in a rage."

"I'd like to see you."

"Perhaps you will — if you're going to school horses for me."

Mrs. Stroud was in the room, her short, straight figure advancing almost relentlessly. Dayborn was moving solicitously beside her, as though he would leave no stone unturned to retain her goodwill. His introduction was characteristic.

"This is Mr. Whiteoak, who is going to give us a job. For heaven's sake put down the kid! This is our benefactress, Mrs. Stroud."

"I don't know why you call me your benefactress. Is it because you have taken a house I badly wanted to let?" Her voice was deep and musical. She had fine grey eyes with black lashes and heavy brows. Her thick brown hair was elaborately done. Surely she must spend hours each day over it. One feature was noticeable which scarcely counted in other women. That was her ears. The hair swept clearly away from them, revealing how flat they lay against her head, their waxen pallor, and the fact they had no inward-curling rim. She was dressed in a black skirt, a black-and-white striped silk blouse with an immaculate lace jabot, fastened by a brooch formed of the name Aimee in wrought gold. She pressed Renny's fingers in a firm clasp. She was thirty-eight.

"You know the houses well, I guess," she said.

"I knew them when they were one."

"Don't you think I was clever to divide it?"

"It is better, I suppose, than having it stand idle. I like things in their original state."

There was a domineering note in his voice that brought an antagonistic tone into her own. "Well, everyone else thinks the change is for the better. And it's given me charming neighbours." She smiled tenderly at the baby.

Renny had set him down and he was staggering about among the legs of the grown-ups as though they were forest trees. He struck at them with a willow wand he carried, as though he would chop them down. He was angelic with his silvery curls and satin skin but he made small, animal noises. Mrs. Stroud knelt in front of him, holding her face, with eyes closed, toward his. He looked at it critically, wondering whether or not to hit it.

Renny turned to Dayborn. "I must talk to you and your sister alone. Will you come to my place tomorrow morning. I'll show you the stables and horses. We'll talk over my plans for breeding. I'm cabling for an Irish hunter I saw when I was visiting relations on the way home."

"We shall be there soon after breakfast. I do hope you'll take us on." Dayborn's thin face showed a painful eagerness.

"I'd like to see both of you ride before I promise anything."

"You'll find that we can ride all right."

Maurice's deep voice broke in — "Mrs. Stroud wants us to see her house, Renny."

"Yes," she put in, "it's such an event, having strangers here."

If she had thought to propitiate Renny by this remark she was mistaken. The word stranger stabbed him like an insult. He turned it over in his mouth as though testing its ill-flavour. Then he repeated it aloud, adding — "Maurice and I were born here and our fathers before us."

"Yes, yes," she agreed quickly. "But I've so dug myself in here that *I* feel like the old-timer. It's so lovely having a possessive feeling toward a place after knocking about for years. Do forgive me!"

Renny did not want his chagrin put into words but he lifted his lip in a smile which he fancied was amicable and said:

"I'd like to see your house. To judge by the outside you must have made a good job of it."

"Tod must come too," cried Mrs. Stroud, but the child's mother picked him up.

"It's his bedtime," she said.

"Well, I shall be back to tuck him up," said Mrs. Stroud. "Are you coming, Jim?"

"I think I'll stay and wash up."

"I'll see you both tomorrow morning," said Renny.

Mrs. Stroud and Maurice had gone on. Renny and Chris Cummings exchanged a look. On his part it was a look of warm interest, calculating appraisement of her possible gifts as a breaker-in of colts. On hers, an effort to appear tough-fibred and capable, softened by the feminine thought that here was a man one could lean on.

Renny followed Mrs. Stroud and Maurice. He heard Maurice saying:

"I used to come here as a child and old Mr. Pink used to make baskets out of peach stones for me. He played the organ too."

"And so does his daughter. She's such a sweet woman but so timid. She teaches your little girl, doesn't she?"

"Yes."

"How delighted the child must be to have you home! What a reunion!"

"Yes. It is nice!"

Good God, thought Renny, the woman knows everything about everyone!

All three went into the house.

From the small square hall opened the living room. It was furnished in a definite colour scheme of blue and brown. It looked pleasantly homelike, a woman's room, after the disorder of the house next door. It glittered with order and cleanliness. The only disorder was the deep settee strewn with blue and brown damask cushions. On these young Eden Whiteoak was lounging. He sat up, his hair dishevelled, unable to conceal his astonishment.

"Hullo!" he said, staring at his older brother.

"Hullo." Renny in his turn was astonished. Eden looked suddenly grown-up. But what was he doing in this room? Smoking too. The cigarette was between his fingers. His lips were fixed in a defensive and nervous smile. He got up and turned to Mrs. Stroud.

"I've brought back the book," he said. "I came right in. I thought you'd be back."

"Oh — did you like it?" asked Mrs. Stroud, her eyes resting for an instant on the only book that was not in the bookshelves.

"Very much." Eden picked up the book. Its title was clear — a popular work on the building of small houses. He flushed and laid it down. "This isn't it," he said. He looked about vaguely. "I don't know where I've put it!"

Mrs. Stroud looked into Renny's eyes. "Perhaps you didn't know that Eden and I are friends. We got friendly over books."

There was an ironic gleam in Renny's eyes. Their glances crossed like fencing foils.

"It is so nice to find a young man who appreciates poetry," she said. "We've been reading Rupert Brooke's poems, and Flecker's. Don't you love them?"

"I don't *love* any poetry," he returned. "But" — his glance added — "I understand women like you."

Maurice said — "I think you've done a very good job in making this place over."

The incident of the book was buried. Mrs. Stroud led them from room to room. Eden came last, his eyes on his elder brother's back.

When he and Mrs. Stroud were alone he ran his hands through his hair and gave her a distraught look.

"I'm afraid I'm going to be a bad liar," he said.

"Why on earth *shouldn't* you be sitting on my settee? Why were you embarrassed?"

"Why were *you*?"

"I wasn't."

"Yes, you were."

"Well — it was just because I could see that you and he were." They sat down side by side on the settee. "Tell me about him. He isn't a bit like I thought he'd be."

Eden caught her hand and laid it against his cheek. "Save me from all soldiers!" he exclaimed.

"Darling," said Mrs. Stroud, "the only one you need saving from is yourself."

IV

THE REINS

THE GRANDMOTHER'S CHAIR had been placed out in the sun for the first time that year. She was ensconced in it, with a footstool at her feet and a rug about her knees. She wore a fur-lined cape and a crocheted wool "fascinator" was wrapped about her head. She actually felt too warm but, on the other hand, she was afraid of taking cold. It had been a long hard winter and she was tender from sitting by the fire. Her sons and daughter had insisted on her being well wrapped and her objections had been affected. She had her role of hardy pioneer to live up to. Now the sun beat down on her with affectionate warmth, for she had been the object of his solicitude for well past ninety years. She felt the benign warmth and she swelled her old body to open its pores. She had survived the winter. Now there was the long summer and autumn ahead.

The sunlight was too much for her eyes and she kept them fixed on the soft green of the grass. She examined it critically, thinking how well she knew it in its comings and goings, its eager burgeoning in the spring, its browning in the fierce heat, its second greenness in September, how it was furred by frost in the fall; drooped, withered, and died in December.

Now it was very pretty with its sharp spears bristling thick and green, tiny clover leaves dotted among it, the insect and worm life again

active. It must be fun for the earthworms when they first slid their rears
up into the sun, began to eat the earth, pass it through their bodies into
neat little piles. But they spoiled the looks of the grass. There was one
now, just beside her footstool! She carefully took her foot from the stool
and planted it on the tiny mound, flattening it. That was better. The feel
of the earth under her foot was good. She took a long look at her foot
before replacing it on the stool. She turned it this way and that, marvel-
ling how foot and ankle had kept their contours, as though still ready
to run or dance. This was the same foot that had sped across the daisied
grass in County Meath, supple and swift.

She peered down at it, wriggling her toes. They felt stiff, a little rheu-
matic inside the soft shoe. As she looked, a small curly head appeared
from under her chair, bent inquisitively to see what she was looking at. It
was the head of her youngest grandson and she remembered with a pang
that she had promised Meg to keep an eye on him. Why, he might have
got into all sorts of mischief while she sat contemplating the contours of
her foot! She peered down at him.

On the supple pivot of his neck he turned his face up to hers. His
mouth was open and she could see right into the moist rosy cavern. She
noticed the young animal brightness of his eyes, the shadow of delicacy
beneath them, the inquisitive nostrils.

"Stay just as you are," she commanded, "and I'll give you something."

She opened a small velvet bag, extracted a peppermint lozenge and
popped it into his mouth. His eyes beamed his thanks.

She was unprepared for what followed — the beam in his eyes turning to a goggling stare. He began to choke. The peppermint had stuck in
his throat. She caught him by the shoulder and began to beat him on the
back. His face grew scarlet. His eyes rolled at her in distress. She grasped
him and tried to stand him on his head. Her chair toppled. She all but
fell on him.

"Help!" she shouted in her vigorous voice. "Help!"

Meg heard her and came running across the grass.

"The baby's choking! Put him upside-down!" In an instant Meg
had reversed him. The peppermint lay on the grass. Wakefield screamed
against her shoulder.

"There, there," she soothed him. "Oh, Gran, how dangerous to give him a small hard sweet! I never do! If I hadn't heard you — but I can't bear to think of it!"

"Bless me, I was all but overturned! You don't speak of what might have happened to me!"

"If I ever leave him — he's always in some danger. Poor darling!"

"Want the candy," said Wakefield, blinking down at it through his tears. "Want the peppymint."

"No, no, darling! Meggie'll get you something nice and soft."

Old Adeline did not like this ignoring of her own narrow escape. "Almost on my head," she muttered, "and nobody cares."

"But Granny, you should have called before — not after."

The old lady peered truculently up at Meg from under the edge of the "fascinator."

"Before *what?*"

"Before you tried to put him on his head."

"He'd have choked to death if I'd hesitated. I saved his life."

"But the peppermint didn't come up till I arrived."

"Perhaps not. But it was me that brought it up."

"Why, Granny, when I picked him up he was choking."

"Nothing of the sort. By the time you got here the peppermint was on the grass."

"It was not."

"It was."

They glared at each other. It was not the first time they had had words over Wakefield.

Adeline was silent for a moment, then said:

"I'm going to have some sort of spell."

Instantly Meg was alarmed for her. She set the child on his feet and bent over her.

"Are you feeling ill? Shall I fetch Uncle Ernest?"

"No, no, don't leave me. There's that man — Wragge — what's his name? Tell him to bring me a glass of sherry." She leant back breathing heavily. The strong hairs on her chin quivered.

"Will you please bring a glass of sherry quickly," Meg called to the man. He wheeled as though he had been waiting for the order and ran into the house. He was wearing an old morning coat of Ernest's and the tails of it flapped behind his knees.

"Some biscuits too," called Adeline after him. "I feel faint."

She watched Wragge's hurrying figure as though she were drowning and he in quest of a life-belt. Wakefield picked up the peppermint and put it into his mouth.

All three waited for Wragge's return. He brought two glasses of sherry on a small silver tray and a plate of arrowroot biscuits. He was only thirty-five but his face was wizened and cynical. He produced a harmless, benign expression on it, as though it were another biscuit. He was determined to make himself indispensible in this house.

Old Adeline stretched out a handsome wrinkled hand toward the sherry. She also took a biscuit.

Wragge addressed Meg. "I thought," he said "as 'ow you might like a little somefink too, miss, seeing as you took almost no breakfast."

Meg was pleased that her delicate appetite had been noted but she was puzzled. He explained.

"I was 'elping Eliza to clear away the breakfast things. I worried when I saw your plite."

Adeline stretched out her hand for another biscuit. "I was just shaping for a bout of something," she said, "but it's passed." She beamed at Wragge. "You were just in time. I may be old and weak but I saved this child's life. It was a terrible effort." Again she put the sherry to her lips.

"It fairly took me breath away, ma'am. It was wonderful." Then he caught Meg's look of irritation and hastened to give her one of understanding.

"Baby have a biscuit," said Meg, offering him one.

"No, Baby has the peppymint."

"Look out!" cried his grandmother. "He will choke again! Reverse him!"

Meg, in trepidation, caught him up. Her wineglass was upset. "Spit it out this instant!" she commanded.

Wakefield began to choke.

"What did I tell you!"

"Put it out, darling!"

"Perhaps I could 'elp," said Wragge.

Meg surrendered the little one and closed her eyes against the sight of Wragge's joggling him by the ankles.

"Stop!" cried Adeline. "It's up!"

Sitting on Wragge's arm Wakefield shrieked joyfully — "Do it again! Do it again!"

"Put him here," said Adeline, spreading her lap. "I will give him a biscuit soaked in sherry."

In the kitchen Wragge said to Maggie, the cook — "That there old lidy is making a spoilt kid of that there, if ever there was one."

"They all are," she returned. "Him being posthumourous and knowing as a monkey."

"Some cooks won't stay where there's spoilt children and old folk to be waited on. Some won't stay where there's a basement kitchen."

She was preparing the vegetables. Now she deeply dug out the eyes of a potato and said:

"No — and some won't stay where there's a useless man hanging about."

He grinned, his jutting chin giving him an impudent look that was not displeasing to her. He watched her plump red hands that looked so clean in the murky water. "I'm going to be a lot of 'elp to *you*," he said."

She glared at him. "Well, I'd like to know *how*."

"Wait and see."

"I'll bet I wait a long time."

"I'll bet you don't."

Masterfully he took the knife from her hand and set about peeling the potatoes. "I can't 'ave you doing dirty work like this," he said.

She wiped her hands on her apron and watched him skeptically. "If you keep on like that you'll pare it all away."

"It's no thicker than yours."

They compared the wet brown parings.

Eliza came down the stairs from above, carrying a tray. She gave them a look of hate. Maggie had been a year in the house and Eliza had liked her less every day, even though she had to admit that she was an excellent cook. Now the addition of this cheeky Cockney to the kitchen made her feel that she was being forcibly pushed out. She had been going anyway but hers was still the will that ruled the housework. She was teaching Wragge how to wait at table, trying to make him understand that his nails should not be broken and dirty, brushing the dandruff from his shoulders before he carried in the tea. She looked down from the height of her long ears of perfect service at this worm, pushing himself in — pushing her out. She was going anyway, worn out in the service of this family, she repeated to herself, but she hated the sight of Wragge.

His very politeness was an insult. Now he sprang forward and took the tray from her hands.

"Allow me," he said, at the same time giving Maggie a wink. "I can't bear to see you carrying that there load. You ain't fit for it."

Eliza surrendered it without thanks and stalked to a window level with the grassy verge above. She rested her knuckles on the table that stood below the window and stared out into the sunny yard. There were clotheslines there and Ernest Whiteoak had hung his spring overcoat on one and was refreshing it with a good brushing on preparation for the season's wear. What did he mean, Eliza thought, by brushing his own coat? That had always been her job. Probably he thought she was too weak. Probably he thought she would fall down if she wielded a brush. A chill rage welled up inside her. Her knuckles grew white on the table.

"You better go," she said to Wragge, "and help Mr. Ernest with his coat."

"Right — o!" sang out Wragge, and he darted through the kitchen door, up the three steps to the yard and bent his solicitous head before Ernest.

"Can I 'elp you, sir?" He got the brush into his own hand.

Ernest was glad because he was standing on the wrong side of the line and the breeze was blowing bits of fluff into his eyes.

"If you would put the coat on, sir," suggested Wragge.

Ernest, with his help, donned the coat.

"Not many gentlemen," said Wragge, brushing furiously, "'ave such a figger as you 'ave, sir, at fifty."

Ernest smiled delightedly. "Fifty! I'm sixty-five!"

"Noa, noa, sir — I can't believe it!"

Eliza could not hear what was being said but she could imagine. "Go on," she sneered, between her clenched teeth, "flatter him — worm your way in!"

Ernest kept on the coat and joined his mother on the lawn. He had given Wragge a silk muffler he had found in the pocket of his coat. The day before he had seen Nicholas give him something. It was not well to let his brother get in ahead of him. He strode out, feeling that he looked well in the coat. His shadow lay on the grass, showing the elegant waistline.

The old lady sat tranquil, Wakefield sunk in the delicious depth of her lap. She dipped bits of biscuit into her glass of sherry and put them into his mouth. He kept his eyes on her face with the unquestioning pleasure of a little animal. Meg sat in a wicker chair reading one of Jane Austen's novels, not because she was trying to be modern or because she thought her books "delicious" or "delightful," but because Jane Austen had always been her favourite author.

Ernest turned round in front of them.

"How do you think it looks? That man of Renny's gave it a good brushing."

"Why don't you buy a new one?" asked his mother. "Your father always bought a new one."

"You must know by this time, Mamma, that my financial position is not what my father's was."

"What's the use of having a good shape if you don't dress it properly?"

"Do *you* think I should have a new coat, my dear?"

Meg pursed her lips. "This one looks very nice, but in the spring sunshine —"

"That settles it," said Ernest. "I shall go to my tailor today and order a new one." He turned suddenly to his mother. "Do you think that Renny is a bit close?"

She peered about her "Nearby d'ye mean? I want to see him."

"No, no. I mean *close.*"

"Close by?" She peered around the edge of her fascinator. "I've a bone to pick with him. Where is he?"

Ernest sighed. "Mamma, I mean *close-fisted*."

Her eyebrows shot up. "I do. He's like my father, I'm sorry to say. My father, old Dennis Court, he'd skin a flea for its hide and tallow. There was nothing he wouldn't do."

"But you are always saying, Granny, how many servants he kept," said Meg.

"He kept them because they couldn't leave him, he owed them so much."

"But I don't think Renny's close. He only has asked questions. Like about the pigs."

"He has been gong over the accounts, reckoning the vet's bill, the feed bill, wondering why there isn't feed enough raised on the place for horses and stock."

"And he home only a week!" cried Adeline. "And with a medal! That ought to be enough for him."

It made Meg unhappy to hear her best-loved brother criticized. Her face flushed as she defended him. "But he must understand the place. After all, it's his. He's got three boys to educate. And Baby coming on."

"Baby wants more sops," said Wakefield.

"Yes, my pet," said Adeline. "This child would never live if I hadn't an eye to him." She filled his little mouth.

"It's quite true," went on Meg, "that the boy's clothes have cost a lot. Their tennis rackets, their skates, their camping trips all mount up. Renny says why can't we give them more stews and fewer cutlets."

"Has he been into all that?" cried Ernest.

"By the time he's middle-aged," said Adeline, "he'll be a skinflint."

"Here he comes," said Meg.

Adeline watched the approach of the tall figure of the Master of Jalna with some uneasiness. She hoped he would not suggest that she might contribute to the family exchequer. She had no intention of doing any such thing. She had her own private fortune and she meant to hang on to it. Her husband had left her a third of his money. The remaining two-thirds he had divided among her three sons, also bequeathing house and land to the youngest and least extravagant. Nicholas and Ernest had made their shares last for twenty years and thought they had done well with it, considering that they had lived in England among people of expensive tastes. They had gone into several ventures to increase their incomes but these had always failed. At the time of their younger brother's death they had come home to Jalna and were settled down quite happily. They had felt that their presence was more or less necessary there. Now that Renny had come home they had, mingled with their sense of relief at his preservation, a stirring of resentment at his obvious desire to take over the reins.

"Renny has ridden too much," observed Ernest, "he's a bit bow-legged."

"Uncle!" cried Meg, "What nonsense! Renny has beautiful legs."

"He has the rider's gait. Back a little bent. Legs slightly bowed. Hard and wiry."

"He'll have his hands full," said Adeline, "if he tries to domineer over this household."

She pushed out her underlip and watched the approach of her eldest grandson. She bent and whispered into Wakefield's ear — "Granny's pet. Mustn't go to soldier man."

"What's he do?" whispered Wakefield.

"Kills people." Her long arm pressed the little body protectively. "Stay with Granny."

Renny came, slapping his hands together. "Hello, Wake! Come and have a ride on my shoulder."

Wakefield burrowed his curly head into his grandmother's side. She hastily finished the sherry lest it should be spilt.

"Go along, darling," urged Meg, drawing him upright. "Go to Renny."

"No. No." He squirmed and burrowed. Renny's eyes hardened. He showed his chagrin. He took Wakefield from Adeline's lap and held him at arm's length. No one was prepared for the shrieks that came from his squared mouth, as though without his volition. His face turned white. Renny set him down. At once he was quiet.

"What in thunder is the matter with him?"

"He's shy," said Meg.

"Shy! He's utterly spoilt."

"He thinks you'll hurt him."

"So I shall — if he doesn't behave himself."

He had been home a fortnight, and to speak so peremptorily! Meg flushed.

"I'm worn out," said Adeline. "I want to go into the house. Give me your arm, Ernest." But she was really amused and exhilarated.

"It hasn't been very restful for you, Mamma," remarked Ernest as he helped her to her feet.

Piers came round the side of the house wheeling his bicycle. A small case was on the carrier behind.

"I'm off," he said, kissing Meg.

"Where are you going?" asked Renny.

Piers returned his look with nonchalance.

"With Tom Fennel — camping over the weekend."

"Who said you might?"

"I told Meg I was going." There was almost effrontery in his tone, and he fourteen. Now was the time for a lesson.

"You *told* Meg you were going?"

"Yes."

"Well — put that bicycle away and next time you want to go off for the weekend, ask me."

Their eyes, bright blue and fiery brown, held their antagonism in mid-air for a space. Then Piers turned, wheeled his bicycle back to the house, went behind it, out of sight, somehow containing the fury that was in him for that space. The he hurled the bicycle to the ground. The case fell off and he kicked it. It flew open. He kicked it till the clothes inside were scattered on the grass. In his blind anger he kicked the pedal of the bicycle and hurt his toes. He kicked the bicycle in its spokes. Just as he did this Renny came round the corner of the house. They stared at each other, neither wishing that the situation might be different. There was a triumphant light in both faces.

"So that's the way you behave when you're thwarted," said Renny.

"Yes," answered Piers. He gave the bicycle another kick.

Renny picked up the strap that had fastened the case to the carrier.

Piers backed away from him, his nostrils dilated.

In an instant he was bent forward by an iron hand on his neck. Blows from the strap rained down on him. He twisted and writhed. He reached for Renny's legs. Renny thought he had never felt a body so resilient. He grinned as he brought the strap down on it.

"Will you do that again?" he asked.

"Yes!" shouted Piers.

Eden, strolling from the cherry orchard, a book in his hand, stood galvanized by the sight. His face had been dreamy but now a look of amused astonishment lighted it.

"Are you going to behave yourself?" demanded Renny.

"Yes." Piers was breathing hard. He straightened himself, his eyes clouded by tears.

"Gather your things and put them away."

Piers picked up a sweater, a pair of pyjamas, a toothbrush. He gave a surly look at Eden.

But now Eden was sorry for him. He found his soap and proffered it. But Piers ignored it.

"Let him do it himself," said Renny.

Piers pushed the bent bicycle before him into a shed.

Eden put the soap to his nose and sniffed it.

"It must have felt lovely," he said.

"What? To get a licking like that?"

"No. To give it. If you have the guts."

An hour later Ernest met Piers in the upstairs passage.

"Why, I thought you were off for the weekend!" he said, simulating surprise.

"Renny wouldn't let me go. You were there when he said," mumbled Piers. "I don't suppose it meant anything to you."

"It did indeed, but I couldn't believe he was in earnest."

"You bet he was."

"My dear boy, I am sorry!"

"So am I. It's pretty hard luck. I'm darned if I'll stand it. He thinks he owns the earth."

"I'm afraid things aren't going to be so pleasant for you boys. I'm afraid your Uncle Nicholas and Meggie and I have spoilt you."

Piers looked lovingly at him. "Well, *he's* not going to, you can see that." Piers almost blubbered.

Ernest's hand went to his pocket. "Take this, old fellow. Go to a film or something." He put a silver half dollar into Piers's hand.

Alone, Ernest felt both pleased and amused at himself. "I've given two presents this morning," he thought. "Two kind deeds. I'm like an absurd old Boy Scout."

V

FRUSTRATED PLANS

RENNY FOUND MEG poking about in the flower border to find out if a certain dark-blue delphinium, given her by Miss Pink, were flourishing. He stood watching her leisurely movements, unseen by her. As she squatted on her haunches, her light-brown hair slightly ruffled, her skin fair in the sunlight, she looked as though she had spent all her days in just such tranquil pursuits. Yet her life had been far from tranquil. Their mother had died when she was a child. She had never got on with their stepmother. She had been unfortunate in her one love affair. She had been hedged in by old people, keeping peace among them, adoring her father. Two deaths and a birth had shaken her world while Renny was in France. Tenderness for her welled up in him as he watched her hands move gently among the leaves.

"Hullo, Meggie," he said.

She looked up at him. Her face clouded.

"Oh, Renny, I did think you were hard on Piers. Not letting him go with Tom Fennel. He must be terribly disappointed."

"He's a young ruffian."

"Have you seen him since?"

"For a few minutes."

She stood up, brushing the earth from her skirt.

"I'm glad you're going to take him in hand. The truth is, I can't do anything with him."

He put an arm around her. "Don't worry. He'll soon find out he can't be high cockalorum here."

"If I try to control him, Gran interferes. She says he is like Grandfather...."

"I'll take it out of him."

"And Eden, he does just as he likes. Uncle Ernest and Aunt Augusta say he's artistic. They encourage him."

"Good God — *artistic!*"

"I don't know what to think about that Mrs. Stroud. He spends a good deal of time in her house."

"Hmph."

"Finch is a dear little boy but he's a great trial in some ways. If you tell him anything it goes straight in one ear and out the other. He can't or won't remember anything. Yesterday he put on his new shoes and ran through the gravel pit. He almost ruined them. Uncle Nick just laughed."

"Hmph."

"It's so lovely having you home again. I have had no one of my own age about for so long."

"Meg, there is something I want to talk to you about."

She looked at him with a little apprehension. She was afraid he might be going to object to the way the place was run. She loathed the words *economize* and *change*.

"Yes?"

"It's about Maurice."

A flicker of amusement passed over her face. After the four years of his absence it was not disagreeable to know that he was once again in his house beyond the ravine, still hopelessly devoted to her. It would not be the first time that Renny had pleaded for him. She looked like a teasing girl now.

"Don't imagine that I want to hear about him. You saw what my feelings were at the railway station."

"You were wrought up. Now listen, Maurice loves you and you think you ought to let bygones be bygones and marry him. He's served his country for four years. I think he deserves some reward."

"I'd be a like a medal to pin to his breast. He could throw back his shoulders and say — 'Well, boys, here is my medal.'"

"Don't be a fool, Meg."

Renny put both arms around her.

"Think of how nice it would be to have a wedding in the house. There hasn't been one for twenty years."

"Don't remind me of that wedding. If you imagine that reminding me of it will make me want another, you're mistaken."

"Well, after all, Dad was very much in love. They were happy and the marriage gave you these young brothers you're so fond of."

She laid her hand on her smooth forehead. "Oh, how unhappy I was! To have him marry our governess! Do you remember, Gran was visiting her relations in Ireland and she came all the way home to stop the marriage but she couldn't. When the hour came my hair was still in the plait I wore it in at night. I went to the church that way. It was tied with a faded blue ribbon. In the vestry Daddy was so annoyed he pulled off the ribbon and threw it under a seat. He shook out my hair so hard it hurt. I was weeping when I went into the church."

He grinned. "Yes, I remember. But that was nothing to do with what I'm telling you. I'm telling you that you should marry and have children of your own."

"I have my hands full. I don't want any more children."

"But Meggie, even if you don't want more children, you should marry. This is the mating season. Listen to those birds."

A jolly jargon of untutored sweetness rose to them from the ravine. Baritone and tenor, soprano and alto, stretched their breasts to make their own part the solo. The very branches shook with the passion of their singing.

"Let them sing," said Meg. "I'm not made that way."

He opened the little wicket gate and led her down the mossy path. At their coming the voices of the bids were stilled but the cool impersonal song of the stream could now be heard. It showed itself between branches of trees and bushes in their spring flowering.

With a somewhat dramatic gesture Meg threw out her hand toward it.

"I'm more like that," she said. "I don't need a mate."

"Don't fool yourself!" he exclaimed. "Just follow that stream down to the lake, in flood time. You'll see a mating that would put the stable to shame!"

"If you're so keen about marriage," she said, "you'd better get married yourself."

It was the last thing on earth she wanted him to do. She was surprised at his answer.

"I'd like to, if I hadn't all these boys to educate and could find the right woman."

"And bring another woman into the house," she cried. "*That would* be the last straw!"

"You'd not have to live in the house with her. You'd be happily married at Vaughanlands."

"So you want to get rid of me!"

"Meg, I only want you to be happy."

"If you think it will make me happy to live under the same roof with that child of his!"

"I've thought that all out."

"And what arrangement have you made?"

"You needn't look so supercilious. I have arranged, if you will marry Maurice, to adopt Pheasant myself."

"Well, I call that charming. I'm to go there. She's to come to Jalna. She's to take my place as the daughter of the house. Oh, Renny, I never thought you could conceive anything so horrible. I'd rather die than do it."

"Very well. Very well. For heaven's sake let's forget it. If you want to spend the rest of your days as you do —"

"I think I lead a useful life."

"Useful. Yes."

"I don't lack affection. The boys —"

"Maurice loves you with a *man's* love."

"He is nothing to me."

Renny fixed his eyes on her. "Nothing?"

She coloured but she repeated with more vehemence: "*Nothing*."

"All right. I don't believe you but this is the last time I shall ever speak of it."

"Thank goodness for that."

She turned and began to ascend the path. He saw that she had really grown much stouter during his absence. She found the steep path heavy going. And she only thirty-four! "I wish you could see a back view of yourself!" he called out derisively after her.

She stopped stock-still but did not look round.

They remained so, speechless and immovable till he flung down the path, crossed the stream, climbed the still steeper path beyond and passed through a small wood of oak trees into a field. The field had been sown with fall wheat. Its bold promise was tempered by the yellow of the mustard flowers. Across it he could see the small figure of Pheasant.

She saw him and came, skirting the field, her brown hair flying about her shoulders. It being Saturday she wore an old dress too short in skirt and sleeve. She looked up into his face eagerly. He cursed himself for having asked her how she would like to be his little girl and come to Jalna to live. He forced a cheerful grin to his lips.

"Hullo!" she called out.

"Hullo! Having a nice walk?

She looked at him gravely.

"No. I've been waiting for you."

"I'm afraid I've kept you a long while. I didn't know that I mentioned any special time."

"You didn't. You only said that by the end of the week something might happen that might settle whether I could.... It's Saturday today."

"Yes. And it has happened."

She gave him a penetrating glance. "Did it — happen *wrongly?*"

"Pheasant — I don't believe you really would want to leave your home — Maurice — and come to Jalna."

"Then ... you think I told lies when I said I would."

"No. But — ours is such a big family. All those boys —"

"But ... when you talked about my going ... you said what fun."

"I know. But there's Maurice. After all, he's your father."

"He'd be glad to part with me."

"Oh no. He's not like that."

She looked down, her lashes quivering. Her child's face marked by deep thought.

"You've been alone too much," he exclaimed.

He put his arm about her and pressed her to his side. But she drew away. She looked into his eyes, as though in wonder. She said:

"I never know what grown-ups mean. It's not what they say."

He answered her almost sternly — "I mean what I say. But I got this affair the wrong way about. I should have made sure that what I wanted would be possible before I spoke of it to you."

She drew her smooth forehead into puzzled lines. "But what is it all about? What was this thing you couldn't make happen? Does Maurice know?"

"Yes."

"That's why he couldn't eat his breakfast. Mrs. Clinch says he's sickening for something."

"This is going to be worse for him than you, Pheasant."

"But what *is* this thing? May it happen sometime?"

"Perhaps. I hope so. Look here … I'm going to tell you. You're not like other kids. Let's sit down."

They dropped on to the young grass that was more cool and moist than the sandy soil beneath. They were in a fence corner where wild convolvulus had shown since sunrise how fast it could climb. Its first frail blossom already hung its head in the heat. Pheasant touched it with her cheek. Then she turned her dark eyes to Renny with a strange mingling of trust and suspicion in them.

"You know," he said, "that Maurice and my sister Meg were once engaged to be married."

"Yes. And I know what unengaged them." An almost cynical smile curved her lips. "She *was* a silly."

"Yes. She was and is." He lighted a cigarette and drew a puff or two in silence. She had made it easier for him to tell her.

"I had the idea," he went on, "that as Maurice has been so long away Meg might change her mind and marry him now if —" He hesitated.

"If I went to Jalna to live?"

"Exactly. I'd lose a big sister and gain a little one."

"No, no," her face was contorted. "It's not like that! It's just that she won't come here if I'm here and she won't let me in there. I understand

and I don't care. I — I don't care." Her face was ugly in her supreme effort at self-control. "I don't want to be anybody's child. I — I'm twelve. I'll soon be a woman."

He took her hand and it lay like a cold little fish in his tense clasp. "I deserve to be kicked," he said.

They sat motionless for a space while her self-control tautened. Then she drew her hand decisively from his. "Goodbye," she said, "I'm going."

"Have you got the little knife I brought you?" he asked.

"Yes. It really wasn't for me, was it? I'll give it back, if you like."

"Good Lord, no! I don't want it back. But I thought kids always lost things."

She smiled at him tremulously, then turned quickly away. She slid through an opening in the wire fence that seemed impossibly narrow. He saw that it sagged a little and was evidently shaped by her continual using.

She ran straight to the house and closed the front door behind her. She had been holding a single sob tightly in her throat as she ran. Now safe inside the door she let it go with a harsh sound that hurt. Her heart stopped its beat in a moment of fear. What if Maurice were in the sitting room and had heard it? But there was dead silence in the house. After the furbishing for his return Mrs. Clinch had allowed it to revert to its usual fustiness. The air was heavy with the smell of old upholstery and damp wallpaper and a something that was suggestive of Mrs. Clinch herself.

Suddenly the door behind Pheasant opened and Maurice was almost on her. He started, then saw her face. "Is anything the matter?" he asked.

She shook her head. She wanted to fly up the stairs, but she stayed where she was, looking up into his face.

"Can't this door be left open?" he asked.

"Mrs. Clinch doesn't like it open."

"Mrs. Clinch be damned."

"It fades things and gives her neuralgia. She's awful when she has it. It goes from her bad tooth right into her ear."

"Damn her ear! I must get someone else to keep house."

"You can't. She wouldn't go."

"She'll have to, if —" He stopped short.

"*That's* not going to happen."

"What?" he stared at her astonished.

"Renny Whiteoak told me."

They stood in a strange unaccustomed intimacy. The door at the end of the passage opened and Mrs. Clinch appeared. She saw the two standing guiltily and the door open. Her whole face tightened, as though she had pulled a drawstring. Then she laid a work-worn hand on the side of her face and after another askance look at the door went heavily up the stairs.

Maurice hastily closed it. The sound of Mrs. Clinch's bedroom door shutting came from above.

"It was strange," said Maurice, "for Renny Whiteoak to speak of such a thing to a child. How did he come to do it?"

"He had promised me — something, if it happened."

Maurice looked at her sombrely.

"And then he told you it wasn't going to?"

"Yes."

"Well — you shouldn't have been mixed up in it." He turned from her and went into the sitting room.

Pheasant flew up the stairs. From Mrs. Clinch's room came the smell of Minard's Liniment.

Safe inside her own room she drew a deep breath of its seclusion. There was a greenish light in the room from the thickness of a cedar tree. She saw her full-length reflection in an old pier glass, like the ghost of a little girl come to meet her. But this glass was never secure in its frame and, at the tremor of her step, it tilted forward and the reflection was lost.

Pheasant put her hand in her pocket and felt the little knife Renny had given her. She took it out and it lay on the palm of her hand.

"I always think," she said loud, "that there's something sad about this little knife."

It was as though she sought to explain away the tears that ran down her cheeks.

VI

EDEN AND MRS. STROUD

STILL WITH THE copy of Dante in one hand and Piers's cake of Windsor soap in the other, Eden walked thoughtfully along the path that led to the road where Mrs. Stroud lived. He was turning over in his mind the changes made by the return of his elder brother. He was reaching the conclusion that he preferred Jalna as it was in the days of the War. Renny's letters from the front had often been amusing. It was right that one of the family should be serving with the Buffs. If the War had gone on for another year Eden himself would have joined up. His father had consistently indulged him because he was like the wife he so tenderly loved. His mother had been the one to spoil all her children. When at fourteen he had been bereft of them both, his grandmother, his aunt, uncles, and Meg had been in agreement to humour the willful golden-haired boy. Now, with this hard-handed veteran of the War set up as master of the house, and apparently determined to force his will, things were going to be very different.

For one thing, too many questions were being asked. Not that his own liberty had yet been curtailed. Each morning he, Piers and Finch, took the train to the nearby town, the two younger to attend a large boys' school, Eden to the University. Eden and Piers were athletic and popular. Eden was a fast runner and a good jumper: Piers, the best of his age in the football field.

In the journeys to town they had had conversations which had produced an odd sort of partnership between them.

Piers was a born farmer. Already he was talking of the day when he would leave school to devote himself to the land. The others might breed horses. He would sow crops, rear cows and pigs; already he knew a lot about them. His blue eyes would shine with pleasure when he saw a lolling sow suckling her plump litter on a field of swarthy stubble.

It would be a good thing for Piers and Eden, their uncles said, to handle money and become accustomed to its careful usage. Eden had, in the last year, bought his own clothes and shown very good taste. Piers had bought bats, balls, racquets, skates, the innumerable things that seemed necessary to him. They had brought home silver mugs for their athletic prowess and added them to the collection already at Jalna.

Eden was, at the moment, wearing an extremely well-fitting grey suit, one of the three he had ordered that spring. He had lately become conscious of his good looks, and no wonder, for since his acquaintance with Mrs. Stroud he had had them compared to Greek sculpture, and deplored as dangerous to woman. Still he was not vain of them. Rather he was amused by Mrs. Stroud's extravagances. He was eager to see her for he had not been to her house for several days.

He vaulted over the gate giving on to the road that led to her house, having put both book and soap into his pocket. Already that road was becoming dusty and he took to the path that ran along the verge. His whistle was clear as that of the oriole that had just crossed the first straws in his nest in the tallest elm.

Mrs. Stroud opened the door herself. Her eyes lighted in surprise.

"Will you let me in?" he asked.

"Do you ask that because you've stayed away for so long?" Her deep moving voice always gave him a sense of something mysterious in her.

"No. Because I've come back so soon. You must get tired of me."

"What have I done to deserve that?"

"But — I don't want to — come too often."

"Why?"

"You have other friends."

"Who are they?"

"Well —" He hesitated and gave a little laugh. She took him by the arm and drew him towards the living room.

"You know that you are the only one who matters to me — in these parts."

He did not know why she had come there to live. Always there was that sense of mystery about her.

Sinking on to the blue sofa he said, accepting the cigarette she offered him:

"I had rather be here than anywhere.... The truth is we've been having some extra lectures."

The truth was that he had met a girl at a tennis match who had interested him to the eclipse of Mrs. Stroud. But, in what a short time the girl had bored him!

"Isn't it funny," he said, after a few inhalations of the Russian cigarette for which Mrs. Stroud had given him a taste, "how little there is in the girls you meet?"

"Very funny." She looked at him between narrowed lids. "It shouldn't be so. You should find them fascinating at your age."

"I don't. Either they're too prim or they're too anxious to be thought sophisticated. They're not a bit like you."

She gave her musical laugh.

"Heaven forbid that they should be!"

But her face and figure relaxed. She pictured, with a clarity that would have surprised him, what had been happening in the past days. She gave a wide smile that showed her fine teeth and asked:

"How is that soldier brother of yours? Is it nice having him home again?"

"It's odd your asking that," replied Eden. "I was thinking, just as I was on my way here, that it's not so pleasant as we had expected."

"I'm not surprised."

"Why?"

"He seems to me an unsettling sort of person."

"I never used to think so."

"Probably you both have changed. He has been through a war and you have grown up — almost."

"Oh, Mrs. Stroud, that last word was unkind!"

She gave him a teasing look. "Do you feel entirely grown-up?"

"Except when I'm with you."

"I wonder how I ought to take that remark," she said musingly.

"Well, I meant it for a compliment — in a sort of way."

"What else besides a compliment?" He gave her his odd smile, in which the eyes had no part but remained speculative and even ironic. A nerve in his cheek twitched. He said — "I wanted to make you a little angry."

"Does that please you? I mean, to make me angry?"

"It makes us seem a little more — intimate."

He saw that she was considering this and he thought — "I wish I hadn't said that! I wish I hadn't. She'll expect — God, I shall feel a fool!"

But she only laid her hand on his knee and said gently — "A nerve in your cheek is twitching. You are tired. You have been working too hard."

"I don't feel it," he said. "Where is it?"

She touched his cheek with the tip of her second finger. "There."

He caught her hand and held it to his lips. "Now," he thought, "what will she say?"

For a moment she left her hand tranquilly in his, then withdrew it and said:

"Tell me about this brother."

"Well, he used to be the eldest son and my father's favourite, but now he's the master of the house. We can't get used to it."

"Who is we? "

"All of us, right from my grandmother down. We'd got a plan of living and it worked out very well. We can't get used to his interference. He's always interfering."

"With such a majority against him I don't see how he can get his own way."

"So far, he has only attacked us separately."

Mrs. Stroud gave a mischievous smile. "Why don't you attack him in a body then?"

"I wish we could!"

"In any case I should think your combined resistance would wear him down."

"You mustn't think we're having rows at Jalna. We're not — yet. But I don't see how we can go on like this. Now just listen.... He's been home for a month. In that time he has had words with Grandmother about Wakefield. He's had words with my aunt over this man Wragge he's brought home with him. Aunt Augusta says it's outrageous that such a fellow should act as butler in her father's house. She says her father would turn over in his grave if he could see him handing about the soup. On the other hand, Gran likes Wragge. She's always against Aunt Augusta. She's fitted him out with an old livery three sizes too large for him and she's encouraging him in his courtship with the cook. Eliza has left."

Eden stopped talking. He began to laugh softly as though at himself.

"You know," he said, "I love talking about us. I think we're maddening but I love us. Don't you think we're lovable?" He looked at her slyly. "Or do you only see the maddening side?"

"I wish I might be invisible in your house for a day. What about your uncles? Are they willing to be domineered over?"

"Not they! They've each had a real set-to with him. Uncle Nick's was about a stallion my father bought. Uncle Nick sold it last year. It wasn't paying for itself. It wasn't a good sire. But Renny wasn't told. Now he's furious. He and Uncle Nick shouted at each other. Grandmother was so excited that she dropped her egg flip and it spilled down the front of her dress."

"In this case my sympathy is with your brother."

"Mine isn't. Uncle Nick did the right thing. As a matter of fact, we needed the money. It seems to get scarcer every year."

"And the other uncle?"

"Oh, Uncle Ernest! He's a dear old boy! He'd never have a quarrel with anyone. But he and Renny had a passage over an armchair that was a favourite of father's. Uncle Ernie took it up to his room and Renny said he missed it from its place by the fire. He said he could just see father sitting in it with one of his spaniels between his knees, pulling burrs out of its ears and hiding them under the chair, where Mother wouldn't see them. Uncle brought the chair down again and now Renny sits in it. But there's a feeling between the two. In fact, Renny's halo of a returned hero is beginning to grow spikes. He's been after me, too, about my tailor's bill. He says that I'm too young to order just what I want, but I've done it for the past year. He thinks Piers has more tennis racquets, skates, and hockey boots than he needs, and so he has! He says Meg has spoilt us. He's told the youngsters that they must ask his permission to do things. I've just seen him giving young Piers a good hiding."

"What had Piers been doing?"

"Kicking his bicycle about."

"Tck! And the baby? The little one?"

"Oh, Renny frightened him so on his first day at home that Wakefield has begun to stammer whenever he sees him. He says — 'P-pl-ease, no! B-b-b-baby says s-soldier must go way!' Aunt Augusta says — 'Poor child, this may change his whole life!' And Gran gives him a nibble of her fruit cake."

Mrs. Stroud's large grey eyes rested on him with commiseration. "Not a very tranquil environment for a young poet."

Eden flushed, but he laughed gaily. "I'm not a poet yet." His flush deepened and he added — "But I did write something last night and I've brought it to show you, if you don't mind."

"You know what I feel about that."

"I hope you'll like it."

She rose and moved a vase of flowers to another position, then reseated herself in a chair opposite him, as for a ceremony, and looked at him with grave attentiveness. Eden took a small exercise book from his pocket and turned its pages nervously.

A quick rap sounded on the door.

"Bad luck!" exclaimed Mrs. Stroud softly. "But I'll not answer it."

They sat in guilty silence while the knock was urgently repeated. Young Dayborn's voice came: "Mrs. Stroud! Are you there? May we borrow your tea kettle? Ours has sprung a leak."

He left the door and moved toward the window. Mrs. Stroud darted to that corner of the room where they would be hidden. Eden pressed close after her. They crouched together. Her bodice was drawn tight across her breast. She breathed quickly. He threw his arm about her shoulders. Between irritation at the interruption, and the ridiculousness of their situation, he began to feel hysterical. He could scarcely control his laughter. Mrs. Stroud laid a firm hand on his mouth. They crouched close together while the knocking was reiterated. Then the outer door opened. Light steps went towards the kitchen.

"He is going for the kettle," she whispered. "When they want anything you can't stop them."

"I hope the kettle is full of boiling water and he upsets it over himself." He mumbled the words against her palm.

The steps were retraced. The kettle struck sharply against the door handle.

"He's gone!" breathed Mrs. Stroud. Eden's lips still moved but now he was kissing her hand. She took it away but flashed him a look that gave more than she had denied. They rose like one and returned to their seats. She looked a little flustered and touched her hair with her fingers. She spoke rather excitedly.

"Really those people are becoming impossible! I have no privacy. They come and go as though we lived in the one house."

Eden was suddenly sulky. He stared at his hands that hung limply between his knees. Mrs. Stroud spoke cheerfully:

"How are those two getting on with the schooling?" she asked.

"Schooling?" he repeated as though he had never before heard the word.

"Your brother's horses. They're pretty good riders, aren't they?"

"Yes, the girl especially. They are training a horse for the Grand National. Haven't they told you?"

"I believe they did mention something of the sort.... But don't let us talk of them. I want to hear your poem."

"Who began talking about them? Not me."

"I spoke of them just for something to say. I couldn't ask you to read your poetry the instant he had gone."

"We might have been silent."

"It *was* stupid of me! "

"It doesn't matter."

"It does."

"I think I'll go. I'll leave the thing and you can read it later, when you're in the mood."

"I'm in the mood now." She spoke authoritatively. "Eden, don't look like that. You're hurting me. Come...." She picked up the book and put it in his hand.

He sprang up and tossed it on to the bookshelves.

"There! That's how much I want to read it! Goodbye. I'm sorry if I'm being disagreeable."

Mrs. Stroud rose calmly. She brought a chair, mounted it, and retrieved the book. She put it into Eden's hands with a smile, intimate and pleading. He accepted it with sudden meekness and turned the pages. He began to read in a low voice:

"I and my shadow found each other.
After the long night.
We —"

His voice faltered. "I can't," he said, and looked at her in despair. He got to his feet.

"I should not have asked you."

"It's all right.... Goodbye."

"When shall you come again?"

"Soon. Tomorrow — if I may."

"I'll be thinking of you, Eden."

A steady noise of hammering began next door. To its accompaniment they parted, he going out by a side door so that he might not be observed by the neighbours. The child could be heard crying.

She watched his departing figure till out of sight. Then she returned to the living room. She plumped the cushions and emptied the ashtrays. She took up Eden's book and held it to her lips. The hammering continued. She gave a vindictive look at the dividing wall.

"I have a good mind," she said, addressing her unseen neighbours, "to throw you out — baby and all!"

But, when young Dayborn returned the kettle, there was no lessening in the kindness of her attitude toward them. "You can't imagine," she said, "what it means to me to have intimate neighbours. Sometimes I get spells of depression. Then I remember you three on the other side of the partition and everything seems brighter."

VII

FINCH AND THE WHITE RAT

FINCH HAD EIGHTY cents. By an iron-willed saving of his pocket money, which was five cents a week, he had accumulated forty cents. Piers had given him ten cents for taking his bicycle to the repair shop; Uncle Nicholas had given him ten cents for finding his spectacles; Meg had given him five for taking castor oil; and he had earned fifteen for helping to sort sound apples from rotten ones. Now he had enough to buy the white rat his heart was set on. The white rats were for sale at a shoemaker's in Steed, the village seven miles away. Each rat had its own cage with a wheel for exercising. Not that his rat would spend much time in its cage. It would be playing about with him, learning to do wonderful tricks, running all over him with its dear little white feet.

His body felt light as air, with the eighty cents in the small leather purse in his pocket. He could not keep his feet on the ground but skipped and leaped like a lamb. There would be seventy-five cents for the white rat and five cents for caramels. What a day! What life and power and joy were his!

It was Saturday morning and he was free. His heart was so full that he made up his mind that he would brush his teeth as a gesture of gratitude to the Providence which ordered his life. He would be good that day if ever he had been good. What would the rat's name be? For it must have a name. Something imposing and nice to say. He would ask Meg. Not that she was entirely sympathetic about the rat but she was kind and quite good at names. She generally named the horses and dogs.

He stood by the washing stand in his little pyjamas with a patch on the seat, his toes curled up from the cold of the square of linoleum that lay before the stand, his hair on end. His own toothpaste was gone and he thought he would take some of Piers's. It was neatly folded at the bottom, plump to squeeze. He laid a blob of the paste on his brush and began violently to rasp it across his large new front teeth. He was cautious about the back ones because of a loose one that ached. It had been the bane of his life for weeks — aching and wobbling — wobbling and aching. The new tooth beneath had pushed it almost out but still it clung. His tongue was sore from its sharp edge. He could not enjoy his meals but he kept the discomfort to himself because he dreaded to have the tooth pulled out.

Even while he was being careful of it the door behind him opened suddenly and Piers came in. Finch started and the brush knocked against the bad tooth. He doubled up with pain. He dropped the brush.

"Ooo — oo — oo!" he moaned.

"What's the matter?" asked Piers.

"It's my tooth! I hurt it."

Piers came to his side. What if Piers should smell the wintergreen scent of his own paste!

"Let's see."

Finch straightened himself and shut his mouth tight. The tooth was jumping.

"It's all right," he gasped.

Piers took him by the chin. "Open your mouth. I won't hurt you," he said softly.

"You promise you won't touch it? "

"Sure. Don't be a little ass."

Finch opened his mouth. The smell of the wintergreen came out. He pointed. "There!"

"You've been using my toothpaste!"

"Just this once. Honestly."

Piers did not look angry. He just stared into his junior's mouth. "It shouldn't be pulled," he said, "while it's aching."

"Shouldn't it?" Finch's fears subsided. He looked trustingly at Piers. "Why? "

Piers hesitated.

"Would it hurt more?"

"No. It wouldn't hurt more. But it would stick in tighter. They always stick when they're aching. I don't suppose it's very loose anyway."

"Oh, it's pretty loose." Something drove him to add — "Just feel it."

Piers's fingers approached the tooth tentatively. "I'd better not touch it. It might hurt."

"I mean, just wobble it."

Piers gently took the tooth between finger and thumb. Then electrically there was a fierce tweak.

"Ouch!" cried Finch. "You beast! You did hurt it after all. It's aching like the dickens. You think it's funny, don't you." He glared at Piers and felt for the tooth with his tongue.

Piers laughed delightedly.

"It's out, you little duffer! I pulled it." He displayed the tooth on his broad palm.

"Out!" gasped Finch. "Out! Gosh, how glad I am! Oh, thank you, Piers!"

"Rinse your mouth with salt and water." Piers laid the little tooth on the washing stand. "And next time you have toothache come to me."

The joy of eating breakfast without the aching tooth! He crunched his toast without a care in the world. Sometimes, with his tongue, he felt for the little hard knob of the new tooth.

There were only himself, Wakefield, Meg, and Renny at table. Grandmother had her breakfast in her room. The uncles and Eden were still in bed. Piers and Aunt Augusta had theirs earlier. The sun poured into the room. The windows were open. There were white lilacs on the table, as many plumes as possible pressed into the tall vase. Meg's blue eyes rested on them approvingly.

"The lilacs are lovely this year," she said. Renny looked up from the account of a polo match in which he had played the day before. He was so interested that he forgot to chew and one cheek was distended by a bite of toast.

"Yes," he agreed." They're lovely."

"What are?" she asked, cornering him.

"Your eyes." He grinned and crunched his toast.

"Baby, eat your porridge. You are just playing with it."

"Baby wants more sugar on it."

Meg weakly began to sprinkle sugar over the porridge.

"More."

"No. That is enough."

"Baby says *more*." He lay down on his spine.

"Sit up," Renny said sternly.

"C-c-can't s-s-s-s—"

"*Please* don't start him stammering first thing in the morning. It will go on all day." Hastily Meg added more sugar. Wakefield smiled seraphically at her. He began to eat. He kicked his heels softly against his chair.

Renny laid down his paper and again attacked his sausages and bacon.

"I wish I might have seen the polo match," said Finch.

"I'll take you next time."

Finch's face glowed. "Oh, thanks, Renny." Now was the time to ask if he might go to Steed. He drew a deep breath. He would ask neither Renny nor Meg, but the air midway between them. He fixed his eyes on that space and got out:

"Please, may I go to Steed to buy my white rat? I have the money all ready. Please may I go?"

"Baby wants a wh-wh-white wat."

"Shut up!" said Finch fiercely.

"Finch, don't be rude. I dislike rats but I suppose you may go."

"He can come with me," said Renny. "I am going to see a man who wants the pony I rode yesterday. I am going in the car."

"How soon?"

"In ten minutes. Another cup of tea, Meg."

It was heaven to be in the car with Renny, flying swiftly toward the place where his loved white rat, all unsuspecting of his coming, waited. He sat small and tense beside his elder, his hand between his bare knees clasping his purse. The fields with their growing crops, the little gardens with their young flowers, road menders with their picks and muscular arms, girls with their hands full of marsh marigolds, made him strangely happy. He felt with his tongue for the space where the aching tooth had been. He knew what he would do. He would buy caramels for Piers from the extra five cents. Piers deserved a present.

Renny was letting him out in front of the shoemaker's. "I'll be back here for you in half an hour," he said.

Finch was in the shop.

There were a dozen mice and rats in cages, but only one he wanted. It was the smallest rat, scarcely larger than a mouse, with a silky white body with black markings, bright eyes, and delicate pink feet. He was so intelligent, the shoemaker said, you could teach him anything.

Now Finch had him, safe in his cage, clasped in his two hands. He walked carefully so as not to affright him. There was five cents left in his purse. He made his way along the village street to the confectioner's.

Outside the shop he thought he heard music. He was not sure because there was a kind of music inside him. His heart beat in time to it. Then he saw an organ grinder with a little barrel organ just ahead of him. A monkey, wearing a tight red jacket, was perched on the organ. Its sweet wistful eyes peered first at Finch, then at the rat in the cage. A quiver ran through the length of its subtle tail. It beamed with pleasure. Its eyes invited the confidence of the rat. The rat, clasping the bars of the cage with its delicate paw, looked at the monkey without fear. The overture from *William Tell* came rushing out of the organ.

The monkey doffed his gilt-braided cap and bowed to Finch. Finch could not help himself. He took out his purse and gave his last five cents to the monkey. The monkey grinned his pleasure. The organ grinder touched his cap. The music changed to a Strauss waltz. Finch, hypnotized, followed the organ from street to street.

Suddenly, Renny's tall figure loomed above him. "You little dud," he said. "I've been all over the place after you. Hop in." He half lifted, half pushed Finch into the car. The car started with a jerk, for he was an abominable driver. A back wheel took the edge of the curb. The rat looked wildly through the bars.

"You're all right. You're safe, pet," whispered Finch, his thin hands encircling the cage.

On the open road Renny dropped a chocolate bar into Finch's lap. "Give me a bite of it too," he said.

"We're off together," thought Finch. "We're pals. He's splendid! He's kind!" He offered Renny a square of chocolate. Renny bent his head and took it into his mouth from Finch's fingers. Finch thought:

"He looks as though he could give a good bite." He asked:

"Did the man buy the polo pony?"

"Yes."

"I'm glad. Can I tell the others?"

"No, I want to tell them myself."

"Do you think the rat might have a bit? "

"Of course. They'll eat anything."

Renny watched the rat take the bit of chocolate in his tiny paws and hold it to his lips, on which the pale whiskers vibrated. The car almost collided with a load of hay driven by one of his own men.

"It would have served him right if I had run into him," he remarked to Finch as they sped on. "Fancy having to buy hay with the amount of land we have! "

"It's a darned shame," said Finch solemnly. Their anger fused together into a flame of comradeship. Finch asked:

"How old do rats live to be, Renny?"

"It depends on how well you treat them."

"Do pet rats live longer than wild ones?"

"Well, they haven't poison and traps to contend with."

"You saw lots of wild ones in the trenches, didn't you?"

"They weren't so wild."

"I don't suppose they lived to be old."

"Not when I could prevent it."

"But you do like this one, don't you?"

"He's a nice little fellow."

Finch saved a square of chocolate for Piers. Piers opened the door of the cage and allowed the rat to run out on to the palm of his hand. It stood breathless in an agony of fear and delight. Finch's heart was filled with envy at the sight of it on Piers's palm.

"Be careful!" he implored. "It'll get away. Please give it to me, Piers! *Please!*"

Piers's lips curved at the delicious tickling of the tiny paws. Then his tilted hand approached the cage and he tipped the rat into captivity.

"He's a nice little fellow," he said. "Don't stuff him with food."

The rat was already nibbling the bread soaked in milk which the cook had provided.

"He's hungry. He likes it. I know what he likes."

Finch took the white rat everywhere he went. He could not bear to be separated from him. He could scarcely eat his lunch for thinking of him. He asked everyone what he should name him. But no names suited. No name was good enough. He decided he would have a secret name for the rat which none but they two should know.

Wakefield begged to hold the rat for just one little minute, and Grandmother insisted that he should be allowed.

"He'll drop it," said Finch. "I know he'll drop it."

"No, Baby won't drop it." He held it close in his little sallow hands.

"You're squeezing it!" cried Finch. Baby dropped it.

There was a wild search. The rat was somewhere in the massive folds of Grandmother's apparel. She was more frightened than she would own. "He'll bite me," she declared, "but I don't suppose I shall die of it. Bother the boy. I wish he'd keep his pets off me!" She peered anxiously into the bosom of her dress.

"There he is!" shouted Uncle Nicholas. Like a furtive thought the rat darted across the room.

"Boney!" screamed Meg. "He's after it!"

All predatory wings and beak, the parrot had swooped from his perch. He hung, like an electric cloud, above the scurrying rat. Finch threw himself between the two and felt his pet scramble to safety under his jacket. His heart and the rat's palpitated beneath his jacket. He shouted:

"I knew he'd drop it. He shan't touch it again! Nobody can touch it! It's mine!"

With a perfunctory slap on the behind, Eden turned him out of the room. He went to the orchard and lay on the warm grass, alone with the rat.

It was growing more and more tame. It no longer quivered under the outstretched hand but gave itself meekly to his caresses. He lay at full length while it ran here and there over him, in and out of his sleeves, through his fine straight hair, or peered at him between the spears of long orchard grass.

As it was Saturday, he knew that Miss Pink would be practising on the organ. He thought he would like to take the rat to the church and show him to Miss Pink. So, when he had tired of the orchard, he trotted along the grass path that led to the road. Every now and again he stopped to tempt the rat with some tidbit, a clover blossom which it rejected, a bit of bread dropped by a bird, a biscuit from his own pocket. Obligingly the little rat nibbled till his sides were broad as his length. He raised his sweet face trustingly to Finch.

The church was pierced by a sunbeam from the west window. Miss Pink was playing "Lead, Kindly Light," with variations. He stole softly up the chancel steps and sat down on a low seat by the organ. The music enveloped him, caught him up as in a cloud. His rapt eyes were fixed on Miss Pink's profile. The rat lay curled in his hand.

Miss Pink knew he was there. She played on and on for his pleasure. She always felt that she played better when Finch Whiteoak was listening.

She was not prepared for the appearance of the rat on the keys. Finch had forgotten him and he had set out to explore. Miss Pink screamed. She was frightened and would not be mollified. Finch regretfully took the rat and trotted out into the churchyard.

There the grass, green as the sea, rose and sank over the graves. The old headstones slanted this way and that, like drooping sails. But the mariners all were asleep. Like the sound of distant surf, the singing of the organ came from the church. Like a lighthouse, the tall plinth that marked the Whiteoak plot rose above the clustered graves. So Finch saw it and leant against the iron chain that surrounded the plot. He put down the rat and it ran in and out among the graves. It perched on the headstone of an infant Whiteoak, and nibbled at something held between its paws. Finch and the rat spent a happy hour there.

As Piers was getting into bed beside Finch that night he said — "You've got the rat in here. I smell him."

"Please let me have him, Piers. He'd be terribly lonely if he was put outside and he scarcely smells at all. Sniff hard and you'll find he scarcely smells."

Piers sniffed and grunted.

"Where is he?"

"Under the bed." There was bright moonlight. Piers rolled over and looked beneath the bed.

"Doesn't he look comfortable?"

"He's awfully fat."

Finch chuckled. "You bet he is. He's had all sorts of good things."

"You handle him too much."

"He likes it. He knows me better than anyone."

Each could see the other's face upside down staring at the rat's cage. Finch's hair touched the floor. It was a pale halo in the moonlight.

"I had white mice once. Do you remember?"

"Yes. One of the dogs killed them. Were you sorry?"

"Yes, — at the time. I've never wanted any more." Piers lay back on his pillow and yawned. He murmured — "I tell you the rat stinks."

"I think it's a nice fuzzy, warm smell."

"It's the last night you can keep him here."

"I'll find a place for him tomorrow."

"All he'll need is a grave, if you go on stuffing him and handling him the way you do."

"Don't you worry about him," returned Finch.

Long after Piers was asleep Finch lay staring at the patch of moonlight by the bed. He would strain his ears if his pet moved. When he heard a faint movement he would lean over the side of the bed and see the tiny creature once more compose himself to sleep.

It was grey dawn with a scattering of raindrops on the roof when Finch woke. He crept out of bed and lifted the cage from the floor. The rat was curled close round and sleek. It was very fast asleep. Finch opened the door of the cage and took out the rat. It lay curled in his hand. It was quite cold. Why — it was *dead!* It lay in his hand with no breath of life in it.

After a little he was able to think more clearly. He made up his mind that he would say the rat had escaped. He would leave the door of the cage ajar and hide the rat till he could bury it secretly. He stole softly to the clothes cupboard and hid the little body in an old shoe. It would be safe there. It lay curled in the shoe as though sleeping.

Finch crept into bed and pulled the bedclothes over his head. In his mind he rehearsed what he would say — "Why — my little rat's gone, Piers! It's escaped. I'll bet I didn't shut the door tight! It's a darn shame, isn't it? But I'm like you, Piers. I don't want another. What I'm glad of is that you pulled my loose tooth."

VIII

SCHOOLING FOR HORSES AND MEN

JIM DAYBORN AND Chris Cummings were going toward the stables for their morning's work, he carrying Tod, she a bundle containing an extra sweater, a rug for the child's rest time, a packet of sandwiches, some biscuits, and a bottle of lukewarm tea. All three wore a businesslike early-morning air that revealed nothing of the disorder they had left behind them in the house. The baby sat on Dayborn's arm with an expression of determination on his chubby blond face. He seemed to feel that the livelihood of all three depended on his behaviour. Dayborn carried him so carelessly that a sudden stride over a ditch all but dislodged him from his perch, but he allowed himself no more than a moment's discomfiture, then gripped Dayborn's collar more firmly.

"I hope to God," said Dayborn, "that the old groom hasn't given that four-year-old sixteen pounds of oats, as he did yesterday. He was like a tornado to handle."

"Whiteoak himself overfeeds them, so what can you expect of the grooms?"

They walked on in silence for a space, leaving dark footprints on the dew-grey grass. Then Dayborn said, the colour rising in his thin cheeks as he spoke:

"He's making up to you, isn't he?"

She laughed. "The groom?"

"You know who I mean."

"If you mean Renny Whiteoak, you're dotty."

He looked shrewdly into her face. "You're a bad liar," he said.

"And you're a bad judge of character. He's not interested in women."

Dayborn gave a derisive laugh. "You should hear what they say about him in the village!"

"Well, when we're together, it's always horses he talks about."

"What do his eyes say?"

"You make me tired, Jim.... I'm able to look after myself."

Tod looked dubiously into their faces, as though he feared a quarrel. They were nearing the stables. In the paddock a groom was leading about a dark bay two years old that scarcely was able to contain itself for the spirits that drove it to eccentric plunges and kicks. It was a recent acquisition and was being schooled as a hunter.

"Look at him," exclaimed Dayborn bitterly. "Ready to jump out of his skin and his belly fit to burst!" He set down the baby, who toddled forward and looked between the palings at the capering horse with the eye of a judge. Dayborn slouched round to the gate and entered the paddock.

Chris Cummings hung her bundle on the palings, divested herself of her cardigan and went into the stables. There were a dozen horses in the various stalls and loose boxes, most of them being got ready for the Horse Show in November. Several of these Renny had bought at a considerable outlay since his return two months before. Toward one of these Chris moved slowly, stopping to give an appraising glance at one or other of the occupants of the stalls she passed. She wondered if Renny had yet arrived at the stables. She strained her ears for the sound of his voice. She passed Scotchmere, the oldest groom, squatting beside a chestnut mare, her hoof between his knees, while he plastered a strong-smelling ointment on a swollen joint. His wizened face grinned up at Chris. He tolerated a woman who rode well.

"It's a nice cool morning," he remarked.

"Yes. It's lovely. How's the leg?"

"Better, but she's fussy, like all females."

"That's a lie, Scotchmere. She's not half so fussy as you are — or her master either. Has he come yet?"

"Yes. He's in the little room next the harness room. He's fitting up an office for himself there. I guess he wants some place where he can be private from his family when he likes."

As they spoke Renny appeared at the end of the passage. The mare whickered and made as though to withdraw her hoof from Scotchmere's knees.

"Whoa!" he shouted.

Between her delight at seeing Renny, whose favourite she was, and her distaste for the smell of the ointment, the mare uncovered her big teeth in a monstrous grimace.

"Whoa!" cried Scotchmere again, and smacked her on her drum-like belly.

Renny nodded to Chris and squatted beside the groom, their two heads, grizzled and red, close together. The mare muzzled the red in a rough caress.

"Well, I must get to work." Chris moved to the last loose box and ran her eye over Launceton, her especial care.

"It's about time," grumbled Scotchmere. "She's wasted half an hour already. That brother of hers let off a stream of cursing because Jerry has a few oats in him. He wants a sheep to ride. What do you think of this here leg?"

Renny fingered it tenderly. "It's fine."

While he held the mare's fetlock he listened to the pleasant sounds of the stable. He felt singularly happy. He realized this morning, as he had not realized before, that the war was over. There would be peace, he thought, for the rest of his life. Things were going better at Jalna. He was fitting into his new niche. There was less friction between him and his family.

Coming suddenly on Chris Cummings had sent a new excitement through his nerves. He went to the loose box and looked in. She was bent over, grooming Launceton, her slim body moving beside the reposeful bulk of his like a reed against a rock. As she heard Renny's approach she worked with even more energy.

Scotchmere, who had followed Renny, exclaimed angrily — "Are you wanting exercise, Mrs. Cummings? That there horse has been groomed already."

"Who groomed him?" she asked, without looking up.

"I did."

"Well, all I can say is, you've left a hell of a lot of dust in him.... Look at it."

An aura of dust was indeed surrounding both the horse and her.

"You can always get dust out of a horse's hide," Scotchmere declared furiously.

"You bet I can when I come after you."

"If you was a boy I'd have something to say to you."

"If you were a man you'd get out of my way and let me finish my work."

"I'll stay here as long as I like."

"All right — if your boss doesn't mind paying you for wasted time."

With a furious look the groom shuffled off, his thin bow-legs bending under him. Chris grinned at Renny as she saddled and bridled the horse. Renny remarked:

"He looks fit."

"He is. I believe he's a winner. He has the best set of pegs I've ever seen."

"And what shoulders!"

They stared absorbed at the horse so charged with quiescent energy. His great eyes mirrored their figures in a look less of curiosity than of noble interest.

"He's a superior being," observed Renny.

"He's rather like you."

Renny gave an embarrassed grin. He passed his hand over the horse's flank.

"Now, I'm wasting my time!" she exclaimed. There was a nervous tension in her voice. She hooked her arm through the bridle and began to walk towards the door. Renny followed her.

"Why are you in such a hurry?"

"It will be hot later on."

In the paddock they found that Eden had mounted the two-year-old. Dayborn was nursing an elbow. "I've had a nasty tumble," he muttered.

"Your brother said he'd carry on for a bit."

Renny frowned. "He doesn't know how to school a hunter."

"That one is as cantankerous as the devil."

There was more hilarity than skill in Eden's handling of the colt who did not approve of the change of riders. His ears were laid back and his tail held tight down. He was going to buck. He began. The violent intermingling of the lines of his powerful body with those of the youth, the distortion of the kicks and the momentary return to immobility while a new series of bucks was generating, held the eyes of the onlookers in fascination. Tod stared between the palings, a dandelion in his mouth.

Eden was on his back on the ground. The horse galloped down the paddock, a stableboy running after him.

"How do you like it?" called out Dayborn as Eden picked himself up and came toward them.

"Fine." His eyes were sparkling. "What do you suppose, Renny? I've had a poem accepted by an American magazine! That's why I wanted Pegasus under me!"

"A poem? Are they going to print it?"

"*Print* it! Why, they've sent me twenty-five dollars."

"Well, that's good," said Renny, but his heartiness carried no conviction. He hoped the boy was not going to be a queer egg. "I didn't know that you sent poetry about?"

"I wouldn't tell you till I had a success."

"Better read us the poem," put in Scotchmere. "I'll bet it don't rhyme."

"Is that baby allowed to eat dandelions?" interrupted Renny.

"Not till it's in print," answered Eden. He passed his hand over his bright tumbled hair of a gold that had a greenish cast. "Well, I'm off," he added. He picked up his coat, vaulted over the palings, and walked quickly along the path toward the cherry orchard.

No one had replied to Renny's question. He picked up Tod, put a finger in his mouth and extracted the dandelion. The stableboy led up the hunter.

"I'll have a go at him," said Chris, seeing how pale Dayborn was. She opened the gate into the paddock and went in.

"All these changes are damned bad for him," repeated Renny. Then to Tod — "If you eat dandelions I shall put you over the fence among the horses."

"Gee-gee," Tod chuckled and filled his hands with earth.

"I'll be all right in a few minutes," said Dayborn.

"Come into my office and have a drink." Renny felt a boyish pleasure in speaking of his office though not till today was it ready for use.

They waited, however, to see Chris ride the colt. The boy held him. The groom helped her to mount. He stood docile a space, then began to buck.

"Ah, he's an ugly brute," observed Scotchmere. "You'll never get a decent price for him, sir."

Chris hit the colt with her crop. There was a struggle — a contest of bucking and reprisal. Suddenly he flew into a grand gallop. She looked thin as a spider on his back. Round and round the field they flew. He seemed magically to be in good humour. She put him over a hurdle. Then another. Then over a thick high fence.

"Hurrah!" cried Scotchmere. "She *can* ride! I take off my hat to her."

They stood watching, Tod with his mouth full of dandelions, Launceton calmly awaiting his turn.

"You ought to be proud of your sister," Renny said to Dayborn as they went toward the office.

"I am. She can ride anything. The colt will make a fine hunter. As to Launceton — if he goes on the way he's begun — he'll be fit for the Grand National."

"God!" exclaimed Renny, his heart in his voice. "If only I could win that."

In the office he took a bottle of Scotch from a cupboard and offered Dayborn a drink. "How do you like my office?" he asked.

"Very much. It looks businesslike."

"See this desk? I bought it second-hand." He opened and shut the various drawers. "Here I shall keep pedigrees, records of sales and accounts. How do you like my pictures?" He indicated a number of coloured lithographs of horses.

"They're fine."

"They belonged to my father."

He sat down in the swivel chair, turning it slightly as he sipped his whiskey and water.

Dayborn said abruptly — "Mr. Whiteoak, I wonder if you know that an affair is going on between your young brother and Mrs. Stroud?"

Renny stared.

"I know it's none of my business," added Dayborn.

"Do you mean Eden?"

"Yes…. And Mrs. Stroud."

"That — woman? It's impossible."

"Impossible? They're male and female."

"She's old enough to be his mother! *An affair?* What sort of affair?"

"He's always there. I hate to tell of it. But there's gossip. I thought you ought to know. One day, for instance, I went to her door. No one answered my knock. I could hear voices. Then I saw him leave the house by the back door. I was talking to her a bit later and she asked me if I had seen him recently. She said she guessed he was studying hard and not going anywhere. Another time I was up with the kid and I saw Eden leaving the house. It was past midnight."

Renny ruefully bit his thumb. He did not want to hear disturbing things about Eden. He was getting on better with him. He was getting on better with his family. He did not want a row. He wanted very much to be happy, to savour the peace of this country life, to adjust himself to his new responsibility. He missed his father continually. That easy good humour, that look of beaming confidence in the well-being of tomorrow, had seemed so permanent a part of Jalna. He sometimes felt himself to be irritable, authoritative and even harsh, yet he burned with a protective paternalness toward the boys left in his care.

"What sort of woman is Mrs. Stroud?"

"Well, she's been kind to us — in a sort of way, but she's too possessive. You daren't call your soul your own. That's one reason I think an affair with her would be so bad for an impressionable poetic boy like Eden."

"Has she told you anything of her past life?"

"Only that her husband was a paralytic for years. I think he led her an awful life. I imagine she's out to make the most of the time that's left."

"Hm…. Well, thanks for telling me. How do you feel now?"

"All right. I'll get on with the schooling."

They found Chris galloping over the course on Launceton. He had been working hard. His sides showed dark patches of sweat. The girl's thin face was pale, but set in an expression of exaltation. She waved her hand.

"He's a wonder!" she cried.

As the heat of the sun increased, the horses were taken into the stable and rubbed down. Chris Cummings's hair clung to her forehead. She went to her child who had curled himself up in the shade and brushed a mosquito from his cheek. She opened her bundle and took out his bottle of milk. He was fast asleep, but the nipple, pressed between his lips, woke him to ecstatic feeding. He gave her a look of deep gratitude, as though she had spent the morning in tending him.

Renny strolled to her side.

"What a good child," he exclaimed." Upon my word, I believe that wholesome neglect develops them."

"I'm not much of a mother," she said. "But I do love him."

"Can he manage the bottle alone? Can you leave him?"

"Of course. Do you want me to work some more?" She rose and adjusted her belt.

"What do you take me for? A slave-driver? I want you to come and see my office. I want to talk to you about something your brother told me."

She looked a little startled but acquiesced. They went into the stable, Tod rolling his eyes after them with a mingling of disappointment at his mother's departure and resignation in the possession of a bottle of rich Jersey milk, fresh from the cows of Jalna and very different from what he had once thought palatable.

In the office Chris stood, hands in pockets, gazing at the desk. She said:

"I can't picture you at a desk."

He sat down at it to show her.

"Well, you look damned queer. And you've got a typewriter too. I can imagine your saying 'whoa' to it."

"More likely 'get up'! Look here." He began slowly to pick out some words on it.

She laughed and came to his side.

"What are you writing?"

"Can't you read?"

She bent closer.

"Your typing's awful."

"It's quite legible. Read it aloud."

She read, "give me A K i Ss."

She said — "Like hell I will."

He painstakingly typed "you have a Horrid tongue, but your lips are adorable."

She asked — "Why is it going off at a slant?"

He answered with a slight huskiness in his voice — "Because I'm trying to see your face."

"Don't try. It's not a nice face." She laid a hand on each side of his head and turned his face toward the typewriter.

He sat very still a moment, then his hands covered hers. He drew her hands down to his breast and raised his face to hers. She bent and put her lips to his half-smiling, inviting mouth. She thought:

"I'll kiss him. Why not? That will be an end to it. How thick and dark his lashes are, and the whites of his eyes are like Tod's."

She felt dizzy before the mystery of his eyes, so close to her own; she closed hers, kept them tight shut while his upturned face was still as the carved face in a fountain, all its vitality concentrated in the passionate mouth.

She pushed her hands violently against his chest.

"Let me go!" she gasped.

He released her and rose with a swift, eager movement. They faced each other.

"Not again," she breathed. "No, not again."

"Why not? You liked it."

"I mustn't."

"Mustn't?"

"I hate love-making. I've had enough."

"Not with me! We've only begun."

"No — I tell you. I hate it."

His eyebrows rose incredulously, but he said:

"Very well. Let's talk about other people's love-making."

She touched his sleeve with her thin brown hand. "Don't think I don't like you.... I like you only too well."

"If that isn't like a woman!" he exclaimed.

"How?"

"They put up a sign — 'Keep off' — then wreathe the sign in roses."

"Look here," she said, "I came here to school horses. If you're not satisfied with me, fire me."

"I'm perfectly satisfied," he answered curtly. He sat down on a corner of the desk and took out a somewhat battered packet of cigarettes. He offered her one. He continued — "If you think I'm one of those men who can't work with a woman without making love to her, you're mistaken."

"I've never thought that," she answered simply. "But Jim suspects us."

"Good Lord," he exclaimed, "Jim seems to suspect everyone. He's been telling me a tale about Mrs. Stroud and Eden."

Chris frowned. "I wish he hadn't."

"You think there's truth in it?"

"I think Mrs. Stroud is out for sensation. She's had a bitter sort of life. I think she's trying to make up for it. She adores Eden's beauty."

"I detest her sort of woman. She'll make a fool of him."

"She thinks he needs her appreciation."

"I suppose she calls him a poet — because he's had one piece accepted. Good Lord, I'd rather he were anything else! His mother was always reading poetry. He's a well-set-up fellow too. He could ride. He could be a help to me if he had the guts."

"He hasn't. Not that sort."

"You know Mrs. Stroud. Tell her to let Eden alone. I've a mind to go and see her myself."

"I think that's a good idea. I'm not in a position to give her advice."

"What do *you* think of her? What sort of woman is she?"

"I think she's a smouldering volcano." He took a quick turn about the room, then said:

"If you are going home now I'll walk along with you."

"All right."

With a matter-of-fact air he followed her out of the office.

They lingered a few moments to admire a foal that had been dropped two days before. It lay curled, bony yet weak, at its mother's feet, its eyes beaming an infantile pride, fearing nothing, the mare nuzzling the silken fringe of its forelock.

"*Isn't* it feeling grand!" exclaimed Chris.

"I've never seen a likelier one," he agreed.

They found Tod staggering around the yard like a drunken sailor, his empty bottle under his arm. Renny picked him up while Chris collected her other belongings. They set off across the fields.

"Has anyone ever called you Kit?" he asked.

"No."

"It's good, as short for Christine. I shall call you Kit. Do you mind?"

"Call me whatever you like," she answered indifferently.

"Why are you so don't-care?"

She set her thin, delicately moulded lips in a firm line. She said — "I'm finished with that sort of thing."

"Do you mean pet names?"

"You know what I mean."

His eyes searched her face. "Are you the sort who thinks herself capable of only one great love?"

"I've never had one."

His mobile brows went up. Then he said — "Why not try?"

"Like hell I will."

"But why not?"

"You're too dangerous."

"Is that why you swear at me?"

"I swear because I can't help it."

"You mustn't let my sister hear you."

"I never see your sister."

"But you will. She's asking you and Jim to tea. Mrs. Stroud too."

"Well, — that's kind of her."

"Will you come?"

"Rather."

They had arrived at the semi-detached house which, unlike others of its sort, not having been built as such, seemed to resent the cleavage. The half occupied by Mrs. Stroud wore a superior air, with its immaculate frilled curtains and bright brass knocker, while the other half looked disgruntled, as though resentful of the fact that its once ordered rooms were now treated so casually by the newcomers. When Tod saw his home he clapped his hands in joy. Renny set him down inside the gate and he staggered off, in his rolling gait, like a cheerful automaton. Straws were sticking in his tumbled tow hair.

"What a dear little chap!" exclaimed Renny.

"Yes." She spoke absently, her fingers playing with the latch of the gate.

"Well, I must face the charmer. Wish me luck."

As he waited before Mrs. Stroud's door he remembered that Meg was going to invite her to tea. He could not make himself unpleasant to a prospective guest. But he must find out what sort of woman she was. Not that he felt himself capable of really understanding any woman. Horses, yes; men, boys; and his grandmother — he believed he understood her. But she was over ninety. A woman surely must acquire something of man's outlook by then. Not that Grandmother was like any man he'd ever met…. He rang the bell again.

Inside, Mrs. Stroud had been clipping a pair of garnet earrings on her wax-white, oddly shaped ears, of which she was vain, and changing the low-heeled shoes she wore for her housework to high-heeled slippers. She hastened to the door.

Seeing Renny on the doorstep her face showed first surprise, then a smile of welcome.

"Do come in," she said. "What a lovely day, but it's turning hot, isn't it?"

He entered, they sat down, she offered him a cigarette. He said:

"I walked along with Mrs. Cummings and young Tod."

"Isn't she splendid?" exclaimed Mrs. Stroud. "The way she can ride and take care of her baby and keep that house going!"

"She rides well," agreed Renny tersely.

"She has a hard life. Her brother is an irascible, irritating young man, not easy to live with. Well, the partitions here are thin. Sometimes it makes my blood boil to hear him raise his voice at her."

"She seems capable of looking after herself. She's not a timid type."

"But I do so hate people to be unhappy. Why can't we enjoy the beauty of life — its poetry, in peace."

"I don't know," returned Renny seriously. "But speaking of poetry — I suppose you've heard about Eden's latest?"

"About his poem being accepted? Oh yes, he came over here at once to tell me. You see, I've been so interested in his poetry."

Their eyes met and remained fixed for a moment, in challenge and distrust.

Renny forced a genial smile to his lips. He said — "It's kind of you to take an interest in him."

She smiled a little sadly. "The kindness is all on his side. He's young and attractive and full of promise. The bond between us is love of poetry."

"I'm not sure," he said, "that all this poetry is good for a young chap who is studying law and who needs to keep his wits about him. I shall be glad if he never has another poem accepted."

Mrs. Stroud could not restrain her disagreement with these words. Her colour rose. "You little know what you are saying!" she exclaimed. "You would put him into a cold, calculating profession and deprive him of what is his very essence — however you may dislike it."

"I never even suggested the study of law to him. He chose it for himself. I guess because he thought it was an easy life."

"I'm afraid you don't at all understand Eden. He has an ardent nature and spends himself recklessly on every thing he goes into."

"The only thing I've seen him spend recklessly is my money," retorted Renny.

She returned, just as hastily — "Well, I suppose he has a right to be educated. He has certain rights in your father's will, hasn't he?"

"I see that he has talked over our affairs with you."

"I have his happiness at heart," she answered simply. She clasped her hands in her lap, and he noticed how soft, white, yet capable they looked.

He crushed out his cigarette and rose to his feet. "I came here this morning, Mrs. Stroud," he said coldly, "to ask you to discourage Eden in his visits. He spent a lot of time in your house last spring when he should have been studying. The consequence is that he barely scraped through his exams. Having some rhymes accepted by a magazine doesn't make up for that."

She raised her fine grey eyes pleadingly to his. "What do you want me to do?"

"Just remember that he is an inexperienced boy and a student."

"Do you want me to tell him not to come here?"

"No, that would probably upset him. He'd know I had been interfering. I only ask you to discourage too frequent visits. You don't want the neighbours gossiping about him and you, do you?"

Mrs. Stroud demanded, in her deep voice — "Has Jim Dayborn been talking?"

"I'm not going to answer that question."

"Or Miss Pink? I expect it's Miss Pink. She has been envious of me from the beginning. She imagines it is she who discovered Eden's talent."

"Miss Pink wiped the slobber off Eden's chin when he was christened. You can't tell her anything about him."

"That was a very revealing remark, Mr. Whiteoak. It shows pretty clearly your attitude toward life."

"I may not think it's as mysterious as you do. But I'm my brothers' guardian and I've got to be as keen for *their* future as for my horses."

Mrs. Stroud laughed scornfully. "The same method for boy and horse, eh?"

"I might follow a worse."

"If you think," she exclaimed abruptly, "that those two next door are what they seem to be, you're mistaken." She added, with equal abruptness — "I shouldn't have said that. But he does annoy me."

"Mrs. Stroud, are you going to send Eden about his business?"

She gave a warm, almost tender smile.

"Of course I will. I want to do whatever is best for him."

They parted amicably and, before he left, she took him around her little garden and showed him how well her delphiniums were coming on. At the gate she laid her hand on his sleeve and her eyes flickered in the direction of her neighbours' windows. She said:

"Did you see that curtain move? I can't do anything without being observed. It gives one a funny feeling."

IX

The Tea Party

Adeline walked slowly about the tea table, examining what was spread thereon with an eye so interested as to be almost greedy. She thanked God that her digestion was good. She was not one of those old people who had to subsist on pap foods. She could eat the highly seasoned curry for which she had acquired a taste in India; she could eat English plum pudding with brandy sauce, or a chocolate éclair, and feel so little the worse for it that she always considered the game had been well worth the candle.

Here was spread just the lavish sort of tea she most enjoyed: chicken, cucumber, and fish paste sandwiches. Hot buttered crumpets with honey. Three cakes — a coconut layer cake, a dark rich devil cake, and a white iced cake crowned with halved walnuts. There was a dish of fresh bonbons. She stretched out a greedy, wrinkled hand, took one of these last and popped it into her mouth. The centre was marzipan and it stuck firmly on her upper plate. She did not mind this but stood, leaning on her stick, her brown eyes goggling a little, while she savoured the sweetness.

But of course she could not enjoy it in peace. Her daughter, elegant in black taffeta and heavy gold bracelets, came in search of her.

"Are you all right, Mamma?" she asked, looking into Adeline's face.

Adeline returned the look dumbly but with rising colour. She would choke rather than give herself away.

Augusta came and took her arm.

"Is there anything wrong, Mamma?"

"Justavin a look a — table," she mumbled through the marzipan.

"Mamma! What — oh, I see. But really you shouldn't."

"Shouldn't what?" demanded Adeline, more clearly and truculently. She swallowed the morsel and no longer tried to hide her face.

Augusta replied with tact — "You shouldn't be asked to wait so long for your tea."

Adeline thought — "I've taken her in." She was pleased and said magnanimously — "I don't mind waiting on occasion."

They moved back to the drawing room together. "Do I look all right?" asked Adeline. "Is my cap on straight?"

Her daughter moved it a quarter of an inch.

"You look very nice."

Nicholas and Ernest were already there. Nicholas was reading a war novel sent to him by a friend in England, Ernest a little ostentatiously holding a volume of Shakespeare in his hand. He rose and went to meet his mother. Nicholas winced as he made the effort.

"Stay where you are," said his mother. "I'll take the will for the deed. How's your gout?"

"A nuisance. I've done nothing to bring it on this time. Been living like a Spartan."

His brother uttered a skeptical, falsetto, highly irritating laugh.

Nicholas glared at him.

"Boys," adjured their mother, "I hear the visitors in the hall."

Meg entered the room hurriedly, then went forward with dignity to meet Dayborn, Chris Cummings, and Mrs. Stroud. She presented each in turn to her grandmother, her aunt, and her two uncles. Before the introductions were over, Wakefield came running after her in a pale blue smock, and slippers of the same colour. He gave his tiny hand to each of the visitors, with an air of putting them at their ease. Meg had all a mother's pride in him.

"My youngest grandson," said Adeline. "A posthumous child. He'd never have lived if I hadn't cosseted him. Whatever his life may be, he owes it to me. He knows that already, don't you, child?"

"Yes," agreed Wakefield. "Owe my life to Gwannie." He beamed at the admiring circle.

"And how is your own health, Mrs. Whiteoak?" asked Mrs. Stroud, sitting down beside her. "Good I hope."

"Ah, I'm full of merit," replied the old lady. "I've fewer pains and aches than any of my three children. My eldest son — him with the moustache — is suffering from gout."

"What a distinguished looking man!" said Mrs. Stroud.

"The other one," proceeded Adeline, "has lit'ry tastes. He's got an idea for a book. He'll tell you all about it. He told me yesterday, but I've forgotten. My daughter, Lady Buckley, is a widow. They've all three spent most of their lives in England. They're too English for me. I'm a real old pioneer, I am." She peered round Mrs. Stroud at Chris Cummings. "So that's the girl that breaks in colts! She don't look strong — but you never can tell. Where's your baby, my dear, and why didn't you bring him with you?"

"Old Scotchmere is minding him for me. He's rigged up a hobby horse."

"Ha, ha, Scotchmere turned nurse! They tell me you can ride like a jockey. I must get as far as the stables one day and see you."

Mrs. Stroud interposed. "Don't go, Mrs. Whiteoak. I did once, and it frightened me to see her. She's too pretty to run such risks."

"It's my job," said Chris, "and I ask no better."

"Ah, that's the spirit!" Adeline's gaze swept the room. "Where's Renny? Why doesn't he come to tea? Where's Eden and the other two? We've waited long enough."

As she spoke Renny came in, his hair flat from the brush, his eyes expectant. Eden followed him, a faint smile lighting his face as his eyes met those of Mrs. Stroud. Meg, taking Wakefield by the hand, led the way to the dining room. He held out his other hand to Mrs. Stroud.

"How sweet he is!" she exclaimed. "And so friendly. Children have an instinct for knowing those who really love them."

Renny, playfully and in a mood to show off his precarious friendship with his youngest brother, picked him up as they reached the tea table and raised him shoulder high. Wakefield stiffened and cried — "Down, down, please! Want d-d-down!" Renny deposited him, far from gently, on the chair next Meg's.

"Now, what about instinct?" laughed Dayborn. "He doesn't take to you."

"Unfortunately," explained Meg, "the poor little fellow was frightened by Renny soon after he came home. He hasn't got over it, but he will."

"He is nervous," added Ernest, "and doesn't see many strangers."

Nicholas said — "Since the death of his parents we have lived very quietly. It's time to change that."

He was sitting next to Mrs. Stroud. She looked into his deeply-lined, experienced face and thought — "What a striking looking man! And a *divorcé!* How could a woman divorce him! Oh, to have been married to a man like that!"

But his table manners did not please her. He humped his broad shoulders above his plate and devoured a fish paste sandwich in two bites. He began to tell her about a fountain he was planning, at the south side of the house, to be ready for his mother's birthday.

"The design is to be a female figure, in Hindoo costume, holding an Irish harp and leaning against a lion. It is to typify the three countries which have most influenced my mother's life. The idea is my brother's. He will show you some sketches he has made for it. But please do not mention it to my mother. It is to be a complete secret till the day. The water is to come out of the lion's mouth."

"How interesting!" said Mrs. Stroud. "But has Canada no part in the design?"

"Canada supplies the water," he replied.

Eden, on her other side, was offering her a crumpet. She was acutely conscious of his nearness. She was contrasting his smooth, young brown hands, with those of Nicholas which, though shapely, shook perceptibly as he raised his cup to his lips.

"Well, and what do you think of us?"

"I think you're fascinating. Much more so than you led me to expect. Why, there's poetry in every one of you — with one exception."

"I guess which one you mean. I must say he'd be relieved to be the exception. But I'm dashed if I can see poetry in any of them."

"Ah, you know them too well. If you had lived the life I have! But that's all over. It's a new world for me. I'm so glad I came here. Now I know your background. It's as different as possible to mine. How charming your grandmother is being to Jim Dayborn!"

The old lady was talking with gusto of Irish hunters. Her harsh laugh broke out as she told him of youthful exploits. She questioned him closely as to what he considered Launceton's chances for the Grand National. She was all for entering him but her sons, her daughter and granddaughter, thought it was too great a risk and expense.

Ernest was telling Chris of his idea for a book about Shakespeare. Quite different from anything that had been done, he declared. He felt himself, from years of theatre going, well fitted for the task. He asked her opinion of Shakespeare's sonnets. She confessed that she did not know he had written any. This confession did not lower her in Ernest's opinion. He was satisfied to have an attractive young woman to talk to of "his work."

"What a nice old boy!" she thought. "Yet he does seem a bit ga-ga on the subject of Shakespeare."

But as Ernest talked, his clear forget-me-not blue eyes did not miss the understanding glances that passed between Mrs. Stroud and Eden, nor the self-conscious pleasure in her as she manoeuvred to keep him by her side when, after tea, they went to see the garden.

Old Adeline established herself on the circular white seat beneath the great silver birch that dominated the lawn. The bed of red geraniums had just been set out and she beamed her approval at it. Then she remembered Piers and Finch.

"Where are the two young lads?" she demanded. "I didn't see 'em at tea?"

Meg replied — "Piers is off fishing. Finch has somehow got tar in his hair and wasn't fit to come to table."

"Tar, eh? The young rascal! He'll have to have his hair buttered. That will take it off. That one's a nice little boy, Mrs. Stroud. But full of music, like his poor mother."

"A musician and a poet, Mrs. Whiteoak! You are lucky in your grandsons!"

"I am that! And in yon horsy fellow too — and the baby. Look out, sir! You are a naughty boy!"

Wakefield had just emptied his two hands, filled with gravel from the drive, into Mrs. Stroud's white piqué lap. She made nothing of it and would not allow him to be rebuked. She was making herself a general favourite.

It was the first time that Renny had seen Chris in anything but shabby riding breeches. Here was a different girl. Instead of the long-sleeved shirt, she wore a pink chambray dress. Her silk clad legs and slender bare arms were graceful. But the hand and wrist were so tanned as to give the impression that she wore coffee-coloured gloves. From whip-like, almost fierce vitality, she had flowered into graceful femininity.

"You're two different people," he told her as they stood beside an old mulberry tree under which a dilapidated hammock had been the recipient, for more than three decades, of fallen berries. Its mattress sagged, its framework was rusty, but it was a sequestered spot that retained a certain poetic essence.

"I pity you, if you're as easily taken in as that," she returned.

"I can't imagine your swearing in this outfit."

"The hell you can't!" she exclaimed, incredulously and without affectation.

"Chris, I do like you."

"Thanks."

"I like you more every day."

"Do you like me enough to raise my wages?"

"I don't let material things enter into my affections."

"That's bad news."

"But, if you want a rise, you shall have it."

"I don't earn a penny more than I get. You've been lovely to me." Her eyes suddenly filled with tears.

He turned his away. He began gently to swing the hammock. "Do you know," he said, "my father and mother were sitting on this when he proposed to her."

"A damned messy spot to choose!"

He returned rather huffily — "It was new then. A waterproof covering was kept over it when it was not in use. My young brothers took it for some of their nonsense, while I was away."

"I'm sorry," she said contritely. "But I have to be horrid to you or — can't you understand?"

"No. Tell me."

She turned her shoulder toward him.

"You understand perfectly."

"You mean that you are on the verge of loving me and have some perverse reason for not wanting to."

"I mean I daren't."

"But you *are* on the verge?"

"I'm going. I've been away from Tod too long!"

He caught her arm and held her. He said — "Kit, this is the first time we've ever been alone together. There was always a horse or something."

She raised her eyes to his. If her nose was slightly insolent, her eyes made up for it by their arresting intensity.

"Renny — Renny — darling, please let me go."

He ran his hand the length of her arm, then released her. He followed her to where the others had gathered in a group about old Adeline.

She remained where she was when the visitors had gone. It amused her to talk them over, comparing them with people she had known long ago. She thought she would like a quite large dinner party next week. The continued fair weather had warmed her through and through, given her new vitality. Her sons were seated on the bench beside her, Nicholas placidly puffing at his freshly-lighted pipe, Ernest watching Augusta who had returned to her *gros point.*

"I do wish I could do that!" he said admiringly.

"I'll teach you, if you like," answered Augusta.

"I doubt if I could learn."

"Nonsense! There is no reason why you should be a whit less clever than I."

"I hope you are not insinuating that I am effeminate, Augusta."

Not at all. But you have a niceness, an exactness about you. Now, if Renny should suggest that I teach him ..."

Renny was lying on his back on the grass, one arm thrown across his eyes. Beneath it his lips had a sombre bend. Eden sat also on the grass, playing with Wakefield and showing off, somewhat provocatively, the little boy's preference for him.

"Go and play with brother Renny," he said. "Make him be a big bear."

"No," said Wakefield decidedly. "Baby not able to t-t-talk properly to him."

"Well, if you can't talk, go and make a naughty face at him."

With timorous mien Wakefield ventured close to the outstretched figure. But he was braver than he seemed for, when Renny suddenly caught him and placed him on his chest, Wakefield sat there pleased with his position and with the steady rise and fall of this new throne.

"The darling!" cried Meg, from where she was picking flowers from the border. "I knew he would make friends with you before long."

"There was never any real fear," said Renny. "It was trumped up to show off. Before long he'll like me the best of the lot." He patted the little boy encouragingly on the back. His eyes rested less genially on Eden. He spoke to his grandmother, slightly raising his voice.

"So you liked Mrs. Stroud, Gran?"

"I did. I think she's a nice, sensible woman, though I wouldn't say she's out of the top drawer."

Eden's face flushed. He said:

"She's the most interesting, intellectual woman I have met."

"What would you say, Gran, if you were told that Eden is having an affair with her?"

"I should not believe you."

"It's true."

Eden threw a furious look at Renny. "For God's sake, shut up!"

Adeline planted her ebony stick firmly on the ground between her feet and leaned forward so that she might miss no word. "Shut up, did he say? I say no! I say out with it! I want to know what it's all about." Her eyes glowed with curiosity.

"I suppose," answered Eden, "it is not the first time in history that a young man has had a friendship with an older woman."

"I agree," said Ernest, "that it has often been and I see no reason why it should be bad for a young fellow. I myself, when I was twenty-three —"

"Five years older than this boy," interrupted Renny.

"We develop younger now," said Eden.

"Develop younger!" Nicholas put in impatiently. "Fellows like you are babies compared to what I and my friends were at your age."

Old Adeline gave her stick a thump.

"You're all babies," she declared. She went on — "Why wasn't I told this before the woman came? I'd have drawn her out!"

"She's one woman in a thousand," said Eden. "I'd rather be with her than with anyone I know. And I intend to be with her. If people choose to have filthy minds, let them say what they like. We'll go our own way."

Nicholas turned to Renny. "What *are* people saying?"

Eden put in vehemently — "And who are the people who are talking? Old gossips like Miss Pink! And dirty dogs like Jim Dayborn!"

Renny put the child from him and sat up. Wakefield trotted after Meg who had gone into the house.

"That's rot," said Renny. "You know very well that you can't spend all your spare time in Mrs. Stroud's house without making people talk. Just tell your family, since you're so above-board, what time you came home last night and how you came in."

"I refuse," said Eden hotly. "I'm damned if I'll be badgered like this." He sprang to his feet. "You can talk me over among yourselves. I'm off."

"What a young cock-a-hoop!" exclaimed Adeline. As he flung off she watched him from under her shaggy brows, her strong lips pursed in a line of ironic reflection.

"That remark of Eden's was very unjust," said Ernest." He has had a great deal of sympathy from his family. Especially, I may say, from myself. I have encouraged him in writing poetry —"

"I wish you'd been doing something else, then," said Renny. "Poetry is at the bottom of all this trouble. He sits at Mrs. Stroud's knee, reading his verses. She recites Browning and Shelley to him. I've heard about it from Dayborn. I shouldn't have mentioned this affair in front of you all but I have spoken to him before and he was on his high horse. If you older ones think it doesn't matter, I'll have nothing more to say. Let him ride for a fall if you don't mind."

"That would never do," rumbled Nicholas. "When and how *did* he come in last night?"

"At one o'clock. Through the study window."

Nicholas whistled softly. Ernest exhaled his breath in a soundless "whew." The grandmother was silent, still retaining her expression of ironic reflection.

Augusta had been silent throughout the scene, though her needle remained suspended. She kept her detachment when she could, for she liked placid and orderly things, but this was too much. Such an experience for a boy of eighteen was not to be tolerated. He was her favourite among her nephews. She liked to think of him as elegant and indolent but she did not like to think of him as without moral conscience. Now she felt more put out at him than ever she had been. But the blame was Mrs. Stroud's.

"What effrontery!" she exclaimed, "to come to our tea party with such a thing on her conscience!"

"Who is she, anyhow?" asked Nicholas. "Has she nothing better to do than pursue a youth?"

"She is renewing *her* youth," said Renny drily. "I don't think she's had any past successes. I gather that she'd pretty heavy going with an invalid husband for a good many years. She's making up for lost time."

"She cannot do that on Eden," said Augusta.

Ernest looked at her for inspiration. He asked — "But what are we to do? He seems quite headlong. And if the disparity of their ages and their outlook does not keep them apart —"

"Something must be done," said Augusta.

Renny observed — "You know that he barely scraped through his exams. You know he's in debt. And I must say you've encouraged him in his extravagance, Uncle Ernie."

Ernest looked flustered. He had, before he was middle-aged, gone through the respectable legacy left him by his father. He brought back that father's shadow to his aid now, exclaiming:

"My father would have taken a horsewhip to him!"

Renny grinned and said — "I'm willing to do that, if you think I ought to."

"Oh no," said Augusta, "the day for violence is past. Except of a very moderate sort."

"Like a kick behind," suggested Renny.

Adeline now withdrew herself from her ruminating, which had taken her far back into dusky recesses of her mind, where were laid memories of certain episodes of her own youth. She said:

"There's only one thing to do with a woman like that. An older man of experience must cut him out."

It took a moment for the proposal to gain a footing in their minds, then Augusta exclaimed:

"What a good idea, Mamma! Ernest is the man, without a doubt. He has had experience of the world. He has distinction. He has charm."

Ernest coloured like a girl at these words. He positively simpered. At the same time he was aghast at the thought of tackling Mrs. Stroud. He said, clasping his knee to keep his hands steady — "Let Nick do the job. Women like *divorcés.*"

"With this leg!" exclaimed Nicholas sardonically. I'd look well, with a guitar on my gouty knee, serenading the merry widow."

"I'll bet you'd have her sitting on the other one in no time," said Renny. "I think aunt's idea is a good one. The woman is lonely. She likes masculine companionship but not the horsy type. She likes poetry. Uncle Ernie can tell her about the book he's going to write. Did you speak of it today?"

"I had little conversation with her. I spoke of it to Mrs. Cummings."

"Chris? I'll bet she'd never heard of Shakespeare."

"Indeed she had, though she does not know his sonnets."

"Mrs. Stroud does. I saw them on her writing table."

"There is one contingency," said Ernest, "which none of you take into account. What if I myself should become smitten with the lady? What then?"

"Marry her, with our blessing!" cried Renny.

Ernest looked offended. So did Augusta. She said:

"If and when my brother chooses to marry, I hope he will find some-one more suitable both in appearance and breeding. In my opinion Mrs. Stroud is squat, and a little common."

Adeline asked anxiously of Ernest — "Do you think there's danger of your getting soft on her?"

"Not the least, Mamma. She is not at all my style. I was only joking."

"This is no matter for jest," said Augusta. "You can see how wrought-up Eden is. There is no time to waste. Today has made an opening. Tomorrow you must call on her. Be frank, tell her you are worried about Eden. Touch her sympathies, then proceed with her conquest. Your instinct will tell you what to say."

"It sounds easy," said Ernest, "sitting here under this tree, but it will be very different when I'm alone with Mrs. Stroud."

"It will be easier," encouraged Augusta.

"For your passion will be roused," added his mother.

"My *passion*!" Ernest was aghast.

"Your passion for achievement, Mamma means," supplemented Augusta.

"You'll have her eating out of your hand after the third meeting," said Renny.

"There is something underhand about it," Ernest said, biting his nail.

"Nonsense," said Nicholas. "She has no scruples. She'd make a mess of that boy without a second thought. Go ahead and do your damnedest, Ernie."

Ernest braced himself. He answered with fervour:

"I will."

"All this has been tiring for Mamma," said Augusta. "She's nodding."

Adeline's chin was indeed sunk on her breast. Her lace-trimmed, beribboned cap was over one eye, but an inscrutable smile curved her lips.

X

ERNEST AND MRS. STROUD

THE NEXT DAY it was raining. There had been several weeks of fair weather which latterly had blazed into summer heat, and the heavy rain of the night before had come as a relief. A fresh bright morning might have been expected, but instead it was dull and a thin rain was falling. There was a lifelessness in the air, and Mrs. Stroud, moving about her orderly living room, felt restless and suddenly alone in the world. The sensation was not new to her. It was one she had had to fight against almost all her life. She had been an only child. Her father had died when she was still a girl, and her youth had been restricted by the care and the whims of a semi-invalid mother whom she had never greatly loved. When she was twenty-six her mother died. Only a few weeks later she was caught in a rainstorm and took shelter under a tree. A man of fifty was sheltering there also. They got into conversation. He was a widower, a retired merchant, comfortably off. She was in a mood for sudden intimacies. In less than six months they were married.

Life with Robert Stroud was little more exciting than the life she had left. His ways were set. His will was adamant. He had made his money rather by extreme care than by enterprise. Once they were married, he had seemed to lose interest in her. She had suppressed every warm impulse in herself in order to fit her life into his. They had been married only three years when he had a stroke and for six years was a helpless invalid. Amy Stroud's life with her mother had been exhilarating as compared to the suffocation that now surrounded her days. When she was not hastening to obey the capricious demands of her husband, she had buried herself in books, poetry, and the old-fashioned novels which had belonged to her predecessor.

Freedom had come three years ago. It had been like a new birth, painful in its sweetness. She had spread herself like a heavy-bodied butterfly fresh from the chrysalis. She had bought herself the dainty clothes she had always desired. She had sold the house and all its stuffy furniture. She longed above all things to travel, to see Italy and Greece, but her husband's long illness had eaten up a large part of his capital. Her flutterings would not be high above the ground. It was a thrill to her, in that first summer, to go to a little lakeside resort and sit with other women on a verandah, gossiping, waiting for their husbands to return from their fishing. The next winter she had actually gone to Florida, repeating on a larger scale the experience of the summer. The following summer she had ventured as far as Quebec, had taken long walks about the Citadel and had sat on the promenade reading *The Golden Dog*. Still she was not satisfied. She felt a well of emotion and eloquence within herself. Yet she had no one on whom to spend her emotion or to move by her eloquence. She had spent more money than she should have done and felt that she must buy a house and settle down. She returned to Ontario, spending the winter in a boarding house, concerts and moving pictures her diversions, and scanned the newspapers for advertisements of houses.

When she saw the advertisement of Miss Pink's house she was interested, for as a girl she had once paid a visit in that vicinity with her mother and ever after had retained memories of its quiet charm, its air of remoteness, its fine old trees. She consulted the agent and he took her to see the house. It was a disappointment to find that it was too large for her and the price more than she cared to pay. Yet there was something about the house that captivated her. She felt that she must have it. She had a naturally extravagant nature but the long years of association with her husband had made her cautious and shrewd. She worried herself till she was almost ill. Then came the illuminating idea of dividing the house into two dwellings and letting the half not occupied by herself. The accomplishing of this, the consultations with a builder, the furnishing of her own side of the house, had given her the freest and happiest days of her life.

It had not been so easy as she had expected to find a tenant.

When Jim Dayborn and Chris Cummings turned up she was delighted. She had accepted a low rent because they were just the sort of people she had always wanted to know. They were young, they had come from families with a background. They had knocked about the world and were unhampered by the standards that had clogged her life. She was attracted by Tod. She had never before been on intimate terms with a child. It pleased her to do favours for the three. She felt that a new era had opened up for her.

Unfortunately they were not good tenants. They kept the place badly and were behind with the rent. Already their relations were not so genial as they had been.

But Amy Stroud was not really cast down by any lack in them. For the first time she was feeling life, as well as living it. Eden Whiteoak had kindled desires, passions in her which she had known to exist, but which she had expected would no more than smoulder all her days. Her spirit was like a volcano that has never known perceptible eruption. Over its mouth was grown dry pale grass, prosaic buildings had been painstakingly erected on its verge. But tremblings were now to be felt, mutterings heard. At night she sometimes walked the floor by the hour, not able to sleep, not wanting to sleep, carried away by the floodtide of her emotional ecstasy.

Yet all her dreams were not crystallized on Eden. She knew that his reciprocation was a faint, egotistical emotion compared to hers. As she walked barefooted up and down the room she would repeat his name, over and over — Eden, Eden, Eden — trancing herself by the music of these syllables. Her stocky figure would gain vehemence in all its movements. Her voice would become husky and tears stream from her eyes.

Yet, when she was with him, she forced herself to be playful and even patronizing, assuming, as she imagined, the role of a weary woman of the world, full of experience. She would have given much to have recalled her first confidences to Chris Cummings. But she knew that Eden saw little of her neighbours, and she risked giving him fanciful glimpses of an embroidered past.

She knew that on this day she would not see Eden. He had gone to take part in a tennis tournament. He had asked her to go with him but she had refused on some pretext. She would not risk having people ask him if it were his mother he had brought with him. Now she fretted aimlessly about the room, moving ornaments, plumping cushions, or reading a paragraph of a novel. She pictured the gay scene of which he was a part and was not sorry to see the drizzle outside. She could not bear to think of him enjoying himself with younger women. She felt a mood of melancholy descending on her and fought against it.

When a knock came on the door she almost ran to it in her eagerness for some distraction. She was astonished to discover Ernest Whiteoak standing in the porch. Rather nervously he asked how she did.

"Very well," she answered, "but I resent this dull day. Everything was looking so lovely. My syringas are quite draggled but it will bring the peonies on. Won't you come in?"

He entered and looked about him, pleased with the feminine order of the room. He said:

"I hope you don't mind my coming. I was walking this way and thought I should like to see you in your own house. It was quite an innovation, dividing it in half."

"How nice of you to come! I don't have many visitors. But I have very near neighbours. Almost too near, at times."

"But they're nice young people, aren't they?"

She gave a little shrug. "Nice enough. I like the woman better than the man, and the baby best of all. I suppose they are at Jalna. What hard work for a girl!"

"Yes. It is hard. But she likes it. Sometimes I think she has more care over the horses than she has over her own child."

Ernest had seated himself near a window. It looked on to a small field gay with buttercups and red clover. He felt nervous with Mrs. Stroud's attention entirely concentrated on him. Yet he had rehearsed what he was going to say. Now he said it.

"It is kind of you to take such an interest in Eden. We all appreciate it."

She felt it necessary to steady herself at the mention of Eden's name. She wondered why Ernest had come.

"Are you vexed at my having him here so much?"

"We could scarcely be that," he hedged. "Intelligent companionship is so good for a youth. Most young people scarcely seem to have an idea in their heads these days."

"Oh, Eden's not like that! He's teeming with ideas. He's alive to his fingertips."

"I take it that you are rather like that yourself," said Ernest, with a warm look straight into her eyes.

She flushed, and acknowledged — "Yes, I am."

Ernest began to feel more at his ease. He said:

"Eden is at the stage when he feels the necessity of being understood. I was like that once. Since then I have reached the point where I think it is better to conceal what you are from the world."

"But were you ever like Eden?"

"Well, I don't think I ever had such an ardent nature, but there was a resemblance. At his age I was more mature. I should think you would find his lack of maturity an obstacle to your friendship. As a matter of fact, I am surrounded by people who take very little interest in my mental pursuits." He hesitated, and then added simply:

"I am thinking of writing a book."

"Are you really! Eden has never mentioned it to me."

Ernest looked hurt. "I have talked of it a good deal to him but I suppose he wasn't deeply interested."

"But I am. Would you tell me what it's about?"

He crossed his legs and his eyes brightened.

"It's about Shakespeare. My book is to be something quite different from all others on the subject. It's a subject that lends itself to endless variety. I flatter myself that I have something new to say. In England my brother and I were confirmed theatre goers. We saw Irving and Terry in their best Shakespearian parts. We had the good fortune to know them in private life."

"How wonderful!"

"Yes. Nicholas is reading the plays aloud to me. My eyes are not strong. He has a fine voice and quite a sense of the dramatic. The effect is surprisingly good."

"How I should like to hear him!"

"I'll bring him over one day and persuade him to read to you."

"Oh, thank you." Mrs. Stroud could scarcely believe that a morning so drab could have blossomed into such a day. She longed to say something that would impress Ernest. But, though her mind strove wildly, it could hit on nothing. She could only gaze at him and repeat:

"Thank you. That will be a treat."

Ernest quoted, in his light, pleasant voice:

"'Poetry is the blossom and fragrancy of all human knowledge, human thoughts, human passions, emotions, language.'"

Mrs. Stroud dared not trust herself to speak. Her eyes glistened with tears. Ernest talked on and on. He loved the sound of his own voice and he had never had such a listener.

She asked him to stay to tea. While she got it ready he walked up and down the room. He thought it was attractive though rather bare. He remembered a little Dresden figure in his own room, and thought he would bring it to her next time he came, for he was now sure there would be a next time.

There was a small crash in the kitchen. In her nervousness she had dropped the tea canister. He ventured to the door and said:

"I hope nothing has gone wrong."

"Oh no, nothing is broken. Won't you come out and see my kitchen?" She was suddenly self-possessed.

He wandered about, admiring everything. It was a novelty to see inside a kitchen and he had never known so pretty a one. He helped her carry in the tea things. They became more familiar and laughed a good deal as they ate their thin brown bread and butter, the sponge fingers, and drank the good China tea.

All the way home Ernest was full of his success. He could scarcely wait to tell the others of it.

XI

Pheasant's Plan

Pheasant's life, from the time she was eight to twelve, had been so monotonous that there had been little to distinguish one day from another except the changing of the seasons. These changes she had watched with an eye more perceptive than most children's. She knew almost the exact moment when the old apple tree by the stream would put out its fragile pinky-white blossoms. She became weather-wise from association with Mrs. Clinch, and could prophesy rain or whether the thunder in the air meant clearing and cooling or another storm. She and Mrs. Clinch had long discussions about the weather. She knew of the various extremities of weather suffered by Mrs. Clinch during her entire life. It was their great and unfailing subject of conversation, the only one in which they met as equals. In winter, sitting by an almost red-hot stove, they passionately discussed the past seventy winters. In summer, when Mrs. Clinch had carried her rocking chair into the open and rocked and fanned to keep the mosquitoes off, Pheasant knelt on the warm grass beside her and they talked of droughts, floods, northern lights, thunderbolts, and people struck and burnt black by lightning.

Pheasant was not much interested in her lessons with Miss Pink. They consisted mostly in learning the minerals of distant countries and the dates of distant battles, by heart. She also had to learn by heart such poems as "Psalm of Life" and "Yarrow Revisited." Mrs. Clinch taught her to darn and hem. But she put none of these accomplishments to any practical use as she did her knowledge of weather, which was a constant help and interest to her.

In these years the family at Jalna were the subject of much speculation. They were so near to her, they might have been so much to her, yet she rarely exchanged a word with one of them. But to meet a member of the family or hear a scrap of news about them changed the colour of the day. They were the second-best subject of conversation between her and Mrs. Clinch. The reason they were not the best was that Mrs. Clinch had so many undertones in speaking of them, so many hints at their pride and arrogance, that Pheasant often felt unhappy after talking of them. Yet individually, when she did meet one of them they were always nice to her, with the exception of Meg whom she had only met face to face twice. Each time Meg had given her, first a startled look, then one of cold scrutiny which had clouded to, what Pheasant felt, was dislike.

Sometimes she and Finch met by chance in the fields and played together a little. She thought of him as somewhat like herself and wished she knew him better. She had met him on the little bridge above the stream one day quite lately. She never ventured into the grounds of Jalna except secretly. That day she had stolen through the undergrowth to see if she could find watercress on the bank and had come upon him suddenly, sitting on the bridge, his legs dangling above the stream and a little white rat darting softly over the patch of sunlight on the boards, within the circle of his arm. She had stood knee-deep in the water staring up at him, wondering whether or not to speak. But he had spoken, as though he were expecting her.

"Hullo, Pheasant. Come and see my pet rat."

She had splashed eagerly out of the water and clambered up the bank to his side.

"Look! He's as tame as can be. I'm going to teach him all sorts of tricks. See, he's not a bit afraid of me. He'll sit on my hand. Look!"

Enchanted, she had watched him and the rat. The joy of being with another child had gone all through her. She had felt it even in her fingers and toes. There was a fluttering feeling in them. She wanted to run swiftly at the boy's side or take hold of him and wrestle with him.

"Oh, Finch, may I touch him?"

He was dubious. "I don't think he'd like it. He only knows me."

"Just one little stroke."

He allowed the caress. Pheasant thrilled to the feel of that warm velvet softness under her finger. But Finch was restless. He must be off with his pet. She often wondered how the little rat was getting on and if Finch had taught it tricks.

Sometimes she met Piers but she liked him least of the boys. He thought nothing of coming to Vaughanlands with his gun and shooting rabbits. She admired his pink and white skin, his blue eyes, but she thought he had a hard, teasing look. When they met he would boast of the things he shot. Once he had caught hold of her and tickled her in the ribs with iron fingers. After that she ran the other way when they met. She heard through Mrs. Clinch that he was unruly, that his sister and uncles could not control him. Mrs. Clinch said that he would shout that he *would* or *wouldn't* do things.

Once Eden had been her favourite.

She had quite often seen him in the woods, murmured a timid hullo in answer to his greeting. She thought his smile was nice but rather sad. Then one day he had been suddenly friendly. He had taken her by the hand and they had walked together among the pines and birches. They had sat down together where there was a patch of wintergreen, and he had eaten the berries, yet made a face over them. He had been amusing and gentle, like no one she had ever known. Just to watch his changeful face had been fun. He had asked her innumerable questions about herself. At last, tossing up a handful of berries and catching them, he had confessed to her that he wrote poetry. He was going to be a lawyer, but in between cases, he had said, he would write lots of poems, and after a while when he had made some money he would give up law, do nothing but write poetry. Perhaps he would write a poem about her.

His confidences made the world a new place for Pheasant. She imagined he was to be her friend for ever. She had wandered through the woods day after day, hoping to meet him again, but when she did he had looked at her absent-mindedly, barely nodded, and gone his way. Had she offended him? She could not bear it. She had run after him and caught him by the arm, looking up into his face in eager questioning. But he had shaken her off and exclaimed petulantly — "Leave me alone!" That had been a year ago and she had not talked with him since.

The old grandmother, Lady Buckley, and the uncles were, to her, beings of a stately and remote world. She had had no commerce with them except when Nicholas had met her, stroked her hair with his large shapely hand, and later sent her a doll as a remembrance.

The grandmother she had often seen, drawn in her carriage by the two sleek bay horses, on her way to church or to pay a call. The old lady would direct a piercing glance at her, but not unkindly. Pheasant would stand stock-still, staring as long as the majestic folds of the widow's veil were in sight and the clip-clop of the horses' hooves beat a rhythm on the road.

She would never forget the day when little Wakefield ran away, over all the winding path to Vaughanlands. He had appeared in the doorway of the kitchen where she was sitting with Mrs. Clinch, holding a skein of wool for her and discussing the drought. He had come in as though he were an invited guest, run about the room and peeped into every corner. Mrs. Clinch had given him a cookie in each hand. He had taken quick eager bites, his curls hanging almost into his eyes. Oh, to have a little brother like that! If only they could have hidden him — kept him for ever!

But a servant had soon come to fetch him. He had been carried away weeping. Pheasant too had felt like crying.

She had felt that life would be different with Maurice at home. It was different but not in the way she had hoped for. Maurice was moody and gave little thought to her. In his own house, the War behind him, he felt his estrangement from Meg more than he had since its early days. He was melancholy and after dinner each night was inclined to drink too much.

One day, out of the loneliness of her heart, Pheasant said to Mrs. Clinch:

"Do you think he will ever like me?"

Mrs. Clinch regarded her with a cold, judicial eye. "He might, if you was a different sort of child."

"Different? How different?"

"Well, you are what you are. I don't s'pose you can help it."

"I'd like," said Pheasant, "to be more of a companion to him, like a daughter should."

Mrs. Clinch looked pessimistic. She said:

"I don't see him hobnobbing with you, if that's what you mean. He's got his own ways and his own thoughts and the less you interfere with him the better — poor young man!"

Those fatal words — poor young man — always ended Pheasant's questions. She turned away, flushing deeply. She wondered what she could do to improve herself, to make herself more companionable for Maurice, more able to think like he did.

How did he think, she wondered. She tried to send out her mind that it might penetrate his, feel as his did. She felt herself coming home from the War, very large, manly, and brave, with Renny Whiteoak at her side. She tried not to feel envious that Renny had a decoration and she not. There was one thing she had anyhow. She had a little girl, all trembling with eagerness, waiting for her. Yet, when she met that little girl, what a disappointment lay in store! A shy, plain child with none of the attractions she had hoped for. And at Jalna, beyond the ravine, Meg Whiteoak whom she could not marry! Meg had been a beautiful girl. Mrs. Clinch said she had never seen a lovelier skin and even now there was none to compare to her. Still Pheasant had an interesting face, if only she were more intelligent!

This trying to penetrate Maurice's mind was not successful. It led always to the conclusion that, if she herself were different, he would like her better, or notice her at any rate. One day he reprimanded her for coming to lunch with her hair untidy. Before the next meal she brushed her hair till it shone and tied a blue ribbon round her head with a bow at the temple. He did not even glance at it.

She tried to talk to him about *Rob Roy* which she was reading. He answered politely but he was not interested. She thought it's too old-fashioned, I must read what he is reading. When he went out she took up a war novel which had been leant him by Nicholas Whiteoak, and buried herself in that. She read something terrible about a wounded soldier being caught in a barbed-wire entanglement and hanging there till a splinter of shell horribly finished him. Her flesh crept with terror of it. She felt sick. If Maurice had seen such things why should he want to read of them? Perhaps he could not get them out of his mind. Her heart was full of pity for him. She asked timidly:

"Do you like that book?"

"Not much," he replied indifferently. "But there are some good descriptions in it."

"Descriptions of what?"

"Fighting."

"Did you see things as — bad as that?"

"Bad as what?"

"Things in the book?"

"Have you been reading it?"

"A little."

"It's not fit for you."

"I just wanted to be able to talk to you about it."

"Talk to *me* about *war!* Good Lord!"

"I thought" — she made a great effort and went on — "I thought the book might draw us together."

Maurice laughed in genuine amusement. That hurt her cruelly. She buried her face in her lesson book, glad of the thick hair that fell forward across it.

Maurice said — "You've been alone too much with that old woman. I wish you had another child to play with."

She wanted to cry out, "It's not another child I need, it's you!" But she clenched her hands together tightly under the table, and her blurred vision sought the exports of Sweden.

Mrs. Stroud had occupied her house for some time before she and Pheasant met. Then, one day as Pheasant was passing her gate, Mrs. Stroud stopped her and asked her if she would like to see a nestful of young wagtails. There was one in her porch. Pheasant, full of excitement, followed her along the pink-bordered path. The air was heavy with the scent of pinks. She stood long, admiring the nestlings. Then Mrs. Stroud asked her if she would come indoors and drink a cup of chocolate with her. Pheasant accepted the invitation with outward dignity but with an inner thrill that made her almost dizzy with pleasure. Mrs. Stroud was the kindest woman she had ever met. Her house was the sweetest, cleanest, prettiest house she had ever seen, far prettier than Miss Pink's which had formerly been her ideal. Mrs. Stroud showed her all over the house. The room that pleased Pheasant most was the guest room with its pink silk bedspread and curtains that Mrs. Stroud herself had made. She said that no one had yet slept in the room. Perhaps Pheasant would come and spend the night with her. The chocolate was the best Pheasant had ever tasted, the cups the prettiest she had ever seen. Pheasant sat very straight, conversing sedately. She told Mrs. Stroud as much of her life as she thought not derogatory to herself. She stayed and stayed, till at last Mrs. Stroud suggested that they go next door and see the baby.

They had chosen an opportune time. Chris was giving him a bath for they had just come back from the stables and he was, as she said, dirty as any stableboy.

But now he was clean and pink! He stood, naked and jubilant, his silvery hair on end. He never knew when he was going to be washed or fed, and, when either blessing descended on him, accepted it with unquestioning joy.

The wild disorder of this house, its gypsy-like casualness, was as thrilling to Pheasant as the charm and order of Mrs. Stroud's. She felt that a new world had opened up before her. She saw new possibilities in life. Only the hour before she had thought Mrs. Stroud the most lovely woman and the kindest she had ever met. She still thought her the kindest and was sure no one else had such a smile. But the sight of Chris Cummings in her khaki shirt and breeches, bathing Tod, filled her with a new admiration. She watched every movement of her lithe body, the bony competent hands, with intensest interest. Even the way her hair, the same colour as Tod's, was licked back behind her ears and curled by her jawbone in a drake's tail, was charming.

Chris accepted her presence with matter-of-fact friendliness. She produced a bag of chocolate caramels, passed it round, popped one into

Tod's mouth, then put a clean cotton garment on him and lighted a cigarette. She felt like hell, she said, for she had had a bad fall that morning.

"Renny Whiteoak says," she observed, "that there's a way of falling so that you don't hurt yourself. I wish I could find it out."

Mrs. Stroud disapproved of such language in front of the child. She shook her head smilingly at Chris, then said:

"Why don't you get him to show you?"

"He's promised to, next time he's thrown."

"From what I hear," said Pheasant, "he's broken pretty nearly all his bones at different times."

"What do you think of Eden's riding?" asked Mrs. Stroud. She never could resist bringing the conversation round to him.

"He has good hands but he's terribly impetuous and he hasn't been brought up to control himself, so you can't expect him to control a horse."

She put an old magazine into Tod's hands. "There, look at that," she said. "I've got to lie down for a bit."

He accepted the magazine with interest though it was worn almost to rags with his handling.

Mrs. Stroud and Pheasant rose and said goodbye.

"You will come and see me again, won't you, dear?" asked Mrs. Stroud as they parted.

"Oh yes, I'll come often," said Pheasant. She ran all the way home, feeling that she must pour out the story of this meeting to someone. But when she was inside the door, smelled the familiar musty smell of the house, and heard Mrs. Clinch's movements in the kitchen, she did not know whom to tell. Not Maurice, surely, as he passed her in the hall with a casual nod. There was really no one. She went out again, but this time slowly. She found the old pony in the field by the stream and put her arms about his neck for companionship.

After this she went often to see Mrs. Stroud. Sometimes there was no answer to her knock. Then she would go to the other house, but often found no one there either. Then she would walk around the two houses, looking in at the windows, longing to be inside. Once Jim Dayborn caught her looking into Mrs. Stroud's living room. He laughed and exclaimed:

"So, you've got on to the racket too!"

"What racket?"

"That she doesn't open her door to others when she has her favourite visitor inside."

"Is Mr. Ernest Whiteoak her favourite visitor, then?"

"Mr. *Ernest* Whiteoak! Why?"

"Because I saw him sitting on the sofa beside her just now."

Dayborn sneered.

"So — she's more than one string to her bow!"

Pheasant did not feel surprised or hurt when Mrs. Stroud did not answer her knock. Without doubt she had seen her coming up the path and naturally she would not want a child about when she was having serious conversation with a gentleman friend. Pheasant had got the expression "gentleman friend" from Mrs. Clinch, and admired it. When she could not get into either house she would go home and return two hours later.

She was never listless or lonely now. She had new ideas in her head and she was constantly turning them over, like a small bird turning the eggs in her nest so that they may come to perfect maturity.

By degrees these vague ideas formed themselves into a definite plan. She made up her mind that, since Meg Whiteoak would not marry Maurice, and, as she herself had not the power of making him happy, she must find a wife for him. She believed there were two ready to her hand, if only she could choose the right one.

At first her mind dwelt with most pleasure on Mrs. Stroud. She pictured her standing at Maurice's side in the chancel of the little church, being married by Mr. Fennel, saying "I will" in her deep moving voice. She found a prayer book and read the marriage service. Much of it puzzled her but she was pleased to find that the real object of marriage was the having of children. Mrs. Stroud and Maurice would have lots of children, little brothers and sisters for her. She would make Vaughanlands into a new place, gay, airy, and full of children. Pheasant loved Mrs. Stroud. Yet, for some odd reason, she did not completely trust her. Deep down in her heart she resented Mrs. Stroud's not answering her knock when she had more interesting visitors. At first she had not minded this. Jim Dayborn had planted the seed of distrust.

She found her thoughts turning more and more often to Chris Cummings. She was young and men liked young women, Pheasant knew. She had a lovely face. She had Tod. Above all, she had Tod. When Pheasant thought of having him in the house she felt weak, as though her bones had turned to something yielding.

She had a great admiration for Mrs. Clinch's perspicacity. She thought she would cautiously sound her on the subject. It was one of Mrs. Clinch's very deaf days and Pheasant was finally driven to shout —
"Which do you most admire, Mrs. Stroud or Mrs. Cummings?"

Mrs. Clinch did not hesitate for a moment. She shouted back, almost angrily — "What a question!"

"But which do you?"

"Do I what?"

"Like best?"

Mrs. Clinch gave a snort. "Like that jockey that goes about cursing and swearing in men's clothes! Not me! Mrs. Stroud's a real lady. She's a newcomer who is a credit to the neighbourhood. She's been too kind to that pair, and if they don't run off without paying their rent you can call me Davy."

Mrs. Clinch's objection to being called Davy was so intense that, when she used the expression, Pheasant never had anything more to say. She made up her mind to ask Maurice himself if he had any preference.

By this time she was so excited that she could not rest till she had made a decision. She sought out Maurice who was putting up a screen door at the side entrance. As soon as he stopped hammering she asked, her voice trembling in her earnestness:

"Maurice, which do you most admire, Mrs. Stroud or Mrs. Cummings?"

He stared at her, then, with no more hesitation than Mrs. Clinch had shown, replied:

"Mrs. Cummings, of course. If you mean looks."

"Well, which would you say has the best nature?"

With equal promptitude he answered:

"Mrs. Cummings. I don't like the other one's ears."

"But one shouldn't judge another person by their ears, should one?"

"I do — in this case."

He began to hammer again, talking under his breath to the door.

"You're screwing it on the wrong side," she said gently.

He stared at it dismayed. "So I am!" He picked up a screwdriver and began to take out the screws.

"It's a disconcerting thing, Pheasant, to discover that you can't do anything right."

"Oh, I think you do everything right, that is, *almost* everything."

He gave his unexpected, boyish smile. "Do you? That's splendid!"

"Mrs. Cummings" — now she was in for it — "admires you very much."

"Does she now!"

"Yes, she thinks you're very reliable."

"I'll be getting conceited." He began to put in the screws afresh.

"She wants to ask your advice about an important matter."

"I'd hate to think anyone would be advised by me."

"This is a peculiar matter that only you can help her in. Would you see her by the rose trellis at moonrise tonight, if she came over?"

"Blast the thing! It goes on better the wrong way than the right."

"Would you see her, Maurice?"

"Certainly. But it's funny she'd want to see me."

"Will you be waiting for her, by the rose trellis just at moonrise?"

"If she's set on it." If the screws would not go in with the help of the screwdriver he would hammer them in. He began.

Pheasant did not delay. She ran all the way to the field that lay between Vaughanlands and the paddock where the schooling was done. She crossed the field cautiously, making sure that none of the women of the Whiteoak family was an onlooker. Only Scotchmere and two stablemen and Piers were there. She came up slowly.

She mounted the lowest rung of the gate and hung over it, watching. Chris Cummings was mounted on Launceton, followed by Renny on the chestnut mare. They were moving in a long swinging gallop at the far end of the paddock. They rose, one after the other, as though lifted by some serene, detached power, and took two gates in succession. They came thudding along the track toward her. She raised herself upright on the gate, holding her breast open to absorb the rushing vitality of their passing. She felt the wind from their swift bodies. She smelled the clean horses and their polished leather. She stared into the faces of the riders, thinking how set and courageous they looked. Chris encouraged Launceton and he galloped ahead, easily out-distancing the chestnut.

"Isn't he a clinker?" asked Piers who had come up behind her.

"Yes. But the chestnut's carrying a far heavier weight."

"She's not in the same class with him. He's going to win the Grand National. You'll see."

They stood waiting till the schooling was over. Renny called Piers and sent him to his office for something. Chris strolled over to Pheasant. This was just what she wanted. Everything was being made easy for her. She felt the elation of controlling other people's destinies.

Chris was mopping her forehead with a handkerchief. She still felt the exuberance of the gallop. She threw her arm about Pheasant's shoulders, exclaiming:

"Isn't he wonderful! I could face the devil after a gallop on him!"

"You do not need to face the devil," returned Pheasant gravely. "It's only Maurice you've got to face."

Chris looked blank. "Maurice? Oh yes, your father! What's the matter with him?"

"Nothing. He only wants to see you about a very important matter."

"Does he want me to break in a colt for him?"

"Goodness, no. This is just something between yourselves. He's got to have your help to do it and you've got to have his help to do it."

"It sounds thrilling. When do we begin?"

"Tonight. By the rose trellis, in our garden, at moonrise. He'll be waiting for you there. He's sorry that he can't ask you into the house but Mrs. Clinch doesn't like visitors, and anyhow it's much nicer out there. I wonder if you'd mind wearing that pink dress. Mrs. Clinch doesn't approve of breeches on a girl."

"Gosh, she sounds a Tartar!"

"Will you come?" repeated Pheasant. "It's terribly important to all of us. But please don't mention my name. Just say you were walking that way and thought you'd come in. He'll know what you mean."

A groom was leading out another horse. Renny shouted to Chris. The horse was standing on his hind legs, pawing the air.

"Coming!" shouted Chris.

"Will you be there tonight?" gasped Pheasant.

"Yes, I'll be there." She ran across the paddock.

Pheasant lingered to watch her mount the balky colt.

But she had now won him over. He cantered down the paddock in well-mannered fashion enjoying the newly acquired discipline. Pheasant thought — "There she rides, little knowing what's going to happen tonight."

She had hallucinated herself by her own imaginings and was now convinced that nothing could prevent Chris and Maurice from falling in love "by the rose trellis in the moonlight." She felt a power within herself and, as she walked back across the fields, she took long strides and held her head high. Of her own will she was changing their lives. The day would come when Mrs. Clinch would no longer be able to say of Maurice "poor young man!" Instead, people would be saying — "How happy Maurice Vaughan looks since his marriage and how that daughter of his has improved! She's not like the same child. It is said that she takes entire charge of her little brother."

She went into the garden that, next to Maurice, had once been the pride of her grandmother's life but was now uncared for. The grass had grown long, weeds choked the paths, the picket fence was sagging. But great clumps of peonies, whose roots had not been separated in the last ten years, were heavy with blooms. Sweet-scented phlox attracted the hummingbirds. At the end of the garden there was a locust tree in flower, its blossoms festooned along the boughs in perfumed chains. This tree sang with the hum of bees, and its flowers constantly trembled from their plundering.

Close beside the locust tree was the rose trellis, over which a hardy climbing rose sprawled, unpruned. Already this year's shoots, finding no tendril hold on the overcrowded trellis, were pushing their way through the grass or thrusting outward towards an imaginary support. The roses grew in clusters, were pink, and had an old-fashioned sentimental perfume.

Pheasant hastened to this spot as to a banquet prepared, standing first at one end of the trellis and then at the other to savour the different aspects of the background for the moonlight meeting.

She knew the time of moonrise from Mrs. Clinch's almanac. Shortly before that hour she retired to her room. It was a little earlier than usual but no one noticed that. She knelt by the window where she could, by stretching her neck, get a fairly good view of the garden. Maurice passed beneath and, looking up, asked:

"Is that girl really coming here tonight?"

"Oh yes. I saw her this morning and she said she could scarcely wait till the time."

"What do you suppose she wants of me?"

"She didn't say. She said she wanted me to keep out of the affair and not have my name mentioned by either party."

"Hm. She sounds a bit unhinged."

He moved on.

The moon rose, deep gold beyond the fir trees, just past its first quarter. It was gaining the power to throw strong shadows, and Maurice, as he stood waiting, noticed the meticulous shadow of a rose cluster on the stone flagging beside the trellis. He had lighted a cigarette and was drawing its last inhalation as Chris Cummings appeared at the end of the path and came toward him, slim and purposeful in her pink dress.

"Good evening, Mrs. Cummings," he said rather stiffly.

"Good evening."

They looked at each other warily, neither one wishing to open the conversation.

He held out his cigarette case. "Have a cigarette?"

"Thanks." She took one and he lighted it for her. In the flare of the match her face looked charming. He said:

"Well, I'm here, you see."

"Yes, and I've come, as you may have noticed."

They smoked in expectant silence.

Then — "It's a nice old garden," she said.

"It was nice in my mother's time. But it's been neglected. I shall have it put in order one of these days."

After another pause she said — "Well, I suppose we may as well begin."

"Yes, it's about time."

"Supposing you go first."

Maurice gave a short laugh. "I don't feel equal to it. It's up to you."

"You do want something of me, don't you?"

"I thought it was you who wanted to see me."

She said, with some embarrassment — "I'll take on any thing you have in mind provided —" She hesitated.

"Provided what?"

"Well, — I don't do anything for nothing."

He looked at her suspiciously.

"Just what sort of fellow do you think I am, Mrs. Cummings?"

"At the moment I think you're rather a queer egg."

"You're evidently used to a more impulsive type."

"I'm used to a man who knows his own mind. What do you think I came here for?"

"That's what I'm waiting to find out. Why won't you tell me?"

She made an exasperated sound. "We seem to be all muddled up. I thought you wanted to see me. That's why I've come."

"I thought —" He stopped abruptly and looked over his shoulder. Renny Whiteoak was coming toward them across the grass.

"Hello, Maurice!" he exclaimed, then drew up in astonishment. "Sorry, I didn't expect to find anyone with you. I'll come again."

"No, don't go."

Chris added — "Please, don't go."

He laughed. "Well, if I were in your shoes I shouldn't want a third party about. You've no idea how romantic you look."

His laugh was not genial. He felt himself deceived to find these two with whom he was in constant association, and neither of whom ever mentioned the other's name to him, engrossed in what was evidently an arranged meeting, and who so plainly showed their embarrassment at being discovered.

The three stood motionless a space, the moonlight choosing one feature of each to play upon, to exaggerate into undue prominence. It chose Maurice Vaughan's eyes, making them appear very large and melancholy and, by contrast, his face pallid. In Chris Cummings it was the mouth, the curl of the lips emphasized into conscious provocativeness. The arch of Renny Whiteoak's nose, the sweep of the nostril, were exaggerated to a predatory sneer. They regarded each other in silence, each momentarily disliking the others, repelled by the distorted aspect of the familiar faces. Then Renny wheeled and moved swiftly away, drawing after him his elongated shadow across the grass, like a mummer's trailing cloak.

"What a ridiculous scene!" exclaimed Chris, at last breaking the silence.

"Why was he angry?"

"I can't imagine."

"I can."

"You seem to have rather a fantastic mind. Your message to me, for instance. You beg me to come here and when I arrive you ask me what I want."

"I didn't send for you, Mrs. Cummings."

"You did."

"I did not."

"Pheasant told me..."

"Pheasant told *me.*"

"What?"

"That you most particularly wanted to consult me about something."

"She told me you particularly wanted to see *me.* I thought it was something about a horse."

"She's a mischievous little fool. I must apologize for her. I'm very sorry."

"It's all right. Just like a kid."

"I don't see anything funny in it."

"She probably does. She certainly had us. Well, I'll be off. Goodbye, Mr. Vaughan. Don't be cross to her."

"She deserves a whipping."

"I forgive her, so I think you might. It was worse for me."

"No, no."

"What will Renny Whiteoak think of me?"

"I'll explain."

They separated, she turning at a tangent from the direction Renny had taken, Maurice going toward the house. He stopped beneath Pheasant's window.

"Are you awake?" he called.

There was no answer.

"I'll have something to say to you tomorrow."

Trembling behind the window curtains she was conscious of the anger in his voice.

XII

BY THE LAKE

WHEN CHRIS CUMMINGS set out to return by a different path she had but one desire, to escape a meeting with Renny on the way home. Better explain the ridiculous affair by daylight. There was a strain of malice in her that made the prospect of his passing a night of chagrin, possibly of sharp jealousy, not unpleasing to her. He had caused her hours of troubled sleeplessness. Now let him suffer.

She would go through the main gate, she thought, and skirting Vaughanlands on the side farthest from Jalna, return home by way of the back road. It was a lovely evening. She would enjoy the solitary walk. Tomorrow she and Renny would laugh together over the child's prank. She hoped Maurice would not be furious with her.

But, when she reached the road, a wayward impulse made her hesitate. The road lay white between the dark pines and spruces, inviting in its emptiness. The air was heavy with the scent of newly mown hay. Puffs of warm air rose from secret places as though the earth, turning in its first sleep, had exhaled its warm and scented breath. There had been a strong wind the day before and a distant murmur told that the lake was still disturbed.

She had had no more than glimpses of it in passing. Now she had a sudden wish to be alone by it. In England she had lived near the sea.

She had a craving for an expanse of moving water. When she had seen the lake it had stretched glassy and impersonal, blinding blue beneath a fierce sun or a dim pewter under a clouded sky. Tonight it was alive and moving sonorously on its shores. She wanted to be beside it and give herself up to thought. She was not often enough alone. There was something in her nature that needed solitude. She walked quickly down the road. She knew that the lake lay two miles away.

What if Renny were walking beside her? What if there were nothing to hinder their friendship, their love?

She had the road to herself. It had branched off and ended abruptly in a small field. She passed through a sagging wooden gate and entered on a sandy path that barely kept its contour among the crowding bushes. Suddenly she was past these. The path had ended. She was on the beach alone. She had a sense of achievement as she saw the unmarked stretch of it. Her feet sank in its warmed depth. The lake was agitated rather than tumultuous, spending itself in broken waves on the submissive sand. The moonlight was less bright than it had been. A cloud shaped like a waterfowl had the sky to itself, as she the beach. Behind it the moon was hidden, though its light illumined the sky, silvered the waves that lay beyond the cloud, and gave a gleaming breast to the fantastic shape of the bird.

She felt herself as adventuring far beyond the two miles she had traversed. Jalna, with all its activities, human and equine, lay far behind. Renny took his place with them, irrevocably bound up with them.

The house where she lived seemed far away; Mrs. Stroud no more than a stranger; Jim — she turned her head as though in pain at the thought of him — seemed far away. Even Tod, sleeping in his cot, was no longer her child but a being who had clung to her and now suddenly had relaxed his grasp and let her go. She stretched out her arms like the wings of a bird and drew in deep breaths of the cool night air. The scent of the clover and the hay was gone. The air had the smell of the lake, of the sparse vegetation that grew along the edge of the shore.

She took off her shoes and stockings and carried them that they might not be injured by the sand. Her toes curled with the delicious sense of freedom as she walked along the lake's verge. She walked on and on, her thoughts becoming tranquil, then scarcely thoughts at all. She felt like a child again. She walked with one foot on the sand and the other in the water, enjoying both at once.

At last she reached a place where private grounds came down to the beach. She turned back, but now she walked with both feet in the water, holding her skirt above her knees. The moon and the cloud had parted company, the moon already beginning to bend toward the horizon; the cloud, estranged from it, elongating the bird's neck, opening its beak as though in a despairing cry. Gazing upward, Chris forgot to be careful of the waves and found herself holding up a drenched skirt.

She gave an exclamation of dismay. Now the dress would have to be laundered. But what of that! The feel of the water against her thighs had been worth it. A desire to swim in the lake took possession of her.

She ran across the sand and, hiding among the bushes, quickly pulled off her clothes. She felt reckless and very young. She ran back across the sand and out into the waves. They were too powerful to swim against. They were rowdy playfellows, rolling over her, dashing up behind her, striving to pull her from her feet. She played and struggled with them, thinking that this was as good fun as riding Launceton. Here were a dozen wild horses careering about her, never to be broken in. She gave herself up to her joy in them.

She waded out to her armpits, facing the long, cool green sweep of the waves. She jumped up, as each one swept over her, keeping her head above them, throwing out her arms across their foam-flecked arch. Then, on the largest that had yet risen against her, she turned and threw herself, and was carried on its crest to the shore. This was the wildest play of all. She lay on the beach panting, getting back her breath. She wanted to do it all over again.

She ran, exulting in the waves, liberated from the chains of living. Again and again she ran out into the lake and rode landward on a wave. "Once more," she thought, "a little farther still." But the sand beneath her declined and she lost her footing. She cried out in terror.

A voice shouted: "It's all right. I'm here!"

She saw Renny running toward her. His face, in the moonlight, looked white as his shirt. He was at her side and had her in his arms.

"It's all right," he repeated.

She relaxed against his shoulder.

"I wasn't really in trouble," she said.

"What?" he shouted.

"I wasn't drowning," she shouted in return.

A wave broke against them, submerging them. She looked up into his face, laughing. "It's fun."

His lips moved but she did not hear his answer. His wet shirt clung to him like seaweed.

"This becomes you," she said loudly.

"What?"

She put both arms about his neck and said into his ear — "You look like a triton or faun or something."

Again he said something she could not hear.

Again a green wall submerged them. He drew her toward the shore. Waist-high she moved away from him. There was a lull in the agitation of the waves that, in contrast to the former sonorous roar, was almost silence. Rising so, out of the troubled lake, she was a figure of enchantment, gleaming marble-white in the moonshine.

"Why did you come?" she asked.

"I followed you."

"But you went the other way."

"All ways are mine in this place."

"Why did you follow me?"

"I wanted you to explain."

"About going to meet Vaughan?"

"Yes."

"It was nothing. A trick of his child's. I haven't the slightest interest in him, or he in me."

"Is that the truth?"

"Yes."

She shivered. "I'm going in."

His arms tightened about her. He asked:

"What do you want me to do?"

"Leave me."

He bent his head to look into her eyes. He drew a finger along the curve of her lips, over the curve of her chin, to her throat.

"Is there nothing more you want than that?" he asked.

She answered almost angrily, catching his hand in hers and withdrawing it from her lips:

"You're making me love you!"

"Why not?"

"I don't want you to!"

"Very well." He released her with a renunciatory gesture. She remained standing where she was, then asked:

"If I had not screamed, what would you have done?"

"Stayed where I was till I saw you safe on shore."

"I think that's rather nice of you."

"I'll go off then. You can follow when you're ready. I want to see you safely home."

She turned passionately to him:

"Renny! Kiss me!"

His face lighted. He held out his hands to her. She came close to him. The waves were subsiding about them. A pocket of warm air, mysteriously released, enveloped them. She raised her face to his in delicious anticipation. His arms drew her close. He had kissed her before lightly — not like this! Other men had kissed her — not like this! ...

He went ahead of her up the sand. He stretched his length beside a sand hummock, pillowing his head on his arm, his back toward her. He waited.

After a time she came to him and knelt behind him. She bent over him and put her lips to his cheek. She said:

"You look as though you'd been drowned — cast up by the waves."

He turned over on his back and smiled up at her. He put both arms about her.

It was past midnight when they left the beach. Long ago the moon had sunk. The few stars gave little light but the sky was of a luminous dark blue. The path, and then the road, lay clear before them. The night was warm. Tomorrow would be hot.

"I wish I hadn't to go back," she said.

"I wonder what your brother would say if you didn't." There was a pause. Then she said in a low voice:

"Jim's not my brother."

"What is he to you, then?"

"He's my husband and — I don't love him!"

In his astonishment he stopped stock-still.

"Jim your husband! But why have you kept it secret?"

"Because it paid us to. He has a friend in England. She's done a lot for him. She paid his way out here and gives him a small allowance, but she gives it on condition that he doesn't marry. If she heard he was married, the allowance would stop."

"But you can't keep this deception up for ever."

"He's always expecting her to die. She's not young and she's delicate. He's sure she'll leave him her money."

"What a position!"

"Yes — but you can get used to anything."

"Did you know about this when you married him?"

"No. He told me we must keep our marriage secret for a few months because his family would disapprove. In reality his family wouldn't care a damn. They're a heartless lot. It's only this Mrs. Gardiner who cares.... I don't love Jim, but I'm sorry for him. I guess, in his own queer way, he needs me. I'm someone to quarrel with.... I've never loved anyone but you.... I think Tod knows everything — all about Jim and me. He looks at us so queerly sometimes, as though his soul were all clear and pure and he knew ours were murky." She spoke with passion, then moved quickly along the road.

"This staggers me," said Renny.

"Does it make you like me less?"

"Nothing can do that. If I live to be as old as my grandmother I shall never forget this night.... I think you're adorable, Kit."

She stretched out her hand and caught his. So linked, they continued their walk. They passed the gates of Jalna. The dark bulk of the house could be glimpsed beyond the trees. The house had a secret air, yet not withdrawn. It was as though it waited, not for the first time in its history, to receive a night-wandering Whiteoak under its roof.

XIII

WANING SUMMER

THIS YEAR SUMMER moved in majesty. Sunrises were radiant, noontides dazzling, sunsets spectacular. Rain, when it did come, fell in a grand downpour. The crops thrived, ripened, were reaped, as orderly as pictures in a book. Colts, calves, and piglets flourished like weeds. There was no devastating heat, no killing drought. In the orchards the trees bent beneath their weight of fruit. The cherries especially, Richmond and Montmorency, were prolific. So much so that, with an abundance in other districts, prices fell. It was scarcely worth the time to pick the cherries. The trees were red with them. Maggie the cook bottled them, made jam of them, even cherry brandy. Still there was great waste of the fruit. The only one who worried over this was Piers. It hurt him to see the ground red with the glossy spheres. He filled baskets and took them to all his friends. He told the village boys to come and help themselves, but they climbed the trees and broke branches and he had the blame.

Wragge had never lived so well in his life. In truth, as he told the cook, he had not known such food existed as he got at Jalna. When he looked at her round red face, her round red arms and clean capable hands, he could have shed tears of joy at the thought of her potentialities in the way of cherry pie, whipped cream, salad dressing, sage stuffing and chocolate soufflé. But she had a violent temper. Already she had threatened to give notice. What if he should lose her! He made up his mind to marry her. Of course she had not all the qualities he desired in a wife. But what woman had? Certainly, in the lottery of marriage, she would be far from a blank. Out of his second month's wages he bought her a bangle bracelet.

His chagrin was deep when she rejected him. What did she want! An Adonis? A millionaire? The shock of it, combined with too much cherry brandy, went to his liver. He had a violent bilious attack. Then he had fresh evidence of Maggie's worth. She fed him delicate broth and orange custard.

Perhaps it was seeing him prostrate, looking more dead than alive, that went to her heart. At any rate when he was about again, though still subdued, she astonished him by remarking almost casually:

"Well, I don't mind if I do."

He turned his head from blowing on the silver teapot he was polishing.

"Do wot?"

"'Ave yer."

"*Ave* me! Ow?"

"In 'oly wedlock."

"Maggie!" He set down the teapot and took her rapturously in his arms. "You've made me the 'appiest man on earth!"

Dinner was late that day.

On the whole, the family were pleased with the proposed marriage. Lady Buckley, however, disliked Wragge. The sight of him in a livery much too large for him which had belonged to a quite exemplary butler of former days, greatly irritated her. His impudent face combined with his obsequious manner was, in her opinion, a disgrace to Jalna.

Wragge did not trouble about Lady Buckley, as she was returning to England in the early autumn, but he did set about winning the approval of Meg. He discovered that she liked to pose as having little or no appetite at table but enjoyed a tray carried to her room. Maids had chafed at doing this. Wragge behaved as though it were an honour. He would arrange chicken sandwiches, ripe raspberries lying on their own green leaves, a few pansies in a tiny vase, with an instinct for the appetizing.

He made himself useful in a hundred ways. To be called from the job he was doing, to another, did not fluster him. He had learned to hate monotony in the War. He soon discovered that in this house many things went on beneath the surface. Every item of smallest interest sent him hurrying down the basement steps to repeat the same to his betrothed. She, from being phlegmatic when she was not in a temper, became as avid for gossip as he. Their life was so full of interest that there was not time for more.

It was arranged that their marriage should take place after Lady Buckley's departure. Renny was to give the bride away.

In these months Ernest varied between pleasure in his acquaintance with Mrs. Stroud, irritation at the responsibility of pushing it to the point where Eden should be undone and still keeping it within the bounds of safety. He was of an indolent temperament and it irked him to rival a being so full of youthful energy as Eden. Also there was something underhand in the situation which he shrank from. Eden trusted him. What if that trust should turn to anger and even hatred! On the other hand, he was doing his best to save the boy from an entanglement injurious to him.

There was no doubt of Mrs. Stroud's pleasure in his company. His visits became more and more protracted. Her door opened to him almost before he knocked. He took her flowers, fruit and books. She was elated by her success. In erotic dreams she played off one lover against the other. In waking moments she told herself that neither was really in love with her. Her husband's greatest compliment to her had been to say that her head was screwed on right. These words came to her mind now and she doubted the truth of them.

As the summer wore on and the paths became more overgrown, the air more vibrant with the song of locusts, the moon in its fullness a deeper orange and seemingly closer to the earth, Ernest found that he was no longer able to put Mrs. Stroud out of his mind when he returned to Jalna. Her image, intensified, remained with him wherever he went. Above all, he found himself resenting more and more Eden's friendship with her. He resented his family's amused approval of his amorous excursions. More than once he positively trembled with anger at some complacent remark of his brother's about "the would-be adventuress." Ernest had to go outside the room and lean against the wall to calm himself.

His old mother was far too clever, his brother knew him far too well, not to see evidence of the change in him.

"I told you," Nicholas said to her, "that Ernest would get soft on that woman."

"D'ye suppose they're living in sin?" grinned Adeline.

"My dear Mother, you're a better judge of that than I am."

"Well, if 'tis so, it's made him more interesting than ever I've known him. But then, it often does!"

Eden, the central figure, was slow to realize the import of these developments. He looked on the sudden intimacy between his uncle and Mrs. Stroud as an effort on Ernest's part to find out, for the family, what sort of woman she was.

Since his outbreak of anger after the tea party was past he held little rancour against his family. He was still a boy and, when they one and all were particularly pleasant to him, he felt relief in his mind and renewed confidence in his ability to conduct this affair in his own way. In fact, he had a new zest for it. The eyes of his elders were on him. They had sent out their emissary. The emissary could not help but feel the charm of the enchantress. Mrs. Stroud repeated to him the gist of all her conversations with Ernest. When Eden made fun of some remark of Ernest's, she exclaimed:

"After all, he's a charming man. I've never met anyone like him. I hope you don't mind my being friends with him, darling. He helps pass the time for me when you're not here. It seems so long."

Eden stared. "Does he come so often as all that?"

"Oh, not very often. But I shan't let him any more, if you don't want me to."

Delicious words to her to utter, placing herself submissively under control of this fair-faced youth. Delicious to him to hear, as he looked at her strongly marked features, her virile body. What lines there were in her face were lines of spiritual endurance and secret eroticism. Her eyelashes were thick, her wide smile showed remarkably good teeth. Her small soft hands were hypnotic in a caress.

She was of so complicated a character that her constant probings of her own depths left her baffled. She was soon conscious of her effect on Ernest. She felt dizzy with the sense of her power. She had always felt capable of fascinating men, if only she had the opportunity. She had given up hope of such when she met Eden. Her friendship with the pliable, poetic boy of eighteen, of what she thought of as "aristocratic birth," filled her days and nights with sensuous delight. She was not to grow old without having expressed in some fashion what she felt within her. When he sat on the floor, his head on her knee and her hand moved over the shining casque of his hair, waves of almost unbearable delight stirred her blood. She would remember how she had sat stroking the forehead of the paralytic till her arm was ready to drop off, and she would almost cry out in her joy.

Narrow as was her experience, it served to make her aware of her increasing influence over Ernest. She began to plan each meeting with him as a move in a campaign. She began to think of herself as living in a network of deception between two lovers, one of eighteen, the other past sixty. Though her intimacy with Eden had not advanced beyond a lingering kiss and that with Ernest beyond the discussion of amorous passages in novels, she was intoxicated by the potentialities of her position.

Again and again she wished that she had a tenant different from Dayborn, or no tenant at all. She pictured the house as she had first seen it, undivided and roomy. If only she could have received her admirers in such a house! She was angry with herself for having hampered the builder who had made the alterations. He had wanted a more solid dividing wall. But she had insisted on cheap materials. Now, in her most cherished moments, Dayborn's voice would penetrate the partition, complaining of the hardness of his work or Chris's cooking. Once Chris herself had shrieked that the sausages were burning and an hour with Eden had been spoilt. Eden had insisted on shouting back — "Bring them here! I like burnt sausages!" He had seemed about sixteen while she had felt an ageing vexation. Once Tod had cried throughout a visit from Ernest. He had been suffering from injudicious feeding. But Mrs. Stroud had never really liked him again.

As summer drew to its close and the grains were harvested, the majestic progress of the seasons disintegrated into violent, changeable, and erratic weather. Surely September brought greater heat than had July! There were storms, floods, fogs, and days of mesmeric heat, when all action seemed to cost an effort beyond its worth. Eden, Piers, and Finch went in each day to college and school. The effort to see that they did not miss their train took more out of Meg, she said, than all the rest of the day. She made no attempt to eat breakfast but, after their departure, was served with a tray in her room by Wragge. He was now definitely known in the family as "Rags," and his position established. Meg, for the rest of the day, sat on the lawn with her needlework or did a little desultory gardening. She had engaged a healthy young housemaid who took much of the care of Wakefield upon herself. He had developed astonishingly during that summer, was forward and mischievous. Meg said that it was more than she could do to cope with him single-handed.

Lady Buckley had left for her home in Devon, Nicholas accompanying her as far as Quebec. His gout for the time being had disappeared and he was glad of the change. He had a weakness for the old French town for he had been born there.

Augusta was greatly disappointed that the affair between Mrs. Stroud and Eden had not been ended, by Ernest's intervention, before she left. She had had a good talk with both her brother and her nephew, placing the dangers of their situation calmly but relentlessly before them.

"You," she said to Ernest, "have shilly-shallied shamefully over this business. To judge from what you say, you have made a deep impression on the adventuress. That letter from her which you showed me proves it. Why do you not insist that she should put an end to her affair with Eden? Nicholas says it is because you are completely under her domination, and that he wishes *he* had undertaken the job."

"Don't worry your head, Augusta. I have the situation perfectly in hand. Before long you will get a letter telling you that all is over between Eden and Amy."

"Amy!" Augusta's jaw dropped.

"And why not? Surely there must be some familiarity where influence is desired."

"I sometimes think it is all familiarity and no influence. But Mamma has confidence in you, so I suppose *I* must."

To Eden, Lady Buckley said — "I am sorry to go away leaving you still enamoured of that woman."

Eden laughed. "I am not enamoured, Auntie. You and the whole family should be grateful that I'm not entangled with some silly girl. If you knew what some of them are like you'd have a real shock."

"I don't wish to know what they or any other female who fancies herself a man killer, is like."

He put both arms about her. In spite of herself she patted his back and said a tender goodbye.

Augusta had mixed feelings as the ship steamed down the St. Lawrence. She was both glad and sorry to be aboard. Memories of many greetings and partings from that port crowded each other in her mind. Surely this river marked the flow of her life. As an infant she had first arrived in her mother's arms, her ayah having died at sea. She had sailed from Quebec as the bride of Edwin Buckley. He and she had many a time made the journeyings to and fro together. Then, as widow, she had come alone. But, of all the voyages, the last had been the most melancholy when she had been summoned because of the death of her brother, Philip. That had been early in the War. She had lent her house in Devon to the Government as a convalescent home for officers. She was leaving behind her vexing problems at Jalna. She wished Ernest might have been the one to see her off, as was usually the case. Fond as she was of Nicholas, Ernest was her favourite and it had hurt her more than she had guessed at the time to see how calmly he had relinquished what had always been his privilege. Was it possible — but no; she put the thought from her mind and turned her face resolutely toward the widening stretch of the river.

Ernest in truth missed Augusta less than he would, a few months ago, have thought possible. Nicholas was to spend a fortnight in Quebec. With brother and sister removed from the scene, Ernest settled down to enjoy his friendship with Mrs. Stroud to the full.

The sudden tropic heat of September, which other people found enervating, agreed with him. The high temperature brought out the delicate pink of his complexion. This made his eyes appear very blue. His pleasing reflection in the mirror was good for his spirits which, in their turn, aided his digestion, his weak point.

As he walked steadily along the path on this Sunday afternoon, exposed to the reddish and still intense glare of the sun, he felt scarcely more than forty and certainly looked little above fifty. He wore a light grey flannel suit and a panama hat. His socks, handkerchief and tie matched his eyes. A white rosebud bravely held up its head in his buttonhole. He felt oddly elated as he knocked on Mrs. Stroud's door.

She opened it and stood dazzled a moment by the sunshine. Then she drew him hastily inside.

"We must keep out the heat," she said.

"You are surprisingly cool in here. The blue curtains help to give the effect of coolness also. And that dress — have I seen it before?"

"No. It is new. Do you like it?"

"Very much."

He touched the material with a new air of familiarity.

"I couldn't resist it," she said.

"I'm glad you didn't."

"It is good of you to face this sun to come and see me. I scarcely hoped to see you before another hour."

"I couldn't wait," he answered with a little laugh.

There was something different in that laugh. There was something new in their relationship. Possibly the cool sequestered air of the room, in contrast to the heat outside, had its share in the advancement. Perhaps the absence of Augusta and Nicholas had cut loose an anchor. Whatever it was, the two found themselves sailing into deeper waters. To bridge the moment Mrs. Stroud remarked:

"The wild flowers are lovely just now, aren't they? Did you notice the Michaelmas daisies at the edge of the wood as you came here?"

"Yes. I should like to have brought you some but I was afraid they might be a little dusty. The goldenrod is coming on too. It makes one realize how the season passes."

"And to think that a year ago we had not met. And now we seem like quite old friends."

"Yes," he agreed. "I can't think of anyone but you living in this house, now. I can't think of myself as not coming to see you."

"And I might so easily have chosen another place! My one trial is my tenant. Listen to that!"

Dayborn's voice came from beyond the partition. "Put paraffin on the fire if it won't go, you idiot!"

Ernest made a grimace of distaste but he said consolingly:

"I should never have noticed if you had not drawn my attention to it. But it is a pity the partition is so thin. What was your builder thinking of?"

"It was my fault. I wouldn't let him spend what he wanted to. How I regret it now — when I want privacy — if ever I did!"

Ernest coloured. He coloured first at the thought of her meanness in hampering the builder, even more deeply at her plain statement of her need for privacy. He found his heart beating quickly. He began to wonder how deeply his punitive expedition was going to entangle him. He agreed:

"I am like you, too. I have a great need of privacy. The walls of Jalna are so built that, when I am in my room, the only person who has the power to annoy me is my brother. I must give him the credit of not often doing it, though occasionally he makes a great hubbub with his puppy. It's a sweet little creature but it does yap."

Mrs. Stroud made tea. It was now the custom for Ernest to carry the tray from the pantry for her. He glanced at the tomato sandwiches with approval. A fresh cream cheese and brown bread looked delicious. When she came in carrying the smaller tray with the tea things he smiled at her almost tenderly and exclaimed:

"Isn't this nice!"

With a new air of ascendancy over him she made him sit down, and laid a little embroidered napkin across his knees, as though he were a child.

"There!" she said. "You mustn't get a speck on that lovely grey flannel."

He could not help himself. He stretched out his hand, caught hers, and imprinted a kiss on her wrist.

She hurried back to the tea table and began to pour the tea, not daring to meet his eyes. But he had come out into the open.

"I don't see why you should mind that," he said a little brusquely.

"It surprised me, that was all."

"After all, any gentleman may kiss any lady's hand. Isn't that so?"

"Yes, but there are different ways of doing it."

"Do you dislike my way?"

"No," she replied in a whisper.

"Some day," he continued with temerity, "I may salute you with an even greater difference. What will you say to that, I wonder?"

Their eyes met. They laughed excitedly. Ernest was enjoying himself. It was just the sort of love-making he liked — neither here nor there, but always on the verge of something. To Amy Stroud it was a nervous ordeal. She enjoyed it as a skater might enjoy skimming over exquisite but brittle ice which might, at any moment, crack beneath his weight. Ernest was a being of a different world from the one she knew. His urbanity always made her wonder what lay behind it. Yet she had no doubt of her fascination for him.

Nearly all her waking thoughts were concentrated on him and Eden. To draw them close to her, to keep them from interfering with each other, was her problem. Already Ernest had touched on the subject of Eden's youth and the necessity for his education to be carried on without interruption from outside interests. There was a certain austerity in his face, when he spoke of Eden, that made her wonder.

She was expecting Eden that evening. He knew Ernest was to have tea with her and was not to set out till Ernest's return. Between visits she would have time to rest for a bit, and lay the table for supper. They both were startled when Eden's face appeared suddenly at the window. He drummed with his fingers on the pane. Ernest made no pretence of hiding his chagrin.

"Why had he to come!" he exclaimed angrily, but under his breath.

"Sh!" she formed with her lips, her eyes on Eden's face.

"How quaint you look," said Eden.

"Do we?" Mrs. Stroud's lips were disapproving, but her eyes melted in tenderness.

"Yes. Like Darby and Joan."

"And you are a Peeping Johnny," said Ernest huffily.

"Shall I come in?"

Mrs. Stroud sprang up and went toward the door. Eden was on the threshold. He put his arms about her.

"Don't!" She breathed in a panic, pushing him away. "Are you mad?"

"Quite."

He followed her into the room.

"Can I have tea?"

"May," corrected his uncle automatically.

"May I?" repeated Eden, with docility.

"I'll make a fresh pot." She had not reseated herself and now picked up the teapot decisively. Her confusion vanished. She felt exhilarated at the thought of a crisis. She would show herself capable of keeping both lovers, for so she pictured them, in good humour.

Left together, they sat looking at each other; Ernest trying to appear not displeased; Eden wearing the veiled smile that sat oddly on his boy's face. Ernest nervously tapped his teeth with his fingernails.

"What are they doing at home?" he asked. "You said that you would read to my mother. She is feeling Augusta's departure."

"I did. And she fell asleep. She was safe till tea time. Meg is dozing too. She's in the hammock, the old one under the mulberry tree. Rags has cleaned it up for her. There was a ladybird sitting on her nose when I passed that way. Piers was making Finch bowl to him. They looked as hot as blazes. The nursemaid has been teaching Wakefield a hymn and he's screaming 'Jesus loves me' at the top of his voice."

"And my mother asleep!"

"He's not near her. He's sitting on Rags's stomach where the clothes-lines are. The cook is in prenuptial retirement."

"And Renny?"

"Where he always is — in the stables."

"Have you no work to do?"

"None."

"Hm…. You don't look very tidy."

"I've stopped dressing up for Mrs. Stroud. She likes me any old way."

There was an insolence of intimacy in his tone which Ernest found excessively annoying.

Eden repeated, as Mrs. Stroud returned with the pot of tea — "You don't mind whether or not I'm tidy, do you?" He ran his hand through his hair, still further dishevelling it and aggressively stretched his legs, displaying his canvas shoes, the lace of one dangling.

Mrs. Stroud gave an indulgent look across him at Ernest. It re-established confidence between them. Ernest smiled. He passed his hand over his own yellowish-grey hair and accepted a fresh cup of tea.

Eden ate greedily. "Church service and Sunday dinner," he said, "leave one famished. I don't know why it is, but I want to eat all day on Sundays."

"Were there many at church?" asked Mrs. Stroud. "I just couldn't face going out in the heat along the country road. Was the sermon good?"

"It was mercifully short. Every time the rector paused Gran struggled to get on her feet, hoping it was all over. I think that unnerved him, for he was very brief."

"It is a sight to see Mrs. Whiteoak arrive at the church in her carriage, behind those prancing horses. It is worth going just to see her."

"The congregation was small," continued Eden, "and the singing would have been feeble if it hadn't been for us. We sang with all our mights, the sweat running down out faces and our backs sticking to the pews every time we rose. I could hear myself singing, but I was really fast asleep."

"This lad is a perfect chatterbox," said Ernest, smiling at Mrs. Stroud, "and prone to exaggeration."

"Yes, I know." Her eyes met Eden's but dared not rest long. His were too teasing, too mocking. There was something in his voice that set Ernest aside. It was hard for Ernest to overcome the constraint he felt. The afternoon was spoilt for him.

"Who read the lessons — with your brother away?" Mrs. Stroud asked of Ernest. "You, I suppose."

"Yes. But later on Renny will read them. It has always been the custom for the owner of Jalna to read the lessons."

Mrs. Stroud exclaimed — "And he will wear a surplice! I shall certainly go to church to see that sight."

Ernest resented the flippancy of her tone. For a moment Mrs. Stroud was to him no more than a rather ill-bred sightseer who had somehow pushed herself into their circle. His constraint deepened.

Eden turned to him. "Mrs. Stroud doesn't like our Renny, you know."

She interrupted hastily — "I do! I admire him very much. But I can't picture him in a surplice."

"You mean, he's so horsy?" said Eden.

"Perhaps that. I'm not quite sure. I know there are fox hunting parsons in England."

"He is filling his niche," observed Eden in a sententious voice.

As he perceived the constraint of the others his own spirits rose in proportion. Sometimes he talked to Mrs. Stroud, making allusions that left Ernest feeling out in the cold. Sometimes he directed his remarks to Ernest, irritating him by expressing too modernistic views on manners and morals. He was restless and moved about the room, sometimes languidly, sometimes leaping over a sofa as he might do at home.

He carried the tea things to the kitchen and insisted on washing them, though he had never had his hands in a dishpan before. He opened the refrigerator and peered into it, exclaiming at the dainty food in store there, wondering who it might be for. Mrs. Stroud was at her wits' end. When she had him alone for a moment she gave him a smart slap on the cheek.

"There! Take that and behave yourself!"

"Uncle," he began, in a complaining tone.

"For goodness' sake don't!" she exclaimed, aghast.

"Kiss me, then."

She took his face between her hands. Their lips met. She grew dizzy in this web of deception.

Ernest and Eden stayed on and on.

They became pensive in the oppressive heat. There was dead silence next door.

At sunset a breeze lifted the curtains. Ernest went to the piano and lowered the old-fashioned stool to suit his height. The instrument had belonged to the first Mrs. Stroud. The husband was always telling his second wife how she had played hymns for him by the hour. Amy Stroud would have sold it with the rest of the furniture but had had no acceptable offer for it. Now it had been tuned and, in place of the yellow velvet drapes it had once worn, its expanse of shining wood was bare except for a slender silver vase containing a single red rose.

Ernest began softly to play "Träumerei."

Mrs. Stroud moved to a low chair near the piano and fixed her eyes on his face. It was his turn to be enmeshed more securely in her net.

"How beautifully you play that!" she said, in deep thrilling tones.

He finished the piece and then said: "I am a very poor performer, but my brother plays really well. Or would do if he were to practise a little more. He says his fingers are getting stiff."

"Will you bring him to play for me?"

"I'll try to persuade him."

"My little brother, Finch, is going to be musical," said Eden.

Ernest turned on the stool to face him. "Indeed he is! He will sit, quiet as a mouse, when Nicholas is playing. I myself have taught him to play 'The Blue Danube'; though he doesn't know one note from another, he plays it charmingly."

"How sweet!" Her eyes glowed. "Do play something more. It's like hearing running water after the heat of the day."

"My repertory is painfully limited." He knit his brows, then began something of Schubert's.

"Music at night," said Eden, "always sends me to the depths. Good music or bad, the effect is the same."

He went and stretched his length on the sofa, his face to the wall.

The thin curtains were wafted into the room. The music was spun out under Ernest's delicate touch. His feeling for Amy Stroud was reaching a point it had not hitherto touched. He had a surge of triumph at the thought that Eden was outside the magic circle. He had done what he had set out to do. That his own feelings were involved took nothing from his triumph but rather enhanced it.

"My two lovers, my two lovers." The words throbbed through her brain. She saw the one, prone on the sofa, the other playing on and on, with that rapt smile on his face. What she could not be aware of was the supreme egotism of both, which made them truly invulnerable to the spell they courted.

As Eden lay with his face turned to the wall he wondered, with growing irritation, what Ernest was up to. In all decency he should have gone an hour ago. Was it possible that he was trying to outstay him? Was it even possible that there was some understanding between him and Amy Stroud? A quiver of laughter ran through him at the thought. This was followed by a shudder of jealous anger. He turned abruptly to his other side and stared at the two by the piano. He could not see Ernest's face, but there was something almost indecent in the droop of his shoulders — by heaven, there was! And why was Amy gazing into his face with that soulful expression? Her eyes were luminous with some emotion.

He rose from the sofa and went to a small table. From it he took a paper knife in the shape of a dagger. Fixing his eyes on Mrs. Stroud he moved stealthily up behind Ernest and made a barbarous gesture as though to stab him in the back. She closed her eyes and kept them so till the piece was finished. She opened them and discovered Eden standing by the window, the paper knife returned to the table. Ernest got up from the piano.

A feeling of lassitude came over all three. There was silence for a space, then Mrs. Stroud said:

"Won't you stay and have some supper?" Her glance included them both.

"I was under the impression," said Eden, "that I was invited days ago."

Ernest answered calmly — "Thank you. I'd very much like to."

With the same feeling of lassitude the supper was prepared by Mrs. Stroud and arranged on the table by the uncle and the nephew. They laid their places on either side of her. In silence they sat down to the meal.

"There's nothing I enjoy more," said Ernest, "than a meal away from home."

"Me too," said Eden. "There's nothing I like so much as a meal away from home."

"How do you manage," asked Ernest, "to have such deliciously crisp salads?"

"By keeping them on ice," answered Eden. "Like she does her emotions."

"How rude of you!" said Mrs. Stroud.

"Am I? I'm so glad. I'm naturally of such a polite nature that it's difficult for me to be rude, even when I want to."

"Do you want to?" asked Ernest.

"Terribly, Uncle."

There was something insolent in his use of the word *uncle*. Ernest looked at him sharply.

"Why, may I ask?"

"The situation is so terribly unpleasant. Don't you find it so?"

"No. But I do find you a trifle so."

"I have an elastic nature," said Eden. "Just now it is drawn to snapping point."

Under the table Mrs. Stroud put her foot warningly against his. He took it between both his own and held it. Under his breath he mumbled:

"Probably he's doing the same on the other side."

Pretending to drop his napkin he peered under the table to find out. Ernest's feet were decorously side by side.

Eden noisily ate a stick of celery, even to the leaves. "I used to call them the feathers when I was a little boy," he said. "I love celery."

"What a pity!" observed Ernest.

"Why?"

"You eat it so resoundingly."

Eden turned to Mrs. Stroud. "Hasn't Uncle a wonderful vocabulary?"

"I refuse to be drawn into this," she answered. She tried to withdraw her foot but he held it firmly. She could scarcely control her laughter.

It was impossible that Ernest, with his sensitive nature, should be unaware of these passages between them. His spirits began to flag. He was tired. But he was not a whit less determined to hold his position. The evening degenerated into a test of which could outstay the other. A distant roll of thunder was heard. The darkness outside was illuminated by a vivid flash. Mrs. Stroud had lighted candles and set them about the room. Curiously, as their three faces became marked by fatigue, they were definitely set into three generations. Ernest's face was dimmed to all his years. Mrs. Stroud, though nothing was added to her years, which the candlelight diminished, looked wearily middle-aged. Eden appeared a pale exhausted boy. Thus it was as though they were father, daughter, and daughter's son, three generations in some morbidly tense situation.

Finally Mrs. Stroud could bear it no longer. Her eyes were full of tears. She said:

"I'm afraid I must ask you both to go. This heat and the thunder in the air has got on my nerves. My head aches."

Even then they were reluctant to go. Ernest asked solicitously:

"May I get you something? An aspirin, perhaps?"

"No, no. I shall be all right. It's silly of me but I must lie down."

Eden plumped up the cushions on the divan. "You can't go to bed yet. Do lie down here."

She shook her head, not able to speak. There was another roll of thunder. Ernest remarked apprehensively:

"We shall be caught in the storm."

She accompanied them as far as the gate. The breeze had fallen and the air was heavy with the approaching storm. She took a hand of each and looked up into their eyes. Her own were glistening with tears:

"How sweet you both are to me!" she exclaimed.

She stood looking after them, her arms resting on the gate. Relief at their going was mingled with triumph at their staying so long. She felt that she never could close her eyes that night. But she did not mind. She had thoughts for the long night through.

She turned back to the house, which at that hour and in her present mood appeared as a glamorous retreat. She raised her arms and stretched them wide, drinking in the night air. Her lassitude had vanished. She was free to brood over the contrasting personalities of her two "lovers," and to calculate her future relations with them.

As she reached the door, a lurid flash discovered Jim Dayborn standing on his own doorstep, the door shut behind him. How long he had been there she could not guess but her anger flared at the sight of his almost painfully thin, sarcastically smiling face. She exclaimed heatedly:

"How you do like to spy on other people!"

Dayborn replied imperturbably — "Well, what else have I to do on a Sunday night?"

"You acknowledge, then, that you do spy?"

"If you can call it spying to stand on one's own doorstep. What you need, Mrs. Stroud, is a house in a wood, with not a neighbour in sight."

She came to the low fence that divided them and placed her hands on two of the pointed palings.

"I am tired," she said, "of your prying presence. You are two months behind with your rent. You can go. I will not ask you to pay the rent but you must be out of here inside of three days. Three days, do you hear?"

She was positively intimidating in her restrained fury. Dayborn was shocked into silence for a moment. Then he repeated:

"Three days! You can't mean it! Why — what have we done?"

"You've made yourselves a nuisance. You've been prying. You've been always in evidence — quarrelling — coming in and out of my house at all hours — borrowing and not returning — behind with your rent — now you can go!"

"But we can get no house about here!"

"Then go somewhere else."

"But our work is here!"

"Your *work*! Breaking in colts! Let them go unbroken — let them go mad — I don't care! Just to be rid of your presence is all that I ask."

He now used a placating tone. "But you've encouraged us to run in and out of your house. You've said you liked to lend us things. You've liked the kid."

She cut him short. "Well, — I don't like any of you now! I've borne more from you than I've ever borne from a tenant in my life."

He was roused. He said sarcastically, "The truth about you is that being taken up by these Whiteoaks has gone to your head. But if you think that either of those men care a curse for you, you're damned well mistaken."

It was with difficulty that Mrs. Stroud controlled herself. She gripped the sharp palings of the fence in her hands and bit her shaking underlip. Then she spoke with comparative calm.

"This is the end. I don't want you to speak to me again — ever. Tell Chris not to come in to see me. Not she or anyone else can change me. Hand me your keys inside of three days."

She turned from him and went into her house, shutting the door behind her. After a time a rap sounded on her door but she did not answer it. Looking out of a window she saw Chris Cummings climb over the fence and return to her own house.

Ernest and Eden said little on the way home. Now that they were alone together they were embarrassed by what had taken place, though Eden the less of the two. His mind was revolving about the events of the past weeks. He would have liked to know what was in Ernest's mind. How much did Ernest care for Mrs. Stroud? How much had the family to do with it? Were they at the bottom of it? Either Ernest was a good play-actor or he was really himself entangled. Eden leaned toward this opinion. What did Amy feel? She and Ernest appeared to hit it off too well for just a casual friendship.

Eden was angry at Ernest's interference. His evening had been spoilt. Was he never again to have the freedom in her house that had meant so much to him? Did Amy love him? Could she love Ernest? His immature mind groped among vague possibilities.

As they reached Jalna there were heavy rolls of thunder. Lightning outlined smallest twigs against the greenish sky. Large drops of rain fell.

"We're lucky," remarked Ernest, "to get under shelter. The rain is coming."

He bolted the door. The gas was turned low in the hall. He examined the dim gold face of the grandfather clock. It was a quarter-past twelve. He gave an exclamation of dismay.

"We did keep that poor lady up late!" he said.

"I never knew her to be tired before," said Eden.

"I suppose it was the weather."

"I never knew her to mind weather before."

"But we haven't previously had any such heat."

"I don't want to go to bed, do you?"

Ernest hesitated. Late hours did not agree with him. But he was excited and it was not pleasant to be in bed during a storm. It was probable that his mother might want him. He went and stood outside her door, which was at the end of the hall. A tranquil snore came from within. It was not so much a snore as the buzzing of a bumblebee in a particularly well-honeyed flower. Ernest smiled. "What shall we do?" he asked.

"Could we have a drink?"

"My dear boy, you're too young for drinking at this hour."

"I feel that tonight is the time to begin."

"I don't know what your aunt would say."

"Come, now, Uncle Ernie, there are just us two! Who's to know?"

"Very well. We'll have a whiskey and soda. It will do us good. There — listen to that!"

A deep roll had ended with a crash that reverberated through the house. Ernest again listened at his mother's door. There was dead silence. Then the bumblebee resumed its rumbling in a more tremulous tone.

"Bless her!" exclaimed Ernest. He led the way to the dining room.

Eden closed an open window and set two chairs together at the end of the long table. Ernest fetched a bottle of Scotch and a siphon of soda from the sideboard. They sat down and Ernest poured whiskey into each glass. Eden filled the glasses with soda water.

"I don't think," observed Ernest, "that the storm will be heavy. The rain is already coming."

The rain, as though a barrier had been removed, began to fall in a torrent, beating against the panes, streaming over the gravel sweep. Beyond its onslaught the distant roll of thunder could be heard.

Eden raised his glass halfway, hesitated, and then said — "To Aimee."

"To Aimee," repeated Ernest, and put his glass to his lips.

Eden lighted a cigarette. "It must be lonely for her," he said, "in that house, in a storm."

"It must be very lonely."

"It's a pity we came away so soon."

"It is a pity." Ernest took a deeper drink.

"Still, if we hadn't come when we did, we mightn't have got away at all."

"You mean stayed all night?"

"Yes." Eden again drank.

"But we couldn't have done that — not both of us."

"I should say two would be better than one."

"You mean more conventional."

"Of course — Uncle."

"You have a curious way of calling me *Uncle* this evening."

"Have I?"

"Yes. I don't quite like it."

"I'm sorry — Ernest."

"Now that's just silly."

"Yes, it is rather. But our position is rather silly, isn't it?"

"What do you mean, silly?"

"Being rivals and all that."

Ernest was perplexed and apprehensive at Eden's bringing what both had striven to keep secret, into the open. His confusion was added to by the fact that a glass of whiskey, such as he had now taken, went inevitably to his head. He poured himself another.

"Why — I — don't know. I hadn't thought about it." Eden looked at him reproachfully.

"Not thought about it! It seems to me we have thought of little else for hours. You're not afraid to admit that you *are* my rival, are you?"

"Afraid! No, certainly not, but —"

"But what?"

"I entered the field for your good, dear boy."

"You mean the family put you up to it?"

"We discussed the matter. All we elders were present."

"And you drew the fatal ballot!"

"I repeat that it was done unselfishly and to save you from what we considered a designing woman…. Since then my opinion of Mrs. Stroud has changed."

Eden leant toward Ernest:

"Uncle Ernie, you are in love with Amy yourself."

The amber of the whiskey glimmered low in Ernest's second glass. He was less disconcerted to have his hand thus forced than he would have been only half an hour before.

"You do rush your fences, my dear boy!" he said with a slight tremor in his voice.

"No, I don't. I only want to bring a salutory candour into the situation. When you first went to see Mrs. Stroud you thought of her as a climber, didn't you?"

"I did, rather. But, as I said a moment ago, I have changed my opinion of her. I now think she is a woman of great sensibility and charm."

"In short, you're in love with her."

"That is putting it too strongly. But I do acknowledge that I am attached to her."

"Do you think she wants to marry?"

"No. I think she would be satisfied with male friendship and understanding. I gather that she hasn't had much of either."

"She's an awful liar!"

"Do you think so? I think she is hungry and illogical, that is all."

"You do understand women! You must have had a lot of experience."

"I never had to learn," returned Ernest modestly. "I was born understanding women."

"God! I wish I did!"

Ernest spoke with benevolent seriousness. "There is plenty of time. Nothing could be worse for you than a love affair now. A detached, cool woman of the world might do you no harm. Mrs. Stroud is a different proposition."

There was a conscious pause. Then Eden said, with what seemed unnecessary violence:

"If she's got to choose between us, let her choose!"

"Nonsense! There is no question of a choice. How can she choose between a crusty old bachelor and a mere boy?"

"It's a matter of dignity! We can't go on like this!"

He sprang up and walked about the room. "Could we have the window open? It's stifling in here."

"Yes. The rain is lessening. Put up the window."

Eden flung it up. The air, purified by rain, came almost palpably into the room. The Virginia creeper that covered the wall was encroaching on the window. A dripping tendril dangled across the open space. Eden picked a leaf from it and laid it on the table before Ernest.

"Look!" he said, "there is a tinge of red in it. Summer is going."

"Yes," agreed Ernest, "the year is on the wane." He spoke with a touch of sentiment.

Eden went through the archway into the sitting room. He returned with a carved ivory dice box in his hand. He rattled the dice as he came. If Ernest had been less absorbed in his own thoughts, he might have noticed the mocking light in the boy's eyes.

"I'll tell you what, Uncle Ernest," he exclaimed. "We'll play for her! Three throws out of five. The one who gets the highest numbers wins. If you win I retire to the background, plunge into my work and am a good boy from now on. If I win, you keep away from Amy, tell the family that you've studied the situation carefully and that her friendship can do me nothing but good."

Ernest's hand was a little unsteady as he set down his empty glass. Eden refilled it for him. He sipped the drink, found it too strong, then said deliberately:

"Very well. I'll do it."

Eden handed him the dice box.

"You go first."

The carved ivory was singularly becoming to Ernest's hand. He shook the box and threw a six and a four.

"Good!" said Eden. He then threw a five and a two.

Ernest took the box, rattled the dice dreamily, and threw a one and a six.

"I'm afraid that will be easy to beat," he said.

But Eden threw only a brace of twos.

"It looks bad for me," he said.

This time Ernest threw a five and a six. A smile of satisfaction flickered across his face. He sipped the drink, which he no longer found too strong.

Eden threw a brace of sixes. He gave a crow of delight. "My luck has changed!"

Ernest rattled the dice decisively. His lips were set in a thin line. He threw a four and a three.

Eden threw a four and a five.

"Even!" exclaimed Ernest. He was now trembling with eagerness. He must, he would, make a good cast! He threw a pair of fives.

Eden's face also was set. His eyes shone. He shook the dice and turned them out. But he could not bring himself to raise the box. Ernest and he eyed each other across it.

"Come, come," said Ernest peremptorily. "Let's see what you've thrown!"

Eden raised the box. He had thrown a five and a six.

They sat staring fixedly at the dice.

Then Eden exclaimed dramatically — "I've won!"

"Yes, yes. It's pretty hard on me. My friendship with Mrs. Stroud has been a great pleasure — more than that — but I'll abide by this. But what am I to say to the family?"

"Tell them it was no use. Tell them you know a great passion when you meet it."

Ernest looked dazed. He rose unsteadily.

"I — I must go to bed. Very tired."

"Shall I give you my arm, Uncle Ernie?"

"Thank you. I shouldn't have taken that last drink. What did you say you threw?"

"A five and a six."

"Well — what a pity!" He stood leaning on the table. "Eden, you've won — be worthy of her!"

Eden took his arm and led him through the door and up the stairs to his own room. He returned to put out the light land found Rags in the dining room laying some silver on a tray. Rags said:

"I'm just taking a little food to Miss Whiteoak, sir. She ate little or nothing last evening. The electricity upset her. 'Ere comes the rain again!"

A fresh rainstorm was beating violently on the windows.

"Put out the light when you come down," said Eden.

"Yes, sir. Do you think Mr. Ernest is all right or 'ad I better go to 'im?"

"He's all right."

"Wot about the windows on the top floor?"

"I'm going up. I'll see to them. Has anyone been in to my grandmother?"

"I closed 'er window, sir. It was very 'ot in there. She murmured somethink about India. 'Er parrot 'ad got off 'is perch and was sitting on the foot of the bed. 'E's a rum 'un. 'E opened one eye and gave me a nasty look and repeated over and over — 'Indiar — Indiar — Indiar.' It *was* unnatural."

"Rags."

"Yes, sir."

"You needn't mention to anyone that my uncle and I had a drink here."

"Ow no, sir! I see you 'ad a little gime of dice, sir."

"It was nothing. Just to settle a dispute."

"My word! Listen to that! I don't fancy these storms. I 'ope it clears before tomorrow."

"Tomorrow?"

"It's my wedding d'y. I'm afraid I shall look a wreck, sir, wot with the loss of sleep and the perturbation natural to the occasion. I shouldn't feel so nervous if we was going to fix it up at a registry office, but this 'ere walkin' up the haisle of the church with the horgan playing the weddin' march makes it a serious business."

"You'll come through it all right."

"I call it kind of Captain Whiteoak to give the bride away."

Eden felt that Rags would stand there, tray in hand, talking till dawn. He said goodnight to him and went up the two nights of stairs to his room.

He stopped outside the open door of the room shared by his young brothers. By their breathing, he knew they slept. A bluish flash of lightning illumined the room. Piers was lying on the bed, flat on his back, his tanned chest exposed, his attitude statuesque. The room was intolerably hot. Little Finch had carried his pillow to the window and was curled there on the floor. He slept so deeply that the rain, actually beating in on him, did not wake him.

Eden shook him irritably.

"Do you want to get your death of cold? Get into bed, you young duffer!"

Only half awake, Finch scrambled obediently to his feet and staggered toward the bed. His wet nightshirt clung to his thin body. A clap of thunder drowned the uproar of the rain.

"Oh, gee," he whimpered, "the storm's awful!"

Eden grinned. "I thought you liked it. I thought you'd like to sleep right out in it."

Finch opened his eyes which he had kept tightly shut. They were met by the fierce glare of lightning. He shut them again and scrambled in a panic across Piers's body. Eden put his pillow beneath his head, turning the wet side down.

"Thank you, Eden." Finch burrowed into the pillow. He pulled the sheet over his head.

Eden jerked Piers's pillow from under his head and plumped it down on his face.

"Take that! You lazy dog!" he said.

He closed the window and went to his own room. He sat down by his desk and leant his head on his hand. He did not close his window but sat looking out into the storm. A feeling of melancholy crept over him. What was it all about? What had happened to him tonight? No great experience was over but something was done with. Why had he made a fool of Uncle Ernest? He had got the better of him. He had shown the family that he would go his own way. But what was that way? Where, oh where, would it lead him?

XIV

Rags's Wedding

After the storm, morning broke fair as a flower. The grass had been washed till every blade shone. The curled petals of dahlias which had been filled with rain now spilled it out as the heavy blooms drooped. There was a wind from the west and round white clouds like chariots were rolled across the sky.

In the kitchen all was preparation for the wedding. Eliza had come back to take Rags's place while he went on his honeymoon which was to be a two days excursion to Niagara Falls. Eliza was disapproving of the union between two people both of whom she disliked. It would have been better, she thought, if neither of them had come to Jalna, let alone being married there and settling down to be as common and as wasteful as they chose. She disapproved still more the family's making their wedding a gala occasion, just as though the two had been serving well at Jalna for years. But the old lady had taken a fancy to Rags, also she liked excitement of any sort, on any pretext. There she was in her room, choosing what cap to wear, just as though it were the wedding of one of the family! She had bought Maggie a fine silk dress and Rags a pair of cuf-flinks. Generally she was close enough. It took a wedding to loosen her purse strings. It was a pity there were no weddings in the family. There was Mr. Ernest who should have been married long ago. There was Miss

Meg who had been treated so cruelly by Mr. Vaughan. If only some other nice man would come along and win her!

There was Mr. Renny! Eliza's lips took a downward curve when she thought of him, but her eyes softened. There was one thing about the affair, she would enjoy doing her old work again for a couple of days, investigating the corners, seeing how Rags kept the silver. Eliza would say this for Maggie, that she had prepared an appetizing array of dishes to tide the family over her absence. But what airs the woman put on, with her hair frizzed and her feet crammed into high-heeled slippers, and a red fox fur for going away in — with the thermometer likely to rise to eighty. Worst of all, Rags had stuck labels from a hotel in Paris on their two suitcases! How had he come by them? Eliza could not trust herself to speak of these. She just gave them a look of scornful unbelief as Rags set the cases, with a lordly air, by the kitchen door for the house-maid to carry out. Still, it was nice to be at Jalna once more, to take the old lady's breakfast to her, to fetch Mr. Renny's shaving water and to see how little Wakefield had made friends with him.

The boys were to miss afternoon school in order to be home in time for the wedding. The preparations for it had given Piers and Finch that feeling of hilarity which made them mislay each of their belongings in turn, dawdle over their breakfast and seem likely to miss their train. Eden was preoccupied and inclined to be irritable with his juniors.

As the three sped along the country road on their bicycles toward the little railway station, Eden felt irked by the monotony of these journeyings. Yet he infinitely preferred them to being in residence in the college. He wished he had Oxford ahead of him. His uncles had gone there but the family exchequer would no longer run to it, or so at least Renny said. For some reason which he did not try to fathom, his mind turned resolutely away from the affair of the night before. The poetic intimacy between him and Amy Stroud he felt was no longer possible. What would follow he did not know. What he did know was that she no longer existed for him as a woman. She had become a symbol. As a symbol he would defend her against — what? Again his mind turned away from the thought.

His brothers were pressing too close behind him. It was understood that he should lead the way. Yet he could see the front wheel of

Piers's bicycle and he gave him a warning look over his shoulder. The freshness of the air succeeding the sultriness of the day before, the hilarity of the wedding preparations, made Piers oblivious to Eden's senior claim. He rode past him through a deep puddle, sending a spray of muddy water over Eden's grey-flannelled legs. Finch, following blindly in Piers's wake, did the same. As he passed Eden and saw the fury in his face, he pedalled with all his might, almost colliding with Piers's back wheel.

"Look out!" shouted Piers.

"You young blighters!" exclaimed Eden.

Finch wobbled distractedly. It seemed that he would topple over and that Eden would crash into him but somehow he righted himself and sped, grinning insanely, after Piers into the station yard.

Eden followed slowly, wishing that he had the two at home. They hurried, exchanging mischievous looks, into the baggage room where they were allowed to keep their bicycles. They stood them against the wall and, not able to control their hilarious grins, watched Eden approach.

"I suppose you think you're funny," he said scathingly.

They stared speechless at his damaged trousers.

"It's hard on a fellow," he said, "to have two such imbeciles always at his heels."

Piers's eyes met his daringly. Finch giggled. Eden banged his bicycle into its place. He continued:

"I had a mind to pull you off your bikes and roll the two of you over into that puddle."

"Oh no, you wouldn't!" said Piers.

"I wouldn't, eh?"

"No, you wouldn't."

"I'd like to know why."

"You might do it to the kid — not me!"

"Not you, eh? Come back with me now and I'll show you."

"All right." Piers turned truculently toward the door. Eden walked close beside him. He said:

"If you come back with me to that puddle, you'll be sorry."

"So will you."

The whistle of the locomotive shrieked at the crossing. Several people, carrying suitcases, hastened across the platform.

"I can't do it in front of these people," said Eden. "I'll see you about it later." He took out his handkerchief and attempted to dry the mud spots on his trousers.

He jostled Piers against the door as they entered the carriage, and had the satisfaction of seeing him wince. There was only one vacant seat to be had. Eden took it and, drawing a book from his pocket, settled down to dignified reading. He ignored the two who had to stand by his side all the way to town. Each time Finch raised his eyes to Piers's face, Piers winked at him.

Ernest slept late that morning. He had slept heavily the whole night through. He felt heavy-eyed and oppressed in spirit when he woke but after a cold bath his depression lifted. In reviewing the events of the night before he felt the exhilaration of one who has had a narrow escape. What might not have happened if his intimacy with Amy Stroud had progressed? He might have been drawn into marriage with her and some instinct told him that she was not the wife for him. He doubted if the woman lived who was the wife for him. He had done his best to win Mrs. Stroud from Eden. He had been worsted. His spirit was tranquil. No more hot walks to her house. No more long fervid conversations that left him feeling tired. He would gracefully fade out of the picture. He would pass the torch to other hands. Let Nick have a go at her!

He sauntered almost jauntily to his mother's room. She was already dressed for the wedding. He bent and kissed her.

"How early you are dressed, Mamma," he said.

"Anticipation is the best part of a wedding," she replied.

"I hope this one will turn out well. While these two are not perfect as servants, they have their merits. She is an excellent cook and he will turn his hand to anything. I hope they appreciate what you are doing for them today."

"I like a party. The wedding breakfast is to be laid on tables on the drying green. The Rector and his wife are coming and the Lacey girls and Lily Pink. Weddings always amuse them. I've also asked that man Dayborn and his sister, and told them to bring their child. Then there's that Mrs. Stroud. I want to see you and her together."

"There will be nothing in that to interest you, Mamma. I've given up."

She stared up at him from under the lace edging of her cap.

"Given up what?"

"Mrs. Stroud. It is useless for me to interfere. Eden and she are attached beyond my undoing. In fact, it is I who am undone."

"D'ye mean to say you can't cut out that stripling?"

"Yes. No one can say that I haven't tried. I have given up time when I should have been working on my book. My own feelings even have become involved."

"Ha! She *is* a charmer then!"

"Of the most dangerous sort, for she has no beauty, though she has fine eyes and an alluring voice."

"I wish we had sent Nicholas to do the job."

"So indeed do I. He would have undertaken it as an adventure. I accepted it as a crusade."

The more Ernest talked, the more pleased he was with the situation. He wished that Augusta might have been there to hear him. But his mother was impressed. He confided to her the details of his many visits to Mrs. Stroud. He told her of the dice throwing of the night before.

Her shaggy eyebrows went up.

"A duel! 'Pon my word it was next thing to a duel! You've heard of the duel that was fought for me, when I was but fifteen. 'Twas between Lord Boyne and young Tim Crawshay. They fought with swords for an hour. My brother Abram held the hourglass in his hand. They fought till they fell down exhausted, but they were such fine swordsmen that neither of them had a scratch!"

Ernest had heard the story many times but he becomingly asked:

"Which did you favour after that, Mamma?"

"Neither. While they fought I sat waiting with a young Lieutenant of the Guards. He was so sympathetic that I took no notice of either of them again."

"I hope that you feel that I did my best, Mamma."

"I do, Ernest. But I wish it had been Nick. Gout and all, I think he would have beat you."

"Mamma, no man living could do more than I have done. I have been tossed like a billow on the brine. Mrs. Stroud is infatuated with Eden."

Adeline thrust out her lips. "Then I will have something to say to her."

By afternoon the breeze fell. It was hotter than ever. The brilliant breathless air enmeshed the countryside in a golden veil in which a thousand crickets, locusts and grasshoppers sang; the fluff of milkweed and pollen of goldenrod hung; the voices of farm workers and neigh of horses were muffled.

Eliza looked cool and collected but the poor bride, after a final encounter with the wedding breakfast, was crimson-faced and, as she herself said, in a lather of sweat. Eliza clothed her in a garment of talcum powder before squeezing her into the new silk dress.

As for Rags, he was wearing a morning suit which had been Renny's before the War. A tailor had cut it down for him but it still was somewhat long in leg and sleeve, and the tails almost reached his knees. However, the tailor had made a good job of the shoulders and, as this part was all Rags saw of himself in the small looking glass in his room, he was in a state of high satisfaction. He was pallid as the bride was flushed, as spare as she was full bosomed, as composed as she was flustered.

Rags walked across the fields to the church with a Cockney groom with whom he had struck up a friendship. Renny drove the bride in the dogcart. He was to give her away. Eden took Meg and his younger brothers in the car, while old Hodge, the coachman, drove the carriage wherein sat Adeline, Ernest and little Wakefield.

There were a number of people already in the church when they arrived, for work on farm and in stables had ceased for the occasion. The friends of the family were in the front pews. There was a scattering of people from the village in the back of the church.

Eden slid into a pew beside Mrs. Stroud who was sitting alone. He made facetious remarks to her under his breath about the groom's costume, the bride's colour and the company in general. Rags was just *not* comic as he stood waiting by the chancel steps. But there was a dignity about him, a *savoir faire*, that induced the negative.

Miss Pink, having scrubbed her hands with her pocket handkerchief, fervently produced the wedding march on the organ. Adeline craned her neck, while holding Wakefield close, to watch the approach of the bride.

Renny, wearing the austere expression of a father who is not positive that he is giving his daughter to a man worthy of her, led the cook up the aisle. She suddenly bloomed into a shy and trustful bride. She savoured every moment of this greatest day of her life. As they passed Adeline, Wakefield struggled on her knee.

"I want to go too!" his little voice piped.

"Hush," she admonished him and pressed his face against the crepe of her veil.

Eden whispered to Mrs. Stroud — "What if it were you and me!"

She coloured deeply and her fingers touched his hand that lay on the seat between them.

Piers whispered to Finch — "I wonder if Eden changed his pants!"

Finch gave a suffocated giggle. The sound of it horrified him. Then he heard himself give another. He clenched his hands till his nails hurt him. The back of his not too well washed neck grew red. He shook with giggles. Meg looked across Piers at him and beckoned. He clambered across Piers's knees and sat on Meg's other side. When he dared raise his eyes he beheld Mr. Fennel, the Rector, performing the last of the ceremony.

Now they were man and wife, grappled together for a long serving of the Whiteoaks. The master of Jalna bent his red head ceremoniously and imprinted a kiss on the cheek of the bride.

The wedding cake, made by the bride but iced elaborately by a confectioner, stood in the middle of the long table. The table was conveniently close to the kitchen so that platters could be replenished with ease. All commonizing articles such as clotheslines and props had been removed from the scene. The grass had been shaved and watered. A great bunch of dahlias stood near the cake.

It was an impressive sight to see Rags escort old Adeline to her place at the head of the table. She had removed her mantle and bonnet and wore a mauve-and-white cap with rosettes of ribbon.

"Who but you, dear Mrs. Whiteoak," said the eldest Miss Lacey who had once been a flame of Nicholas's, "would have thought of doing anything so charming!"

"It's not the first party I've given for my servants."

"Indeed, I remember others. But this is especially kind as they have not been with you very long."

"Time flies when you're past ninety," returned Adeline, "I'll not be here to give them a silver wedding breakfast."

"I wish Nicholas had been here."

"I think he stayed in Quebec to avoid it. He has no taste for such junketings."

"I declare," said Miss Pink, "my fingers stuck with heat to the keys of the organ! I thought I'd never get through with the march. What a pretty thing that young Mrs. Cummings is! But how strange of her to have brought her baby to a wedding."

"I invited him. To my mind there's no more appropriate guest at a wedding than a baby."

"Oh yes," agreed Miss Pink faintly.

Ernest found himself beside Mrs. Stroud. He was not distressed by this. He was his usual detached, urbane self. She was conscious of a change in him but could not have named what it was. It was probably, she thought, the presence of his family. Eden, on the other hand, was so openly attentive to her as to be embarrassing. Yet she gloried in his attentions.

It was an irritation to her that Dayborn was seated opposite her. His expression was stony. He spoke only in answer to questions and then taciturnly. Chris looked heavy-eyed, as though she had shed tears. It was characteristic of Amy Stroud that the scene of the night before had finally closed the door of her friendship against them. Their plight moved her to no generous impulse.

Renny was rising. He said:

"It is with real pleasure that I propose the health of the bride. Not only for her own sake and the sake of her husband but for the sakes of all of my family. Four times every day I bless her. In the morning with her good porridge inside me I go to my stables as ready for work as any horse there. At noon I return, knowing that a delicious joint and a tempting sweet await me. At tea time I know that the tea will be hot and that there will be plenty of it. At night — well, her suppers invariably fill the bill. What more can a man want in his bride — except beauty and charm and, if anyone doubts that Mrs. Wragge possesses both, let him look at her smiling there. As for Rags — he is in some ways a better cook than she, because she has to have good materials and plenty of them (I know that because of the bills I pay) but, when Rags and I were at the front and he said 'There's not a blasted thing to eat, sir, but what's in this tin, and the carcass of a hen' — then I knew that a particularly good feed was coming. I foresee a long happy union for these two and I have great pleasure in proposing the health of the bride."

He sat down.

"Hear! hear!" said the Rector, who had eaten a particularly large meal.

"Very good," said Ernest, thinking how much better he could have done it.

The bride's health was drunk. She blushed furiously.

"Now then," urged the best man, kicking the groom under cover of the table.

Wragge rose with trembling but conscious of the elegance of his appearance. He bowed profoundly. His emotions gave a touch of poignancy to his Cockney accent.

"Lidies and gentlemen, I want to thank you very much for your good wishes to my wife —"

He was interrupted by loud applause, led by Piers. He bowed again and proceeded:

"My wife and myself. This 'ere getting married is new to me and that there ceremony at the church a greater hordeal than shell fire. I little thought, when I came to Jalner, that I'd get 'itched up so soon but I believe I've made a good choice. Mrs. Wragge and I feel like old family retainers. When I first went to Captain Whiteoak as 'is batman in France, I says to myself — 'That's the gentleman I'm going to stick to in 'ealth or — blown to bits!' And so I 'ave and so I will." He sat down and wiped the perspiration from his face with one of the dozen silk handkerchiefs which were Meg's present to him.

The cheering, led by Piers, was vociferous.

The day continued fine and hot. The married pair set out for Niagara Falls. Eliza took the reins into her hands. The gramophone had been brought out and Finch put on one record after another, till the three pieces of wedding cake he had eaten began to have their effect on him. He went down to the washroom in the basement and was sick. The family and their friends retired to the house, leaving the rest of the guests to enjoy themselves unhampered. Dayborn seized the first opportunity to draw Renny aside.

XV

Contrasting Scenes

"I want to tell you something," said Dayborn. "Can we go in here?"

He jerked his head toward the open door of the sitting room. The folding doors between it and the dining room were shut. Renny nodded and they went in, closing the door behind them.

"What's up?" asked Renny, wondering if Dayborn again wanted an advance of wages.

Dayborn answered in a tense voice — "We've got to go."

"Go! When? Why? What do you mean?"

"Mrs. Stroud has given us notice to get out of her house. She gives us three days."

"The hell she has! How much are you behind with the rent?"

"Two months. That has nothing to do with it. She doesn't want such near neighbours."

"D'you mean the noise?"

"Lord, no! Just the proximity. She doesn't want her doings spied on."

"Do you spy on her?"

"If you call it spying to stand in your own door before you go to bed. Your uncle and your brother were both there last night. You may say there's safety in numbers but I say the woman is a bitch. I'd put nothing past her. I wish you'd heard her fly at me when she discovered I'd seen things. There was no innocence there. She simply raged. Told us to get out. If you want my opinion of her I'll give it."

"Yes?"

"She's no better than a prostitute. Not as good, for there's no necessity in it."

Renny knit his brow. For the moment his chief concern was that Dayborn and Chris had nowhere to go. He said:

"It's a devil of a mess. There's not a vacant house anywhere about. There's no one who takes lodgers. How long does she give you?"

"Three days."

"She was in a temper. She's probably over it now."

"Not she. She hasn't spoken to either of us today."

"I'll see her. Perhaps something can be done. But first I want to see my uncle. Find him, will you, and tell him I want to speak to him here. How are Launceton's legs?"

"He's still nibbling at them. It's just nerves. They're not filling up."

"He's been working too hard in the heat. Tell Scotchmere to bandage them."

"All right. I'll send your uncle here first." He opened the door. Mrs. Stroud's rich laugh came from the drawing room. Dayborn stood with his hand on the doorknob. "In the first place," he said, "she's a social climber and so I told her."

"You blasted fool," said Renny.

He stood motionless thinking till Ernest came. He closed the door behind him.

"What is that young Dayborn so mysterious about?" he asked.

"There's no mystery. Mrs. Stroud has ordered him and his family to leave their house in three days. There was a row last night after you and Eden left."

There was no embarrassment in Ernest's face. He replied urbanely — "Really! I'm sorry for that. But we can't do anything about it, can we?"

"*Do* anything! I can't part with Dayborn and Chris now. They're too important to me!"

"If the rent is paid I don't think Mrs. Stroud can force them to go without a month's notice."

"Of course not! Why didn't we think of that! I'll pay the rent and they'll have the month for looking about for a place." His face cleared, then darkened again. He said:

"Dayborn says Mrs. Stroud is a devil. What do you think?"

"I think she probably has devil enough in her to be stimulating."

Renny gave him a shrewd look.

He asked:

"How much longer is it going to take you to cut Eden out?"

"I've thrown up the sponge. I've tried and I've failed. I look on the affair as very serious."

The colour in Renny's already high-coloured face intensified. He exclaimed hotly:

"The young fool! With a woman that age!"

"What about yourself at eighteen?"

"I deserved a thrashing. My father was too easygoing. The woman is a pest. She has turned out Dayborn and Chris and roped in Eden. I shall have a word to say to her, and to him too."

"I wish you were more cautious. You may do more harm than good. I sometimes fear I have."

"I'll be crafty."

There were voices in the hall. Someone was going.

"I had better go back to our guests," said Ernest. "The Laceys are leaving."

"Uncle Ernest, I wish you would tell Chris I want to speak to her. She must be very upset. Bring her here, will you?"

Renny walked impatiently about the room. Through the window he could see the Miss Laceys departing. What a hot walk they had ahead of them. Why had no one thought of taking them home in the car. He stuck his head out of the window.

"Wait a moment!" he called. "Someone will take you home. It's as hot as blazes."

They came over to the window.

"Oh, how kind of you!"

"That will be nice."

"It's been such a delightful afternoon —"

"And quite picturesque —"

"I always think a meal out of doors —"

"Dear Mrs. Whiteoak is wonderful. She said to me —"

"And she even had a piece of the wedding cake. I said to her —"

"No, it was I who said —"

They chattered on, interrupting each other, as all his life he remembered their doing. They would think nothing of spending an hour by the window. He heard Chris enter the room. He signalled to her behind his back. She took his hand in hers.

The elder Miss Lacey was saying:

"I remember a garden party at Jalna. It was just such a September day as this. Your grandfather was still living and he —"

"What a good-looking man," interrupted her sister. "D'you know I think that Piers —"

"But, if I may say it, I think that Piers will never have the —"

"How could he! Life and manners are —"

"To be sure, but as I —"

Renny ruthlessly interrupted the amiable flow of words. He felt Chris's lips against his palm.

"Just wait a moment, will you," he said. "I'll get one of the boys to bring the car."

He withdrew his head. Chris was in the shadow behind him. Silently he held her close.

The younger Miss Lacey's voice came clearly: "Certainly *he* has not his grandfather's manners. Did you notice how —"

"*Did* I? And the abrupt way he —"

With a rueful grimace at hearing himself so criticized Renny pushed Chris farther into the shadow. "Back in a moment, darling," he whispered.

He looked into the drawing room. His grandmother, uncle and sister were there with the Fennels and Miss Pink. He went to the dining room. Eden and Mrs. Stroud were standing beneath the portrait of Adeline. They were talking in a low tone but met his eyes without embarrassment. He said:

"Sorry to interrupt but I want Eden to drive the Miss Laceys home in the car. I'd send one of the men but they're playing games of some sort out there."

"Much better interrupt us than them," said Mrs. Stroud with an enigmatic smile.

Eden said deliberately, — "All right. I'll take Mrs. Stroud too. It's a good idea."

He left the room. There was a moment's somewhat embarrassed silence. Then she remarked, looking from Renny to the portrait — "There is a resemblance between you and your grandmother, isn't there?"

"It has always been remarked," he replied stiffly.

"It must be extraordinary to be a member of such a large family. I have lived alone so much. I have never had more than one other person in the house with me since I was a child."

"That partly explains you," he said.

She was on the defensive. "What do you mean?"

"I mean that, if you had had young brothers, you would know a boy for a boy when you met one."

She flashed him a look of anger.

"Perhaps Eden is less of a boy than you think."

"I don't see," he said, "how you can be interested in him. However, if you are, you are, and that's that. There is quite a different matter I should like to talk to you about. I'll come to see you this evening, if you don't mind."

For a moment she felt that she must refuse him. She was conscious of a kind of harsh dexterity in him that might worst her in a conflict. Yet how could she refuse? She heard herself saying:

"Yes, I'll be glad to see you. Any time this evening."

Eden had returned. He gave Renny a swift look as though to penetrate what was going on in his mind, then said to Mrs. Stroud:

"I've brought the car around. Will you come?"

"Yes. I must say goodbye first."

Renny bowed gravely to her as she passed him. He went through the folding doors into the sitting room, closing them behind him. Chris was still standing where he had left her.

"They've gone, haven't they?"

He looked out of the window.

"Not yet. Mrs. Stroud and Eden were in the dining room. I'm going to see her tonight."

"It won't do any good. She's adamant. If you had heard the scene she made with Jim last night!"

"But she has been very kind to you in the past, hasn't she?"

"Yes, but she's changed. She's quite different now. What do you think we had better do?" She raised her eyes trustingly to his face.

"We'll find a way out. Don't worry. Time enough, if I can't induce that woman to change her mind. Eden will go home with her after he's put down the Miss Laceys."

She looked about the room. "What a nice room! Are all those pipes yours?"

"Just two of them. The rest were my father's."

"Was he like you?"

"Not a bit. Much nicer."

"Then, to judge by what the Miss Laceys and you say, your family is deteriorating. I don't believe it. I believe that you're the flower of the flock! Anyhow, I love you. The thought of having to go away makes me sick." She put both arms around his neck.

He laid his profile against her cheek.

"My pretty heart!"

"You do say such nice things, darling!"

"Not to anyone but you."

"Well, you must say nice things to Mrs. Stroud tonight. Don't let her turn us out! If it weren't for Tod it wouldn't be so bad. God! I wonder where he is! I must go and find him!"

After some searching she found him sitting on Scotchmere's knee, a currant bun in his hand, watching a game of quoits. Scotchmere said:

"You're a fine mother, aren't you!"

Tod held up his arms to her. She took him and wiped the crumbs from his mouth.

"How are Launceton's legs?" she asked.

"Filling up," he answered sourly. "You worked him hard yesterday."

"Like hell I did," she rejoined. "Where's my brother?"

"Over yonder, by the cider barrel. He don't care what becomes of the baby."

"Thanks, Scotchmere, for looking after him."

"Ah, he always makes for me, no matter how many other folk there are about. He knows who his friends are, don't you, Tod?" He took the child's foot in his hand and patted it. Tod beamed down at him, then nibbled the currant bun. Chris went to Dayborn's side and, after a little, the three disappeared along the path that led through the orchard.

Contrary to Renny's expectations, Eden was home for the evening meal. Their grandmother had retired for the night. Ernest, weary after the strain of the preceding day, was ensconced in his own room with chicken broth and biscuits at his side and his writing folio in readiness for a letter to Augusta. He had much to tell her.

Eden was lively and apparently exhilarated. He directed his conversation to Meg. She liked him in this mood and laughed at his imitations of the Miss Laceys. He avoided Renny's eyes. Mrs. Stroud had told him of the meeting to take place that night. He anticipated it with suspicion. Finch was lost in dreams, staring into space. Piers eyed Eden warily. He wondered if he had forgotten what had happened that morning.

It was not often that Eden chose to make himself useful but this evening he purposefully unrolled the garden hose and set about watering the flower borders and the grass. Meg approved of him. She wandered in and about, followed by her father's spaniel, directing the stream toward ailing plants or dry places on the lawn. He stood docile, doing her bidding.

There was the sound of hooves, at a walking pace. Renny, on his favourite Cora, rode along the drive. She did not quite like the hose and, lifting an expostulating foreleg, took a few side steps. Meg turned.

"Where are you going?" she asked.

"Just for a little exercise. You know Cora hates taking it in the paddock. We'll not be long. Turn the hose into the shrubbery, Eden. She doesn't like it."

As Renny spoke, Piers and Finch appeared, walking slowly from behind the house. They had been pals all the day and Finch was immensely proud. The stream from the hose moved swiftly and Eden, with his mouth drawn in a malicious smile, turned it full on Piers.

For a moment he was galvanized by the shock. Then he wheeled and began to run in the direction whence he had come. Eden ran after him, dragging the hose. The spaniel set up a volley of barking and ran in front of Piers. He fell, sprawling on the gravelled drive. Eden turned the full force of the hose on him. The spaniel, in a transport of delight, raced round and round his prostrate body, barking now at Piers, now at the stream of water.

Meg screamed. Renny shouted — "Look out! What in blazes!" Cora reared. Piers gathered himself up and fled. Finch stood grinning hysterically. Then Eden turned the hose on him. Meg shrieked.

Finch ran to her for protection.

"Go away!" she cried. "I don't want to get wet! Eden, stop it, this instant!"

Finch ran to seek cover behind the horse.

"By Judas!" shouted Renny, "if I lay my hands on you!"

He warded off Finch with his riding crop. Finch, a small drenched figure, ran despairingly towards the house, the relentless stream following him. Half blinded by water, he fumbled at the door handle. He could not open the door, but it was opened from the inside by Eliza. She staggered back from the full impact of the hose.

Eden, seeing Renny like an avenging centaur rearing toward him, dropped the hose and disappeared into the shrubbery. The final spiral stream flicked Cora on her drum-like belly. Dipping her head she kicked out behind her, just missing the spaniel, then galloped furiously down the drive. The gate was shut. Gathering herself together, she cleared it like a stag and thundered along the road.

XVI

RENNY AND MRS. STROUD

SHE WAS WATCHING for him through the window curtains. She had powdered her face and clipped long gold earrings on her flat, transparent-looking ears. She felt a perturbation which she tried in vain to quiet. She did not know what sort of interview to expect but she was determined to hold her own. Although Ernest and Eden had often spoken of Renny to her, what they had said had been confusing rather than enlightening. "He is such an individualist," Ernest had once said, "that he sometimes seems taciturn or erratic when he is neither. He's very tender-hearted. He has my mother's keenness. It has been rather a handicap to him that he attracts women with so little effort." But Eden had said — "I'm always up against his matter-of-factness. He's fond of his horses and of Jalna. But he has an awfully cruel streak. He never reads a book except on the subject of horse breeding. He and you would find nothing to talk about." Yet Eden had said that very afternoon, — "He'll persuade you to let Dayborn stay on. You'll see." She had returned, — "No one can do that." And Eden had laughed, — "Old Redhead has a way with him."

Well, she would be impervious to any ways of his. Her heartbeat quickened in anger when she thought of Dayborn. She went to the glass and examined her reflection, wondering whether some little curls she had made at her temples became her.

The waning light cast a peculiar greenish shadow over her face. "Surely," she thought, "I am not that colour!" She ran upstairs to examine herself in the more kindly mirror in her bedroom. Yes, she was quite different in this. What fine eyes she had! The curls became her.

The photograph of her husband was watching, it seemed cynically, from the dressing table. She saw the soft, drooping nose, the common mouth, the shrewd little eyes. She suddenly felt that she could not endure it there. She took it to the wardrobe and laid it on the top shelf. She drew a deep breath, whether of relief or of apprehension, she hardly knew. Her emotions were so intensified in these days that her nerves were suffering. "I was repressed too long," she thought. "I can't bear real living. I wish it had come to me earlier."

He had arrived without her knowing it. She heard his knock on the door and looking out of the window saw his horse tied to the iron ring in the worm-eaten post by the gate. A caller on horseback! How romantic — if one could associate romance with the man Eden had described! She wished their interview were on some pleasant subject. But no, let her take life as it came! It would be fun to tell Eden all about this meeting.... There was a louder knock.

She said aloud — "Impatient, aren't you? Well, it will do you good to wait." But she ran quickly down the stairs.

His face cleared when he saw her. He said, — "I was afraid you had gone out."

"I suppose," she said with faint sarcasm, "that you are accustomed to doors being thrown open to you at once but, you see, I don't keep a maid."

"Oh no, I'm not," he answered apologetically. "It's only that I'm anxious to see you."

They went into the living room.

She sat down facing him, with an air of gravity. She was not going to make it easy for him. As though to aid her Dayborn's voice came from the other side of the partition singing "Keep the Home Fires Burning," in a high tenor.

"They are rather close to you, aren't they?" Renny observed.

She shrugged. "Oh, I'm willing to put up with that sort of thing. It's his spying and his insolence that I can't bear."

"You do like Chris, though, don't you?"

She spoke almost violently. "Mr. Whiteoak, I have been kind to those people. Ask them if I haven't. They can't deny it!"

"They don't deny it. It's your former kindness that makes this hard to understand."

"If you'd lived here all these months you'd wonder how I'd put up with them for so long. They don't even pay their rent!" Instantly she wished she had not said that and hastened to add, — "Not that that has influenced me in my decision."

"But it's very important that rent should be paid," he objected. "I'm willing to advance Dayborn the necessary money to pay it. I think Dayborn is willing to promise to mind his own business."

"Then he's promising the impossible. He no more could mind his own business than I —" She hesitated for a comparison.

"Than you could be unreasonably cruel," he supplied for her.

"I'm not unreasonable!"

He laughed. "Then you're not a woman!"

"Can you say that, with such a grandmother, aunt and sister as you have!"

"All three of them are unreasonable."

"I suppose you think *you* are reasonable."

"Perfectly." He gave the ingratiating smile so like his grandmother's.

She smiled too, then said, — "Surely you don't ask me to keep a man in my house who spies on the comings and goings of my friends and makes remarks from his doorstep. We might as well be living on barges. It's degrading."

"Dayborn was a year at the front from 1914. He was gassed. It's probably affected his temper. He's not really a bad chap."

"I wish you could hear the things he says to Chris!"

"I do."

"When?"

"When we're schooling the horses. I gave him a punch one day."

"And yet you think he isn't a bad chap!"

"I'm tolerant."

She looked at him in surprise. She said:

"I had thought of you as the very reverse."

"Oh, I have a quick temper."

Her lips curved. Her eyes rested almost mischievously on his hair.

"Yes," he agreed, "they go together."

With a note of intimacy in her voice, she said, — "I have never seen such dark eyes and lashes go with it before."

"I inherit those from my grandmother," he returned complacently.

She laughed outright, her eyes searching his face, wondering what there was in it that made his presence in the room dim the images of those who had preceded him. Ernest, Eden, Dayborn, they became suddenly shadowy.

A silence fell between them.

He sat so quietly in his worn riding clothes, his wiry alert frame so composed, that it seemed he could remain thus indefinitely. He was looking through the window at his horse, tethered by the gate. He was thinking about Eden. No, he would not bring Eden into the conversation. Let that come later!

She said, — "I feel that I must tell you something about those people. I think that it's my duty."

His eyebrows shot up. "Yes?" He looked at her enquiringly.

She said, her voice deepening impressively:

"Those two are not brother and sister. They are *man and wife.*"

"Oh yes," he returned simply, "I've known it for some time."

"Known it!" She stared, transfixed.

"Yes."

"How did you find out?"

"As for that, how did you find out?"

"Dayborn gave it away by something he said to Chris. I couldn't help hearing."

"When you decided to make this house into two, why on earth didn't you do it properly? It must be like an eggshell." He rose and rapped the partition sharply with his knuckles.

Dayborn, in consternation, ceased his singing.

She gave a little laugh and said, — "He's not usually so amenable."

"I think he will behave in future. I think Chris will see that he does. She has a lot of influence over him."

"Well, it's time she began to exert it." She had spoken tartly; now she added, in a somewhat consciously intimate tone:

"What do you think of their marriage?"

"I think she's too good for him, but what wife isn't!"

She gave her deep, musical laugh. "I wonder what sort of woman you will marry."

"One with as nice a laugh as yours, I hope."

"Don't think you will influence me by flattery."

"I have never flattered any woman."

She leant toward him. "You must have heard strange stories of me. I wish you would tell me just what you think of me."

"I'll tell you when you have told me whether or not you're going to let Chris and the kid stay on."

"You speak as though they are the only ones who matter."

"They are — to me. And to you too."

"Dayborn matters to me."

"I'll make him promise to behave himself."

"He can't."

"Give him a chance."

"It's no use asking me."

"Very well. I think you'll be sorry." He rose.

At this moment she wanted above all things to impress him. Her craving for experience led her to reach out toward a man in whose presence she felt only unease and self-distrust. She felt that, if she submitted to him, she would instantly pass out of his thoughts. Only by opposition or an attitude of wavering could she hope to hold his interest.

She clasped her hands together in her lap and raised her eyes appealingly to his. She said:

"I'll do this. I'll let them stay on for another fortnight. I'll try to endure him that long — perhaps longer. Will you come to see me in a fortnight? I'll tell you then if I can go on with it."

"Good!" He looked down at her almost tenderly. "That is kind of you! I'll go straight and tell them. Would you like an apology from Dayborn?"

"No. I don't want to speak to him."

"But you will speak to Chris?"

"Yes. Must you go?"

"Chris will be anxious to hear. I'll come again. Must I wait a fortnight?"

"Come whenever you will."

He took her hand. "Thanks." His eyes were searching as he looked into hers. He might have worn some such expression as he examined a new horse, wondering whether it would be a hard- or light-mouthed puller.

She followed him to the door. Night had descended on them. The dark form of the mare was barely visible. The air throbbed with the sounds of night. He put his leg over the low fence and, waving his hand, went to the neighbouring door.

It was ajar. He tapped on it with his knuckles, then pushed it open and entered. Chris was alone in the living room. She came toward him, her face small and pale in the lamplight.

"Where's Jim?" he asked.

"He's gone to post a letter. What did she say?"

"At first she wouldn't hear of your staying on. Later she agreed to another fortnight. If Jim behaves himself everything will be all right."

"Is she angry at me?"

"Not specially. It's all Jim. I think you might write her a little note and thank her."

"Very well. But I hope we can find somewhere else to go. I hate this place now."

"I'll find somewhere else for you. Why are you so pale?"

She put her hands to her temples. "My head aches. I feel tired."

"No wonder your head aches." He turned off the light nearest them and took her in his arms. She stood close to him, trembling.

"Take a day off," he said. "Rest tomorrow."

"It's not rest I want — it's you! I love you so, Renny!"

He kissed her. His hands held her close. He said:

"I thought you'd be happier when I told you you might stay on. Poor darling!"

"What would you say if I were free?"

"I'd say, thank God!"

"Why?"

"What a question!"

"Do you think you'd want to marry me?"

"Yes. I'd love to marry you."

"I don't believe you."

"What have I done to deserve that?"

"You don't really need me. You don't need me as much as poor Jim does."

"Will you rest tomorrow?"

"No. I don't want to rest. I want to be with you. Do you remember that night by the lake?"

"Kit!"

She felt him tremble. He picked her up, then sat down with her in his arms. He buried his face against her breast.

"I wish you were unhappy too," she said. "It's horrible of me but I want you to be unhappy, like me. Then I might feel more sure of your love."

He raised his dark eyes to hers. "If you want me to be unhappy — I will be."

She put her fingers on his eyes and closed them. "That's ridiculous."

"It isn't! I'm getting unhappier every moment. Feel me crying."

She felt his breast heave. "How dare you!" she exclaimed.

But, when she took his face between her hands and looked into it, she saw that there were tears in his eyes. She stroked his hair with a mothering gesture.

The mare neighed. They heard Dayborn's steps on the path. Chris went toward the door to meet him. A malicious smile lighted his thin face when he saw Renny.

"Well," he asked, "what's that hag next door got to say?"

"Ssh!" exclaimed Renny and Chris simultaneously.

"I expect she has her ear against the partition."

"You don't deserve," said Renny, "to have anything done for you." He raised his voice and spoke very distinctly. "Mrs. Stroud has been very kind. She agrees to extend your time here to a fortnight. In return she expects you to attend to your own affairs and leave her to manage hers. I'm pretty sure that you can stay on indefinitely, if you behave yourself."

Dayborn, seeing what was expected of him, also raised his voice.

"I'm sure we're very grateful to the lady," he said in a nasal whine. "Being the undeserving poor, we lap up all favours and try to prove ourselves worthy of them."

"Like hell you do," said Renny under his breath.

"But Jim," said Chris, "it is a good thing, isn't it, that we don't have to move out of here tomorrow?"

"I don't know what's good and what's bad," he returned. "I only know that life is sweet and that I damn well want a drink."

He opened the door of the sideboard and took out a bottle of rye whiskey. He set three glasses on the table. He filled them with whiskey and water, then picked up his own. Raising it he turned, so that he faced the partition.

"Here's to you, kind lady," he said, "and mud in your eye!"

The toast was drunk.

Yet a strain of conventionality in Renny made him resent the toast. He felt that Mrs. Stroud deserved some gratitude for what she had done, and he himself a little, as the bearer of good news. He remained for a time while they discussed the horses and, as a second glass was emptied, the possibility of Launceton's winning the Grand National.

They went to the door with him and the stream of light from it fell on the waiting mare. The satin smoothness of her shoulders was illumined. Her large ears that gave her head a look of intelligence slanted expectantly toward Renny. She gave a loud whinny.

"Good night," said Dayborn. "It's nice to have visitors of our own for a change. One gets envious of seeing the other people have all the visitors. One wonders what one has done —"

Chris took him by the arm and dragged him back into the hall. Across his shoulder she threw a kiss to Renny.

He mounted the mare who cantered eagerly toward her stable, oblivious to the beauty of the night, longing only for the comfort of her stall.

XVII

THE CANOE

EDEN WAS IN a state of not unpleasant lassitude that sometimes bordered on melancholy. His mind was filled with thoughts which he longed for the leisure to clarify. He wanted to write poetry, but each morning when he woke the routine of the day lay ahead of him, the lying in bed to the last possible moment, the scrambling into his clothes and through his breakfast, the race for the train, the sitting through lectures that, more often than not, bored him, the return home, the snatched hours with Amy Stroud. There were so many books he wanted to read, so little leisure for reading them. He was not yet nineteen. He had grown fast. Sometimes as he hurriedly dressed in the morning, after too little sleep, he felt alternately excited and weary, elated and depressed. Above all, he felt a distaste for responsibility, a longing to enjoy the lovely autumn weather in his own way. He longed to spend hours each day with Mrs. Stroud. His triumphant, if theatrical, winning of her from Ernest had made her more desirable to him though less real. His feelings toward her, as toward himself and his family, were so subtle as to be apparently contradictory. Yet what he wanted was simplicity and freedom.

He resented his young brothers accompanying him on the train. If it were not for them he would be able to escape for an occasional day. Time and again he thought of plans, only to discard them as hopeless. But at last he invented a fellow student whom he called Powell. He spoke of him several times, envying him his drive to town in a motor car. The car was Powell's own and he was an earnest student. A little later he told Meg that he had been invited to join Powell sometimes in the drive. There was no trouble at fall with the family. Meg said she was glad Eden had found a serious-minded friend. Renny observed that Powell's father must have more money than sense to give a boy of that age a car. Eden at once killed off Powell's father. He was the only son of an indulgent mother. The two lived in the country, so Eden would have to wait for the car on the back road.

On the first morning when he accomplished this, he stood in a little thicket by the roadside till he saw Dayborn and Chris pass on their way to the stables. He then jumped over the fence and swung along the road to Mrs. Stroud's. He felt light-hearted and unscrupulous. He had told her the night before to expect him. He hated being surprised himself, so he would not surprise her, perhaps in a dusting cap doing her floors. He wanted everything prepared for him.

The road was elastic and moist after a rain, and gay with the goldenrod and Queen Anne's lace growing by its side. The air was vibrant with the twitterings of a flock of swallows assembling for their journey south. With each gust of the variable wind a few bright coloured leaves detached themselves from the bough and floated tranquilly through the air. He had filled his pockets with apples in the orchard.

She opened the door, smiling.

"Oh, how naughty you are!" she exclaimed.

"And how happy!" he added.

They stood on the doorstep in the arching sunlight. She breathed deeply, feeling at the moment no older than he.

When they were inside she asked:

"Do you know why your uncle doesn't come to see me any more?"

He looked at her blankly.

"Doesn't he?"

"Never."

"How funny!"

"Have I offended him?"

"How could you?"

"I should think it would be easy. He's so sensitive — I was wondering —"

"What?"

"If he is — but that would be ridiculous."

"Jealous, you mean. But, after all, I was here first —"

"Have you said that to him?"

"Well, if you want the truth, we gambled for you. Threw dice."

Her expression for a moment was outraged. Her jaw dropped.

"How funny you look!" He laughed delightedly.

"But it's disgraceful!" Her puritanical past revolted at the thought. Then suddenly colour flooded her face. Why — it was like having a duel fought for her! "And you won?"

"Yes, I won."

"And he isn't coming here again?"

"How funny you look! No, he isn't coming again. He's taken his defeat gracefully and settled down to his work, as he calls it. He writes a little and plays a little at backgammon with my grandmother. I really think he's relieved. It's no joke, you know, for a man of his age to have a love affair on his hands."

"It wasn't a love affair," she said in a trembling voice. "It was a very pleasant friendship and I shall miss his visits." She sat down, looking at her clasped hands.

He knelt beside her and put both arms about her.

"Aimee, darling, I'm so sorry you're hurt. I've put the thing crudely. But the trouble is, we couldn't go on as we were. It stuck in my gizzard to have Uncle Ernest as a rival. He isn't capable of loving you and I am. Don't you agree that that was a horrible evening we all had together?"

"Yes, but some day you will desert me. Then I shall be alone."

The last word had its poignant effect on her. She began to cry.

"I shall never leave you," he said fervently. "It's been a wonderful experience, the times we've had together in this room, hasn't it?"

"Yes, but it's made me too emotional. I can't control myself. I find myself crying or getting angry, I scarcely know why." She laid her hands on his shoulders, pressing him close to her.

"Well, you're neither going to cry nor get angry any more. You're going to be happy as the day is long. I wish we had some way of getting out on the lake! It's as blue as a harebell these days and as smooth as silk. My family have never enjoyed it as they should. They think that if they have two picnics on the shore in the season they've done well. I wish I had a canoe. Oh, Aimee, I saw one advertised in the post office the other day! If only I had the money, I'd buy it for you! We'd paddle and drift about for hours, reading poetry and talking."

"*I'll* buy it," she exclaimed. "It would be heavenly! I have never been in a canoe in my life."

"No, I can't let you buy it. I'll get the money somehow." He put his fingers against his knit brow and thought deeply. "I'll tell you what. You buy it now and I'll repay you when I can get hold of the money. It gets scarcer in our house every day since the War. Renny spends more and more on the stables. He's had new drainage put in and now he's installing electric light. You couldn't believe how close-fisted he is in other ways."

"Tell me about him," she said quietly.

"That's just what I've been doing, isn't it?"

"I mean — what sort of man is he, really?"

"I don't know him very well myself. You see, he only came home last spring, and when he went away I was a kid."

"He persuaded me to allow those people next door to stay on, just as you said he would do. Did he tell you?"

"He tells me nothing except his usual table talk about his horses. But I wish you hadn't let him persuade you. I shall have to go on dodging them and eventually, I suppose, they'll see me and give the whole show away."

"I detest Dayborn," she said almost bitterly.

"Then why did you let him stay on? I'll find you a new tenant. One who'll pay his rent. I wish I could take the place myself! Wouldn't it be lovely if I lived there, Aimee?"

"Divine."

"If they stay on the family will be sure to find out that I'm not going in with Powell."

"What is this Powell like?"

"Like nothing on earth. He doesn't exist. I invented him. Don't you think I'm clever?"

"I think you're terribly reckless. How much is the canoe?"

"Sixty-five dollars. A beauty, and like new."

"How do you know?"

"The advertisement said so. Shall I go and look at it today? Will you trust me? Are you sure you want it? I can't bear to lead you into anything you'll regret."

"Of course I want it."

Eden had an idea for a poem in his head. He sat down at the writing table in the corner and stared at the clean sheets of paper she had laid in front of him. She crept about on tiptoe, afraid of distracting him. But she need not have feared. The idea was flown. He drew a dog's head on the paper, then thought it looked more like a cow and added horns to it.

After a while she cautiously came near.

He crumpled the paper in his hand. "It's no good. I hate it. I'll write another."

"But don't destroy it! Let me see it."

There was a small struggle between them for the paper. He exclaimed: "Why, how fierce you look! I didn't know you *could* look like that."

At once she relinquished the paper, at the same moment smoothing out her face. He tore up the drawing and threw it into the wastepaper basket. An hour later he left, with sufficient money in his pocket to buy the canoe.

She took the torn paper from the basket and pieced it together. She sat staring at the result. She felt angry at him, not only for deceiving her but for being such a boy. If only he were even five years older!

She delayed lunch an hour, waiting for him, then ate hers alone and without appetite. She hated the sight of the dishes she must wash and put away. She felt like smashing them. Unexpectedly, Dayborn returned to his house. He began to hammer loudly. What on earth was he doing? Something deliberately to annoy her, she felt sure of that. He was moving things about. She heard a small crash. She strolled to her gate, staring at the house, wishing he would come out so that she might tell him to leave the next day. Then she saw that he had broken a pane of glass in one of the windows. It seemed the last straw. She could hardly restrain herself.

She saw Eden coming along the road, walking fast. Dayborn would be sure to see him. She opened the gate and almost ran down the road to meet him. He held out both arms to her.

"I've got it!" he cried. "I've got it!"

"Are you insane?" she gasped, avoiding his arms.

"Absolutely. With joy! It's the loveliest thing you ever saw. Graceful and beautifully shaped. We must go out in her now. I persuaded them to take fifty-five dollars. Here's your change."

He thrust a ten dollar bill into her hand. "Let's take some food with us. I've had nothing but a milkshake. How I hate milk!" he beamed at her.

But she would not let him return to the house with her. It was arranged that he should wait at the nearest crossroad.

She flew up the stairs to her bedroom, feeling like a girl having a secret love affair. She changed into a white flannel skirt, shorter than any she had yet worn, and white shoes. She had pretty feet and felt that the new style became her. She put on a striped shirt, knotting the tie carefully, and a white linen hat. She covered herself with an apron while she made the sandwiches. She was excited and happy when she met Eden at the crossroad.

He strode quickly along the dusty road, talking the while of the hard bargain he had driven, never noticing how difficult it was for her, in her high heels, to keep up with him. She had never walked much and had little liking for the exercise. But, when they reached the boathouse where the canoe lay, she forgot her weariness and felt only pleasure when she saw awaiting her the fragile boat that moved gently on the ripples. Did she really own such a thing! For an instant her mind flew backward and she pictured her dead husband's dismay at the thought of such a purchase. She smiled recklessly up at Eden as he helped her into the canoe and placed the cushions for her.

She had a moment's trepidation as the shallow craft, like a living thing, skimmed forward into the deep water. She felt that the slightest movement on her part would overturn it. She sat very still, resigning herself to Eden's care. He had been on canoeing trips and could paddle well. He had rolled up his sleeves, his shirt was open at the throat. He had never looked more attractive to her.

"Don't go too far out," she begged. "I can't help being a little nervous."

"You'll soon get over that. We'll go out almost every day. I'll teach you to paddle. Isn't the air glorious?"

It was fresh and sweet in contrast to the air on shore, dimmed by dust, carrying the weight of pollen, the chaff from harvests. The shore looked mysterious and beautiful. Here and there a reddening maple burned against the blue of the sky. In the distance they could see a freighter, dark and purposeful, with its banner of smoke. Quite near there were two yachts becalmed in the still air. But the lake was faintly ruffled. Tiny wavelets gurgled beneath the canoe.

She had got a coat of sunburn when she reached home. She felt happy and reckless. Her qualms at Eden's deceiving his family had vanished. Let him do what he liked! They would drift as they had drifted in the canoe.

A week passed and they had had three such outings, one of them in the evening. He had spent the day with her, he had written the best poem he had yet done, or so she thought, and at sunset they had walked to the lake to where the canoe was kept. She had bought heelless rubber-soled shoes and now enjoyed the walk. She was learning to paddle. She told herself that she had never been so happy in her life, then thought grimly that she had never been happy at all, until this summer. She was conscious, too, that her intensified emotions were reaching out for something more passionate than the affair with this boy which could never develop and which might, at any time, be ruthlessly ended by his family. She felt something ruthless in them, else how could Ernest have dropped her as he had? That had been a blow to her pride, for she had felt in herself the power to fascinate him. Still, she did not regret him, for nothing Ernest could have given her would have equalled the delight of those romantic driftings on the lake with Eden.

Three weeks had passed since Renny's visit to her. She had a secret desire to force him to intervene once more on Dayborn's behalf. She desired the pleasure of refusing him. Although their meeting had been amicable she felt something antagonistic in him toward herself, something that had nothing to do with Eden. She could not forget his presence in the room, how it had obliterated all that had gone before.

Deception, she told herself, was wearing her out, yet she had been so enmeshed by it in the past months that she wondered how she would ever exist without its stimulus. She had a leaning toward the belief of reincarnation and imagined that, in some earlier life, she had moved in the intrigues of a royal court.

The morning after her evening paddle, with Eden, the weather changed. She woke half frozen in her bed, for she had fallen asleep with only the sheet over her. She could scarcely believe her eyes when she looked out of the window. It had been raining, and now a cold wind blew. Trees bent, if they were slender; waved their branches, if they were stalwart. The garden path was strewn with drenched leaves. She looked mournfully at the purple clouds and knew that fall had come.

She ate her breakfast in this mood but a flicker of sunlight on the floor cheered her. After all, there was Indian summer still to come. She would look no farther ahead than that. She lighted a cigarette and settled down with the morning paper.

She heard voices outside and glanced out of the window. She saw Renny Whiteoak at the gate. With him were the two children, Pheasant and Finch. He left them there and came toward the house. Her heart began to beat heavily. She folded the paper neatly, looked at her reflection in the glass and went to the door.

Her first thought on opening it was how impervious to weather he looked. It seemed that weather had done its worst to him, that its worst had no more than toughened him, whipped his skin to a high colour, his frame to endurance, and given his eyes a look of wary pleasure in its companionship. This morning became him, she thought, seeing his bare head, the russet of his leather leggings. She invited him to come in. Then she called out:

"Good morning, Pheasant! Why do you never come to see me any more?"

"I don't know," the little girl answered slowly, but there was reproach in her eyes. Mrs. Stroud was embarrassed. They both knew that her visits had been discouraged.

"Won't you come in now? And Finch too?"

"I think they had better wait outside till we have talked business for a little," said Renny. In the dining room he said warmly:

"I want to thank you for letting Dayborn stay on. It's been most awfully kind of you, because I know you don't like him."

"That is putting it mildly. I detest him. I've good reason to."

"I know — I know. But he's been pretty good lately, hasn't he?" He looked anxiously into her eyes.

"Not so objectionable as formerly. But they can't stay on."

"Of course not," he agreed.

"I've been wanting to see you about that."

"And I've wanted to see you." His brown eyes still had that warm gleam in them. "As a matter of fact, I've heard of a place that will suit them, but they can't get into it for a few weeks. About three." He looked at her almost pleadingly.

It was beginning to rain again, a fierce squally shower.

"Do say yes," he urged. "This would be awful weather to move in — especially with a baby."

She looked out of the window.

"How long do you think it will last?"

"About three weeks."

No canoeing, she thought, for three weeks! She said:

"Very well, I'll try, but, if I send for you in the meantime, you mustn't be surprised."

"You'll not be forced to send for me, I promise you. I can't tell you how grateful I am. I should have come to see you about them before this, but I've been working hard and playing polo a good deal." His face fell. "Did you see that the American team beat us on Wednesday?"

"Yes," she lied, for she had no interest in sporting news. "I was so sorry. But you put up a splendid game, didn't you?"

"Yes, we gave them a run for their money. But we were up against superior ponies. I'm breeding some now which I hope will make a difference. I've got one grand pony. You could pull his head through his chest and he'd never lose it!"

"I wish I could see a polo match."

He looked at her commiseratingly.

"What a pity! We've finished for the season but you must see one next year." He knit his brow and then asked, — "Have you been to the Horse Show?"

"No, but I'd love to go."

"You must come to our box. The Show's in November." He gave a start, exclaiming:

"Those kids! They're out in the rain! I must go." Before she could speak he was at the door.

She pressed ahead of him and threw open the door.

"Children!" she called gaily. "Come right in! You must be wet through."

Renny grinned approvingly as the two children, who had been sheltering under a small inadequate maple tree, scampered along the path and into the house. They were bareheaded. The wet had made Pheasant's hair wave over the top of her head but Finch's was plastered down almost into his eyes. He smiled shyly at Mrs. Stroud but Pheasant retained her air of gravity. The two made as though to sit side by side on the sofa but Renny stopped them.

"You're too wet," he said. "Sit on the floor by the fire."

There was a coal fire in the small grate. Mrs. Stroud was glad she had lighted it. It gave the room a homelike, cheerful look. The children sat on either side of the fire, their innocent profiles giving them an air of aloofness.

Renny looked down at them indulgently. He looked, Mrs. Stroud thought, as though he were so used to children that he felt their presence only as an agreeable addition to the atmosphere. She herself felt some resentment at their coming yet, in a curious way, she felt a new familiarity with Renny.

There was a scratching on the outer door. Finch said:

"It's Fan. She was at the back when we came in. Shall I open the door?"

"Yes, do," said Mrs. Stroud.

"She was my father's dog," explained Renny. "Now she's attached herself to me. She's almost always with me. I hope you don't mind."

The spaniel entered with an air of assurance, her fringed legs and long ears dripping from the wet grass.

"Fan's back is just like your head, Pheasant," laughed Renny.

The little girl gave him an adoring look. She stretched out a thin hand and laid it on his knee.

"Look what Fan's got!" cried Finch.

It was the yellow claw of a fowl. With attention drawn to it, Fan laid it on the rug and raised her eyes to her master's. Renny sprang up, gave the spaniel a gentle cuff and laid the fowl's leg on the fire.

"I'm so sorry," he apologized.

"Isn't it lovely the way it sizzles."

"Wait a minute and you'll smell it," said Finch. He gazed rapturously into the grate.

The spaniel seated herself and resignedly watched the destruction of her treasure.

Silence fell in the room. Then Mrs. Stroud said:

"I'm trying to see a resemblance between any of you brothers. I can't find it. It's extraordinary that no two should be alike."

Renny answered, with the vivacity that a discussion of his family always produced in him:

"Well, it's not so extraordinary. I'm the spit of my grandmother, as they say. Eden looks like his mother. Piers resembles our father. Meg is like him too. Wakefield is very like a picture of Uncle Nick at that age. Finch is just himself."

"He looks as though he might be musical." She did not dare quote Eden as saying this. She wished, too, to appear discerning.

"That's clever of you, to see that," answered Renny. "There's quite a lot of musical talent in my family. My sister can sing and both my uncles play the piano. Uncle Ernest has taught this fellow to play the 'Blue Danube.' Play the 'Blue Danube' for Mrs. Stroud, Finch. Would you like to hear him play the 'Blue Danube'?"

"I'd love to." She smiled encouragingly at the little boy.

Colour suffused his face. He began to tremble. "I can't," he muttered, hanging his head.

"Go ahead," urged Renny. "Don't be a duffer!"

"I can't."

Mrs. Stroud leant toward him, her eyes compelling. "Just to please me!"

"Go on, Finch," said Pheasant, poking him with her elbow.

He shook his head, staring down at his hands.

Renny stretched out a long arm and drew Finch to him. "Play it, and I'll give you a quarter," he whispered.

Finch tried to draw away, his breath came quickly. "I can't," he repeated.

"Play it or you'll get a good hiding," Renny whispered in Finch's ear. Across the boy he smiled amicably at Mrs. Stroud. He pushed Finch toward the piano.

Finch sat on the stool, swallowed up in misery. He stared dumbly at the keyboard. As he stared he forgot the others in the room. He laid his small hands, brown from the summer sun, with nails cut too short for comfort, as Meg cut them, on the keys. He began to play. He played the waltz through. He played it delicately yet boldly, with a kind of innocent fervour. When he had finished he remained seated at the piano, his head hanging.

Mrs. Stroud clapped her hands delightedly. She gave Renny an expressive look. She formed the word *wonderful* with her lips.

"It is pretty good, isn't it?" Renny said with pride. "Considering that he doesn't know one note from another?"

Mrs. Stroud opened a drawer and took out a box of chocolates. She offered them first to Finch.

"Perhaps you'll be a great pianist some day," she said.

"God forbid!" said Renny "But it's nice to be able to play the piano. My uncles have had a good deal of pleasure from it."

"Are you fond of music?"

"I'm not what you'd call musical," he returned with diffidence, "but it's nice to hear when you come into a house after a day in the stables. The only time I don't like it is when the band blares out at a Show and I'm riding a novice."

The squall had ceased. Pale sunshine threw the shadow of a branch on the wall. The spaniel was noisily licking her paws.

"It's beginning to roast now," said Pheasant, regarding the fowl's foot.

Renny got to his feet.

"We must be off. Come, kids."

"Oh, don't go yet!"

"We must. We're on our way to the church to inspect a leaking roof. I keep the roof in repair."

At the door he thanked her again for what she had agreed to concerning Dayborn. She stood in the doorway watching him disappear down the road, a child by either hand, the spaniel at his heels.

When she returned to the room she stood thinking with crossed arms, her chin in her hand. She felt sure that she had attracted him. She felt in herself the power to draw him closer — to hold him. Here was a man! She had met no other like him! She was passionate. She had experience. What if she could win him — become his wife — the mistress of Jalna! The room turned slowly round with her. She put out her hand gropingly on the back of a chair and steadied herself.

XVIII

Discovery

FROM THE CHURCH, Renny turned homeward with Finch. Pheasant had run along the road toward Vaughanlands, waving her hand as she climbed over the gate that led into one of Morris's fields. At home Renny found that his grandmother was still in bed. She disliked this sort of day and had a slight cold. She was not, however, feeling ill or depressed. She was propped up with pillows and had bed table across her knees on which she had laid out the cards for her favourite form of Patience. Her parrot, Boney was in his cage for it was one of his irritable days and he had, soon after breakfast, bitten Ernest. Now he was systematically throwing the seeds out of his seed-cup with a sidewise jerk of his beak, in search for a particular variety which he sometimes had as a treat. Each time he threw out a portion, he cast a piercing glance over the bottom of the cage and muttered an imprecation in Hindustani.

Adeline ignored Renny's presence, except by a nod, continuing to turn up the cards in threes, glancing across the board each time she did so with an expression ludicrously like her parrot's. Renny, observing this, gave a chuckle of delight and seated himself on the side of the bed.

"Glad you think it's funny," she said.

"What, Gran?"

"Me not being able to work the thing out."

"I wasn't laughing at you, but at Boney."

She peered at the parrot. "He's disgruntled. He gets that way. He bit your Uncle Ernest this morning, so his tonic must be ordered from the chemist."

"That's not the way I treat horses that bite."

"What do you do to them? "

"Sell them, if I can."

"Ah, I couldn't part with Boney. Could I, love?"

He gave her a glassy stare, then went on throwing out his seeds. She put down her cards and clasped her handsome old hands on her stomach. She turned her large nose toward Renny.

"You smell of the outdoors," she said. "Lean over and let me sniff you."

He bent over her and she drew a deep breath. She fingered the lapel of his coat and looked into his eyes. "Tell me," she said, "have you ever been in love?"

"Often."

"Of course — passing fancies. I mean the real thing."

"Yes. Twice."

"When? "

"Well, once in France."

"Oh, the Countess! You told me about her. When was the other time?"

"That's a secret."

"No, it isn't! Not from me. You're in love now."

He patted her knee. "Go on with your game, old lady."

"I suppose it's that Mrs. Stroud. Ernest confesses that he had an attachment for her."

"It's not Mrs. Stroud and never could be."

"Is it that Cummings girl?"

He shook his head.

Adeline gave a triumphant chuckle, then looked serious.

"You mustn't think of marrying her. When you marry, it must be to a woman of position and means."

"The combination seems rare hereabout. Anyhow, I prefer good looks and similar tastes."

"Now you've proved it. It is that girl. Don't you dare think of marrying her."

"I'm not."

"For one thing, she has a child."

"No harm in that."

"I wonder!" She repeated the words under her breath several times, then began to shuffle the cards. As she laid three out, she remarked:

"Something's got to be done about Eden."

"I don't think he often goes to Mrs. Stroud's now."

"Doesn't he? Doesn't he?"

"Who says he does?"

"Never mind. I have my ways of knowing what my grandsons are up to."

Rags tapped on the door, then entered, carrying a glass of hot cinnamon water on a tray. Adeline stretched out her hands to it. She sipped it cautiously.

"Ha, it's hot!"

"It will do your cold good, ma'am."

Rags stood watching the old lady with an expression of deep commiseration. Looking across the tumbler she examined his features and demanded:

"Why do you look like that? D'ye think I'm shaping for influenza?"

"Ow, naow, ma'am. You'll soon be fit again. I was just thinking wot a pity 'twould be to give you anything to worry about."

Her eyes gleamed. "I'm used to worry. I've worried for over ninety years. What mischief have you to tell, my man?"

Rags scratched his chin and looked enquiringly at Renny.

"Go ahead," said Renny. "It's a dull day."

Rags bowed gravely.

"There's no young gentleman," he said, "I admires more than Mr. Eden."

"Yes," said Adeline. "What's he been up to?"

"I admires 'is book learning. There's nothing I like better than to polish the silver cups 'e's won for running and jumping."

"Out with it, Rags," said Renny.

"I've nothing to tell of against Mr. Eden. It's 'is friend, sir."

"The lady friend?"

"Nao. The gentleman. Mr. Powell 'is nime is."

Renny frowned. "What about him?"

"Just that 'e daon't exist, sir."

"Stop beating about the bush, Rags, and explain."

"Well, sir, it was like this. I 'ad to go on a message to the Rectory the other day. It was one of them lovely days when its 'ard for a 'igh-spirited young man like Mr. Eden to stay indoors. I saw 'im walking a'ead of me towards the back road where 'e was to meet Mr. Powell. But Mr. Powell wasn't there. Nor did Mr. Eden look abaht for 'im. 'E just marched straight on to Mrs. Stroud's."

"Ha!" exclaimed Adeline. "The young whelp!"

"Go on," said Renny.

Rags warmed to the disclosure. "'E went in. As I'd been sent out on a message I didn't dare waste my time watching outside the 'ouse, but the next day, when 'e set out to meet Mr. Powell, I set out after 'im, 'aving explained to my missus that I was off on a mission relating to the family welfare. Mr. Eden went straight to Mrs. Stroud's, like 'e 'ad before. I 'adn't long to wait. They came out together, she very smart in a white costume, and made down the road, me following. They never stopped till they reached that boat 'ouse at the end of the road. There they got into a canoe and paddled out of sight. The next time I couldn't get away but yesterday I did. It was such a weary wait that I came 'ome again. But towards evening I took another stroll in that direction and 'ad the un'appiness of seeing them set out again. There's no young man I admires more than Mr. Eden, and I don't like to see 'im trapped in a spider's web and never put out a 'and to save 'im."

"You did right to tell me," said Adeline. "You can go. We must talk this thing over."

Rags out of the room, she turned her eyes enquiringly to Renny.

"What shall you do?" she asked.

Certainly, he thought, not what he felt like doing! He must be careful not to anger Mrs. Stroud or she would probably send Dayborn and Chris packing. He could not do without Chris for two reasons. First, he loved her. Second, Launceton loved her and worked for her as for no one else. If he ran in the Grand National, Dayborn was to ride him. He must be cautious, and he hated caution. Where was Eden today? Had he gone with the boys? Or was he spooning with that damned interloper? His voice was hard as he said:

"I'll attend to this, Gran. Don't say anything of it to the uncles or Meg."

"Bring the boy to me! I'll lay my stick about him!"

"There's nothing I'd like better. Oh, damn that woman! But I must go carefully. There's Chris to consider...."

Adeline sat staring at him, her jaw dropped, her aged mind trying to take in the circumlocutions of his. Which woman was he damning? But she would not acknowledge her bewilderment. She pulled her cap over her eyes so that he might not see how baffled they were, and muttered:

"Yes, yes, we must be careful! Go slow but certain. We'll put the boy in his place and still win the race. Poetry, eh? It's lucky to make a rhyme. Why didn't Ernest manage things better?"

He bent and kissed her, then left the room.

He was furious with anger against both Eden and Mrs. Stroud. Eden was a deceitful puppy. She was ... he made a grimace.

In the hall he met Meg and asked her if Eden had taken the train that day. He had, she said, and looked glum about it, poor boy. He did so hate cycling in the rain. She added reproachfully — "I kept Finch at home because he had an earache last night and then you took him out with you."

"I didn't take him, he ran after me. He never spoke of his ear."

"What is the matter, Renny?"

"Nothing." He smiled at her, then took his hat from the rack. It was hard to keep back the story of Eden's deception.

For the next three days Eden went to town each morning with his brothers. Gales and rain scarcely ceased during those days. Renny's anger intensified. At breakfast he would ask Eden, solicitously, if he were going by train or with Mr. Powell. His tongue lingered almost affectionately on the name. On the fourth morning, stormier still than the others, Eden returned casually:

"I'm going with Powell."

Renny stood in the hall smoking a cigarette and caressing the dogs while Eden put on his raincoat.

"Filthy morning," he remarked.

Eden gave a resigned shrug. "Yes, I envy you at home."

As soon as he was gone Renny shut the dogs in the sitting room, put on his own hat and coat, and strode swiftly in the direction Eden had taken. He saw him ahead walking leisurely along the path toward the road.

Renny was stopped by one of the stablemen and stood talking to him for a moment, in case Eden looked back. But he moved steadily on, his head bent to the rain. He took his time, as though the day were fine. Renny stopped behind a tree as Mrs. Stroud's house came into view. Eden passed it, however, on the other side of the road, without a glance. Renny inwardly cursed Rags and expected to see Eden picked up by a car at any moment. Added to his anger against the youth he had a sudden resentment at his responsibility for him. Then he wondered how his father would have tackled the situation. For an instant the scene was blotted out and he saw only his father's face, with its expression of indolent good humour. But what a temper he had when he was roused!

Eden at last turned into a tiny shop, kept by a Mrs. Brawn, in the front of her cottage. Probably he was going to buy cigarettes. How long did the young fool think he could loaf about the countryside like this, without arousing suspicion? Renny could see him leaning across the counter talking to Mrs. Brawn.

At last he came out and retraced his steps in the direction of Mrs. Stroud's. Renny had a mind to stop him before he reached the house, so that he might be obliged to put less restraint on himself, run less danger of antagonizing her. But Eden was now walking so fast that he would have been forced almost to run to overtake him. And he was turning into a meadow, evidently intending to approach the house from the back.

Now he had disappeared. Renny stood motionless, watching the house, grimly giving them time to get their greetings over. Then he went to the door and knocked. He noticed for the first time that the knocker was the head of a woman with snakes coiled about it. What a choice! Certainly it had not been there in Miss Pink's time. No, she had had a nice little brass bell that you twirled round. He knocked again.

There was silence inside the house.

He knocked more loudly. No answer. This was something he had not been prepared for. The rain was coming down harder than ever. It was pouring off the brim of his hat across his eyes. He tried the door handle. It was locked. What did it mean? How serious was this? He went round to the back door and knocked on it with his knuckles.

The door opened and Amy Stroud stood there, her lips pale but curved in the semblance of a smile.

"Are you alone?" he asked.

"Yes."

He stared at her steadily through the rain dropping from his hat. She drew herself up. Her lips quivered but she returned his stare without flinching.

He said, in a restrained voice — "I saw Eden come in here less than ten minutes ago."

She gave a quick exhalation, then a little laugh. She said:

"Then you've found him out, poor boy! Mr. Powell did not come along this morning and Eden was left stranded. He came in here for shelter. When he saw you at the door he begged me not to answer it. He thought you'd be angry. But now we're discovered, you'd better come in, hadn't you?" She had regained some composure. She opened the door wide.

"What a morning!" she said, looking at the sky.

He stepped inside the little porch and shook the rain from his hat. He stared inside the hat as though he might discover there what to do next. The necessity of continually propitiating her, because of Dayborn and Chris, intensified his anger.

"Do come in," she said, leading the way through the dining room to the living room.

Eden was standing in the middle of the room, his face flushed, his hands trembling.

"Powell didn't turn up this morning —" he began.

Renny cut him short with a flourish of his hand.

"Don't lie to me!" he said. "Powell doesn't exist."

Eden drew back as though he feared a blow but he smiled and said:

"Oh, he doesn't, eh?"

Mrs. Stroud put in — "I'm afraid I've been terribly to blame."

Renny ignored her. He said to Eden — "Put on your hat and coat. I want to have a talk with you."

She interrupted — "But I must take my share of the blame. I should not have let him come here as I have. But I was so sorry for him."

Renny turned to her.

"Why?" he asked.

"Because it's hard to see a poetic nature harnessed to routine." She felt proud of herself for that. She was regaining confidence. She felt that she might yet control the situation. She even felt a certain exaltation in the scene.

Renny looked at her. He considered her words. "Good God!" he exclaimed.

"It's true!" she said passionately.

"It may be, in your opinion, Mrs. Stroud. In mine, Eden has been acting like a young fool, wasting his time and my money. I don't know how much pleasure you have in his company but I must ask you to forgo it until the holidays. By that I mean that I forbid Eden to come to this house again during term."

"What are you accusing me of?" she demanded, her eyes flashing.

"Nothing, except being too attractive," he returned coolly. With a glance at Eden, he wheeled and went out of the house.

Eden and Amy Stroud were left facing each other.

"What are you going to do?" she breathed.

"Go, I guess. There's nothing else to do." He went to where his coat was hanging and began to put it on.

"Isn't it awful?" she whispered. "When shall I see you again?"

"He didn't say we couldn't meet outside the house. We'll have to meet at weekends. What damned bad luck!"

She put both her arms about him and pressed his cheek to her lips. "Poor boy! Was what I said all right?"

"You were splendid!"

"I'm shaking like a leaf. Feel me." She put out her hand. He touched it absently. His mind was on himself.

"I have a nice row to face," he said.

There was a sharp knock on the door. They started apart, then, with a wave of his hand to her, Eden followed Renny. In the road he asked:

"Was it you who knocked on the door just now?"

Renny returned grimly — "Yes, and I'd rather it had been on your head."

They walked in silence along the muddy road. The wind was now so high that it tore the words from the mouth of a speaker so that it was impossible to talk. Eden was thankful for this. Now and again he stole a glance at Renny's profile. "Blast his red head!" he thought. "I wonder what he is going to do to me!"

When they reached the point where the path branched to house and stables, Renny turned toward the latter. He raised his voice above the wind.

"We can talk in my office."

The door opened and banged behind them. They were in a different world. Here the storm was almost inaudible and the streaming small-paned windows gave a sense of isolation. The floors were moist and clean. A stableboy was sweeping some straw into a little heap, with meticulous scratchings of his broom. A row of well-groomed rumps and glossy tails were visible along the passage between the stalls. They belonged to polo ponies. The one nearest raised his head and looked over the partition. He whickered and arched his neck at sight of Renny. Having no notice taken of him, he began to gnaw the top of the partition. Renny stopped to cuff him, then followed Eden into the office.

Renny took off his coat and hat and threw them on a chair. To Eden the room felt damp and chill. Like a prison, he thought. The lithographs of horses seemed staring at him in hate. He felt utterly wretched. It's Dayborn who has got me into this, he thought.

Renny seated himself on the corner of the desk and looked sternly into Eden's face.

"Are you such a fool," he said, "as to imagine you could I get away with this sort of thing?"

"I've only done it a couple of times."

"I want you to tell me what sort of woman that is. I don't think you've slept with her."

"Lord, no!"

"She's a good woman, eh?"

"Yes. She's my best friend."

"Your best friend! Yet she'll let you waste day after day in her company. She was the cause of your almost failing in your exam. She connives with you to deceive me. She is making a liar and a fool of you. Yet you call her friend!"

"She loves me."

"I'll bet she does! She loves anything in trousers whom she can try her charms on. She'd love me, if I'd let her!"

Eden flushed. "Don't be so sure of that."

"I wish I were as sure that you'd run straight."

"When we spend a day together we do a lot of reading."

"Yes. With your head on her knee and she toying with your locks! Now I tell you this — you are not to enter her house till the Christmas holidays. Perhaps by that time she'll have cooled off or found some other youth to pet."

"You don't understand her — or me. I don't expect you to."

"I understand you better than you understand yourselves. She's a woman without experience who's struggling desperately to get some. You're a young ass who thinks the first experience he has is important."

The telephone, newly installed, rang. Renny turned to it with a look of relief. As he listened to the voice at the other end, his face cleared. A genial smile overspread it. He replied:

"Yes, do come along and see her.... Oh yes, she's in faultless condition ... fifteen hands high ... lovely shoulders.... Right. I'll meet the train at three. You can't make a mistake in buying her. Goodbye."

He turned again toward Eden, the smile lingering on his face. There was a blank moment then he said coldly:

"Well, now you know what you've got to do. The first thing is to catch the eleven-ten into town. You'll be in time for your afternoon lectures."

"Good heavens, must I go in today?"

His outraged expression implied that the punishment far outweighed the crime. An instant later he found himself in a steel grip. He was being shaken, then given a push against the door.

"Yes, you must," Renny said composedly.

Eden gathered himself together, threw a look of fury at his brother, then flung out of the office. Scarcely seeing where he was going, he strode from the stable and toward the house. Imprecations Renny had brought home from the War, Eden now fitted to his tongue, sneering them between clenched teeth. He got his bicycle and rode in the direction of the railway station but, when he reached a certain path, turned aside and went swiftly to Mrs. Stroud's. He knocked at the door. She opened it.

"Eden! What's the matter?"

He glared at her. "I should think you'd know."

"But what has he done?"

"Given me a shaking and thrown me against the wall."

"My dearest — are you hurt?"

"A little — not much. It's the whole thing. A fellow can't get over it in a moment. God only knows what he'd do if he knew I'd come here. I'm supposed to be on the train."

She drew him in and tenderly helped him to take off his raincoat. He had thrown his hat on the floor. She treated him like an injured man, bringing him a glass of sherry, making him lean back in the chair. He poured out the details of his encounter with Renny.

When he had finished she sat down on the floor at his feet and laid her head against his knees, in the attitude which was usually his prerogative. She began to cry softly.

"Oh, Aimee," he said, pronouncing the name in the way she loved. "Don't! I can't bear it."

"Everything is over for me. I'll be so lonely."

"But you mustn't cry." He leant over her, trying to soothe her.

"I can't help it. What am I to do, in the long wet days? Then there's the canoe and all we'd planned for Indian summer!"

"But I won't stay away! He can't make me!"

"He'll have Dayborn spying on us. Dayborn is at the bottom of this!"

"Put Dayborn out."

She raised her head. "I will. He'll go tomorrow. I'll bear nothing more!"

She sprang up and walked resolutely to the door.

"Wait!" said Eden. "Don't go yet."

She wheeled. "Why not?"

For an instant Renny's face came between her and Eden. Eden wavered between the desire to see Dayborn punished, to get even with Renny, and a primitive fear of the consequences to himself. To gain time, he said:

"Dayborn won't be at home."

"He came back an hour ago. I saw him."

She was at the door, her face set.

Eden began to walk up and down the room. He said excitedly:

"What had we better do? Let's think! Don't be in too great a hurry. Listen — if we turn Dayborn out, it means —" He stopped, winced, and pressed his hand to his shoulder. She came to him. "What's wrong?"

"It's my shoulder. I wonder if it's dislocated."

"Oh, Eden, let me feel!" She pressed her fingers cautiously across his shoulder.

He gave an exclamation of pain. "There! It hurts there!"

"Take off your jacket."

He took it off, undid his collar and drew his shirt from the shoulder. The golden-brown smoothness of his flesh, its elastic firmness under her hand, went through her like an electric shock. "How beautiful you are," she breathed.

He was embarrassed. "I'm damned uncomfortable." Gingerly he felt his shoulder. "There's nothing broken. It's only muscular."

"But look! Those marks!"

"That's where he gripped me, the red-headed devil!"

"Oh, I'll get even with him!"

She pressed her lips to the marks. She closed her eyes and seemed scarcely to breathe, but rage and sensuality seethed within her. She longed to give herself to Eden. Yet, looking into his eyes, her own suffused by passion, she saw no answering desire but only his boy's mouth pouted in self-pity.

With all her emotions concentrated into hate of Daybom she covered Eden's shoulder and almost ran from the room. He saw her hurrying through the rain, opening her gate, opening the neighbouring gate, heard her knocking loudly on Dayborn's door. He listened, bending his head by the partition.

He heard the words — "This is the end.... You leave this house tomorrow.... Contemptible spy!" Then such a confusion of voices that all sense was blurred.

She was in the room again, her back against the door, panting, her wet hair plastered on her forehead.

"That didn't take long," she gasped. "I wish you could have seen their faces. They looked as though the end of the world had come and I was the avenging angel. They tried to justify themselves, or plead their case or whatever you like to call it, but I had my say and left them gaping. To think that tomorrow that house will be empty! Aren't you thankful, darling?"

"I wonder where they will go," he answered thoughtfully.

"They can sleep in a ditch, for all I care! She's no better than he is. When I think how kind I was to them — but it's all over. I hope to God I shall never see their faces again — nor their starved-looking bodies! I've never told you this before, Eden, but I'll tell you now. They're man and wife! A woman in England pays him a hundred pounds a year to stay out here."

"Does Renny know this?"

"Yes. She told him. She's in love with him. Anyone can see that. They'd better be careful! They've got me to deal with. If this woman in England finds out Dayborn's married, the remittance will stop. What fools they are! Having a secret and not being able to keep it! Oh, how happy I might have been here if it hadn't been for them! Never mind, honey, we'll be happy still. I know we shall."

She walked up and down the room, her arms stiff at her sides, her hands clenched. Through dilated nostrils she drew deep breaths, as though in an ecstasy of exhilaration.

As Eden watched her he felt repelled. Her short strong figure with its ungraceful movements, her damp hair flat on her forehead, her face blotched by passion gave him a feeling almost of repugnance. He passed his tongue over his dry lips and sought for something to say, but could find nothing. That did not matter. He was the focus of Amy Stroud's dramatization of herself. His mere presence was sufficient.

He had ceased to listen to what she was saying. He began to feel tired and dejected. He wanted only to get away.

She came to him and put her arms about him.

"You must come and lie down," she said. "I'll read to you. We'll put all this out of our minds. Tomorrow they will be gone!" Her eyes turned toward the partition as if she had a mind to return to Dayborn and repeat her eviction. From the other house came the sound of Tod's laughter, rising and falling like a bird's song.

Eden said — "I can't stay. There'd be the devil to pay. There's no use in our making things worse than they are. I'll be back tomorrow."

He made her see the reason of this. He found himself out in the rain again. He was pushing his bicycle, for it would have been impossible to ride in the downpour that had now set in. The rain came down savagely, as though after a prolonged drought. Eden pulled his hat over his eyes and plodded dejectedly homeward. It seemed to him that days had passed since he had risen that morning.

He put his bicycle in its place and went into the house. The voices of his grandmother and uncles came from the sitting room. Rags was laying the table for the one o'clock dinner. Eden went softly up the stairs. As he passed the door of Renny's room, Renny came out of it and they were face to face.

Renny stared at him astounded. "What are you back for?"

"I didn't go. I couldn't. I wasn't well. There's something wrong with my shoulder." His eyes fell. His lips trembled.

"What's wrong with your shoulder? Do you mean that I hurt it?"

"I don't know. Something has. I can't lift my arm. I'm going to lie down."

"I'll have a look at it."

He followed Eden into his room. Eden felt ready to sob with self-pity. He winced as he took off his dripping coat and hat and threw them on a chair. He undressed. He was wet through.

"There's nothing wrong with your shoulder," Renny said, after examining it.

It seemed to Eden that Amy Stroud's kisses might well have left a visible mark. But there were only the marks of Renny's fingers. He put on his dressing gown and lay on the bed.

Renny looked down at him curiously. The boy did not look sullen. He did look ill. Well, he was one of the highly-strung sort. Let him sleep it off. No use in being too hard on him. He unfolded the quilt that lay on the foot of the bed and threw it over Eden. He said:

"I'll send Rags up with some lunch."

"I don't want any."

"Rot! Of course you want something."

"I tell you I don't want anything!"

Eden's voice broke. He threw himself across the bed, his face to the wall. Sobs shook him. Renny looked down on him, biting his lip. Then he said, not unkindly:

"I hope this means that it's all over between you and that woman."

Eden did not answer. The gong sounded. Renny went slowly down the stairs.

XIX

Hospitality

Dayborn sat sipping a glass of steaming toddy, a faded travelling rug about his shoulders, his eyes watering, and his usually pale face flushed and feverish. A cold was prevalent in the neighbourhood and he had got it. He had been forced to return from the stables. Tod also had the cold and Chris had not dared take him out that morning. She looked from one to the other in dismay. How was she possibly going to get ready to move the next day, and where could she find shelter for them?

In the months in this house, she and Dayborn had indiscriminately thrust whatever was at hand in the nearest drawer, or tossed on to a cupboard shelf. Her housekeeping had been of the sketchiest, partly from lack of means, partly because, when she came home from the stable, she was tired out and had a tired baby to bathe and put to bed. Dayborn was incorrigibly untidy, leaving his clothes in a heap wherever he took them off. He knew no order but Chris sometimes had a longing for it. She repeated what she had time and again said in the last two hours:

"What can have happened?"

"The woman is mad, I tell you. It's just come to a head."

"Nonsense. It was something you did."

"Good Lord! Have I got to hear that again! I've done nothing. But you'll heap the blame on me till the end of time."

She scowled, and went on with the sorting of things in suitcases. There was silence, except for Tod's small chucklings over his building bricks and his occasional sneezes. Then Dayborn asked sarcastically:

"Where do you think you're going?"

"I don't know." There was a childish tremor in her voice.

Dayborn looked at her inquisitively. Was she going to cry? But she bent her head so that her straight fair hair fell across her eyes. Tod came and offered her a brick with a picture of a duck on it, as though to comfort her.

"Thanks, Tod," she smiled at him.

Delighted, he trotted back to his bricks and examined them carefully, that he might choose the next best one for Dayborn. He chose one with a bear on it. He trotted to Dayborn's knee and offered it timidly.

"A bear!" laughed Dayborn. "A bear with a sore head. That's me all right."

Tod clapped his hands with joy at his good choice.

"What a pity," said Chris, "that Renny is in town. He'd do something."

"He may be back. Look here, you had better go to Jalna right away. If he isn't there you can leave a message for him."

"Right. I'll do that." She rose, eager to do something different. "Look after Tod. Don't fall asleep."

The idea of his being able to sleep, in his disturbed state of mind, inflamed Dayborn's irascible temper. He did not stop talking till Chris was out of the house. Even after she had banged the door, he told Tod a few home truths about her. Tod, listening with great gravity, laid one brick on top of another with the air of a builder who would say — "This will endure for ever."

Chris was glad to be out under the sky, even though it sent rain and wind to drench and buffet her. She bent her head and tramped doggedly along the road through the deepening puddles. The grass at the roadside was sodden. Even the strong goldenrod drooped and its plumes took on a brownish colour. A branch of an elm was blown down and lay across the road. Chris thought of her life in England, in the States and Canada. Looking back over it, it seemed a long life, long and meaningless. The best thing in it had been Tod. She had felt somehow settled in this place.

It had seemed that at last she had a corner that she could call her own, real friends. No one could have been kinder to her than Mrs. Stroud had been. Yet today she had looked formidable in her hate, even frightening. She must have looked frightening or Jim would not have gone white as a sheet. Well, she was an enemy now and no mistake! Chris wanted nothing so much as to leave her house.

As she neared Jalna, her heart leaped ahead of her. She longed for the sight of Renny and for Launceton too. Tod, Renny and Launceton. She smiled as she thought of the contrast between the three beings she loved. Yet they had one quality in common. There was a reliability, a staunchness, like a hard glowing kernel in the heart of each. Surely Tod was a reliable baby, if ever there was one! Surely Renny was staunch and would never turn against her. The very thought of him brought him so close that she could almost feel him walking beside her, feel his hand on her arm giving her courage, and how much more beside! And Launceton — what a horse he was! Not only powerful and swift but as true as steel. You could do anything with that horse. The thought of him brought him close too. She could feel him between her knees, gathering himself together for a jump, rising, bounding over the barrier like a buck!

In the stable yard she met Scotchmere. He wore a rubber cape and his face was screwed in misery. This weather gave him rheumatism.

"Hello," she said. "Is the boss back yet?"

"No. But he's on his way. He telephoned half an hour ago. Ain't this weather terrible?"

"You bet. I think I'll wait for him in the stable."

"You're looking peaky. What's the matter?"

"Scotchmere, don't tell any of the others. But Mrs. Stroud is on her high horse again. We've got to move out tomorrow and I'm damned if I know where we're going. To make it worse, my brother and the baby have colds."

"So you're turned out and have sickness too! It was me that told Jim to go home. And the poor little feller, he's caught it, has he? You'll be the next. Don't you get sick. Golly, your face don't look much bigger than my hand now!"

As they turned toward the stables, Scotchmere suddenly stopped. "I've got an idea. There's empty rooms over the garage. It's to be turned into a flat for one of the married hands. But money's been too scarce to finish it. You could put your furniture in there and make shift until something better turns up. Come, and I'll show you." He led the way.

Chris was delighted with the rooms. The fact that they were cold, the windows veiled in cobwebs and that there was no bathroom, mattered nothing. It was a haven. She and Scotchmere were as excited as two children over the project.

While they were still there, Renny returned. He came running up the steep narrow stairway. His face lighted when he saw Chris. She told him what had happened and of Scotchmere's suggestion. He looked dubious.

"But it's a wretched hole," he exclaimed.

"It looks lovely to me. And I'm used to discomfort. I'll set right to work to clean it." She began to take off her short leather coat, then added — "That is, if you'll let me have it?"

"Of course you can have it. But don't take off your coat. One of the men will come in and clean it. Go and send one of them, Scotchmere."

Scotchmere disappeared down the stairway.

"How could you think I would let you undertake such a job?" he asked reproachfully. He put his hands inside her coat against the warmth of her body, and pressed her to him. "Give me a kiss, Kit."

She kissed him with passion, clinging to him as though desperately. He said:

"You must come to the house. My sister will give you tea."

"Will she? How nice of her!"

She walked about the bare rooms. "This looks heavenly to me. And there'll be no rent to pay, will there? I wonder why Mrs. Stroud went off the deep end like this, after being peaceable for weeks."

"To get even with me. I had an interview with Eden in front of her. It upset her."

"Anyhow, we've got a roof over our heads. If only Jim and Tod hadn't got those colds!"

Her head drooped, as though from the weight of her responsibilities.

"Come along," he said, almost impatiently, "you must have some tea."

The house was very warm. The thick walls and drawn curtains, the sound of talk and laughter, the three dogs stretched on the floor about the glowing stove, gave a sense of remoteness, not only from the stormy weather but from the outside world. Chris thought — "It feels as safe as a church here and as hot as Hades. I suppose that's for the old lady's sake. It's funny, but Renny looks as natural here as he does in the stables." She said:

"What a good laugh that man has!"

"That's Uncle Nicholas. Come into the sitting room. I'll find Meg. Then we'll have tea."

He left her and returned with his sister. She shook Chris warmly by the hand. She was being a kind sister for Renny had asked her, for his sake, to be her nicest to Chris.

"I hear you've got to move," she said. "What a nuisance! And in such weather! They say it's going to last for weeks." Her blue eyes looked serenely into the girl's amber ones. Chris thought, — "How matronly her body is and how young and innocent her face! I'll bet I look like a hag beside her."

"Renny's been telling me," Meg was saying, "that your baby and your brother both have colds. They must not be exposed. You must stay with us while you settle in the flat. You and the baby can sleep in the spare room and we'll fix up your brother somehow. There's an attic room with a cot bed in it. Do you think he'd mind that?"

"Oh, how kind of you!" Chris's mouth was distorted like a child's who is trying to keep from crying. "I never was so kindly treated in my life. Are you sure we shan't put you out terribly?"

"Not at all. I'd love to have you."

Renny beamed at his sister. She stood firmly, her unclouded brow the soul of magnanimity. Chris felt like imploring, — "Take me in! Keep me — let me be one of you!" But to be one of them she knew she would have to begin her life over again. With all their hospitality she felt that their circle was somehow impervious.

They went into the drawing room. The grandmother sat close to the leaping fire, a beaded fire screen protecting her face from its heat.

Ernest was seated by a table, changing old photographs from one album to another. Nicholas was recalling amusing incidents of his past life in London for his mother's benefit. Rags had just carried in the tea. Meg bent and whispered in Adeline's ear. She turned to Chris, showing her double row of artificial teeth in a benign grin.

"So you're coming to stay for a while," she said. "That's good — I like visitors."

XX

SWIFT CURRENTS

THE FOLLOWING DAY Eden remained in his room. He had drawn the bed across the window so that he might be looking into the trees and across the fields. Little of them was visible beyond the blur of the rain. The old cedar tree outside his window had taken on an unnatural dark green as though it were turned into some fabulous water plant. When the rain lessened he sometimes could see the stables or glimpse the bent figure of a groom.

He was in a mood of deep dejection. He felt lonely in his spirit and that, in his life, he was going to be a failure. When he considered the poetry he had written it seemed to him worthless. He looked forward to the study of law with abhorrence. No study of any kind attracted him. In any profession he would be trapped and futile. He felt that downstairs the family was talking him over. He imagined his Uncle Nick saying, — "Gave the boy a good shaking, did you? Just what he needed, by gad!"

He lay hour after hour, staring out of the window, feeling himself impotent to grapple with life. He wished he might go away to some foreign place. He thought with longing of Paris, of Athens, of Rome. Would he ever see Rome? He was convinced that he would see nothing, but drag out his life misunderstood and alone. All the others would live to be old, old like Gran, but he would die young. For a time the thought of death possessed him. He wished he might will himself to die at this moment. They would come to his room and find him lying pale and still, his unseeing eyes fixed on the window. After his death, Meg would keep his few manuscripts in her own desk, for the sake of sentiment. Years later someone, perhaps young Finch, would find them and discover something poignant and deeply touching in the immature poems.

He could not bear to think of Amy Stroud. Her sudden exhibition of violence, her changed face, coarsened almost beyond recognition, her amorous kisses on his shoulder, had shocked something fastidious in him. He felt afraid of her.

When Meg told him that Dayborn and Chris had come to Jalna he pictured Amy Stroud alone in that house. She would be expecting him but he would not, could not, go to her. He heard Dayborn coughing and shuddered. How he hated the sound of coughing!

Meg told Renny that Eden was listless and looked feverish. Should they send for the doctor? Was Renny sure that he had not injured him?

"The shaking I gave him wouldn't have injured Wakefield. He's just feeling sorry for himself. Let him sulk for a day or two. He'll get over it."

But the days passed and still Eden refused to come downstairs. He ate next to nothing. Finally Renny came to his room. The rain had stopped but the air was heavy and grey. All colour seemed washed from the landscape except the watery green of the cedar tree.

"How are you feeling?" asked Renny, sitting on the foot of the bed.

"Rotten."

"Any pain?"

"No."

"Where do you feel the worst?"

"I don't know. I just feel rotten."

"Want me to send for the doctor?"

"No. I'll be all right."

"You're wasting a lot of time, you know. I think you'd feel better if you got up."

"I can't." Eden's voice broke.

"I've a letter for you. It just came. I have an idea it's from Mrs. Stroud." He handed Eden the letter.

Eden glanced at it, then thrust it under his pillow. "Just leave me alone," he said petulantly. "I'll get up tomorrow."

Renny gave him a penetrating glance. "Would you like me to return that letter to her, unopened?"

"Lord, no! I couldn't do that."

"But you'll not know what to say to her. You can be sure that she's begging you to come and see her. You know damned well I'll not stand any more of that."

"I don't want any more of it," said Eden hoarsely. "I wish to God I could go away somewhere for a while!"

"Look here, I've an idea! How would you like to go into residence in the University? That would settle things. I'll write her a letter. You need not have any responsibility. Will you do that?" There was an unexpected warmth and understanding in his tone.

Eden rolled over, burying his face in the pillow. He got out "Yes," in a strangled voice. His hand touched the letter. He thrust it blindly toward Renny.

"Take the letter," he said. "Write to her for me. I can't see her."

Renny's gesture of comfort toward anyone in bed was to draw the covers close over him. He did so now, almost covering Eden's head.

"You just leave the lady to me," he said. He stuffed the letter into his pocket and went to his office in the stables.

Seated in his swivel chair, he considered the situation. He was not ill-pleased with what he had done. He had found a roof for Chris and her child. One of his farm wagons had brought the scant load of furniture to the flat above the garage. It was installed there. The curtains were up. The place looked habitable though not fit for a girl of Chris's breeding. But she was happy to be away from Mrs. Stroud and — to be so much nearer him. The thought of her slim body, with its reckless vitality, stirred him. He felt between her and himself a curious resemblance. Perhaps it was only that she was more straightforward and sincere than other women. She understood him and he understood her. Perhaps, because of the way they had worked together with horses, their conception of each other was unclouded and direct. They needed few words for explaining it. Sometimes a glance across the stark heads of the galloping horses, a word above the thunder of hooves, would set their hearts thumping.

Dayborn and Tod were still under the weather. The little family was thought much of at Jalna. His grandmother had taken a fancy to Chris. Jim was making himself agreeable to Meg. Everyone loved Tod at sight. Wakefield and he played happily together. Now it seemed that the problem of Eden was to be settled. Renny had a moment's pride in the thought of how he had handled the boy. He'd been firm but not harsh. He'd considered the nature he had to deal with. He'd won the day. Now let the witch stew in her own juice! He took her letter from his pocket.

He held it to his bony nose and sniffed the scent of verbena. It was pretty strong to overcome the smell of Jeyes' fluid in the office. He looked at the writing, large and firm, on light-blue paper, the flap of the envelope caught by sealing wax of a darker blue stamped with her monogram. He wondered what was inside. With a sigh he laid it down.

Slowly he took a sheet of notepaper from a drawer. He hesitated a moment to admire the business heading. Then he wrote, in his small crotchety hand:

MY DEAR MRS. STROUD —

I do not think I need explain to you why I am returning your letter. If Eden read it, it might make things worse than they are and I can't risk that. He is anxious that his acquaintance with you should come to an end and has agreed that your letter should be sent back to you. He is going away for a time.

Yours faithfully,
R.C. WHITEOAK

Without rereading the letter he put it in its envelope and gave it to Scotchmere to post.

Meanwhile Amy Stroud was in a state of excitement that made her days tense and her nights restless. She could not understand why she had had no message from Eden. She had expected him to appear at any moment and kept herself in readiness to receive him. Every time she passed a mirror she touched her hair, arranged her collar or threw back her head in the gesture of gallant recklessness with which she meant to greet him. She powdered her face so often that it began to look as though covered by a mask. Her feet ached because she would do her housework wearing her becoming high-heeled shoes.

The emptiness of the house next door now actually preyed on her nerves more than the noise of her former neighbours. Every few hours she was drawn to go through it. Yet each time she was filled with rage by the state of windows and floors, the marks on the wallpaper. Her hate for Dayborn became so intensified that it was like a livid aura about him. Even the faces of Chris and Tod were hatefully illumined by it. If only they had never come into her life how different everything might have been!

Her one consolation in these days, her one calming thought, was the thought of the extreme discomfort in which Dayborn and his family must now be living. She had found out, from the men who had moved the furniture, that it was going to an unfinished flat above the garage at Jalna. She looked on the lashing rain and wild wind as her allies in Dayborn's punishment.

By the third day she began to wonder if Eden were ill. She made up her mind that he was. How could he be otherwise — treated as he had been and soaked to the skin! She pictured him tossing on his bed in a fever, calling for her. She endured a day of this new anxiety, then set out to call on Miss Pink and find out from her what was happening. She knew that Miss Pink was intimate with the family at Jalna.

As she plodded along the muddy road the landscape looked more dismal to her than, a week ago, she would have thought possible. The leaves were falling fast. The fields were sodden and the cattle grazing there watched her pass with melancholy gaze. She felt out of breath when she had climbed the hill beyond the church and stood in front of the cottage where Miss Pink now lived. The door was opened by a neat young maid.

"Is Miss Pink at home?"

"Yes'm. She's busy teaching but if you'll come in I'll tell her."

The little parlour was overcrowded with the furniture Miss Pink had brought from her former home. She herself came in, looking nervous and somehow not friendly.

Amy Stroud forced a smile to her lips and gave her low musical laugh. She said:

"I hope I don't look as awful as I feel. What weather! How do you manage to pass the time?"

Miss Pink appeared not to see the extended hand. She answered stiffly:

"I find plenty to do. There's the church organ. And giving music lessons. I teach little Pheasant Vaughan, too. She is with me now. I am afraid I can't ask you to stay."

Her small pink face was blank as she regarded Amy Stroud.

"Well, then, I must be off." She managed to control her hurt and anger. "I hope dear old Mrs. Whiteoak is well. This weather must be trying for a woman of her age."

Still with that blank look, Miss Pink returned, — "She is very well. I had tea there yesterday. I have never seen her better. She is having great pleasure in her visitors." The look of blankness left her face and was replaced by one of cool dislike.

"Her visitors?"

"Yes. The people who lived in your house. The ones you turned out. They are staying at Jalna."

"At Jalna! In the flat above the garage, you mean."

"Oh, the family would not allow that in such weather. They are staying in the house. They are very welcome, I can assure you."

"How nice! And Eden," — she must find out about Eden no matter at what cost to her pride, — "is he better?"

"I didn't know he'd been ill. I believe he's going away for a time. Really you must excuse me." She moved toward the door.

Out on the road again, Mrs. Stroud ground her teeth at the thought of the indignity she had just experienced. All else for the moment fled her mind. She pictured herself slapping Miss Pink's fresh-coloured face, leaving purple fingermarks on it.

But, as she trudged on, this anger was swept aside by the bitter chagrin of knowing that Dayborn and his family were snugly ensconced at Jalna, in the house where she had twice been as a welcome guest, and where probably she would go no more. What tales he would tell of her! He would make fun of her as she had heard him make fun of other people, caricaturing their little oddities. The circle about the fire would laugh. She was settled here for the rest of her days and this affair of Dayborn might cut her off from the social intercourse she most desired. She must try to retrieve her position. She must see Eden. Above all things she must see Eden. She did not believe he was away.

When she reached home she found Renny's letter awaiting her with the groceries in the kitchen. She opened and read it.

She read it carefully, twice over, then sat with it crumpled in her hand staring straight in front of her. Its effect on her was the reverse of what might have been expected. It calmed and steadied her. She considered what her next move should be, as though she were engaged in a momentous game of chess. She pressed her fingers against her forehead and gazed broodingly at some mental image. Rain was dripping from the eaves in musical repetition of three treble notes. The bass was provided by the low gurgling of water through a small gulley at the edge of the garden.

Her own letter, returned to her, caught her eye. She took it up and sniffed its scent. She then tore it into small pieces and threw them into a wastepaper basket. Renny's letter she put in the pocket of her jacket. She stood a moment, savouring the contact of this letter with her person, as though it were some sort of talisman that would keep her from wasting her energy in futile anger and, at the same time, intensify her bitter resentment.

She thought she heard a noise in the next house. She often thought that. Sometimes she could have sworn that she heard Dayborn's laugh. Once in the night she had been woken by the sound of Tod's crying. She had been so sure of it that she had risen and dressed and gone into the house to investigate. Now, again, she went there.

It was empty, cold and desolate. Certainly she must get a tenant for it. It was a dead loss, standing vacant. What a comfort it would be to have nice companionable people living there! How was she going to face the winter in this place, with everyone against her — Eden snatched away — Ernest's friendship withdrawn — the neighbourhood prejudiced against her! And all because of Dayborn! She pictured him as, at this very moment, entertaining old Mrs. Whiteoak and her sons with stories about her. She would get even with him, if it took her the rest of her life to do it.

Now she wished that she had accepted the rent owing, which Renny had offered to pay. Then she would not have been able to turn Dayborn out so peremptorily. He would not now be installed at Jalna. She would not be in the position of a persecutor — and after all she had done for that trio! She saw a heretofore unnoticed stain on the wallpaper, behind where the lumpy sofa had stood. There, Dayborn must have rested his head, greasy with sweat from his hard riding. Dirty brute! Mrs. Stroud clenched her hand and struck the spot a blow. It must have been a hard one, for she doubled up with the pain of it. She seemed to hear Dayborn's jeering laugh.

As she turned to leave the house she saw that there was something in the letter box. She opened it and found an old country newspaper and a letter. That was just like the boy from the shop, to have left the post in an empty house. But he probably had not known they were gone. She took newspaper and letter and went back to her own house.

She was still wearing her outdoor things. She now took off her hat and jacket. She took Renny's letter from the pocket and placed it inside her blouse. She sat down by the kitchen range and put her feet, which felt very cold, against it. With a ruthless gesture she cut the string that so tightly bound the newspaper and unfolded it. Without knowing what she read she ran her eye over the headlines. She knew that this paper was sent once a week to Dayborn by an aunt. He always spoke of her as "dear Aunt Katie." Two pansies had been pressed in the folds of the newspaper and they now fell on to her lap. They lay there, fragile and faded but with their petals still perfect in outline, staring up at her like tiny malicious faces. She crushed them in her hand then, lifting the lid from the stove, she sprinkled them over the hot coals. She saw that the kettle was boiling. She took the letter and held its flap over the steam. After

several cautious experiments she was able to open it without marring it.
It was just what she had expected, the quarterly cheque from Dayborn's
benefactress. It was for twenty-five pounds. A small enough amount,
Amy Stroud thought, but how precious to him! She would put an end to
all that! As she had read the headlines of the newspaper without com-
prehending them, she now read the letter accompanying the cheque. All
she wanted was the name and address. She went to her desk in the living
room and wrote:

Mrs. Gardiner,

DEAR MADAM —

I know that you are interested in James Dayborn
and his welfare. I know that you send him a cheque
every three months on the understanding that he keeps
steady and does not marry. His wife told me this. She
too is English and they have been married for some time.
They seem to think it a joke to obtain money from you
under false pretences but I take a different view of the
matter. They are known here as brother and sister. I once
heard Dayborn say (I happened to be in the same house
at the time), when he received one of your cheques, —
"Thank God, the old girl has ponied up again!" I think
you are an honourable woman and I consider it my duty
to inform you of this deception and ingratitude. As I
don't like anonymous letters I am signing my name to
this. I shall give you the name of a nearby solicitor, in
case you should want to make investigations. I am also
sending you the name of a detective agency.

She added the name of the solicitor and of a detective agency once
employed by her husband. She found mucilage and sealed the letter she
had opened. She then sealed her own. She had a sense of deep relief. She
took it at once to the post office which was nearly a mile distant, and was
combined with the small grocery shop. As she was leaving she saw Finch

Whiteoak buying a chocolate bar. She followed him out of the shop.

Outside he began to run in quick, uneven spurts, like a lamb gambolling. She felt wonder that anyone could feel happy on a day like this when she herself was so miserable. She called out to him:

"Finch! Wait a moment."

He stopped and looked over his shoulder.

"Wait a moment," she repeated.

"I can't," he answered and began to run again.

"Please wait," she cried, "I want to ask you something."

He waited, looking shyly up at her out of his grey-blue eyes.

"How is Eden?" she asked, as she reached his side.

"Better, thank you."

"Has he gone away?"

"He's gone to live at the University."

"Oh. Was he really ill? Did the doctor see him?"

"No — just Renny."

She forced a smile to her lips. "Surely you saw him! Did he seem unhappy?"

He gave her a puzzled look. "No — not unhappy — at least — I don't know —"

"What did he look like? What was his expression?"

"I can't remember."

"Are Mr. Dayborn and his sister and the baby still at Jalna?"

"Yes. Please, I must hurry." Touching his cap he almost fled along the road. She saw him climb a fence, as though to make certain his escape. As she passed that spot she saw him loitering, peeling the silver paper from his chocolate, as though untold leisure were before him. She said to him as she passed:

"You weren't in such a hurry after all, were you?" She muttered to herself, — "Another one turned against me! It will not be Dayborn's fault if I am not completely ostracized."

XXI

THE DINNER

AT FIRST EDEN felt glad of the seclusion of the University. He wanted nothing so much as to escape from the attentions of Amy Stroud. She had so repelled him in their last meeting that he felt no desire ever to see her again. But, as the weeks passed, he began to think with longing of his free home life, almost unrestricted by rules. Say what he would against his family, they were a thousand times more congenial to him than were the earnest young men among whom he now lived. He was unfortunate in not finding even one who attracted him. Their minds were already set in a rut that, if adhered to long enough, would supposedly lead to success. They made brilliant achievements out of each of their little triumphs. They laid down the law about morals, economics, politics and literature. "I'd rather," thought Eden, "have Uncle Nick's past than the future of the whole bunch of them." He had no community spirit, he hated teamwork. Because he was supple and swift in his movements, he had excelled in certain forms of athletics. He had been one of the best runners, in a short dash, one of the highest jumpers, in his college. He hated the grind and self-denial of training. What he liked to do was to appear at almost the last moment and win a race or a high jump, apparently without effort. In games he was always perversely amused to see the downcast faces of the team he was playing with, when defeated. Seldom a game passed that he was not reprimanded by the umpire for breaking rules.

The wet weather endured for some time, as Renny prophesied. Then, in late October, Indian summer came with its mysterious deep gold sunshine, its hazy, hyacinth sky and the burning scarlet and gold of the woods. Eden went home for a weekend and on his return felt the bonds of his new life almost unbearable. He lapsed into complete indolence that sometimes became melancholy.

He was in this mood when the morning's post brought him a letter from Mrs. Stroud. Lying in bed he read it.

MY BELOVED FRIEND —

For you always shall be beloved by me — even though my love is returned by coldness. But I can't think you have forgotten our happy times together and I'm going to ask you a favour. I am staying in town for a few days and it would give me something beautiful to think about in the long lonely days if you would dine with me here. If you will come, we shall make no reference to any unhappiness of the past but just enjoy ourselves in our old carefree way. Eden, my darling, do not refuse me this. If you do, I'll know that I have offended you deeply and bitterly. I shall eat my heart out, wondering how.

Any day will suit me. Come at seven.

Your
AIMEE

Eden was surprised to find that he was glad to get this letter. The boredom of his present life pressed all about him. The thought of meeting Mrs. Stroud again came as a return, even though somewhat tarnished, to an old and pleasing relationship. He forgot their last meeting and remembered only the times when he had the freedom of her house, when she prepared him delicious little meals. He was too shrewd not to guess that she was staying at a hotel far beyond her means, in order to tempt him there.

After all, he thought, he had treated her rather badly. She had done nothing more to deserve it than to offend his sensibility. He could not let her go on worrying herself ill. They must have one more meeting. It would leave her less humiliated. Perhaps their friendship might continue, on a more temperate level.

He sprang up with a feeling almost of exhilaration. The morning was lovely. He would dine with her the next night. Possibly he would take her to a play later on. He wrote her a brief note telling her the day of his coming.

After that the hours dragged. He wondered how he could have lived through them had he not had the meeting with her to look forward to. Promptly at seven o'clock he arrived in the lounge of the hotel.

It was a comparatively new one, with a conscious magnificence. An orchestra was playing and waiters moved quietly about bearing trays of cocktails. He would not have recognized her had she not risen to greet him. She wore a dinner dress of the fashionable short length. It was of a bright Chinese red and she wore long red earrings. The precise waves of her hair showed that she had been to a hairdresser. But her fine grey eyes were the same, and her deep caressing voice. She took his hand in both of hers. Her eyes were full of tears but she smiled. She said:

"How prompt you are! It's the very first time you have appeared at the hour I set."

"I must make up for my former delinquencies," he said.

She gave him an expressive look, then said, — "You have nothing to make up for. Your presence at any time was all I asked."

They sat down on a deeply padded settee. A waiter approached. They ordered cocktails. As they sipped them they were, at first, at a loss for words. Then Eden laughed and said:

"How sophisticated we must look! If that waiter knew the few cocktails I've had he would despise me."

She laughed gaily. "But they're good, aren't they? Do you think this dress becomes me? I bought it specially for tonight. I wanted to look as though I hadn't a care. I thought you would like me best so."

"Aimee — how sweet of you!" He laid his hand on her knee. He felt the glow of the spirits all through him.

The ice was broken. Their estrangement seemed a thing of the past. They laughed and talked excitedly, as in a reunion of lovers. She looked so young that no one would have taken her for twenty years his senior. They recalled little incidents of their former meetings but neither Renny's nor Dayborn's name was mentioned.

There were a number of people in the dining room but she had reserved a table for two in the corner. She was at this moment doing what she had long dreamed of doing, entertaining in a fashionable hotel with an air of what she thought *savoir faire*. It pleased her to order the most expensive items on the menu. She told the waiter to bring a bottle of champagne. As he drew the bottle from its icy shelter and uncorked it she felt confident and happy. By her own strength of character, her own vital charm, she would undo the harm Dayborn had done her. She would re-establish herself in the esteem of her neighbours. She felt that nothing was impossible to her.

Eden's spirits were so lifted by the change from the scholastic atmosphere to one of gaiety that he thought of nothing but the moment and to make up to Amy Stroud for what he now began to consider his cruel treatment of her. The orchestra was playing dance music and a few couples were on the floor.

"Will you dance?" he asked.

"Do you think I do it well enough?"

"You dance beautifully."

He led her out. He himself had taught her all she knew of dancing. It had seemed a cruel thing to her that in her girlhood she had known nothing of this pleasure. In the past months she had profited so well by Eden's teaching that their movements were followed with admiration by more than one.

When they returned to their seats the waiter refilled their glasses. Mrs. Stroud had an air of possession toward Eden. Her eyes roved boldly about the room. Presently she laid her hand on Eden's arm.

"Look, darling, at that table over there — the third on my right. Two men and a woman. Did you ever see such a proud head as that on the man with his back to us? I wish he'd turn round."

Eden craned his neck to see. The man turned his head so that his profile was visible.

"Good God!" gasped Eden, almost dropping his glass, "it's Renny."

Mrs. Stroud turned pale. Her hands shook. Then she gathered herself together.

"What if it is?" she said. "I'm sure he hasn't seen us. Your back is to him. If he did glance round he wouldn't recognize me in these things. I'll hold the menu before my face."

But relaxation was now impossible. Try as they would they could not forget the figure three tables away. Mrs. Stroud laughed and chatted determinedly but her eyes were inevitably drawn in that direction. Eden exclaimed:

"I do wish you wouldn't keep looking at him! It's getting on my nerves. I think we'd better go."

"We can't, without the risk of being seen. Wait — I think they're going!"

But they were not going. The woman, young and sleek-haired, was going to dance with Renny. The music was "Three o'clock in the Morning," a popular hesitation waltz. There was nothing to do but to remain seated and hope to escape notice. Fortunately the two dancers glided in an opposite direction and might have been lost to view but for Renny's height and the colour of his hair. The husband, stout and calmly affluent, sat absently fingering the stem of his wine glass, the pouches beneath his eyes accentuated by the light from a lamp at his side.

Whether because of the champagne or because of his inborn perversity, Eden now had a desire to be discovered. The expression on Renny's face would, he thought, be something to cherish for the rest of his days. It would be well to prove, too, that he was not to be treated like a mere boy. Better show Renny that if he wanted to continue this precocious affair, nothing Renny could do would stop him. Mrs. Stroud exclaimed:

"Quick — put your hand to your face!"

She herself was holding a menu as though to shield her eyes from the light. Obediently Eden raised his hand but, between the spread fingers, his eyes looked out, bright with insolence and daring. Their attitudes were so obvious as to draw the attention of all who passed. As

Renny and his partner moved directly in front of them, the music ceased. Renny's gaze was attracted by the hidden faces; he halted. Recognition gleamed in his eyes.

His face, however, still kept the expression of interest it had worn as he listened to the animated talk of his partner.

Now he spoke to her and they came straight to the table where Amy Stroud and Eden sat. Renny introduced them to Mrs. Denovan. Her husband had, that day, bought one of Renny's hunters for her. They were Americans. She said:

"Couldn't your brother and his friend come and sit at our table? There's lots of room."

"Yes, that would be nice," agreed Renny, staring hard at Eden.

He and Mrs. Stroud rose, with an air almost submissive, and followed the others. The music was beginning again. When introductions were over and they were seated at the table with Mr. Denovan, he ordered coffee and liqueurs. Amy Stroud felt a strange exhilaration. Renny's imperturbability on discovering Eden and her, the meeting with these strangers, the potency of the wines, transformed her momentarily into the woman she was always striving to be.

"Are you a neighbour of these gentlemen?" asked Mrs. Denovan.

"Yes," she returned. "Though not for long."

"They've got a lovely old house and a wonderful old grandmother. Why, she conversed with my wife and me like a woman of seventy."

"She's more interesting than any woman of seventy I've ever known."

Eden saw a shade of resentment cross Renny's face. He thought — "Renny doesn't even want to hear Gran *praised* by these people. That's what's the matter with him. Everything that he loves, he wants to keep from the outside world. For all my deceptions, he's got a more secret nature than I have.... Gosh, he's asking Amy to dance!"

Eden had an almost hysterical feeling as he saw Renny take her hand, place his arm about her waist. Certainly she had courage. He threw her a look of approval. He hoped she would acquit herself well. Old Redhead was a good dancer. He turned to Mrs. Denovan and asked her to dance. She was light as a fairy. She was like thistledown on his arm. He gave himself up to the pleasure of the dance.

Under circumstances less extraordinary, Amy Stroud would never have felt sufficiently sure of herself to have danced with Renny. Tonight was different. Though she was not intoxicated, she was in a state approaching it. She wanted to snatch the pleasures of the night with both hands. Her life in the past month had been so lone, so torn by agitation, that she felt, in her flame-coloured dress, like a butterfly newly emerged from the cramping darkness of its chrysalis. Yet, as she waited with her hand in Renny's for his signal, she had to set her teeth to keep her lips steady. She was afraid he might feel the trembling of her limbs.

The orchestra was playing "The Song of India." Eden had hummed it to her. Now she recognized its savage rhythm. The signal passed from Renny to her. They moved down the room where now only a few couples were dancing. Neither spoke.

At first Amy Stroud's one desire was not to disgrace herself. A deep sigh of relief parted her lips as she realized that, even had she been less skilful than she was, she could have fancied herself a good dancer with this man. She had thought Eden's dancing perfect, as they moved up and down her small sitting room to the accompaniment of his whistling. Tonight she had felt the exhilaration of dancing with him to an orchestra.

But this was a new experience. She had a sense of shock in the vital grace of Renny's dancing. She was being swept along. She had no will of her own. "The Song of India" was her very heartbeat. And near her heart was the rhythmic throbbing of his. He was like one of his own racers who, having learnt an artificial gait such as pacing or trotting, took a conscious pleasure in exercising it. They finished the dance at the far end of the room.

"That was marvellous," she breathed, her eyes glowing. "I'm so glad you asked me to dance."

He returned, somewhat stiffly — "I did not ask you to dance with any idea of pleasure in it, for either of us."

She still clung to his arm. She was scarcely rebuffed by his remark. She was bewildered by the ecstasy of the dance. Eden passed with Mrs. Denovan, looking admiringly down at her. He might have been a stranger, for all the effect his passing had on Amy Stroud. She remembered how, when Renny had come to her house, those who had been there before him had been obliterated. Here was a man, she thought, she could have loved with her whole soul. Yet how often she had a feeling of hate for him! "It is my passionate nature," she thought. "Oh, if only he would ask me to dance again!"

He said:

"I want to talk to you about Eden. When can I see you?"

Her heart beat in anticipation. Another meeting with him! Would it be better to meet him in her own house or in this hotel? Her mind wavered between the two, decorating both imagined scenes with provocative embellishments.

"When can I see you?" he repeated.

Better meet him at the hotel! In it something of tonight's atmosphere might still be felt.

"Will you be in town tomorrow?" she asked.

"Yes. Are you staying here?"

"Yes. Could you have lunch with me here?"

"Thank you, I'm afraid I can't. May I come some time in the morning?"

She did not want to see him in the morning. "I must be out all day. Can you come in the evening?"

He gave her a penetrating glance. She felt that he saw through her. She compromised. "I think I might arrange to see you in the afternoon."

"Very well. I'll come about three."

It was like him, she thought, to have chosen that most uncomfortable hour.

"Could you make it four?"

"All right. It shall be four."

They returned to their table. Mr. Denovan, as though feeling cheated of his guest's company, turned decisively toward him and began to talk of horses.

"Shall we go?" Amy Stroud asked of Eden in an undertone.

"No, no, I want to dance."

He did indeed want to dance but apparently not with her. Once again he led Mrs. Denovan on to the floor. Amy Stroud sat between the two men, almost ignored by them.

But she had no feeling of isolation. She was tingling with life.

But when Eden again invited her to dance she refused. She had heard Mr. Denovan ask Renny to go to the smoking room, where they could talk in peace, and Renny's acquiescence. Mrs. Denovan was tired after travelling and was going up to bed. Amy Stroud rose and said goodnight. She left the dining room, followed by Eden. In the corridor he said:

"Thank God, old Redhead let me go in peace! I've felt pretty low in the last half-hour, expecting a row with him."

"He's having it with me."

"With *you*! When?"

"Tomorrow afternoon. Here."

"I wonder what he'll say."

"I wonder."

Eden gave her a curious, slanting look.

"I believe you're looking forward to it."

"I am — in a sort of way."

"He has that effect on most women. I thought you were different."

"I don't know what you mean," she said angrily. "I am looking forward to proving to him that I'm not an adventuress."

They had reached the door of her room. He lounged against it, laughing.

"*You* an adventuress! Oh, Aimee! "

Her voice was icy.

"Why not?"

"You simply couldn't be."

"Your family think I am."

"No, they don't."

"What do they think?"

He tried to say something to soothe her.

"Well — they think you're a dangerous *good* woman."

"Then I must undeceive them."

"As to which quality?"

"I'll talk that over with your brother."

"Aimee, you're angry with me ... and after such a lovely evening?"

Both sought to regain the happy mood of the early evening but they parted with coolness.

Whether it was the different environment or some change in herself, Mrs. Stroud could not tell. Whatever it was, she slept well that night, dreamlessly and long. She woke with rested nerves and clear eyes. She was pleased with her reflection in the glass. How lovely to lie in bed and have your breakfast carried to you! Her own house seemed far away. She felt that this life would go on forever.

She got a novel from the lending library but she read little. It was a pleasure to her to sit in the lounge, watching people come and go. She had a glimpse of the Denovans but drew back in her chair. She shrank from speaking to them. In the writing room she found picture postcards of the hotel, and sent one to each of the few acquaintances of her past whom she considered worth the trouble of impressing.

At a quarter to four she secured a quiet corner and established herself there to watch for Renny Whiteoak. He arrived promptly. After their first words of perfunctory politeness they sat in silence for a space, she waiting for him to strike the note of the conversation, he controlling his desire to speak to her as his grandmother would have counselled. Finally he said:

"Mrs. Stroud, do you mind telling me how serious this affair between you and Eden is?"

"It is a friendship that has been very dear to me."

He answered impatiently — "I didn't say *has been*, I said *is*."

"It is still very dear."

"I suppose you know that I sent him to live in the University to get him away from you."

"Yes. It was not necessary."

"Do you realize that he's only eighteen?"

"He'll be nineteen in a few months."

"What of that?"

"Men have married at nineteen."

His eyebrows shot up. "If you have marriage in your mind —"

"I haven't."

"Would you mind telling me what you have?"

She answered, almost inaudibly — "I want to do what you want me to."

He stared at her, as though scarcely believing his ears.

She went on — "I asked Eden to have dinner with me here, because I had to find out if he still cares for me. You see, I had been terribly hurt. I found out that he cares for me as much as ever. It made him very happy to be with me again…. Then, last night, something happened. I suddenly realized how you must feel about it. I began to feel that, as you are Eden's guardian, you have the right to forbid him going about with people you think are dangerous to him."

"Yes," he agreed, looking intently at her.

Her eyes filled with tears. "I'm a very lonely woman, you know. You can't understand that, because you're one of a large family."

"You ought to live in town."

"I love the country!"

"You had neighbours, Mrs. Stroud, and you turned them out. If you're so lonely, I should think you would have hesitated to do what you did — even if common humanity hadn't prevented you."

At the mere thought of Dayborn, her heart began to thud quickly against her side. However, she said steadily:

"I have a temper. Jim Dayborn brought out the worst in me. I've often regretted what I did. Are they still at Jalna?"

"They're in the flat now." Some thought absorbed him, made him forget her very presence.

She must bring his thoughts back to her. She asked:

"How is Launceton getting on?"

His eyes lighted. "Oh, he's doing wonderfully. The problem is his training when winter comes. But we'll manage somehow. He's a grand fellow."

She was afraid that the interview might be wasted in talk about the horse. She felt that his difficulties with Eden paled before his absorption in Launceton. For a moment she was helpless. Yet his physical attraction for her was intensified. All that had gone before in her life seemed but a preparation for this, a passive and pale introduction. What had Eden ever given her! Nothing comparable to what she had given him. She felt a fire in herself, a passion for living that would make defeat impossible.

"I'm going to promise you," she said, "never to see Eden again, without your permission, on one condition."

"Yes?"

"That you will be my friend instead of my enemy."

He thought — "I wonder what the devil you mean by that?" He said:

"That's very kind of you. But I don't quite know how I am to show you friendship. What do you want me to do?" He looked warily at her.

Her voice had never been more musical, more moving.

"Just not to forget my existence! To come and see me sometimes. You promised to take me to the Horse Show, you know. I don't want you to forget that."

He still looked wary and a little embarrassed. He said:

"All that's very easy to promise."

"There's another thing. I want you to let me give Eden my canoe. It's of no use to me now."

"But I can't let you do that. Surely you will be able to use it next year."

"I'm too nervous to go out in it alone. I can't continue to pay rent for something that will be of no further use to me."

"I will buy it from you, then."

She said, almost gaily — "Let's forget about the canoe for the present. It is enough for me that things are different between us."

Her large eyes looked deep into his. She laid her hand on his arm. His eyes turned to an approaching figure. It was the American, Mrs. Denovan, followed by her husband.

With relief at the success of his conversation with Amy Stroud, relief, too, from the embarrassment of her emotional reaching out to him, he rose and greeted the newcomers. He suggested that they should have cocktails.

They were joined by several others who had come to town for the Horse Show. Amy Stroud found herself in a new world.

XXII

NEWS FROM ENGLAND

THIS WAS AN afternoon in early December. White and purple clouds were moving steadily southward but all day the sun somehow had managed to evade them and to send its brightness on the brown fields, the stable, the weather-cock that flicked from south to south-east, as the cold breeze whistled against his side. Nicholas Whiteoak had just returned from a solitary ride along the lake shore. He had enjoyed it and there was a good colour in his long flat cheeks. He looked well in his riding clothes which were immaculate, in contrast to the worn coat and breeches of his nephew who strolled forward to meet him. A stableman held the horse while Nicholas dismounted. The horse lifted an eager foreleg, his mind on his evening feed.

"Hullo," said Renny. "Had a good ride?"

"Fine. The road was quiet. I met scarcely a soul. Had a little chat with the Lacey girls who'd been at a Women's Institute meeting."

"Oh yes, Meg was there. Like to see the ponies? We're just finishing with them."

They went toward the paddock. The sun was getting low. A saffron light lay across the fields. The hoof-beats of the ponies swept like soft thunder across the turf. There were three of them, ridden by Chris, Dayborn and Piers. A row of kegs had been spaced on the paddock and the three were weaving their way in and about them at full gallop.

Nicholas leant against the palings watching them with delight; the youth and skill of the riders, the strength, abandon and grace of the ponies.

"Gad," he exclaimed, "that girl can ride!"

Renny acquiesced by a muttered monosyllable.

"That's a cantankerous little beast Piers is riding. He handles him well."

Again the approving monosyllable. Then he shouted, — "Enough for today!"

The ponies came to a standstill, their sides heaving, nuzzling each other.

"Admirable!" shouted Nicholas. "Good boy, Piers!"

"That fellow's a handful, I can tell you," said Piers, coming to them. Dayborn had taken Piers's pony as well as his own into the stable. Chris was bent over, examining a foreleg of her pony.

"Anything wrong?" called out Renny.

"Just a graze. I'll put something on it." Her voice came high and childlike on the frosty air.

"There's Matthews," said Piers. "He's been to the post. I'll see what he's got." He ran off eagerly, though he rarely had more than a half-dozen letters in the year.

"Well," said Nicholas, "I think I'll go in. How is Launceton?"

"Grand. Come and see him tomorrow. He'll take your breath away."

Nicholas frowned. "I think it's a hare-brained scheme, entering him for the Grand National. I've seen that race run too often not to know the pitfalls of it. He'll have no chance and you'll have wasted a lot of money. To begin with, you paid an exorbitant price for him. If he's in good condition I advise you to get your money out of him now — if you can."

"Oh, do you?" said Renny, turning away.

He felt bitter at the continued opposition of his family to this dearest project. Time and again they had had evidence of Launceton's amazing powers. Yet, because his father and his grandfather had bred show horses, not racehorses, they resented his enterprise. As to extravagance, good God, his uncles had each frittered away their fortunes. His father had never added anything to the family fortunes, and every member of the family had some share in dispersing what was left.

A great saffron lake had formed in the western sky. Its reflection illumined his face as he went slowly toward the stables. All activity had suddenly ceased where so short a time ago the very earth seemed vibrant with hoof-beats. Now it was black and still.

By a projection of the stable wall he came on Dayborn and Chris, standing close together, waiting for him. She still held her pony by the bridle, while it looked enquiringly at her out of its dark liquid eyes, and occupied itself by pawing a groove in the frosty earth.

"I hope it's not going to freeze hard," Renny said as he approached them.

Neither answered. He saw that Dayborn's face was ghastly. Chris had a drawn look. She twisted a lock of the pony's mane in her fingers. She said:

"Jim's had awful news. He's heard from his friend in England. Instead of sending the quarterly cheque, she sent a letter saying she knows all about us. I've told Jim that you know. It doesn't matter now."

Renny was aghast. "Is she going to cut off his allowance? "

"Yes," said Dayborn. "This is the end."

"How did she find out?"

"Oh, don't start him again!" said Chris miserably.

"It's that Stroud woman!" Dayborn's voice shook with rage. "The bitch! The fiend incarnate! I'll get even with her — see if I don't. I'd kill her if I didn't know I'd swing for it!"

"Don't talk so wildly," said Renny soothingly. "Come into my office and have a drink. Did your friend mention Mrs. Stroud's name? "

"She didn't need to! She said she'd had a letter from someone who knows us well. She's had a lawyer and a detective on my trail — as though I were a murderer. God! I feel like one!"

"Does she know about Tod?"

"She knows everything. What a fool I've been!"

Chris stood plaiting the pony's mane, her lips quivering. She said to Renny:

"I tell him we'll get along somehow. We can, can't we?"

"Of course you can. We'll find a way out. Come along, Jim." Renny took him by the arm and steered him into the stable.

Chris followed, leading the pony. It gave a low whinny of delight and nuzzled her cheek. She put it in its stall and followed the two men into the office. Dayborn had a glass of whiskey and water in his shaking hand. He was saying:

"It isn't just the money. It's the feeling that she's been after us all these months. Trying to harm us. Lying low for us. Prying and writing letters about us. I said from the first that she was a snake but Chris wouldn't believe me. It was Chris's fault she found out about our marriage."

"It wasn't!" retorted Chris. "It was your own fault. She heard you say something when you were angry."

"Well, it was your fault for making me angry. You never give me any peace!"

"Shut up," ordered Renny. "I won't hear her talked to like that."

Dayborn glared at him. "Oh, and what are you going to do about it? Fire me, I suppose!"

"Keep your shirt on, Jim," said Renny. "You do no good by going on like this. No man ever had a better wife than Chris, and you know it."

"There are different sorts of goodness," muttered Dayborn. "I'm not so sure about her sort."

Renny refilled his glass. Dayborn became calmer. He said:

"I'll tell you what I'm going to do. I'm going straight to her house to have it out with her."

"You'll do nothing of the sort," said Renny. "You're not sure she did it. I don't believe she did. I don't believe she could."

"Oh, she's got round you! She's a serpent, if ever there was one! First it was your brother — then your uncle — now you! You took her to the Horse Show! You go to her house! She writes little scented notes to you! Oh, I've seen through the whole affair. She tried her hand on each of the others — then she tackled you — she's got *you* just where she wants you! Chris, you've no chance against her, don't imagine you have!"

Renny sprang up from his chair. He took Dayborn by the coat and pushed him out through the door.

"You go to hell out of here!" he exclaimed.

Chris followed them into the open. She suddenly remembered Tod. She ran toward the garage. Over her shoulder she could see the two men striding, side by side, along the path. She ran up the stairs to the flat. It was almost dark in there. For a moment she saw no sign of Tod. Then she found him sitting on the floor with his building bricks. He had piled seven, one on top of the other, the tallest tower he had yet achieved. He turned toward her smiling. He was beginning to talk.

"Tall, tall," he said. "Nice."

She caught him up and held him to her cheek. He sniffed. "Pony," he breathed. "Nice."

Dayborn was saying to Renny — "You're always ready to make excuses for women. And the reason is clear. You don't understand them. I do understand them, and I hate them."

"Yet," returned Renny, "you're willing to take favours from them."

"I've been driven to it," muttered Dayborn. He lengthened his stride and added — "When I've told Mrs. Stroud what I think of her, she'll not look so pleased with herself. Your attentions have made a complete fool of her. I believe that's why she wrote that letter. She wants to drive Chris and me out of Jalna. She's jealous because we're your friends. I'll bet she's made up her mind to marry you."

"You know you're talking rot. Mrs. Stroud is a lonely woman. She promised me not to see young Eden again. She's kept her word. I had to be decent to her."

"I suppose you'll go right on being decent, even after this!"

"I'll never see her again!"

"I'll tell her that! I'll tell her you said she could not —"

"Yes, do! Make a greater ass of yourself than you already have! Now look here, Jim, you are not going to see Mrs. Stroud. She has tried to injure you —"

"*Tried!* She's succeeded, hasn't she?"

"For the time being, she has. And nothing will please her more than for you to tell her so."

Dayborn ground his teeth.

"The only thing to do is to behave as though she doesn't exist. I don't want ever to speak to her again but if I'm forced to —"

"You go to her now! Tell her what you think of her."

"I'd look well, shouldn't I? No, the important thing is to show her that she's a failure. You must come into the open and acknowledge that Chris and you are married. Say you've kept it secret because of family disapproval. Now, I've an idea! I'll get my sister to write to your friend and tell her what we think of Chris and the kid. We'll send a letter that will prove that marriage has been the best thing in the world for you."

"She'll never forgive me," groaned Dayborn.

"Is she in love with you?"

"Not a bit. She's one of those strong characters who never change their mind."

"Then she should still be your friend."

"She can't! Mrs. Stroud told her that she heard me say, when I got one of her cheques — 'Thank God the old girl has ponied up again!'"

"Did you say it?"

"Yes!"

"Well, you must deny it. One more lie won't damn you."

"Yes, yes, I'll deny it! The letter from your sister will be fine. Ah, Whiteoak, what a good friend you are!" He squeezed Renny's arm. His fingers felt thin and hard as bones. "But I'll repay you! I'll win the Grand National for you, or die in the attempt!"

They were opposite Mrs. Stroud's. Into the frosty green sky the white smoke from her chimney curled comfortably. The windows of her living room glowed warmly through the drawn curtains. The other half of the house stood blank and empty. A new sign bearing the words "To Let" had been fixed to the gate. They stared at it for a moment in silence, then turned back toward Jalna.

Having parted with Dayborn at his flat, Renny returned to the house. It was now dark. In the hall his nostrils were greeted by the pungent smell of hot tomato catsup, rising from the kitchen. He sniffed it and hung up his hat. Three dogs were about the stove. Fan, his father's spaniel, had carried in a large bone and was guarding it between her paws. She had a far away look but her mind was alert. The big young bob-tailed sheepdog, Ben, which Renny had acquired since his return, lay facing Fan, his eyes twinkling at the bone, through his long hair. On a high-backed chair the Yorkshire terrier puppy belonging to Nicholas sat shivering in excitement. Warning the two larger dogs not to fight, Renny tucked Nip under his arm and went into the drawing room.

Old Adeline was dozing in her chair by the fire. It was her custom to relax after a good tea. Nicholas and Ernest were just finishing a game of backgammon. Ernest indicated his victory to Renny by a gesture of triumph. Nicholas yawned and felt for his tobacco pouch. Meg was making herself a blouse with frills down the front. She was so absorbed that she scarcely noticed Renny's coming. He tossed the terrier on to Nicholas's knee and tucked his cold fingers inside Meg's collar. She hunched her shoulders and said:

"How cold you are! Please don't! Go and warm yourself. There are muffins keeping hot for you and Rags will bring you a fresh pot of tea. What kept you?"

"I'll tell you later." He bent his head and looked into his grandmother's face. Her lips were pouted and she was blowing through them gustily. There were crumbs down her front but her hands, clasped on her stomach, were so handsome and so richly ringed that her mien was not without dignity.

The old bell-cord made a rasping sound when pulled. It might wake her. Renny left the room and went to the top of the basement stairs. He shouted:

"Rags! Tea!"

Returning, he noticed that the sheepdog had got into the chair lately occupied by the Yorkshire terrier. The spaniel lay with her chin on the bone. Her eyes were closed.

Renny was so hungry that he had taken a muffin from the dish and eaten it as he went through the hall. Swallowing the last of it, he returned to the drawing room and sat down near Meg. As he ate his tea he told what had happened that afternoon. What annoyance Meg might have felt at having been deceived by the Dayborns was lost in her pity for their fresh misfortune. She had long felt nothing but distrust of Mrs. Stroud. She regretted that such a woman had pushed her way into the neighbourhood. She blamed poor Miss Pink not a little for having sold her her house.

Nicholas was inclined to be jocular on the subject, especially as Ernest had been involved in the affair. He pulled a long face and asked his brother, in a hoarse whisper, if he thought he had given Mrs. Stroud any grounds for a breach of promise suit. Vehemently though Ernest denied this, he was greatly agitated and began to pace up and down the room, reviewing in his mind every note written to her. Oh, to have them back! Their slightest friendly phrase now loomed incriminating to him.

"What a dangerous woman!" he exclaimed.

"But what made her do it?" asked Meg, puzzled. "She had already turned them out of her house. Surely Dayborn must have given her some fresh cause."

"I think," said Renny, "that she blamed him for my finding out about Eden. But it was Rags who told me."

"What a useful man he is," said Meg. "And so devoted to us."

Rags now entered with the pot of fresh tea. He carried his head on one side as though, by this posture, he further emphasized his respect for the family. There was silence till he left the room.

"What I want you to do, Meg," said Renny, "is to write a nice letter to this friend of Dayborn's and tell her how abominably Mrs. Stroud has behaved. You must tell her what you think of Chris and the baby, and what a hardship it will be on the three of them if the allowance is cut off. Will you do that, Meggie dear?" He laid his hand on hers.

"Of course I will! I'll tell her that Chris keeps him straight and that, if it were not for her, he would probably have gone to the dogs."

"Good for you, Meggie!" He gripped her fingers.

"And I'll write and tell Aunt Augusta about it, and ask her to use her influence."

"The very thing! Why — the lady lives in Exeter. Not forty miles from Aunty."

In his excitement he had forgotten to control his voice. Old Adeline woke with a snort. She stared truculently at them.

"What a to-do!" she said. "One would think it was the middle of the day."

"It's only six o'clock, Granny."

"Bless me, I thought it was midnight. What a long day!"

"Yet you were saying, Granny, just before you fell asleep, what a short day it's been!"

"Long or short, it's all one to me," returned Adeline huffily.

Renny came to her side and sat down. Briefly he told her what had happened. Perhaps he told her too briefly, without the details she loved. Perhaps there was just something in him that day which she did not like, as sometimes happened. However it was, she listened with an uncomprehending stare and then turned to Meg.

"Tell it properly," she said. "He's talking in a funny way. I believe he's tight."

Renny's already high colour deepened but he controlled himself and sat silent while his sister repeated, at greater length, what he had said. When she had finished, Adeline remarked:

"A pretty kettle of fish. The woman ought to be ducked in the horse pond!"

The fact that the horse pond she had in mind was far away in Ireland signified nothing to her.

"And don't you think," finished Meg, "that it is a good idea for Aunt Augusta to see this Mrs. Gardiner and tell her what we think of Mrs. Cummings?"

"Mrs. Dayborn," corrected Ernest.

"Better still, for the young man himself to see her," said Adeline.

"But Aunt Augusta is so convincing."

"Mrs. What's-her-name doesn't love your aunt. Apparently she is very fond of young Dayborn. He is the one to see her. Write to your aunt. If she can arrange a meeting between them he must go over."

"I suppose you'll pay for his passage," Renny said sarcastically.

"No!" she retorted. "You will."

They glared at each other.

"I've been thinking," she went on, "about this scheme of entering Launceton for the Grand National. I knew a great deal about horse racing before you or your father were thought of. I tell you that you can't train him properly in this climate. If you're determined to try for it, why don't you send him over now? Wait — don't interrupt. What was I saying? Bless me, it's gone right out of my head!"

"You were saying," returned Renny, "how simple it would be for me to send the horse and Dayborn to England for the winter."

"I didn't say England! I said Ireland. My cousin Dermot is eighty. His house is falling to pieces but I guess his stables are still standing. You've heard about them."

"Why, Gran, I visited him when I was on leave. He's a grand old boy. By Judas, what an idea! Cousin Dermot will be delighted to keep Launceton. I'll follow in February. It's the very thing." He sprang up and heaved her bodily out of her chair. "What a wonder you are! If I win the Grand National, I'll buy you whatever you choose. Come, Gran, come, let's do a dance together!"

With his arm tightly round her waist, he waltzed her down the room.

"Steady on, Mamma," said Nicholas.

"She likes it, don't you, Gran?"

She clutched his shoulder. She was gasping, laughing, but her legs were suddenly agile, her shapely feet supple. Twice the length of the room she showed him something of the dancer she had been.

XXIII

LAUNCETON

IN THE MIDDLE of December there was a heavy snowfall. Even Adeline could not remember such a heavy one at that time of year. It came almost without warning. The white clouds that for a week had been moving majestically across the sky, ceased to move. They gathered together and shut out the sun, stilling the land in a chill purple hush. Through small crevices in the now complete cloud, the pale sun might be traced in his descent. As the men locked the stables and went to their evening meal, a few large flakes were falling. Next morning they discovered a changed world. Without wind, without bluster, the snow had fallen deep and silent. It had obliterated the paths and made the roads impassable. Trees looked like decorations for a Christmas cake: houses, like houses on a Christmas card. But there was no bright Christmas sky. The purple clouds drooped with the weight of still more snow. It was the hush, the sustained pause, that Amy Stroud most minded. She had been lonely enough before the snow came. No neighbour had set foot in her house since the day she had turned the Dayborns out. Even the boy who brought her groceries was different. No one had a smile for her. She did not get a letter, though with painful eagerness she had watched for one from Renny. She had written, asking him to come to see her. It was on a matter of great importance she had said. The matter was that the desire to be with him was tormenting her beyond bearing. She told herself that he was all she had left. She magnified their few meetings into passionate episodes. The pleasure she had had from the visits of Eden and Ernest paled to nothing compared with that night at the hotel when she had danced with Renny; that afternoon at the Horse Show when she had applauded his riding so fervently, with so possessive a smile, that the people near her turned to her and smiled in sympathy. Then there was the day they had met on the road. He had walked with her and talked confidentially of his hopes for Launceton. There was that other day when she had wandered into his own grounds, had met him and asked if he would show her his horses. He had shown them all, drawing her attention to their best points, while she, with an effort, looked at them instead of at him. Now she had written him, the second time imploringly, begging him to come to her. He had not answered. She would write again telling him she was in great trouble. She would have to invent something — investments gone wrong or something of the sort. But why had he not answered her letters?

Suddenly, with a shock, came the memory of her letter to Mrs. Gardiner. She had actually forgotten it! What was coming over her that she could do a thing like that and then forget it? She recalled how her husband had said that her head was screwed on right. What would he say if he knew how she was carrying on now? She didn't care. She would see Renny! Nothing must come between her and him. It could not be because of her letter to Mrs. Gardiner that he was treating her so. If Dayborn had had trouble from that quarter she would have heard from him. The thought of the scene he would make suddenly frightened her. She had never felt in the least afraid of Dayborn, but now a chill ran through her and a prickling sensation across her face. She would deny to Renny that she had ever written the letter. But what if her name were mentioned? She must see him today. She went again to the window and looked out at the snow. It was late afternoon. What a day she had had!

She put on her hat and coat and, without having glanced at herself in the mirror, left the house. Fortunately for her a snowplough had passed along the road. But even so, the going was heavy. It was heavier still when she reached Jalna but she never faltered, plodding doggedly along the path broken by men's footsteps, to the stables.

She turned the heavy iron handle of the door and entered. The first person she saw was Scotchmere. On his shoulder he had a sack of something that bent him almost double.

"Well, ma'am," he said glumly, "are you wanting something?"

"I want to see Mr. Whiteoak."

Scotchmere was about to say that he was in town but at that moment the door of the office opened and two horsy, almost disreputable-looking men, appeared on the threshold.

"So long, Captain," one of them called out, "see you later."

"You can depend on us," added the other. "Goodbye."

Renny's voice came, — "Goodbye and good luck!"

Mrs. Stroud pressed past the two men and entered the office.

Renny's expression changed from good humour to hostile surprise.

"You —" he said, "I did not expect to see you here, Mrs. Stroud."

She closed the door behind her.

"I had to come," she said.

"Well," he said tersely, "tell me why you came and have done with it."

"You know, without my telling you!" She spoke in a strained, gasping voice.

He turned away.

"Tell *me*," she went on, "why you did not answer my letters?"

"You don't need to ask that."

"But I don't know."

He wheeled and faced her.

"What about the letter you wrote to Mrs. Gardiner?"

Her face flamed to a telltale red. She said:

"It was horrible, but I couldn't help it. I couldn't help it."

"You were quite mistaken about its being Dayborn who told me of Eden's going to your house. It was my man Wragge who told me."

She threw back her head with a desperate gesture. "It doesn't matter. It would have been the same. It was jealousy that drove me to it."

"Jealousy?"

"Yes." She tried to steady herself, to think clearly. If she could make him believe that love for him had driven her to desperation he might forgive her. "I wanted to get that girl away from here. I love you so."

"That's a lie," he said fiercely.

"It is the truth! I've worshipped you — ever since that night we danced together."

"Another lie! The letter was already written."

She stared at him blankly a moment, then began to cry.

"So it was," she sobbed. "Have the truth then! Force me to tell it! I've loved you since the first moment I saw you."

He made a gesture of exasperation. "You're altogether too emotional, Mrs. Stroud. By tomorrow you'll be saying you hate me."

"Never — never," she sobbed. "If you were to take that whip and beat me — I'd love you all the more."

"I don't doubt it. But I've no intention of doing anything of the sort. What I'm *going* to do is to put you out of here."

He grasped her by the shoulders, faced her about and propelled her toward the door.

Writhing in his hands, she managed to turn her head so that her face was close to his. Her streaming eyes were distended. Her mouth was thickened and pouting.

"Kiss me," she gasped.

"I wouldn't kiss you," he returned, "if you were the last woman on earth. You tried to seduce my young brother. Now you're trying it on me. It's no go. You must find a fresh field for your activities."

Detaching a hand from her shoulder he opened the door and pushed her through. He shut and locked the door.

She stood bewildered for a space, then Scotchmere's voice came, close by. "This is the way out, ma'am." He was grinning at her. She threw him a vindictive look.

She stumbled out into the snow. It was almost dark. She plodded hurriedly along the path that was strewn with lumps of blue-white snow. A dog ran out from the stable and followed her, barking. He grew more and more angry as he followed her. She felt a tug at her skirt. She screamed loudly. It was a relief to scream.

Scotchmere whistled for the dog and it ran back to him, joyously wagging its tail. Her brain seethed, now one thought boiling to the surface, now another. That grinning groom would tell Dayborn of her humiliation and they would laugh together. She could never again face any of these people. How she hated them! They all had been against her from the first. And she so alone — so lonely! Eden was a deceitful boy. He was a wastrel. He would come to no good. His poetry — bah! Ernest — the old dandy, — the opinionated old bore. How he had tired her — tired! The grandmother — decked out like an idol — that horrid little boy Finch who had run away from her. That grinning groom who had had his ear to the keyhole.... That brute of a dog! Renny's hands were like iron.... No resisting them.... If only he had kissed her! She heard his words — saw his outraged expression. If only she had some different sort of memory to cherish! She would never see him again. Her head felt as though it would burst. In spite of the cold, she was on fire.

Again she felt something tugging at her skirt. It was that dog! She turned to face him but no, he was not there. She discovered that she had wandered from the path and was in the middle of a field. She had ploughed through snow almost to her knees. The tug at her skirt had been the weighing down of the snow. She could see her own tracks deep and icy-blue in the fine whiteness. They went round in a circle, like the steps of a lost person. She thought — "If I walked round and round here till I fell down and died, no one would care."

But she was not lost. On her left spread the fields and woods. On her right, the orchard. Behind her, the stables. All she had to do was to find the path and go straight home. But she shrank from what would happen at home when she really let herself go — in the loneliness — with that empty house next door. She wondered how long she had been wandering about the field. She turned and looked back at the stable. It had been lighted when she had been there. Now it lay in darkness, except for one small bright window.

He was there alone. Going over in his mind, as she had been doing, all that had happened. He was alone. If she went back to him now, no one would know. She would control herself — talk to him calmly and coolly — by degrees make him forget the mad things she had said to him. She would tell him the story of her life — from its very beginning. If he knew everything he would pity, not blame her. Her husband had said her head was screwed on right. She would finally prove that it was. She would undo all the harm she had done. She would offer to take the Dayborns back into her house. She wanted them back. Oh, she wanted them back! Better them, a thousand times, than the cavern of that empty house.

She would not surrender. She would not be defeated. She would knock calmly on his door and, when he opened it, she would be standing there in complete control of herself.

She began to make her way back toward the stable. She placed her feet in the depths of her former footmarks. She trembled for fear the dog would run out at her again, but all was silence. She went round the corner and looked in at the office window. He was not there but his hat was lying on the desk. He must be somewhere in the stable.

Gently she lifted the latch and the door swung back. She closed it behind her. A dim light was burning at the far end. By it she could see the rows of stalls and loose boxes and, here and there, the stark outline of a head or the hairy swish of a tail. The air was full of soft noises made by big bodies. A deep sigh, a comfortable crunching, the movement of a hoof on the floor. Then she heard voices. They came from the loose box where Launceton was kept. She walked softly along the passage and listened outside. The voices belonged to Renny and Chris. They were talking about the horse. It was not easy to make out what they said. Their voices were low and muffled.

There was a crack by the door. She put her eye to it and could see them plainly. Renny's back was to her. He held a lantern in his hand and its beam illumined Chris's slim figure as she stood leaning against Launceton. Her face looked thinner and whiter than Amy Stroud remembered it, but her eyes were beautiful and her delicate lips smiling happily. She was saying:

"It seems too wonderful to be true. Especially after all we've been through."

"Everything will turn out right," he said. "You'll see! Launceton's going to make our fortunes, aren't you, old man?" He ran his hand along the horse's neck.

"And to think that Jim and Tod and I are going with him to Ireland to stay with your relations! And that you're following in February! Darling, it will be glorious!"

Renny gave a little laugh. He caressed the girl's bright head as he had, with the same hand, caressed the horse.

"I wish I had a picture of you, standing beside Launceton. I do love you, Kit!"

Anything else that was said was beaten down by the drumming in Amy Stroud's ears. She leant against the wall, her knees trembling. She heard them leaving the loose box. Barely in time, she stepped into a stall beside it. The horse standing there pricked his ears and looked at her askance. She pressed herself against the side of the stall. The beam of the lantern travelled down the passage. She heard Renny ask Chris if she were tired. Ask her in a gentle protective tone.

Hate and jealousy surged up in her. Now she knew she was defeated but her spirit, she told herself, was not broken. Somehow or other she would prove that.

Her head was screwed on right. Anyone who hurt her would meet his match.... The stable door clanged. The horse beside her ignored her, munching his hay. She could hear Launceton moving about in his loose box. What was she going to do next?

Like a moving picture reel, projected again and again for her torture, she saw the scene she had just witnessed. Every inflection of the voice was stressed. Every gesture was suspended just long enough for her avid mind to drink in its import. Jealousy, hatred, devoured her.

The horse beside her moved closer. Its flank pressed her against the side of the stall. With a cry of fear she darted out into the passage. The horse turned his head to look after her, a wisp of hay dangling from his mouth. She heard movement all through the stable. From the poultry house came the feeble crow of a cockerel.

If only she could do something to Launceton that would prevent his running in the Grand National! If only she had some paralyzing poison she could inject into him! That would be revenge in earnest. She had heard of horses having been hamstrung. The word was savage but — what did it mean? Whatever it was she knew she could not do it, even if she knew how. She dare not go into the loose box beside that great creature. Again came the picture of the girl leaning against him with Renny's eyes fixed in love on them both. She paced up and down the passage between the stalls.

Then the thought came that she would turn Launceton out into the snow. He was as carefully guarded as a child. She knew that. Perhaps he would get a chill that would lay him up for weeks, even prevent his running in the race. In any case it would give them a terrible shock to find their darling, their hope, wandering about in the bitter cold. For it was getting terribly cold. She was shivering all through her.

She went down the passage and opened the big double doors and fastened them back. Her head was screwed on right. Not many women would have remembered to fasten back the doors! Then she went back to the loose box where Launceton was. When she opened the door he made no attempt to come out. She stood waiting; then clapped her hands and said "Shoo!" to him, as to a fowl. He stood looking out at her, a gleam of what seemed to be amusement in his great liquid eyes. She repeated the word and clapped her hands with all her might but he would not move.

In a fury, she took a long-handled brush that was leaning against the wall and struck his flank, then darted out of the way. He only gave her a reproachful look and walked slowly out into the passage.

"Get along, you brute!" she cried. "Shoo! Shoo!" She drove him down the passage and out of the door.

He stepped delicately through it and stood silhouetted against the snow. She threw down the brush and stood in the doorway, regarding him. He looked at her. Then he trotted in a leisurely gait into the open. He gave a whinny of delight. He had not been out of the stable all day.

Suddenly, as though galvanized, he raced along the path. He galloped as though the goal of goals was in sight, his mane and tail flying, no bit in his mouth, no rider to check him. Mrs. Stroud ran after him, eager to see which way he would go. She forgot all fear. All other feelings were swallowed up in her triumph.

He flew past the orchard. The thought came to her that she might open the gate at the end of the field and let him out into the road. But now he threw himself on his back in a snowdrift and joyously rolled, his hooves in the air like a flourish of iron weapons. She toiled along the path after him.

He made as though to rise. Then sank back. He floundered, his hooves in the air. Then sank back and was still. She ran to him, as though solicitously.

He raised his eyes searchingly to hers.

Why — what was wrong? What could have hurt him — for she was sure he was terribly hurt — why could he not get to his feet? A shudder ran through him. With a deep sigh that seemed to come from the innermost part of his being, he settled himself into the snowdrift. She ploughed through the deep snow to his side. She squatted there, looking into his face. He was dying.... In a moment, he was dead....

Scotchmere found him in the morning.

He ran, as he had not run for years, along the snowy path leading to the house. It was barely light. He knocked loudly on the kitchen door. Rags opened it, in shirt and trousers.

"I've got to see the boss!" gasped Scotchmere.

"What's the matter?"

"The horse is dead! Launceton."

"*Dead!* What are ye givin' us?"

Scotchmere pushed him aside and came into the kitchen.

"'Ere, you can't go up now. W'at killed 'im?"

"I don't know. But he's dead. Out in the snow. I've got to tell the boss." He hurried up the basement stairs. Rags followed him. In the hall he managed to push past him. It was he who knocked on Renny's door, then opened it.

Renny lay on his back, one arm across his forehead, like a man warding off a blow. They stood, one on each side of the bed.

"What's up?" he asked.

"It's Launceton, sir. He's dead."

Renny looked up at them, dazed. He tried to wake. He threw out his arm and moved his head sharply on the pillow. But the two men did not disappear. They were still there, looking down at him. Rags said:

"I got the scare of my life, sir. Scotchmere came pounding at the door and I leaped up. My missus said —"

Scotchmere interrupted — "He'd got out of the stable, sir. He's lying in the deep snow. He's ruptured hisself!"

Renny's lips were pale. He sprang out of bed and looked about the room, still dazed. Rags began to hand him his clothes. He pulled the garments on, one after the other. He said:

"Are you sure he's dead?"

"I know a dead horse when I see one," answered Scotchmere bitterly.

Nicholas appeared in the doorway.

"Launceton's dead," Renny told him. "Scotchmere found him in the snow. How did you say he got out?"

"God only knows! The stable doors were fastened back. Some fiend has done this to us, sir." He began to cry.

"But this is awful," said Nicholas. "Why, I can't believe it!"

"I had the scare of my life, sir," said Rags. "My missus —"

Ernest, Meg, and the boys were coming out of their rooms. Renny hurried past them and ran down the stairs.

Everything was in dim tones of grey and white. Launceton lay dark on the snow. Some had fallen during the night, had first melted against his warmth, then outlived it. His dark mane was whitened. There was snow in his still-open eyes. Renny knelt and kissed him between the eyes.

"Dear old man," he said.

They found snowy footprints inside the stable. They were the footprints of a woman wearing high-heeled galoshes. They found the same footprints about Launceton where he lay. It was Dayborn who shouted:

"It was Mrs. Stroud! There isn't the faintest doubt."

"She gave me a murderous look when I showed her the door last night," said Scotchmere.

"Was she here last night?" asked Dayborn.

"Yes," answered Renny, "she was here. But she couldn't have done it, Jim! No one, with a heart in their breast, could have done such a thing — let alone a woman."

They were in Renny's office. Chris came running in to them.

"It was Mrs. Stroud!" she cried. "There are two sets of footprints. You can trace her everywhere she went. Nothing would melt in this stable last night. We must telephone for the vet. Three of the horses and one of the ponies are shaking all over."

"Telephone, then," said Renny.

The three men stood watching as she telephoned in a steady voice. She hung up the receiver and said:

"He's coming at once. The men are already making mashes. The horses are blanketed. God, what a fiend!"

"This time," said Dayborn, "no one can stop me. If I'd had my way with her she'd never have lived to do this."

He almost ran out of the office.

"I'll come with you," said Renny.

There was a ruddy streak in the east as they went through the snow. A little knot of men were standing by Launceton's body. Renny averted his eyes. Dayborn kept repeating:

"All our hopes — everything — everything — all our hopes —"
Tears ran down his cheeks.

"Hang on to yourself, Jim. Let me do the talking."

They reached Mrs. Stroud's house.

As they stood on the doorsill, Dayborn was shaking with excitement. He gripped Renny's arm to steady himself. Their two pairs of eyes were fixed on the spot where they expected Mrs. Stroud's guilty face to appear. But she did not answer the door.

"She's run away," said Dayborn.

"No. There are her footprints going in. There are no others."

He knocked again.

"I tell you she's gone!"

They listened intently. There was no sound inside the house.

Dayborn turned the handle of the door and threw it violently open. There were snowy footprints in the hall. They went into the living room. It was cold and, at the first glance, appeared empty.

Then they saw Mrs. Stroud, sitting on a low chair in a dim corner. She wore coat and hat. She sat, with her hands clasped in her lap, as though waiting for them. She fixed her large grey eyes on Renny's face with an expression of deep melancholy. Dayborn shouted at her:

"Do you know that you'll go to the penitentiary for this? You're a murderess — that's what you are! I knew from the first that you —"

She interrupted, — "Mr. Whiteoak, will you tell him to go away. I want to see you alone."

"I'll not go," said Dayborn. "This means as much to me as to him."

Still keeping her eyes on Renny, she repeated, — "Tell him to go away."

"If you think," sneered Dayborn, "that you can get around him you're mistaken. Do you know what ought to be done with you? You ought to be hanged from one of the rafters in Launceton's stall! And left there dangling! By God, I'd like to do it!"

She smiled mournfully. "I don't blame you.... But please go. I want to see Mr. Whiteoak alone.... Just for a few minutes.... I must see him alone."

"Go outside, Jim," said Renny.

He spoke so authoritatively that Dayborn flung out of the room without another word. He banged the front door behind him. But he did not go far. He placed himself before the house he had once occupied, staring at the windows of the room where he had left Renny and Mrs. Stroud.

She drew a deep sigh, then rose and stood facing Renny. She said, in a hoarse voice:

"I've killed Launceton."

He took a step backward, as though he was afraid she might touch him. "Yes. You've killed him."

"Would you like to see done to me — what Dayborn said?"

"You deserve it."

"Do you know why I went to the stables last night?"

"To find me."

"Yes. I found you there — with that girl — and the horse. I wanted to do something that would hurt you both — terribly. So — I let Launceton out. I thought he might take a chill and not be fit to race. I'll not keep back anything! I didn't care if he died."

"I could forgive you," he said, "if you'd put a bullet into me. But — that horse — who'd never harmed anyone!"

"I'd bring him back if I could. I've no hate or jealousy left in me. I'm dead in here!" She clutched her coat above her breast. "Except — except — for my love — oh, I love you still!" She began to sob.

"What a liar you are!" he said bitterly. "You don't love anyone but yourself. You don't know what honest feeling is."

She clasped her hands tightly on her breast. "I know I deserve everything you can say. But I wish I could tell you my life.... From the very beginning.... I think I could make you understand ... and it wasn't as though I were an ordinary woman.... Those years ... I wasn't changed by them.... Something in me just smouldered and waited its chance.... Then the chance came and — it is you who have suffered."

"Yes." He turned away his eyes. He could not bear to look into her face.

"What are you going to do to me?" she whispered. "Have me arrested?"

He stood, with his hand to his mouth, his eyes averted. The jangle of sleigh bells came from the road. He stood silent so long that it seemed to her he was struck dumb. At last he spoke:

"No," he said. "Not that. But you're to go away from here. Never show your face again. Never as long as you live. Will you promise that?"

She answered in a strong voice — "I promise. I'll go. Far away. You're very kind.... You're very, very kind...." Her voice took on a sort of sing-song. "You're kind ... kind."

He looked at her startled. He felt afraid of her.

"Very well," he said. "Then — this is the end."

Her eyes were closed. One hand moved gropingly toward him. "Don't go," she said hoarsely.

She opened her eyes. He was gone.

The red sun swam up into the clear sky. The snow was rosy where the sun touched it, deep blue in the shadow. Dayborn walked close to Renny. He never stopped talking. Renny strode through the snow, not hearing. When he tried to think of Mrs. Stroud or her act, he could make nothing out of the confusion in his head. All that was clear to him was that Launceton, so full of fire, so noble in his simplicity, was dead.

When they reached the stable the vet was there. The horses that had been chilled were being treated. None was in a dangerous state. Rags was there, imploring him to go to the house for breakfast. He refused and Rags brought a pot of tea to the stable. It was noon when he went to his office and sat down at his desk, his head in his hands.

He did not raise his head when Chris and Dayborn came in. They stood looking at him. Dayborn said:

"If you'd listened to me, this would never have happened. I told you what she was, long ago. But you always will do your own way. I don't want to rub it in. But you're a lot to blame."

"Shut up, Jim," said Chris.

"You're to blame too," continued Dayborn, in his hectoring voice. "You were always reminding me how kind she'd been to us. It's damned hard that I, who saw through her, should have to suffer with the rest. That night when she —"

"Shut up!"

"Shut up yourself!"

The door opened. Scotchmere stuck in his grizzled head. "Will Mr. Dayborn please come. The vet wants to see him." The groom's eyes accused Dayborn of slacking.

Dayborn went, his shoulders sagging in weariness, the tail of his shirt dangling ludicrously outside his riding breeches.

Chris came to Renny and drew his head to her breast.

"Poor darling," she whispered. "If only I could do something!"

He pressed her hands to his throbbing temples.

It was evening before Dayborn and Chris could persuade him to return to the house. He had eaten nothing but had drunk a great deal. Under a glittering new moon they steadied him, one on either hand, along the wide path shovelled by the men. The snow at the sides was waist-high. They were both so thin, so nearly of the same build, that he was not sure which was which. He patted both their backs.

Old Adeline, on her way to bed, heard him coming. He was singing at the top of his not very musical voice:

> "D'ye ken John Peel, with his coat so gay?
> D'ye ken John Peel, at the break of the day?
> Peel's view-halloo would waken the dead
> And the fox from his lair in the morning."

She opened the door to him.

XXIV

CHRISTMAS

MEG AND HER grandmother were in the sitting room going through a box of decorations for the Christmas tree. It was a large box and some of its contents dated back to the time when Meg and Renny were children. One of these was a fat wax cherub, now grown rather dingy and with his nose gone, but dear to all the family. There were the gay-coloured cornucopias for the Christmas sweets. There were tinsel streamers some of them rather tarnished, though, when the candles were lit, they shone as brightly as the best. Not one in the family could see that box without a certain excitement. It meant that Christmas was at hand, the last rites were being performed.

Adeline was extricating a silver fish from a tangle of tinsel. Meg, with one corner of her handkerchief wetted by her tongue, was washing the cherub's face. The air was heavy with the scent of the tree and of the spruce and hemlock boughs that had been placed above the pictures. A basket in the window was heaped with still unopened Christmas cards from the post.

"Thank goodness," said Meg, "that Renny has got over the worst of his disappointment before Christmas. I think that, on the whole, he bore it pretty well, don't you, Gran?"

"I do. He bore it like a soldier."

"But he did get terribly drunk! It was a shock to me."

Adeline threw up her hands. "And to me, too. Bless me, when I opened the door and he came feather-stitching along the hall, he reminded me so of my own father that I all but fainted! Before I could stop myself, I called him by my father's name. I said, — 'You ought to be ashamed of yourself, Renny Court.'"

"And what did he say, Gran?"

"He said, — 'I wish I had been Renny Court, for I'd have been dead forty years. Better be dead,' he said, 'than live to see this day.' Then he came and put his head on my shoulder and cried. And I said, — 'Cry away, my dear, 'twill do you good.' And what do you think he said then? He said, — 'Oh, Gran, the War was terrible!' His poor brain was completely moithered with all the trouble that was on him, as my old nurse used to say."

"Poor darling! It was wonderful the way you soothed him and the uncles got him to bed. It is strange how he never wants to speak of Launceton now. And, if anyone so much as mentions Mrs. Stroud's name, he gives a black look and closes right up. I think it is good to talk over one's troubles, don't you, Gran?"

"Eh, Meg, but you've never wanted to talk over Maurice Vaughan, have you?"

Meg coloured deeply and bent her head over the box of decorations. Her grandmother looked at her shrewdly. "I believe you still love him, Meg."

Meg did not answer. There was silence except for the crackling of the fire and the rustle of their hands in the tinsel.

At last Adeline spoke. "I'm wondering what sort of Christmas that Mrs. Stroud will have."

"Miserable enough, I should say, with such a dreadful thing on her conscience."

"She ought to thank her stars that she's not locked up."

"Renny was too soft-hearted in letting her off so easily. But, as he said, no amount of punishment could bring Launceton back."

"Well, she's hid herself completely. No one seems to know where she's gone. I wonder who will buy the house now. How well I remember when it was built! Little did old Mr. Pink guess such a queer woman would come to live in it. But bad as she was, she wasn't made of the right stuff for a sinner."

There were footsteps in the hall. Meg shook her head. "Sh, Gran. Renny is coming. We mustn't be talking of her.... I think the snow has stopped, don't you?"

Renny came in. She turned smiling to him while holding up the cherub for inspection.

"I've been washing his face, Renny. Does it look clean to you?"

He examined the waxen face critically. "It's a bit smudgy but it'll look clean in the candlelight."

"I hope Wakefield won't scream when he sees Uncle Nick as Santa Claus. He did last year."

"He'll not scream. I'll hold him on my shoulder."

"What do you think of Finch's hanging up his stocking? Piers says he's too old and that the tree is enough. But I can see that he wants to. I really think he still believes."

"Let the poor little devil hang up his stocking."

He hesitated, then took a paper from his pocket. He said: "This came just now. It's a cable from Aunt Augusta. She's seen Mrs. Gardiner and advises Dayborn to go to her as soon as possible. She says she's sure he can put things right." He gave a short laugh. "Not much chance for Dayborn to go to England now."

"When I think," said Meg, "what that woman has done to those poor things —"

"Did the girl know, before she married, that there was this woman in England to be reckoned with?" asked Adeline.

"No," answered Renny. "Dayborn told her nothing till after they were married. He's a mean dog, but I like him."

Adeline spoke in a shaking voice. She said:

"I'll do it."

"Do what?" asked Renny.

"Pay their passage. And their expenses. The three of them."

He stared at her incredulously. "Gran, you don't mean it!"

"I do. Go you, Renny, and tell them that your grandmother is full of goodwill this Christmas and wants to prove it by helping them. Heigho, but 'twill take a deal of money!"

Renny folded her in his arms and laid his cheek against hers. "Gran, you've never done anything better than this. They'll be grateful all the rest of their lives. And so shall I! I can't tell you how I've been worried about them — since — this affair."

She peered up at him shrewdly. "How much do you think of that girl Chris? Tell me that."

"So much that it will hurt like hell to give her up." With a defensive glance at grandmother and sister he went toward the door.

When it had closed behind him, Meg said, — "I wonder how true that is. Of course I know he thinks it's true. But men deceive themselves even more easily than they deceive women."

Adeline shut her eyes. Her lips moved. She said, — "I get all mixed up when I try to calculate how much it will cost. But I know it will be a lot. Well, well, I'll have to grin and bear it. I wonder what your uncles will say!"

Meg patted her hand. "I don't see how they can help being glad. They both admire Chris and are sorry for her. And they know the baby's future may depend on this. For my part, I think you're showing the real Christmas spirit."

Adeline looked slyly at her granddaughter. "It isn't only for their sakes," she said. "The young man must be protected. Yon redhead."

Meg stared. Then she exclaimed, — "Oh, Gran, how clever of you! I always say that whatever brains I have, I inherit them from you!"

Chris was waiting near the gate when Renny appeared, driving one of the farm sleighs drawn by a lively gelding. Seeing the open gate it was determined to go through without stopping.

"Whoa," he shouted, tightening the reins.

The gelding, forced to a standstill, danced heavily in the snow, its thick neck arched in make-believe fear of the tree Chris held upright. It was a Christmas tree, somewhat taller than she, its roots wrapped in a sack, its thick-spreading branches tapering to a perfect spire. She was bareheaded and, with the medieval cut of her straight fair hair and her dark jersey and breeches, she made an arresting picture against the snowy landscape. Her face, too, was arresting, with its look of fragility and endurance, purity and experience. Renny stared at her and the tree without speaking.

"Will it do?" she asked.

"It's a beauty." Now his eyes looked only into hers. He was torn between the desire to tell her the good news and the pain of telling her they must part.

"I chose it myself. Somehow I couldn't bear to have it cut down. I made the men dig up roots and all. Now, if Pheasant likes, she can have it planted again and it will live."

"What a good idea! The kid will love that."

"After Launceton dying I can't bear to think of anything young and beautiful being killed."

"I know." He kept his eyes on her. He said:

"Do you know what I'm doing, Kit? I'm making a picture of you in my mind — to keep always — just the way you look at this minute. You've no idea how lovely you are. You're the most unself-conscious girl I've ever known. This picture of you will never leave me — no matter where you go. It's — sort of symbolic."

She smiled up at him. "Renny, you've been beautiful to me. If only I could have helped you win that race!"

"It would have been grand." They gazed spellbound into space for a moment, visualizing that dream of victory. Then, with a sharp sigh, he jumped out of the sleigh and took the tree from her. She sprang on to the seat just in time to grasp the reins and restrain the gelding.

"Stop it, you devil," she said, without emotion.

Renny lifted the tree into the sleigh. He remarked:

"There's only one thing I don't like about you, Kit. That's the way you call horses hard names."

"I just can't help it. They understand. They know I love them."

"Here come Jim and Tod," exclaimed Renny.

"He said Tod could be with him in the stable." She called out to the approaching pair, — "Why are you coming here?"

Dayborn answered, — "You'll have to mind him. I've got to go and buy myself a pair of boots. My feet are right out of these."

Tod smiled apologetically at his mother. He wanted to be with her, yet feared she might welcome him no more than had Dayborn. She patted his cheek with her thin chapped hand. Dayborn put him on the straw beside the tree. He beamed up at it.

"Choose a good pair of boots, Jim," said Renny. "You've a long journey ahead of you."

Dayborn stared uncomprehending.

"My grandmother is going to pay your expenses to England. She told me so this morning."

"But why — why —" Dayborn could only stammer.

Chris said, — "But she mustn't do that. It's too much."

"She wants to," said Renny. "It's her Christmas present to you."

"Are Chris and the kid to go too?"

"Of course. I think they'll be your greatest assets when you meet Mrs. Gardiner. I've had a cable from my aunt. She has met your friend and is sure you can patch things up. She says she's a motherly person."

"She is!" cried Dayborn fervently. "She's been an angel to me. God, how glad I shall be to see her and make everything right."

"Tod will do that. Just look at him."

He had grasped the trunk of the tree in his little mittened hand for support. A scatter of snow from its branches was clinging to the fringe of hair that gleamed from beneath his woollen cap. "Tall, tall," he said complacently. "Vewy nice."

"I must go straight to Mrs. Whiteoak and thank her," said Dayborn. "Or had I better wait till I get my new boots?"

"Get the new boots first," said Chris. "And put on your other coat and your blue tie. Give her my love and tell her I shall come to thank her."

"You ought to come now."

"I'd rather go alone."

"Right! Oh, what a woman she is! I adore her. Chris, isn't she splendid!" He put both arms about Chris and hugged her. He looked across her at Renny, with a possessive air. A malicious smile flickered across his small, irregular face. "I haven't been blind, you know," he said.

Chris slackened the reins. Jake plunged forward. Dayborn looked after them still smiling, then turned toward the village. The reaction from bitter disappointment was almost too much for him. He could not clearly see his way. The sun came out in dazzling brightness. There were bells on Jake's harness. He could hear them jingling across the snow.

Renny squatted between child and tree, a hand supporting each. Clots of snow from Jake's hooves were thrown back into the sleigh. Fine snow, like spray, rose from the runners of the sleigh. The bells were deep-toned and melodious. Above them, Renny said:

"Are you really glad, Kit?"

She did not answer. Then she turned her face and looked at him over her shoulder. Tears were running down her cheeks. She turned her face away again. Neither of them spoke. Tod still stared up into the tree. "Tall, tall," he said.

They left him in the sleigh and went into the porch. Before ringing the bell Renny took out his handkerchief and dried her cheeks.

"Why are you crying, my darling little heart?" he asked.

"You know very well.... We shall never meet again.... I feel it here." She struck her hand on her breast.

Pheasant had been watching for them. She threw open the door.

"Oh, you've brought it!" She cried in delight. "Maurice told me you were bringing me a tree. He went to town and bought decorations for it. And something in a box which I'm not to open till the morning!"

"He'd better," said Renny grimly. He put a package into her hand. "Here's something else that must not be opened till the morning."

"Oh, how lovely! And I have one from Miss Pink! And Mrs. Clinch has crocheted me bedroom slippers. What a Christmas! Maurice home and a tree loaded with presents!"

❧❦

She was alone with the tree. It was evening. She had stayed up later than usual and had come to have one last look before she went to bed. The tree stood, round and thick, and as full of confidence as though it were still in the middle of the wood. It was wonderful to think that it was not destined to die. Its roots were there and it could be planted in the earth again. She would keep it all her life. When she had children of her own she would point to it, where it rose tall and stately, and say — "That was my first Christmas tree when I was a little girl." Probably it would be her last. She did not think she would want to have another. The joy of it was too deep, too disturbing. It hurt her.

Maurice had bought such pretty decorations but he had forgotten to buy candles. It was just as well, for Mrs. Clinch had a horror of fire. But she herself had gone to the kitchen and fetched the pair of old brass candlesticks from the mantelshelf. She had put candles in them and set one on either side of the tree. Now she lighted them.

How holy the two little flames looked! They reached up into the darkness and threw a soft radiance into the dimmest part of the tree. The boughs gave out their scent. It was like the breath of Christmas. The unopened packets lay clustered on the lowest branches. Five. She thought she would sing a carol. She stood very straight, her brown hair hanging on either side of her face, the candle flame reflected in her eyes. She sang, in a small sweet voice:

"Once, in Royal David's city,
    Stood a lowly cattle-shed,
Where a mother laid her Baby
    With a manger for His bed.
Mary was that mother mild,
Jesus Christ her little Child."

The scent of the tree rose like incense. From the road came the sound of sleigh bells.

THE END

The Jalna Novels
by Mazo de la Roche

In Order of Year of Publication	In Order of Year Story Begins
Jalna, 1927	*The Building of Jalna*, 1853
Whiteoaks of Jalna, 1929	*Morning at Jalna*, 1863
Finch's Fortune, 1931	*Mary Wakefield*, 1894
The Master of Jalna, 1933	*Young Renny*, 1906
Young Renny, 1935	*Whiteoak Heritage*, 1918
Whiteoak Harvest, 1936	*The Whiteoak Brothers*, 1923
Whiteoak Heritage, 1940	*Jalna*, 1924
Wakefield's Course, 1941	*Whiteoaks of Jalna*, 1926
The Building of Jalna, 1944	*Finch's Fortune*, 1929
Return to Jalna, 1946	*The Master of Jalna*, 1931
Mary Wakefield, 1949	*Whiteoak Harvest*, 1934
Renny's Daughter, 1951	*Wakefield's Course*, 1939
The Whiteoak Brothers, 1953	*Return to Jalna*, 1943
Variable Winds at Jalna, 1954	*Renny's Daughter*, 1948
Centenary at Jalna, 1958	*Variable Winds at Jalna*, 1950
Morning at Jalna, 1960	*Centenary at Jalna*, 1953

From *Mazo de la Roche: Rich and Famous Writer* by Heather Kirk

INTERNATIONAL BESTSELLERS
BY MAZO DE LA ROCHE
BACK IN PRINT!

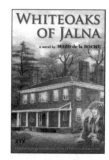

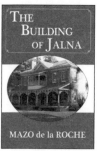
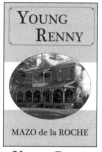

Tell us your story! What did you think of this book? Join the conversation at www.definingcanada.ca/tell-your-story by telling us what you think.